Praise for *Lady Anne's Dangerous Man*

"Jeane Westin brings Restoration England to life in a sweeping tale of passion and adventure."
—Lauren Royal, author of *Lost in Temptation*

"An old-fashioned swashbuckling romance with smart, sexy overtones." —Suzanne Enoch, author of *An Invitation to Sin*

"Stories like this don't come along often. Jeane Westin weaves sharply observed historical detail into the tale of a seductive battle between a rascal and a bluntly spoken young lady. It's a true pleasure to read!"
—Eloisa James, author of *Kiss Me, Annabel*

LADY ANNE'S DANGEROUS MAN

Jeane Westin

A SIGNET ECLIPSE BOOK

SIGNET ECLIPSE
Published by New American Library, a division of
Penguin Group (USA) Inc., 375 Hudson Street,
New York, New York 10014, USA
Penguin Group (Canada), 90 Eglinton Avenue East, Suite 700, Toronto,
Ontario M4P 2Y3, Canada (a division of Pearson Penguin Canada Inc.)
Penguin Books Ltd., 80 Strand, London WC2R 0RL, England
Penguin Ireland, 25 St. Stephen's Green, Dublin 2,
Ireland (a division of Penguin Books Ltd.)
Penguin Group (Australia), 250 Camberwell Road, Camberwell, Victoria 3124,
Australia (a division of Pearson Australia Group Pty. Ltd.)
Penguin Books India Pvt. Ltd., 11 Community Centre, Panchsheel Park,
New Delhi - 110 017, India
Penguin Group (NZ), cnr Airborne and Rosedale Roads, Albany,
Auckland 1310, New Zealand (a division of Pearson New Zealand Ltd.)
Penguin Books (South Africa) (Pty.) Ltd., 24 Sturdee Avenue,
Rosebank, Johannesburg 2196, South Africa

Penguin Books Ltd., Registered Offices:
80 Strand, London WC2R 0RL, England

First published by Signet Eclipse, an imprint of New American Library,
a division of Penguin Group (USA) Inc.

First Printing, January 2006
10 9 8 7 6 5 4 3 2 1

To Georgia Bockoven, author and always supportive friend;
and
Ellen Edwards, my editor, who recognized the fun and romance;
and
Henry Purcell, Restoration composer, whose CDs provided a musical background as I wrote Anne and John's adventures;
and finally,
my son-in-law, Sgt. Bob, who called this novel "cool!"

Chapter One

Flight from the King

The Lady Anne Gascoigne paced the marble hall outside the queen's withdrawing chamber, clutching Edward's urgent message to her breast. She wished with all her heart that tonight was not just another tryst, but the night she and Edward would be joined in the marriage bed. How could she wait another three whole days to be loved and safe from her king?

The thought of Edward's arms about her bare body at last made her ache with imagining, and threatened to produce a hot tremor. Her wedding night would put an end to weeks of anticipation, and to Edward's practiced way of arousing her to a shocking passion with a sly kiss here and a touch there. At last, all that would cease, and she would bestow upon the love of her life the one thing she held most precious, her womanly chastity, that which once pierced could never be restored until another heaven should come again.

She heard the swish of her best scarlet silk petticoat, the front panel exposed to show the brilliant-colored silk stiffened with gold and silver braid, to delight Edward. She cocked an ear for the sound of his footsteps, but heard nothing beyond her own desire to hear. Without meaning to, her fingers crumpled his note. "'Fore God," she said, damning the clock that struck in the tower across from the gallery. This waiting was unbearable.

Nothing in life had been easy of late. It had been most arduous to remain virginal with such a handsome and insistent suitor as Edward Ashley Carter, Earl of Waverby, especially in this modern year of 1665, when chastity was not so prized, and more especially in the court of King Charles II. But she had made a vow of purity at her mother's deathbed, and she meant to keep it, though it was the most difficult vow a maid of twenty-three years could keep.

Anne stopped by a huge multipaned window through which the setting sun slanted its rose-tinged rays. It overlooked the Royal Horseguards Parade between the Thames River and Whitehall Palace, its paths filled with sauntering, resplendently dressed courtiers. She looked hard for Edward's tall, slender form or for the graceful bow that represented the most obliging manners in all England.

Where was he?

The clock chimed the quarter hour after six of the evening. She uncrumpled the note and checked again. There was the hour of five writ as plain as before. Was he not coming, after all? Was he disturbed about last night? Angry? No, surely not. He had asked for this tryst to reassure her yet again. Sweet, sweet Edward.

She'd been desperate to tell someone about the king's latest advances, which grew bolder by the day. Who else but her betrothed could she turn to? The king had enormous power, and she had only her maiden's scruples.

It had been Edward's sensitivity to the king's public advances that had first drawn her to the earl. He'd offered his protection, and, within days, his love. At first, he'd maintained that the king's attentions were his way of showing a royal regard, and she should be glad of it.

Anne had wanted to believe Edward. But yesterday, the king had followed her into a garden arbor and attempted to show her far more than his regard. He'd fumbled at the lacings on his breeches, and only the arrival of the queen and her ladies had saved Anne from the worst possible indignity, although the royal entourage had, with all delicacy, pretended not to see what they plainly saw.

Anne was still humiliated that evening, and withdrew from the dancing. Edward followed her and, on hearing her tale, had knelt at once, promising his husbandly protection, even if it meant banishment from the court.

Still, Anne felt a nagging question that he'd hesitated in the first place, and then deep shame for doubting his devotion to her.

Maybe she should have gone with the other ladies-in-waiting to the queen's chapel. Yes, most definitely, she should be on her knees this minute giving thanks for her good fortune. Lord Waverby, besides being the handsomest man at court, was a peer of the realm, and the man to whom her father owed his recent preferment as a high justice. Yet it wasn't Edward's power or fine features that she loved, but the man who made her long to be a woman in truth.

A great groan escaped her. Surely he wasn't gambling again. Just last week he'd lost another thousand pounds to Lady Castlemaine at basset, a game at which she cheated outrageously. Still, Edward's faults were undeniably minor ones. Even gossip of his occasional visits to certain ladies of the town shouldn't bother her overmuch. That they did at all showed her how hard she would have to work to be a modern woman, one who accepted that a gentleman must have his gentleman's diversion even after marriage.

Anne twisted Edward's emerald seal ring on her finger, slipping it off and then on again so that she could enjoy the wondrous excitement of its return.

"God's bowels! Where are you?"

Her words bounced along the empty marble corridor, startling doves upon the window ledge. She had not meant to swear aloud like a coach driver, which is exactly where she'd learned the naughty phrase as a little girl. Though a woman grown for several years, she still delighted in what managed to be shockingly profane and quite unruly, too.

As if in response to her curse, muffled voices drifted from beyond the turn of the hall.

Anne froze, unwilling to believe her ears. It was Edward's voice, yes, but he was not alone. The tapping and scratching of tiny claws on the marble floor signaled the spaniels that went everywhere with the king.

Anne raced to the door of the queen's apartments, praying for enough time to slip through it undetected, happy that the customary guards had followed the queen to chapel. She glanced back to see Edward's note lying on the floor but had not a second left to reclaim it. Inside, she rushed to the wardrobe in the outer chamber and jumped in, hastily draping the queen's heavily brocaded gowns in front of her. She raised a hand to her nose to stifle the overwhelming scent of a dozen French perfumes. To her horror, the wardrobe door came off its latch and swung lazily aside as the apartment door was flung open, and heavy heels sounded upon the marble floor.

Anne squeezed her eyes together and compulsively sucked in a shallow breath, trying to contain her hurt. Why was Edward bringing the king to their tryst? Hadn't he believed her, after all?

"I am vexed with you, my Lord Waverby," the king's indolent voice announced above the yapping of his dogs. "You promised me a kiss from this beauteous minx of yours."

"And so you shall have it and thrice over, Your Majesty. Here is my note, perhaps dropped in haste. She must have been called away to some grave business."

"What graver business than waiting for you, eh?"

Anne could hear their footsteps drawing closer, and the dogs scratching and snuffling everywhere at once.

Edward laughed. "I assure Your Majesty that Lady Anne is quite besotted with me. She will do whatever I ask, and that means whatever you require for your diversion, sir."

Anne went rigid, her hurt now mixed with fear and so many other emotions; her head whirled with them. Oh, false heart! Edward had deceived her, or worse, plotted the betrayal of her womanhood with the foremost lecher in the realm.

One of the dogs was clawing at the gowns around her feet. She bit down on her lower lip, almost crying out.

"Ha!" the king shouted. "Fubbs, you naughty little baggage! What will the queen say if you ruin her gowns?"

Suddenly, a beringed royal hand appeared between the folds of the perfumed dresses surrounding her, prodding and poking, narrowly missing contact with her leg. His voice was petulant. "Surely, Waverby, this lady's singular modesty would not stoop to hide from my royal prerogative. Or is she a secret Puritan that she would deny a troubled monarch his comforts?"

Holding her breath and clutching at her breast, Anne eased against the back wall of the wardrobe, her nose twitching from the heavy spice scent rising from the nearest gown. Her mouth felt as dry as old straw.

Edward chuckled. "Anne will become far more agreeable after our marriage, sir, once relieved of her tiresome maidenhead."

In one heart-stopping second, the king's hand brushed Anne's own gown and lingered, caressing the satin between two royal fingers. Then the hand withdrew, the wardrobe door clicked shut, and the king replied testily, "So you have promised me quite regularly, my lord."

"I swear it on my honor, sire."

"In truth, the Lady Anne's impudent charms do rack me needlessly."

Anne could imagine the king's dark eyes measuring the man in front of him, the droopy eyelids and amused mouth, which did not necessarily indicate the king's pleasure. She could see Edward's refined bow, his hand upon his heart. False, false love!

Charles II laughed. "What fish would my good earl hope to catch if he baits the hook with his own bride?"

"Why, simply to be of service to Your Majesty would make me the happiest man in all your dominions." Anne shivered with rage at Edward's calculated tone.

The apartment doors opened and the voices and dogs moved to the corridor. "You are a great liar, my lord," the king said with good humor again, "but if your future countess makes me merry, then you will not be a poorer one."

Anne waited for long minutes after the last cruel word had rung along the shining marble hall and the clatter and scrape of dogs had receded. Cautiously, she stepped from her hiding place, shaking with anger and grief, knowing that this present great distress would rest forever at the bottom of her heart.

Never again would she trust a man with her love and honor. The maidenhead that was hers alone to give would go to the grave with her before any pretty rogue would have it. Her lips scarcely moved, but the words rang with terrible fierceness throughout her body and around the cavernous room: *"I swear that no man shall take what is now more precious to me than life itself."*

Anne swiped at a tear that threatened to bathe the bitter curve of her lips. Edward could never have loved her. All of his sweet words, the gentle caresses, the tongue that searched the shell of her ear, all had been lies. The sure knowledge of that fact charred to a cinder the last trace of her desire for him.

A guard's measured tread echoed in the hall outside, and Anne looked wildly about the room. What could she do? Who would help her? Queen Catharine would advise her to do her duty to her betrothed, and would hear nothing ill of the king, not even what she'd seen with her own eyes. What other way could a still-barren Portuguese wife survive in an alien court?

And Edward, Anne knew now as certainly as she knew

anything, would betray her virtue for gain at a flick of his lace *de Venise* handkerchief. It was all suddenly clear to her. He had long coveted a royal land grant in the Virginia Colony and dreamed of a tobacco plantation to help him rebuild his Oxfordshire estates ravaged by Cromwell. And yet Anne's mind could hardly conceive of such deceit. How could the man she'd loved so easily exchange her honor and his own for a land full of forests and savages? And after the king, in how many other beds would she have to whore for Edward's advancement?

Horrified at these thoughts and others too dreadful to put to words, Anne knew she must escape from the palace; to have time to think what to do, to plan how to defy both a charlatan earl and a lecherous king. She left Edward's seal ring on the floor where it dropped, and throwing a hooded cloak about her blue silk court gown, raced through back corridors and down stairs, along outer walls of gathering shadows to the least-used gate at Whitehall Palace.

"Stand! Who goes?" the guard challenged.

"Step aside, my man," she ordered, imitating the low, imperious voice of the Countess of Castlemaine, the king's chief mistress.

"My lady," he said, thrusting a lantern at her face. "Where is your escort?"

Anne knocked away his lantern arm. "The king will hear of it if you stop me. I am on urgent business of life or death." It was not a lie.

The guard stood dumbfounded before her, his arm dangling the light.

She clapped her hands sharply. "A sedan chair, and quickly, unless you fancy your head atop a Tower pike."

Muttering, he obeyed, but she knew that he would go straightway to his captain and the hue and cry would soon be raised. Then they would discover that it was Lady Anne Gascoigne who was gone. A lady of the court did not leave it without royal permission.

Helped into the sedan chair, she urged her bearers forward into the twisted, narrow, rapidly darkening streets beyond St. James Park. A linkboy ran ahead to light the way and discourage footpads.

"A silver penny for each man," she called to them, "if, for God's sweet pity, you hasten."

By the time she reached her father's chambers at the Inns of Court, her neck ached from constantly looking over her shoulder, expecting at any moment the sound of mounted men in close pursuit.

Titus, her father's footman, had heard sounds of pounding feet in the courtyard and calls of "Make way!" and was waiting at the door.

"Pay them in silver, Titus," Anne called, dashing past him. Gathering her skirts, she raced on her high red heels through a warren of rooms to her father's library, and burst in unannounced, tears of fury and betrayal spilling from her eyes.

Sir Samuel Gascoigne was still wearing the robe and periwig of a king's justice, but his face was consumed with curious alarm. "Why, m'dear girl—" He got no further because Anne threw herself into his arms, sobbing and talking, hiccuping and angrily incoherent.

He held her, shushed her and smoothed the fashionable auburn curls at either side of her head. "There, child. Now sit down by the fire." He held a chair for her and poured a glass of Madeira, which he tipped up against her lips. "Now, what's this about Edward? You've had a lovers' quarrel, is it? You must tell your father all, and I will speak to the japes rather harshly."

The strong amber wine was sharp against Anne's throat, and its spreading warmth helped her to collect herself and begin. She choked out the story, all of it. She told how the king had waylaid her in the garden, and how, when she confided her danger to Lord Waverby, he had forsworn his oath of protection.

The judge listened without a word, his fists clenching and unclenching, until the moment when Anne told of the conversation overheard in the wardrobe, especially the king and Edward's plans for her debauchery. He jumped up, stripped off his robe and reached for his ceremonial sword over the mantel. To Anne's horror, he held the sword in front of him like a crucifix. "Damn me, but I'll kill the ungodly bastard, if I go to the gibbet for it," he said, grating the words through clenched teeth. Then he bent and kissed the sword to seal the vow.

Alarmed, she clutched at his sword arm. "Father, that is treason!"

"I do not speak of the king. He's a Stuart rakehell with more bastards than a dog has fleas, but he is my anointed ruler, and I would give him everything but my daughter. But Waverby, the scoundrel, deserves to die for his perfidy." Sir Samuel blanched. "Damn me, I have signed the marriage portion, and he can take all your Essex estates."

"Father, I care naught for estates."

"But you'd be without a portion. How could I make a good marriage for you?"

"Father, you cannot, *must* not challenge Edward. He is an accomplished swordsman. I have seen him easily disarm men in play."

"Do you hold my honor so slight that you think I would not defend your name and fortune?"

"Please, Father," she begged, clutching his sword arm with both her hands. "No one honors you more than I, but I would not have you killed or sent to the Tower. Think you if not for your own sweet life, then for mine. With you out of the way, Edward and the king would surely work their will with me."

He stroked her shoulder soothingly. "You speak truth, daughter, but Lord Waverby needs chastising as a babe needs the breast." He sat down suddenly and put his face in his hands.

"This is my fault, all mine. My pride and ambition put you in Edward's clutches, and I must free you of him if it costs me everything."

"Do not blame yourself, Father," Anne said softly. "I did love Edward, to my everlasting shame. I will never think that I know a man again." Her entire body grew as cold and hard as winter. "And I swear that I will never love another."

"Hush, Anne. You are but three and twenty, and—" She shook her head violently, and thought to speak again, but he raised a finger. "Wait, sweet daughter, I must think."

For long minutes, he sat without moving, while Anne watched, occasionally glancing above the mantel at the portrait of her Puritan mother, Prudence, dead these three years of smallpox, a smile for her loved ones captured forever by brush and paint. The portrait, the warm fire, and the smell of leather-bound books did not work their usual calming magic. Anne's breathing was shallow and rapid, and her head was suffused with a light, sick feeling.

Finally, Sir Samuel spoke: "I must have time to get to your uncle, the Bishop of Ely. Only he can set aside the marriage banns, and then we will together gain Castlemaine's ear and appeal on your behalf. The king is much under her thumb, and she does not welcome beautiful rivals unless she easily controls them, and control is not so easy with you, m'dear.

"Meanwhile, you must be well hidden. But where? Edward will turn over every stone in every hamlet in the kingdom to claim you. His vaunting pride as well as his ambition demands it."

Anne pulled her cloak more tightly about her, even though she was already warm. Where in all of England would she be safe from either man's need? She did not realize she was talking aloud until she heard the sound of the words. "I would rather die by my own hand than submit my virtue to Edward or the king."

"Do not, dear daughter, say such words to me." He

moved quickly to her and embraced her protectively, and she could see the deep furrows of worry between his eyes.

"Did I do wrong, Anne?" he mused in a most agonized tone. "Have I unfit you for the world and your place in it? You had the brain of a boy, and it was my delight to nurture it. But what good will your Latin and Greek, your philosophy and poesy do you now? Your uncle, the Bishop of Ely, swore that such study would cause brain fever. He will say this is the result."

"Father, six hours a day of plying my needle would have burned my brain to ashes. You made no mistake with me; I will always have the learning you gave me."

He nodded, but again he did not speak for a long time. Had she wanted, she could not have penetrated that superior mind once it began to wrestle with a problem. At last he spoke. "I think I know what is to be done. But you must be brave, Anne, for it is a desperate plan, yet for that very reason has a faint hope of success."

"What plan?"

"Come, Anne, we must leave at once for your safety's sake." He signaled Titus to have his coach brought around. "Your courage will be tested these next few weeks, but all will soon be well again. I promise you on my oath."

Her voice held a strange echo that made his heart shudder. "Yes, Father, one way or another, all will be well."

Chapter Two

A Highwayman Hangs, or the Obscene Verse

It was a good day for a man to hang, if hang he must.

John Gilbert moved his neck gingerly within the noose, then threw back his head and laughed heartily. He could easily imagine happier thoughts for his last minutes on earth. Damned if he couldn't. For example, that savory baggage Nell Gwyn, masked and leaning from her carriage near the gallows, the sun glinting on her gilded curls newly escaped from under her hood. He caught her eye and gave her his best insolent grin and a rakish wink.

Oh, how women loved their rakes, even here on Tyburn's unfriendly hill, no matter their demure protests. Give a real woman her choice between a debauched man and a gent, and she would choose debauchery, and then with great effort attempt to reform that which first attracted her lust. Women, bless them, had been the ruin of love for one John Gilbert.

He had ever been crazy to get next to their scented flesh and crazier still to get away again. His lips curved into a regretful grin, because he would never be able to turn that phrase in witty company.

He raised his bronzed face up to the hot sun, feeling his scalp prickle. "Whoa, boy," he told the horse twitching flies at the head of the tumbrel, "don't pull away and cheat me of my final minute on this good green English earth."

The hangman bent toward him. "Although ye be a highwayman, and deserving the worst, Gentleman Johnny Gilbert, I can make it quick for ye. Those shiny black Spanish boots there on thy feet, if ye give them to me now, I won't have to take my chances with the guard's dice once ye swing."

The executioner's ale-sour breath reached the doomed man's finely chiseled nose, and he inclined his head away. "I'll meet the Lord well shod, hangman. These boots are too good for the likes of you."

"Too good, ye say? And ye the unclaimed bastard son of the Duke of Lakeland and a milkmaid."

The doomed man's muscles seemed to swell against his shackles, his hard eyes filled with fury, and the hangman shuffled backward in alarm.

"I will not die with that foul epitaph, bastard, ringing in my ears."

"Ye will die as I say," the executioner declared, regaining his courage and stepping forward again. Then he cruelly twisted the knotted noose to one side of John's neck. "There, my fine would-be lordling, this will promise ye a merry dance. Why, a strong, young man like thyself could break me record and last longer than nine minutes."

Proud words rasped from between the highwayman's teeth, unusual for their whiteness, and due mainly to a store of fine tooth cloths he'd lifted from a Hollander merchant careless enough to cross his path on the highroad. "Then watch me dance, and marvel, Sir Hangman. The ladies say I do tread lightly to any music."

A warder stepped past the two-wheeled tumbrel. "Now hear our good King Charles's warrant," he shouted. "John Gilbert, alias Gentleman Johnny, has robbed our loyal subjects of their property on the highways of this realm, to their detriment and in defiance of the King's Majesty. The penalty is death by hanging on Tyburn's hill this thirtieth day of May, in the year of our Lord Sixteen Sixty-Five, and of our reign the fifth. Signed by the king's justice, Sir Samuel Gascoigne."

John straightened, adding steel to his spine. No man would see him falter this day. Then he felt his shirt of fine Flemish cotton and lace stripped away to hang from his waist, to save it, he supposed, from the inevitable frothings.

The ladies in the crowd, waiting for the day's entertainment to begin, gasped at his exposed chest and daintily covered their eyes. Except one. The masked lady in the gilt carriage stared boldly, appraisingly.

She called to him in a taunting tone, "Is it true, my pretty pillicock, that you have not only eluded the king's magistrates for all these seven years, but also cuckolded most of them?"

Bless you, Nell, he thought. At last, an epitaph that he could die with. He bowed as best he could, inevitably tightening the noose about his neck. "As you see with your own eyes, my sweet, it must be true."

She inclined her golden head. "'Tis undoubted that your form is engaging, sir. You have the face of an angel and the body of a devil."

He bowed again, further tightening his noose, but he didn't care. Civility made its demands in even so unlikely a place.

"And is it further true," she continued in a voice that easily overreached the crowd, "that you were only brought to the bar of justice because you played a role in the latest of Nell Gwyn's plays in the Drury Lane, by name *Madame Rampant, or Folly Reclaimed*?"

Again he bowed, and drawled, "Foolish of me, perhaps, but it *was* a good role with a great actress."

The lady's eyes flashed. "Can you then be that highway-

man about whom tavern maids make the bawdy rhyme"—
her voice quavered in a comic cockney accent that had once
been her own as Orange Nell in the pit of the Theater
Royal—

"Nor are this Johnny's lusts above his strength;
His sword and cock are equal length?"

The crowd hooted and began to chant. "Gentleman
Johnny—Gentleman Johnny!"

The highwayman stared at the lady, a smile flickering
about his lips, and delivered a speech that would soon be repeated from Drury Lane to Westminster. "You do me no
honor, madame. I'm *twice* the man that you describe. And if
you'd care to rid me of this paltry string," he jiggled the
noose, "I'll give you pleasure that would satisfy . . . a
queen."

The crowd roared again and turned as one not to miss the
masked lady's reply.

"Merrily said, Sir Highwayman. May you rest in the eas-
iest room in hell."

Scowling, the hangman chimed in, "Here, now, enough
o' that. This be not the Theater Royal. This be serious king's
business."

He raised the whip above the horse's rump. The crowd
hushed and gawped as the highwayman lifted his proud
chin.

John Gilbert fixed his eyes on the lady, who had dropped
her mask to expose tears.

A porter in the crowd yelled, "It be Nell Gywn herself!"

"No tears, Nellie," John Gilbert called to her. "I'll die
with my eyes on your lips." He strained forward against the
rope, as if he would taste her feminine flesh a last time.

Drums rolled. The hangman's whip quivered in the air,
and absolute stillness enveloped Tyburn Hill, hushing even
the birds in midsong. The whip descended toward the
horse's flank.

"Hold!" The shout came from a carriage just arrived and

parked beyond the crowd. A robed judge alighted and hurried toward the tumbrel. "This man will not meet his maker today," the justice announced.

John, who had given himself up to an analysis of Nell's lips and found them arousing even at such a final hour, drew in a deep breath that he had not expected to breathe.

The hangman objected, "This man be condemned, Sir Samuel." His sputtering voice announced his disappointment. "Where be the king's pardon?"

The judge handed over a parchment, a seal dangling by a scarlet ribbon. "The prisoner is not pardoned, but will remain in my custody He has promised to show us where he has hidden his treasure. Don't delay There is my name on the king's warrant, and here is my name on the stay of execution." The judge's voice grew harsh with authority. "Now put him in my carriage, but leave him shackled. Quickly, man!"

Some of the crowd applauded, but others muttered angrily because they had been cheated of their sport.

Sir Samuel tossed the hangman a gold guinea, which seemed to lend wings to his feet.

John no longer felt the weight of the noose, and then he was clasped by rude hands and unceremoniously tossed into the judge's carriage, which raced away, pulled by four fast horses. He leaned out the window and awkwardly blew a kiss back toward Nell Gwyn, whose mouth was in a pretty pout. He had made verbal love to her, then cheated her of a climax. Perhaps one day he would make such amends as would win her forgiveness and much more.

The judge watched this exchange, frowning. "I would think you'd thank your god instead of such a woman," the judge said. "You are indeed a cold knave, sir."

The sun passed behind the clouds and an afternoon shower began to fall as the carriage careened down a road made thick dust by a dry spring.

The highwayman grimaced. "I am happily colder, sir,

than the place you planned to send me," John replied, no trace of gratitude in his voice. Yet his blood coursed hot through his body as he breathed deeply of the earthy green rain scent streaming in the windows. "Sink me, Sir Samuel, if I ever complain of this good English chill again." He tried to don the cloak the judge tossed to him, then gave up. "Will you kindly remove my irons?"

"Not until we are arrived at our destination. You are altogether too familiar with getting in and out of carriages on the highways."

The prisoner stared curiously at the judge. "You condemn me one day and release me the next. Can't you make up your lawyer's mind?"

"I will answer no questions until I am ready, and your insolence will not provoke me," the judge said, staring out the window as the road began to parallel the Thames River. Mile after mile, he steadfastly refused John's questioning entreaties, and, finally, they drove on in silence, the highwayman leaning back against the rich tapestry seat, trying to anticipate an opportunity to escape. If the judge thought to extort treasure from him, Sir Samuel was doomed to sore disappointment. John Gilbert had given his last pound on this earth to Nell for a new costume.

Just at dusk they drove through the carriageway of a small half-timbered, thatched inn off Oxford Road.

The judge pulled a key from his waistcoat. "Have I your word, sir, that you will not escape?"

"Would you trust the word of a highwayman?"

The judge slipped the key into the wrist shackles, and then bent awkwardly to work at the ankle irons. John smiled down on the older man's gray head. "You are no doubt a superior judge, Sir Samuel, but a poor gaoler. I could easily overcome you in that position."

The judge straightened, his work complete. "You could, but then your curiosity would not be satisfied. You are actor enough to want to see the climax of this drama."

John rubbed his wrists where the shackles had dug painful red grooves. "You know me too well, Sir Samuel." It was not jest but true, and the highwayman felt altogether uncomfortable with this discovery, although amused in spite of himself.

The two cloaked men passed through the public room, climbed the narrow stairs behind the landlord and entered a small sitting room adjoining a bedroom. A hot eel pie, some cheese and bread, and a bottle of sack awaited on a table by the fire.

John had thought never to eat another meal, and the memory of the thought alone was enough to make him ravenous. He ate while the judge talked about his daughter. It was an amazing story, too amazing for John not to credit it fully. Though this judge had sentenced him to death, it was the least punishment the law allowed. He could have gone to the gibbet to hang in chains until the flesh dropped from his bones, or suffered drawing and quartering.

John had no reason not to trust the judge, although Sir Samuel obviously trusted his daughter too much. It was unlikely that the lass was as pure as he proclaimed, not if half of what he'd heard of the court were true. But then, every father wanted to believe his daughter a virgin until her belly swelled beyond doubt.

Finally, Sir Samuel fell silent. The highwayman took a very deep drink of his tankard of sack, rolling the sharp taste about with his tongue, and turned to meet the judge's eyes. "Let me see now, Sir Samuel: You want *me* to hide your chaste and no doubt pious daughter from the king's desire and from the man to whom she is legally betrothed, to whit Lord Waverby, a peer of the realm, a court favorite, and a famed swordsman."

The judge shifted uncomfortably. "That's one way of viewing it."

John Gilbert's eyes glittered, unbelieving. "Those things are of no consequence, but there is something that is. You are telling me that you would entrust the Lady Anne Gascoigne to me, sir, a felon and a bastard."

"I hold no man's birth against him."

"Then, sir, most men of your station would find you immoral." John threw back his head and laughed heartily for the second time that day. The judge half stood, his hand on his sword, but the highwayman raised his own hands placatingly, trying to control his laughter. "Yet, sir, even if you discount my dishonorable birth, then my reputation alone is not such that—"

The judge snorted. "Think you that I cannot measure a man beyond his outer guise? I was schooled with your father at Oxford, and I know the branch does not stray far from the tree. Further, I know that you have never killed unless in a fair fight, you have never stolen from the destitute—"

"Although from quite a few judges," John admitted.

"And," Sir Samuel went on, determined to finish, "if your public songs do you a justice, you have never taken a woman without her consent."

John was no longer amused. "I would happily plead guilty to all charges. Still, I must point out that men of honor abound in this isle. Why me?"

"You are a man with nothing more to lose."

John rubbed his neck ruefully. "That is debatable. Once a man's neck is saved, he prizes it all the more."

"And because," the judge continued with resolute deliberateness, "I cannot jeopardize the lives of my family and friends. Lord Waverby is obviously a ruthless man."

The highwayman turned and put his feet up on the fender of the fireplace to warm them.

"And of course," the judge continued, speaking now to the younger man's strong profile, "there is an even more obvious reason for my choice. You escaped the best of the king's men for years. It is said you have a hideaway in Whittlewood Forest that not even the best hunting dogs could find. I want you to take my daughter, the Lady Anne, to that place, until I can have her betrothal annulled and until the king has been newly charmed by one of a host of willing doxies at the court."

John pierced a final bit of cheddar with his knife and swallowed it, not taking his astonished black eyes off the fire, because he didn't dare look into the pleading face of the desperate father in front of him. "Sir, my men are unmannered and my camp is rude. It is certainly no place for a lady of tender virtue, especially virtue guarded at such a price to herself." He put his chin in his hand and leaned against his knees, and the firelight exposed the sharp angles of his frowning face. "Tell me why I should do this thing. If I'm caught again, the king will dispense with a nice, clean hanging and have me racked. Very untidy, they tell me."

"Better a death delayed than one set for tomorrow," the judge threatened. "My men surround the inn."

John laughed, facing him again. "Do you think to frighten a man who has cheated death? The memory of the rope might lend wings to my feet if indeed there are truly men without. No, Sir Samuel, you'll have to do better, much better. I want a pardon, or at least an exile, and transportation to the colonies—Jamaica, I think. They say a gentle breeze blows in every season, that it cools the ale and enflames the women, that a man can pull a meal off the trees."

"At best, I can offer you nothing but a few more weeks of life."

John stabbed his eating knife into the plank table and left it there, quivering. "Then take your virgin daughter and be damned, sir!"

"It is you who will be damned, sir!"

John shrugged and leaned back in his chair, no care showing on his face or in his demeanor.

The judge stared at him, clenching his teeth. "I do believe that you are a man who would trade his life unless he gets what he thinks right. I am all the more convinced that you are a man a father can trust."

John was not so certain. Such trust made him uncomfortable. "Do we have an agreement then, Sir Samuel?"

"You have my word on your freedom if you succeed. You have nothing, not even life, if you fail. Hide the Lady Anne, keep her from harm, and I will use all my powers to have your sentence commuted to exile. I will meet you here in exactly a fortnight. That should give me enough time to do what must be done."

The judge produced a clean shirt and a sword hung from a broad baldric, which John quickly donned, having sorely missed the weight of steel against his hip in Newgate Prison.

"And now, Sir Samuel, when am I to meet this paragon of maids, this saint of prim lasses? I confess that I am aflame with anticipation." He swept the judge a mocking bow.

"You will meet me when your lewd manners are much improved, sir."

John jerked upright at the unmistakably husky, feminine voice. A cloaked figure walked softly from the adjoining room into the flickering firelight; a woman of such yielding translucent beauty and shimmering green eyes as to make John Gilbert fully understand why the king was so persistent despite the lady's advertised frigidity.

Sir Samuel embraced his daughter. "Do not worry, Anne. In weeks, perhaps days, I'll return. I'm going at once to your uncle, the bishop. He will help us. But now you must go with Master Gilbert. It is all arranged. He knows what he must do."

"But Father . . ." Sir Samuel hushed her with a gentle finger laid along her cheek. She looked toward John and he bowed again, an even more exaggerated bow to hide his consternation.

He had supposed her such a resolute guardian of virtue that her face had already set into the hard lines of priggery, and now, here before him, was a face to set his wits jangling. Glorious auburn curls peeped from under the hood of her velvet traveling cloak, ringing her delicate face with an angel's firelit halo. John swallowed hard and remembered John Donne's line about love that made "one little room, an everywhere."

Still, he kept a tight grip on himself. Ah, a man's flesh was always at war with his mind. A log fell forward on the grate, and sparks crackled and danced on the hearth.

The woman stepped closer to Sir Samuel. "I'm sure Master Gilbert knows what he must do, Father, but does he know what he must *not* do?" she said, her voice as light as air, that same substance a man must have to live.

Withdrawing inside the hood of her cloak, Lady Anne Gascoigne was presenting a composure she was far from feeling. She could not believe that the man in front of her, whose smoothly handsome features, faultless narrow mustache and long, curling dark hair belied his coarse occupation, was the same man about whom tavern girls and ladies of the court sang, the one they called Gentleman Johnny, the one who was lover to the famous actress Nell Gwyn herself. Anne's face flushed hot as she remembered those overheard ditties mostly singing the praises of his manly part, and she tightly gripped the ivory pommel of a pretty Italian knife sheathed at her waist, sweeping aside her cloak to reveal it to him.

"Sir, I will not hesitate to use this steel if you tend to impudence or think me a proper testimony to your manhood." The artificially brave words threatened to strangle her.

He inclined his head slightly, his face serious. "I would do nothing, my lady, to disturb your admirable modesty, especially when so many of your sisters do honor me with their eagerness and flourish so under my tender care."

In an exaggerated courtly gesture, he placed one hand on his sword, extending a sinewy and well-shaped leg. "I do swear by all I hold dear that your chastity will remain yours so long as you wish it."

But his appraising eyes and scarcely hidden sarcasm did not reassure her, and her hand remained on the dagger's hilt.

Indeed, if she had removed the hand, its tremor might have given away her true state of mind. She was drowning in dread, about to take a desperate gamble, to leap into an unknown abyss with a strange and dangerous man. But she could betray her feelings to no one, certainly not to her father, who had so many worries, and certainly not to this highwayman, who would be the first to take advantage of any feminine weakness.

Minutes later in front of the inn, Anne's father kissed her cheek and handed her into the saddle. For one long moment, she clung to his safe hand, to the child's security she had always known. He turned worried eyes up to her, but she forced a smile and straightened in the saddle.

At the stirrup, John saluted the judge. "I admire you, sir, although you strike a strange bargain. It pains me to say that you have no chance against the king and his pimp. There will be those who wonder aloud about your part in my escape."

"That is my concern."

"As you will it, then." John sprang up behind the lady Anne, gathered the reins, and kicked the horse into a gallop.

Suddenly, she was enveloped by his arms, pressed by his legs and sensing wave upon wave of his damp, warm breath on her neck.

Behind her, he wondered at his immediate excitement, and put it down to the feeling of renewed life coursing through his body, and perhaps a little to the half-bottle of sack he'd consumed with his dinner. It certainly wasn't this pious wench, who'd run away from her lawful king to save the feminine bauble that was lost every minute in this kingdom, which he himself had taken from not a few willing maids. Could this Anne Gascoigne, though she sat in his arms like a stick, be without love's passion? Nay, if he was any judge, and he was. She would make a fine tumble. He would stake his life on it.

But that thought raised a second question. Could what

she guarded so closely just be worth losing a chance for the colonies and a new life?

He shook himself sharply and veered off the road onto a narrow forest track. If this woman could make him think of breaking his sacred oath and other such brain-sick thoughts, she was dangerous. He must keep his wits about him. Besides, Sir Samuel spoke true. John Gilbert had nothing to lose in this life, because he'd been bred with nothing—no parents, no inheritance and no name. A bastard is born to be bitterly alone, and best he remember.

Anne felt him moving forward in the saddle and tried to lean away, but his hard-muscled inner thighs tightened and she was in a vise, and for a moment she wondered if it were not more tenacious than the one from which she'd fled at the palace.

Back in the upstairs room at the inn, Sir Samuel took his ceremonial sword out of the cleansing fire and pushed it through the fleshy part of his left arm. Shuddering, he wrapped the bloody limb in a clean kerchief. Now let the king's magistrates dispute that John Gilbert had fought his way to freedom before revealing where he'd hidden his treasure.

Chapter Three

Into the Forest Encampment

In some way, it really felt quite good. Anne, exhausted from two days of terror and a night's riding, drowsily leaned back against John Gilbert's chest. She would never have believed such an unyielding hardness could provide this peculiar comfort. Nor could she have believed that this man, whom she should despise ... did despise ... could impart a curious strength through his touch, adding steel to her purpose.

No experience in her court life had prepared her to understand a man like John Gilbert, a man who seemed devoid of any true sensibility one moment, and yet—and this was most uncommonly strange—a man who had valor without brandishing a sword about or talking overmuch. Her father had seen it and believed it, or he would never have given her over to the highwayman's care.

Whittlewood Forest grew denser, and Anne Gascoigne tilted her eyes up to see the green canopy of trees slowly closing over her head, thick enough now to blot out the gathering first light beginning to slant between the branches.

"Sit up," John said, his voice unexpectedly deep and harsh from a cold night's disuse. He cleared his throat and went on in his normally irreverent tone. "My apologies,

Lady Anne, but every man in my band, woman, too, must pull a man's weight."

She sat suddenly and rigidly erect, every one of her vows securely in place. "I am in no doubt, Master Gilbert, what you require of a woman."

John regretted the removal of her soft, curving shoulders from his chest, but could not fail to take up her saucy challenge. "Then it will not surprise you that I now require you to be blindfolded, just in case a turn of heart would compel you one day to exchange the whereabouts of my secret hideaway for a king's favor."

If she'd been able to turn inside his iron grip, she'd have thumped him soundly with her fan—if she'd had a fan. The habits of court would be slow to fade.

He reined the weary horse beside a swift-flowing stream rimmed in bracken, and quickly draped his finely woven French handkerchief across her eyes and nose. She could feel his hands deep in her hair, tightening the knot.

Her nostrils were of a sudden drowning in some strange and manful skin scent, part sun and breeze, part horse and a blot of good claret hidden in the folds.

He urged the horse forward into water; she heard the splashing for some time and knew they were traveling the length of the stream. "No wonder the dogs couldn't find you," she said, to confound his superior sense of secrecy.

"If I must, I'll stopper your ears, too," he said firmly.

She took him at his word, but she didn't stop listening and straining to see through the handkerchief, until at last her eyes adjusted to the gauzy pictures in front of her. She must remember to taunt him with how poor a blindfold his fine kerchief made.

John Gilbert rode the familiar route to his camp, wondering why he saw no guards posted high up in the lookout trees. Everything in the forest was too quiet, as if hunted and hunter alike were yet asleep in some false security. It wouldn't last long, he knew. Once Sir Samuel reported his escape, the high sheriff of the shire would post every road in or out of Whittlewood. He smiled to himself. Fortunately, the sheriff didn't know every exit. Spurring the horse under them, John left the stream and finally halted in front of a mountainous tangle of briars.

Anne felt him dismount; the sudden loss of his weight against her made her almost fall backward. She hadn't realized how much she'd relied on his strength of carriage, and she determined not to do so again, for any reliance on a rogue such as Gentleman Johnny could be perilous.

But John Gilbert seemed not to notice her. He studied the briar patch, which she could just barely make out as like a giant deer copse, the safe forest place does use to give birth to and to nurse their fawns. He groped inside the brambles and grasped a large black iron ring, which he pulled with both hands. A huge door slid slowly open, screeching along a metal rail. She gasped as the hiding place yawned open.

"Lie against the horse's neck," he ordered.

"I will go no farther, sir, until you remove this uncivil blindfold."

A rude hand pushed her forward into the horse's mane and held her there, while he nudged the horse into the door of the copse. Then the door grated shut behind, and suddenly the blindfold was gone. She blinked hard in the yellow light of a lantern. She was surrounded by an earthen cave, as near as she could tell, dug out of a hill behind the mock copse, its sides and roof shored up with timber, and with a passage big enough to pass a horse and sitting rider.

She couldn't stop the admiration that crept into her voice. "If this is your doing, Master Engineer, you are a cleverer man than I thought. Surely your skills would have gained you honest preferment with some lord, if you had tried."

John walked on toward the lighted opening some yards ahead, pulling the reins behind him. His tone made no effort to hide his annoyance. "Why is it, my lady, that your sex does always seek to improve that which needs no improvement? If you admire a thing, then admire it for itself, and not for the seal that presumed men of quality could put on it."

She was deeply offended. She had intended to honestly compliment, and he had chastised her as he would any ignorant oaf. How dare he? Her next words were haughty enough to do Lady Castlemaine justice. "I do not think that I need lessons in deportment from a jackanapes highwayman."

"My lady, you need lessons in just about everything."

She struck out with furious words. "I do not choose to take them from such as you, sir."

Without stopping or facing her, he bowed, the very bend of his head an outrageous insult. "Nor would I choose to waste my talents on a lady of your station, one who thinks pure blood an excuse for mean spirits and bad manners. I will hide you, as I promised your father, and keep your person safe, but I will not enjoy your company, no, not one minute, if this past night be any portent." He bowed again, and this time the mockery was all too clear.

Anne clenched her lower jaw and did not deign to answer. He had handled her roughly and spoken impudently. Why, if she were still a lady of the court, he would have been on his way to Newgate Prison twice over for his behavior. She had never met a commoner with so little regard for his betters. Look at him! He held himself more erect than Edward.

She flushed with grief and anger at the memories that name conjured, and could make no excuse for his faithlessness these many hours later. At least this highwayman practiced a rude honor, though he scorned to own it to his face.

They exited the far end of the tunnel and came into a small green vale ringed with steep, forested hills, so thick with trees that a man could scarce walk between. As Anne's eyes adjusted to the full morning sunlight, she saw with amazement what could only be described as a tiny thatched Cotswold village before her, cook fires curling lazily from wattle-and-daub chimneys, a grassy common where milch cows grazed near the prettiest little bowling green.

"Johnny!" A huge gray-bearded man roared from the three-sided smithy on this edge of the village, and came running toward them as fast as his bulk and belly would allow.

"Joseph," John called, dismounting to be nearly crushed in the bigger man's embrace.

"We thought ye dead on Tyburn, yesterday noon, Johnny, my lad."

"It's a long tale, Joseph, and I'm not sure you'd believe it."

"That's as may be. But let me look at ye." The smith patted his huge hands along John's shoulders and arms, as if to make sure that he was in one piece. "If these were the days of the old religion, I'd light candles in the church and pay the priest for a mass of thanksgiving. God's tears, if I wouldn't!" He turned his emotion-glazed eyes to the woman on the horse. "And look ye here. I might have known you'd bring a wench from your hanging."

John reached for Anne's waist and lifted her down, holding on tightly until she got her legs firmly under her. "Joseph, this is Sir Samuel Gascoigne's daughter, Anne, lady-in-waiting to her majesty, Queen Catharine. She will be with us for a time."

Anne could hardly stand. She was stiff from the night's ride and the necessity of holding herself away from John Gilbert's touch.

"A lady, is it? Ye don't say," Joseph said, without the bow courtesy demanded but with a very broad wink.

"I speak true, Joseph," John answered impatiently. "Lady Anne will have my quarters, and I will bed down with you in the smithy."

Joseph raised two bristled eyebrows. "As will be, Johnny, but I fear the hangman rattled ye, if ye let a maid this fair sleep alone."

"You can loose me now, Master Gilbert," Anne said,

coolly pulling John's hands from her waist, preferring to hold on to the horse than be held by a highwayman.

Joseph laughed. "Master Gilbert, eh? So that be the way of it."

John didn't laugh. His tone was that of a commander. "Why aren't the sentries out?"

"Ah, Johnny, ye know the lads. They rode for London to rescue ye from the king's rope or bring your body back for a decent Christian burial among friends."

"Then send our lasses to the lookout posts, Joseph, and when the men return they'll forfeit their shares for the next month to their women," John said grimly. "The first article everyone puts his mark to is that a man not endanger the company by foolhardy rescues. I knew the chance I took when I made my masquerade at the Theater Royal."

Joseph flushed red. "I couldn't stop them, Johnny. You're the only one they'll heed."

"Damn me, but they *will* do that," John declared. "And now I must rest. I was awake two nights in Newgate. A sentence to the noose takes away a man's desire for sleep." He smiled wearily, swept another of his mocking bows to Anne, and strode away toward the smithy. "Take care of her, Joseph."

Anne sagged against the horse, too tired to take further offense, although much offense had been offered before she'd even set foot in this hideaway village.

Joseph watched the receding John Gilbert with a puzzled frown. "Never seen our Johnny with such a case of spleen." He looked suspiciously at Anne.

"Take me to my quarters, Joseph," she said, and her manner showed that she was used to being obeyed.

Without a word, he walked toward the green. She stumbled stiff-legged behind, passing a knot of whispering women milking a cow, the rhythmic splashes of milk in the pail matching her footsteps.

Joseph stopped at a cottage, newly thatched, with leaded

glass windowpanes and fresh gillyflowers in a tub beside the ironbound plank door. Joseph stepped aside and motioned her into the cot. "Thank you," she said, crossing the threshold. "I do not wish to be disturbed, especially by Master John Gilbert."

Joseph smiled and bent to close the door, filling the doorway from frame to frame, blocking the morning sunlight. "All that know him be calling him Johnny, my lady."

"That I *never* will do," Anne said.

"Never be a long time in Whittlewood Forest, Lady Anne," he jested.

"It will be as long as I need it to be."

Joseph closed the door softly, but Anne heard him chuckling as he walked away. Let him think as he would; she was too tired to fight his ignorance. She barely stopped to remove her red heeled shoes. Could it have been but two days since they had trod Whitehall's marble corridors? Now they lay by the bed of a humble forest cot, scuffed from stirrup and bramble. For a moment, images of the king, of Edward and of her father flickered painfully across her mind, and then she sank down on the feather mattress. She felt the softness of clean, fine linen sheeting under her hands and sniffed the faint scent of crushed rose and violet and lavender on the pillow, wondered at the man who slept so, and then slipped into a deep, exhausted stupor.

It was dusk when Anne woke, having nearly slept the clock around, and for quite a long moment she didn't know where she was. She stretched and yawned.

"My lady?" It was a question from the shadows.

Anne sat up and suddenly clutched the sheet to her breast. She was naked as a newborn babe. "My gown, my hose!"

"They be naught but tatters," said the woman's voice. The speaker lit a candle and placed it on a small table. "I'm Beth, my lady. I took thy clothes and brought these. He sent them for ye to wear, and a request for your company at table." The woman laid a satin gown, deep rose in color and with a yawning décolletage, across the bed.

Anne was in no doubt as to who "he" was, and she had no intention of being at his beck and call. "Tell Master Gilbert that I am pleased to dine alone in my lodgings."

The woman stepped into the candlelight. She was quite pretty in a country-bred, milk-fed, rosy-cheeked way. "I don't think he be liking that," she said softly.

"It is not for him to like or dislike, Beth," Anne said, determined to establish the natural authority of her rank at this place, before any more of it was eroded.

Looking a bit frightened, the woman bobbed a curtsy and left. Anne stretched again, her muscles still stiff but less so. She inadvertently touched the fabric of the gown at her feet and found it to be the finest satin, and obviously of the latest fashion, the undershift overflowing the bodice and clasped there with jeweled brooches. Stolen, no doubt, or purchased for some Drury Lane moll, or both. Well, she would not wear it. She had no need to tantalize a man ever again. Those days were behind her.

The plank door opened, and Beth reentered. "He says, my lady"—the voice hesitated—"that ye are to dress and come to break bread, or he will truss ye and carry ye naked to table."

Anne thought she heard amusement in the woman's voice, therefore firmness was even more in order. "A Gascoigne does not respond to the idle threats of a gallows bird."

Beth's amusement was gone. "No idle threat, Lady Anne. He never gives a counterfeit word, as many have learned to their dislike. I think ye'd better come, my lady, or there'll be trouble. The lads are back, and they bring grave news of London. Also Black Ben be here."

"Black Ben?"

"A bad one, Lady Anne. It would not do for him to think ye didn't obey John Gilbert. Ben has twice our men and none o' our scruples. Please, my lady, if I come back without ye—"

Anne interrupted triumphantly. "John Gilbert would beat you, would he?"

Beth looked startled. "Oh, no, not that, but I can't disappoint him. Not after all he be doing for me."

The woman, little more than a girl, really, was obviously in love with the highwayman, from the look on her moon face. Anne could too well imagine what he'd done for her; or better, she tried not to imagine too well. "Then hurry—bring water for washing and a comb. Fresh hose, too."

"All here, Lady Anne. Then I can tell him that ye be coming?"

"I'd have no one in this place think a Gascoigne was too timid to face a rabble of thieves."

It was full dark when Anne emerged from the cottage with a lantern, and following the raucous sounds of laughter and the scent of suckling pig, crossed to the bowling green. Long trestle tables lit by silver candelabra were ringed by several dozen men and women, in the most colorful and appallingly mismatched finery she'd ever seen outside the gallery of a London theater.

John Gilbert, his darkly natural hair thick and curled to shame the best wigmaker, advanced toward her, taking her hand to escort her to the table. She pulled away, but he grasped her fingers in a vise. "On your peril, Lady Anne, you must follow exactly what I say and do."

For one too-swift moment, he allowed his eyes to absorb her appearance, the red glint of hair brushed into soft side curls, the bodice pushing up two orbs of quivering flesh like an offering of rich cream custard to the gods. On his life, he had never seen another woman of less lucidity or more beauty. The unbidden thought angered him, and he pulled her along the greensward before she spoke the loud complaint even now forming on her lips. At table, he propelled her into the high-backed chair next to his.

In the face of this strange company, Anne tried to compose herself. Behind her in the shadows, Joseph stood. Opposite her chair, a man lounged, his hand on a large tankard.

"Ben, may I introduce the Lady Anne Gascoigne," John Gilbert said. "My lady, Master Ben Skirret, Black Ben, as the sheriff's men do call him."

She was confronted with an unshaven rogue, wearing a full yellow French wig, ill-fitting and badly curled, and a dirty blue satin cloak that hung with tarnished foreign medals. Here was a drunken, farcical imitation of a courtier. But it was no buffoon whose face turned up to hers. She shrank from the evil hardness in his squinting black eyes, his gaping smile only making his visage more brutal.

"So this be the lost palace virgin on every London gossip's tongue."

"Not lost, sir, but found, as you can see." Anne inclined her head coolly, and Black Ben laughed, sending quivers along her spine.

"A pretty tongue, Gentleman Johnny, I swear. No wonder Lord Waverby offers a reward of a hundred pounds for her return. Not nearly enough, say I."

After John filled her pewter plate, she sat quite still under Ben's bleary gaze, pretending a consuming interest in the sallet of lettuces and fruit and a huge slice of coney, which she was forced to eat with a knife. She gripped her tankard and took such a deep quaff of claret that she became instantly lightheaded. Hungry or not, she must eat if she was to keep her wits, and keep them she must.

Black Ben filled his tankard, and with a leer, splashed more wine into hers. "Ye must count yourself among the lucky ones, my lady. Thy virtue may have saved more than thy maidenhead. There's bad plague in London."

A young man at the end of the table stood. "That's right, Johnny. We heard naught but plague talk when we went for ye. The dead be doubling every day and now must be buried in common plague pits."

John Gilbert leaned back and swung a leg over his chair arm, but it was far from a relaxed pose; Anne could see that he was very much alert in every limb, his hand never far from his sword.

"We're safe here, lads," John announced. "The air is fresh. None of the ill humors of London, and if we have need, we can fumigate with tobacco smoke."

Black Ben sneered. "I was taking the mercury at Mrs. Fourcard's pox baths in Leather Lane, and saw a man dead of plague with a tobacco pipe in his mouth."

John bent to pop a morsel of honey-dipped bread into Anne's open mouth, and her eyes flashed her dislike. How dare he behave toward her in this common manner? She was about to speak her mind when her ankle received a sharp blow from the toe of his boot. Blinking back the pain, she decided to say nothing now, but she would store up words for him later.

Black Ben sputtered and coughed with laughter. "So she's found her swain at last, 'as she? I envy ye such a dandilolly, John." The man lifted his tankard to them.

John Gilbert grinned at Ben, winking broadly, and popped another bit of honeyed bread into her mouth. He would gladly fill that luscious mouth to keep it shut. She was no match for Black Ben, but she wouldn't know it. She knew only the conversation of the court, where sly innuendo was the hidden language of love, not an invitation for rape. The only way he could keep her safe was to pretend a conquest. No highwayman broke the code and took another's woman or betrayed her whereabouts for gold, and the jest of John Gilbert's having a judge's virgin daughter would distract Ben until he could be busied slitting throats on some king's highroad.

John didn't blame the lads for bringing Ben and his men to Whittlewood. Joseph had told him how it happened. Drunk and wenching in the stews around Drury Lane, they'd been badly outnumbered and outguessed when Black Ben and his men found them. Any resistance would have meant instant death, or at the least had the watch down on them, followed by a quick trip to Tyburn's hellish tree.

Sweet music now intruded over the sounds of merry-making, and John was relieved to see Beth make an appearance with her lute. She'd mellow the raucous crowd. Willing hands hoisted her high onto the table, where she gave them some lively country airs that most of the company knew, and sang loudly. Then she turned to softer song of love and loss. For a moment, John was entertained at the unashamed tears that flowed down Ben's cheeks, but only for a moment.

One of Ben's drunken men sitting below Beth reached for her in midchorus and pulled her into his lap. With a roar, Ben was on him, and before the man's sword was free, he was run through and squirming, pinned to the ground in his death agony. John heard Anne's gasp of fear above the murmurs of his own men, as Ben wiped his bloody steel on the man's jerkin.

Joseph whispered in the stunned silence that followed. "Shall I give the signal to fight, Johnny?"

"No," John answered, and Anne was astounded at his cowardice. Warily, he stood, his hand lightly on his own sword, his voice as droll as if he spoke lines from Mr. Wycherley's new comedy. "You do use your men most severely, Ben, when there is an excess of song and an absence of good swordsmen in these woods."

Black Ben filled his chair and his tankard again, and looked cannily over its rim at Anne. She sat very still in her chair, as rigid as the wood that held her. Ben grinned his snaggletoothed grin. "Why, never fear me, your ladyship. I think ye have more to fear from our Gentleman Johnny here." Ben looked at John Gilbert. "You wouldn't be planning a tumble or two ere you turn her back to her father?"

John Gilbert gripped Anne's knee under the table as he bowed in Ben's direction, leering like any plowboy. "Why,

Ben, you do know me better than that. Would I take a virgin behind her father's back?"

Everyone within hearing roared, "Aye!"

John took Anne's hand in a strong grip. He bent over and kissed it, whispering for her ears alone. "Smile on me!"

Anne was half decided that the two outlaws had planned this playacting scene between them, but caution kept her from testing her theory. She imitated an infatuated smile, showing too many teeth.

Black Ben belched, not taking his eyes from her. "There is still more pressing business than wenches. What be a plague to some, friend John, be the clink of gold in the pocket to us. What say ye and thy band? Shall we join forces? The roads from London will soon be clogged with great carriages carrying quality and all their baubles away from the plague. It be a simple matter to send them on their way the lighter for having met us."

He laughed, and his men with him, and John Gilbert could see most of his own lads joined in with enthusiasm.

"I'll think the night on it, Ben."

Black Ben stood. "Then we will let ye to thy pleasant work."

He bowed his drunken parody of courtesy to Anne, then with an added leer in John Gilbert's direction, Black Ben staggered away, with his men carrying their dead comrade toward a ragtag of tents pitched in the common.

"Come, my lady," John said, and with an iron grip on her arm, he guided her quickly to the cottage.

Once inside, she felt herself shaking with rage and fear. "How dare you expose me to such murderous company, sir, and hint to that base blackguard that you're my lover. It mocks all that ever I stood for."

He removed his long waistcoat and hung it on a peg, taking his time to face her with a lazy smile. "On my soul, I am grown weary of your ignorance, my lady." His smile disappeared. "Don't you know that if I leave this cot tonight, you'll have another in my place, one who has not sworn to protect you and your divine jewel?"

Her rage mounted at his sarcasm. "You call *this* protection, sir? I am witness to foul death, held up as a strumpet to rabble you refuse to fight, and now you think to spend the night in my cottage."

He bowed, and she was nearly maddened to see that the smile now flickered at his mouth. "*My* cottage, my lady, and lower your voice, or Ben will think we're having a lovers' quarrel and decide to take the advantage. He would not match my scrupulous conduct."

She was breathing rapidly, her mind searching for a way out of this. "Are you telling me, John Gilbert"—she spat out the words, but her voice was lower—"that you have no control in your own camp? Call your men, sir, and have this Black Ben thrown out."

He thoughtfully smoothed his already perfect mustache. "For a nobly bred woman, you send good men to their death most readily. I could not do so. Besides, I am not lord here. My men are free men, and they have a vote according to our articles." She started to speak, but he overrode her. "Tomorrow, they will vote to join Ben and his lot, because he offers them adventure and gold. And I will lead them to see that they are not cheated of their gold or their lives."

"I do not believe you."

He shrugged. "It is no matter, my lady, whether you do or you don't. I will turn my back while you disrobe and get into bed."

"I will do no such thing."

He turned his broad back to her, and it looked like a barricade beyond her ability to storm, or five husky men moreover. God's bowels! She bit her tongue, but she was well provoked. John Gilbert was maddening enough to make her think of words no lady, except of the street, would ever utter. Watching him closely to see that he didn't glance about, she quickly unlaced her bodice and threw the dress over a chest. Then she slid onto the bed with a catlike motion.

A hot flush crept up her neck as she watched him loose the ties on his shirt and breeches, remove his fine black boots and settle into a chair in front of the fireplace, the banked coals glowing in the dark. He laid his baldric and sword across his knees, leaned back and closed his eyes without once giving her a glance, but she was not deceived. This was all a charade, some playacting that he thought her too ignorant to discern. Slowly, she inched her Italian knife from under the pillow where she'd left it earlier. From this night on, she would never be without it, and if she had to, she'd use it.

He didn't speak, but his silence only made her more alert. He was waiting until she slept to fall on her and spend his passion, although to be honest, he had never even flattered her, never made an ungentlemanly move toward her person. Quite the contrary, he seemed often to want her out of his sight. She set her mind against such denial. The man was a rogue, capable of the greatest tricks.

Guttural singing burst on her, almost at the door. Before she could gather herself or grip her knife, or even fill her lungs to scream, John Gilbert, her protector, had o'erleaped the space between them, landing in the bed on top of her, capturing her breath with his own mouth.

Chapter Four

All the Bed's a Stage

The door flew back on its leather hinges with a force to knock out windowpanes, and Black Ben advanced to the bed and leaned his drunken red face over it, his wig askew, his close-set eyes darting everywhere.

"I owe ye apologies, John," Ben's voice boomed. "I doubted ye were the man to bed this icy wench."

John Gilbert lifted his mouth, a smirk on it, from Anne's. "As you see, Ben, you underestimate my ability to fire her blood."

"She has a bawd's way, then?"

Anne was just catching her breath and trying to squirm from under John, when he pressed his body full against hers and kissed her again. Then he ran his tongue over his lips, tasting, frowning. "Perhaps in time, Ben, but I doubt she'll ever have the skill for a man of your parts."

Black Ben didn't look so sure. He was trying to lift the covers.

"Why, Ben," John said with an easy smile, "I'm surprised that a brave gentleman of the highroads would disturb a fellow larcenist about to spill his passion."

"Then with a kiss from yon wench I'll be gone. Surely ye can spare old Ben a single kiss, John Gilbert."

"Only if the lady chooses."

Anne could hardly believe what she heard. Not only was John Gilbert stretched atop her, kissing her with no pretense at playacting, but he would not fight this blackguard for her honor. She was so angered that her arms seemed languid and sapless, incapable of any defense. But as Black Ben's dark face closed on hers, anger demolished revulsion, her hand grasped her knife and she brought the point to Ben's throat in one swift motion.

Ben reared back with a roar, his hand pulling at his sword hilt.

John spoke in a low, clear voice. "Ben, think well before you spend your rage on this ninny, albeit a judge's daughter, under my protection. I would be obliged to kill you, or if I died instead, the sheriff would hunt you down no matter what share of the spoils you offered him. The whole of English justice would thirst for your blood."

Ben hesitated, then pushed his sword back into its leather. "Ye be right, smart John, but I be not like to forget this night or this bawd." He gave her a last leer and stamped out the door, closing it behind him with taunting softness.

"Are you mad? Get off me, sir," she hissed.

"Gladly," he whispered, rolling to one side but putting his finger to his lips. "Quiet. Ben's lurking about the cottage."

She shuddered suddenly, but for more than her close call. The memory of John Gilbert's body was as disturbing as the real thing, making her reaction to his perfidy even more bitter. "You would have allowed that horrible man to kiss me."

"Better a kiss than a dozen dead men, especially if one of them were me. Who, then, would befriend you and your bad temper, lady?"

She despised him even more when he made sense. "You are no gallant, sir."

"You're not going to weep, are you?" he whispered, frowning.

"You'll never have that pleasure," she said, but she was gulping tears as she denied them.

"Good," he said, "because I must ask you for yet another display of your considerable pique, my lady."

"I will do anything if you will leave my bed, sir."

"I would, and nimbly, too, but I cannot just yet. And further, you must help me convince Ben that you are truly my woman in all ways."

"You go too far, sir!"

"A pretense, no more, one I'll like no more than you." He said it, but he knew that even this cold lady's pretension had moved him strangely.

"What pretense?" she sniffed.

"I have some skill upon the stage. Nell Gwyn herself was my teacher, as I would be yours."

The bragging rogue was actually enjoying this, Anne could tell. She showed him her steel, and he widened his eyes in supposed fright. Damn his insolence! And then she heard Ben's footfall outside the window, and resisted an impulse to cringe against John Gilbert. "What would you have me do?" she whispered.

"Bluff, sham, fake love's climax, my lady, as some of your sisters do, although I swear never a one I ever loved."

"I don't need your rogue's biography, sir, but want simple instruction to end this farce."

He reached for her. "Then turn—"

She pricked his hand with her steel, and he winced, sucking at the drop of blood.

"You are *not* to touch me," she said, "not once."

He raised his hands in surrender, and his mouth twisted in a most engaging way. "You are a woman to try even my great skill, Anne."

"I am the Lady Anne to you."

He smiled. "Must we obey the proprieties even in bed?"

"Especially in bed, sir."

"Then we begin."

"How?"

"Let me hear you moan, as if your fantastic fancies moved you to the pleasure of true love."

Though she thought it silly, the memory of Black Ben's thick, moist red lips near hers and the continuing sounds of his footfalls outside made her try, but her throat behaved as if it had a lock on it.

John drew closer without touching her. "That, Lady Anne, was the sound of a squirrel squeaking."

"Remember, you named me ninny, so you do better, sir," she whispered angrily. He looked so disdainful, she could have cheerfully strangled him.

"This is a moan," he said, beginning to rhythmically move upon the creaking rope springs and groaning wood. He moaned, first softly, then with mounting intensity, until she longed to look at anything but his face, but she could not. It was a moan that rose and fell, that had a heart's pulse, an eager, melting fire that threatened her limbs with bliss as it supposedly made them safer from it.

At the height of the moan, he increased the rhythmic bounce, setting the bed's rope springs to creaking harder and its wood to groaning louder.

Obviously, she had overdrunk at table to be feeling this hot-blooded. Her mother had always told her that lewdness lay at the bottom of a wineglass.

"Now," he said, leaning insolently on one pillowed elbow, "can you do that?"

"Of course I can." The brag overcame her doubts. She would show him acting excellence that his mistress Nell Gywn had never dreamed of attaining, and the idea of besting that celebrated lady took hold and brushed her throat with velvet.

Anne's moan started with a murmuring that soon began to grow, but slowly, so slowly. She actually enjoyed the change in his face as her skill mounted, and determined not to shift her eyes until she'd taught him not to scorn her abilities. She filled the moan with eager desires and longing for what might have been had this been her wedding night, and had the man she'd once loved not proved a treacherous scoundrel. The moan began to tremble as it soared, to quaver with a languorous joy, and she could see the highwayman's practiced gaze ignite under her false passion. She did not stop until she was sure that lightning had touched him in that nether part that would never in this life pierce her.

Breathing with difficulty and limp with heat, she whispered, "Well, Master Gilbert, where is your applause?"

The sound of her words shook him from his attention, which had been total. He moaned, a most natural and desirous sound that he couldn't stop, as he couldn't stop his stiff cod from its want. Damn, oh, damn, but he was undone! His hand reached out for her, only just remembering his promise and stopping, floating, a bare whisper above her face. His fingers traced her outline, her eyes, her nose, and her lips, her ears, her neck, and then her heaving bosom. He heard her moan again, not the proud moan of a woman learning her powers over a man, but one as helplessly real as his own; he heard his own stripped voice answer again, quickly followed by hers, until all playacting was gone between them and the cottage was filled with unfeigned passion. He knew that any true woman must burn as he did.

Anne thought that if the highwayman did not touch her soon, she would surely lose her maidenhead to the flame that flared at its entrance.

And when he spoke in the dark, so near to her, she was strangely and gently moved by the unfamiliar huskiness in his voice. "Come live with me and be my love—"

She answered with the poet's next line. "And we will all the pleasures prove—"

Sink me! The woman knew Christopher Marlowe. Was there no end to her attractions? "I would almost rather be killed in a duel with Black Ben than believe such sweet, womanly passion was meant in jest," he said.

She was confused. "But, sir, the *jest* was of your own making."

"Then you've become its tyrant, Anne," he said, bending toward her face across the chasm of inches.

"*Lady* Anne," she corrected, fighting the invisible rope that pulled her toward his perfectly hewn face. Oh, the seasoned rake! He must have known that playful pretense often turned to real passion. Yet even mindful of his probable deception, she closed her eyes and turned up her mouth to his lips. The Italian steel lay forgotten beside her hand.

John stopped himself by some inhuman exertion just short of violating his oath to Sir Samuel. For if he really kissed this woman with all the craft at his command, there would be nothing between him and her arms and legs, and the breasts that cried out for a tongue to sport with them. He slipped from the bed, and the chill night air tempered his senses.

"Go to sleep," he told her harshly.

"I hate you, John Gilbert," she said, her voice choked with shame and need.

He cursed himself as he went to the window to determine that Black Ben had tired of his game and gone off to bed or a wench. Seeing nothing, he sank into the chair beside the fireplace. He had nearly allowed this fatal woman to take from him the only thing his Lakeland family had left him: his honor. A bastard's honor, true, but all he owned of a centuries-old heritage. Sir Samuel would have his daughter back in less than a fortnight, chaste and unloved, and there was an end on it.

Long after her steady breathing told him that Anne slept, he thought of the warm breezes and warm women of the Jamaica colony. He sat awake all night.

*   *   *

John Gilbert was gone the next morning when Anne awoke, and she was glad of it. If he had been there, had spoken, had touched her even by accident, she would have run like a spooked mare. As her face flushed a bright red in recollection, she knew that running had been far from her thoughts when he had been in her bed last night. She had fallen in with his shameful scheme like any London trollop plying her trade along the Strand. Only her mind's stark image of Black Ben's face, still firmly genuine this morning, convinced her that she had not been the butt of one of John Gilbert's japes. Not that she put such a thing past him.

She stepped to the chest to don the rose satin gown, only to find it gone, and in its place a gray dress of linsey-woolsey, with a long white kerchief collar, perfectly sober and suitable for country visits. He'd thought of everything.

The door opened and Beth barged in with a bowl of water. "'Morning, my lady."

Anne smiled at her. "Please, Beth, do knock before entering a bedchamber."

The young woman flushed. "I didn't know. At home there be only the one room for all of us."

"Of course you didn't know," Anne said, regretting her ever quick tongue. "Pray, where is your family?"

Beth looked painfully pleased, and Anne felt a twinge of guilt that normal good manners could be taken for personal interest by a servant.

"They be all gone, my lady, to the Cornish mines. I were too young and the recruiter didn't want me, so I eventually came here."

"I see," Anne said, wondering what had happened to the pretty dairymaid between her family's departure and taking up with highwaymen. Nothing good, she feared. "Thank you for this dress," Anne told her, smoothing its rough folds.

"He said—" Beth stopped, looking at Anne wide-eyed, swallowing compulsively.

"He said what? Come, Beth, I don't sting."

"He said," Beth doggedly continued, "that ye be helping out with the—the milking." She ducked back toward the door.

Anne was stupefied. "The milking? With cows?" And then she laughed, or more rightly, she howled. Not content with her acting demonstration of last night, John Gilbert sought to challenge her to another task of which he thought her totally incapable. So it was to be a test of wills, was it? She smiled, pleased at the prospect. The highwayman held a high opinion of himself if he thought to best a woman who had defied a king and an earl both on the same day. "Lead on, Beth. I have longed to be a milkmaid for my complexion's sake. It is well known that they never get the small-pox."

"It's the cowpox we be getting, Lady Anne, and then we be safe somehow."

Anne dressed hastily. "Perhaps it should be required that every lady of quality spend a season in the dairy barn."

Beth held the door for her. "I never knew a lady like you before," she said shyly.

Anne swept past her. "Neither has John Gilbert, as he will learn to his utter chagrin . . . or should I say *udder* chagrin," she added, laughing merrily for the first time in days, impulsively linking her arm through Beth's.

Beth was obviously shocked, but Anne kept a firm grip. "What a fine morning," she said, and, indeed, she meant it. The warm sun sparkled on the dew that wet her stockings, its rays chasing clouds across the trees on the hills surrounding this hidden village. She breathed deeply, turning up her face to taste the scent of wood fire and the morning's first yeasty bread thick in the air.

When they reached the common, the cows now tethered there were already being milked by two other women, who nodded but pretended that it was their normal routine to work with ladies of the court looking on.

"What do I do first?" Anne asked, pushing up her sleeves

and pulling up her skirts and tucking them under her bodice as the others had, although her ankles were now in complete view.

"We be taking the full pails and pouring the milk into the standers," Beth said, emptying hers into a large shallow wooden bowl. "The cream rises, my lady, and then we be skimming it off for the churning."

Anne examined the wooden plunge churn before her. It looked easy to operate. The man who thought she could not do this simple work had never seen her dress a sobbing queen or learn the steps to six different French dances while sidestepping the dancing master's hands, and all in a single afternoon.

When the cream was in the churn, Anne insisted cheerfully that she would do all the churning. At first the plunger rose and sank effortlessly, and she asked Beth and the others dozens of questions, almost as curious about their lives as they were about hers. The movement of the plunger was actually enjoyable, a use of force that gave her a good sense of her bodily strength, strength she would have much need of before this grave business was settled.

A bell rang loudly. "What's that?" Anne asked.

"We must go, my lady, to the voting. It be decided whether to join Black Ben and his band for the next ride. Can ye carry on by thyself for a time?"

"Certainly," Anne said. "Why must *you* go?"

"In this band, my lady," Beth said very importantly, "women vote with the men. Our Johnny says we share equal in all and must needs be a part of all, since if we be caught our necks will stretch like any man's." She ran toward the smithy and caught up with the other women.

Anne worked the plunger for a long time, and felt the liquid beneath her hands begin to change, become heavier. Women voting? She had never heard of such a thing. Even Cromwell had not thought of such a freedom. The king would think it a great joke and make a witty couplet. But the astonishing idea took hold of her mind and would not let go. Where had John Gilbert learned such strange practices?

By the time the sun was high, the plunger moved very slowly, and her arms and shoulders were rapidly growing achingly numb. She looked into the churn through the air-holes in the top and saw loose butter lumps floating. She would never again be able to eat butter without an appreciation of the anonymous maids who churned it.

Weren't the others ever coming back? She was thoroughly exhausted when Beth and the two women appeared.

"Why, the butter's come, my lady, and right well," Beth said, and showed her how to scrape down the sides of the churn to collect every lump, and then to add the salt and press it into firkins. Afterward, they sat about on the grass and ate new-baked oat-cakes hot from the beehive oven, dripping with her sweet butter and with flower honey. She thought she had never broken a fast so well in all her life.

After eating her fill, she stretched upon the soft green, more than ready for a nap, when a shadow blotted the sun. She opened her eyes, shielded them and saw John Gilbert looking down at her from a great height.

John had never seen her so lovely. All her satins and fine lady ways had not stirred his blood as much as the heat-flushed maid on the green grass below him, tendrils of auburn hair sticking damply to her forehead, her sea-green eyes hot with defiance, her rosy lips shiny with butter, and a crumb of oatcake nestled in the corner of her mouth, waiting to be licked away by some fortunate man.

Beth offered him a buttered cake. He took it, smiled at her and ate it, smacking his lips. "You've done a fine job with our new dairymaid, Beth. I think I'll have you instruct her in all the arts of a country lass, and we'll send her back to London with skill enough to earn her way in the world. Think you, good Beth, if the palace could make its own butter, the king wouldn't have to tax the commons so hard."

Laughing, he bent and kissed Beth's furiously blushing

cheek, turned on his booted heel and strode away toward the smithy.

Anne sat up and watched his receding back, broad and straight inside a shirt that she recalled right well was open to the navel. Yet she had a dairymaid's impulse to throw a brimming milk pail after him. That was gratitude for you. She'd slaved since early morning over the churn, and he'd acted as if it were nothing.

She felt Beth's hand on her shoulder. "He be jesting, my lady."

"I pay the man no attention. It would be too much to expect a thieving highwayman to have real sensibility." She rubbed an aching shoulder.

"Ye be very tired, Lady Anne," Beth said, her voice full of sympathy. "I will finish the washing up while ye have a little lie down."

Anne struggled to her feet, appalled at her unaccustomed stiffness, but her pride rising nonetheless. "While you work, I will work."

She soon had cause to regret both pride and promise. She and Beth gathered the wooden pails and standers. The two other woman hoisted the churn between them, and they all four headed for a stream several furlongs away in the thick woods.

The stream widened into a pool at the green place where they stopped, and a little waterfall dropped suddenly onto a wide, smooth, shallowed-out rock below, providing them with a natural basin. Beth showed Anne how to pick mare's tail to scrub the milk pails. Pig-bristle brushes, Beth explained, would be too stiff and would eventually eat away the wood utensils, which were milky soft.

When they finished, the water felt so cool and fresh on Anne's feet that she longed for a good wash herself. "Beth, let's bathe. No one will see us."

Beth and the other women shook their heads violently.

"No, my lady," Beth said, "it could unbalance the humors, and with the plague about—"

Anne laughed. "Plague take the plague! I will bathe alone, then, if you can manage the pails." She stripped off her dress, draped it on an overhanging limb, and waded into the middle of the stream where the current was swift enough to tug at her smallclothes.

She closed her eyes and let her arms float at her side, paddling a bit to stay upright. This was heaven, the first time she'd felt herself whole and clean for days. For a few minutes, she would rest both afflicted body and mind. She would forget that she was paying a penance for having loved the wrong man, she would forget that her anointed king had shown himself a lewd wretch, and she would cease to wonder and worry about her father, using all his influence at this very moment to placate the king and extricate her from her betrothal. For just a few minutes, she'd forget. Even the lowest rabbit in Whittlewood Forest needed occasional respite from the drudgery of survival.

John saw Beth and two of the women return from the stream, and for a moment he panicked. Where was Anne? Ben had gone ahead to scout the main Oxford road from London and pay his annual tribute to the sheriff, but he could have doubled back. There, good Beth was smiling, so nothing could have gone amiss.

Still, he walked quickly toward the stream, only to hide in the trees on sight of Lady Anne.

She was standing center stream in a mass of sunlit bubbles, water swirling about her pointed breasts, tugging at their lacy covering; her sweetly curved arms were held high above her head as if she were some water nymph offering herself to the gods. He stared, immensely fascinated by the image of such loveliness as he had never known before.

He had determined just this very morn that he would stay as far away from her as he could. And yet all this day, he had made excuses to see her.

"Damn me," he breathed. He'd always prided himself on his self-control, and here he was, with all he could do to keep from jumping into the water and taking her wet body into his arms, bending his lips to her breasts and sucking new life into himself to replace all that he had lost since first he met her, all that surety of purpose that he had felt leave him at every sight of her, though he tried mightily to remember that she was only a way to cheat the hangman.

Still, he watched hungrily like a loin-sick boy at his first lass, as she waded out of the stream, her smallclothes molded to her pink-and-white flesh. But he was not that boy, nor was she that lass, He was a bastard, though well born, still no match for the likes of the Lady Anne Gascoigne, betrothed to an earl, a scoundrel, true, but without the bar sinister of a bastard on his coat of arms. And that would make all the difference to the likes of Anne Gascoigne.

Some poet had said that there was never Bedlam so awful as for a man to want a woman that could not be his. Fortunately, he had never known this madness and was determined not to know it ever. He smiled at the memories that proved his confidence. Not for John Gilbert the hopeless desire that drove men, young and old, to act like tame monkeys and clowns. He would have none of it. Aye, he had naught to fear on that score when he contemplated the lady's manner. Though the Lady Anne had the likeness of an angel, she had the tongue of a harpy. Why, just the way she said his name was akin to screeching blackbirds. When the time came, he would have no qualms ridding himself of the lady and her confounded chastity.

He made so much noise angrily stomping back through the woods that Anne thought a bear had come upon her, and grabbing her gown off its limb, raced in the opposite direction until she heard the bear no more.

Chapter Five

A Milkmaid En Garde!

The next day was like the first, and the next, too. Anne rose at first light, worked with Beth at the milking and churning, fed and watered the animals and changed their straw bedding, ate her supper as far as possible from John Gilbert's seat at table, and fell, exhausted, into bed at dusk.

He spoke not a word to her, and she was glad of it. From a distance, she could see him staring at her ofttimes, but she was thankfully spared his unflattering wit, not to mention his unwelcome attentions. Still, her heart raced when she recalled his hard, commanding kisses in her bed.

Once, she walked toward the smithy where he stood talking with Joseph, and he stepped forward to meet her, obviously anticipating some discourse. At the last moment, she veered away, as if suddenly remembering a more important task. The startled look on his darkly handsome face proved worth the effort. It was some satisfaction to know that in this small instance, she had subdued him.

She denied feeling the slightest guilt for the trick. Hadn't he taken her mouth—twice—until she could literally feel the heart being sucked from her body? And then, not yet content, he'd trifled further with her emotions, something no real gentleman would do.

It wasn't until a week later that she had the time and energy to take a good look at the contents of the cottage. A restlessness gnawed at her, and she satisfied it by intense examination of her surroundings. The one room was neat for a man's lodging, especially a man with no body servant, although she knew of several women in camp who were obvious and willing slaves to his comfort. She set her mouth disapprovingly at the thought.

Near the foot of the bed, she found a chest of fine white shirts, satin breeches, matching coats and handkerchiefs of the finest lawn and lace point. Did the rogue fancy himself a lord?

"Come," she said, answering a knock at the door, just as her hand struck a hard object. The bottom of the chest was lined with books. She was holding one when Beth entered. Anne bent to replace it.

"Johnny wouldn't mind if ye read from his books, my lady," Beth said earnestly. "He tried to teach me letters once, but I had no head for them."

Anne picked up a King James Bible, Mr. Milton's *Paradise Lost*, a quarto of Shakespeare's plays, work by a playwright long considered stiff and old-fashioned unless rewritten for modern audiences, and a Latin grammar, which she had once studied herself. On the flyleaf of the grammar was written: *To John Gilbert, scholar. For excellence. Wm. Pennyman, Master, Baliol, Oxford, 1658.*

"He went up to Oxford?" Anne asked aloud, scarcely able to credit her own eyes. "Who could believe," she murmured to herself, "that a thief consorting with the likes of Black Ben had a gentleman's education?"

"Aye, he be. a gentleman, Lady Anne," Beth said, her voice fiercely loyal. "The finest and truest gentlemen that ever lived."

Anne couldn't disagree aloud with Beth, since her eyes shone with such partisan fervor, but Anne's face must have spoken her doubts for her.

"It be true, my lady, as I've good cause to know." Beth frowned and dropped to her knees beside Anne, straightening the clothing in the chest, her hands lingering lovingly on the folds of fine material.

Anne touched her arm. "You love him true, don't you?"

Beth shook her head furiously, a telltale flush suffusing her neck. "Johnny's not for such a one as me." She looked into Anne's face, her light blue eyes rapidly blinking away tears. "He needs a fine lady. As for me, I'm content to serve him as he wills."

Anne was moved by the milkmaid's selfless ardor, and consumed with a curiosity about John Gilbert that she quite suddenly realized was nothing new. She just hadn't put that name on the feeling before. "Tell me about him."

Beth's face flamed again, but her back straightened where she knelt. "He found me whoring in the London stews and brought me here. Ye cannot understand, my lady."

Anne stood and walked to the window, which was open and filled with a riot of sweet williams and violets. Her hand trembled slightly as she picked one and tucked it into Beth's kerchief collar. "I understand quite well. He recruited you for his pleasure in this forest. And you thank him for it?"

"It be not that way at all, my lady. No man lies with me here unless I will it. Those be his rules."

Anne did not look around. "Surely Master Gilbert himself—" She left the thought unfinished, but the meaning was clear.

Beth was silent, and Anne looked around to see if the girl understood. She had, most obviously. Gone was the blush. Now Beth's face was full of sadness, and her voice thick with it. "No, my lady. He will not lie with me. He says that he loves me as a sister, but that cannot be. I am fair and all his family is . . . dark." Her voice caught on the last word.

Quite suddenly, Anne wanted to hear no more. This was not the story she'd expected, and she didn't know what to make of it. Moreover, she didn't want to know. She could not have been wrong about John Gilbert. He was a notorious rakehell whose famous mistress had come to his hanging, where they had both engaged in shameless and ribald banter. His men, new returned from London, had repeated the story endlessly until she was thoroughly sick unto death of hearing it. Now Beth would have her believe that such a man rescued whores and gave them protection and a healthy trade as milkmaids. Even if simple Beth thought it true, the story was too much for Anne to credit.

"Beth, you have been kind to me, and I would be a good friend to you. In some ways I am more of the world than you, and I warn you to be on your guard. Men, even those you think gentlemen, are capable of great deception."

Beth looked fascinated. "Were you so deceived, my lady?"

"Yes, Beth, most cruelly, by a man I honored and loved above all other men. Yet without regard for my tenderest feelings, he would have betrayed his vows and mine for his own gain. I will never again place my trust in any man but my father."

Beth turned up her moon-round face, its faith and love writ for all with eyes to see. "Ye can trust John Gilbert, Lady Anne. He knows what it be like to suffer betrayal. Bastard or no, the duke, his father, loved him and left him three hundred a year, and Burwell Hall and its deer park. But his half brothers changed the will, cheating him of his rightful inheritance. And when he threatened to take them before the courts, they accused him of stealing the crest ring the duke had given him. He had to flee Oxford or lose his life, and thence, as ye see him now, to become a captain of the road."

The story had all come out on several long breaths while Beth knelt, smoothing John Gilbert's clothes with her work-reddened hands. She stood abruptly when she was finished, plainly embarrassed by the lengthy speech. "I almost forgot why I came, my lady. He says you be joining us at the women's swordplay on the green."

Anne was astonished at this new evidence of John Gilbert's strange ideas about women. "Does he think us Greek Amazons?"

"I do not know these Amazons, my lady, but he be wanting the women of the camp to defend ourselves if the men be gone." She opened the door, and on her way out added, "And he says for you to don a pair of his breeches."

First he would make of Anne Gascoigne a milkmaid, and then a woman-at-arms. He was insufferable! While it was true that London women of a lower order and actresses sometimes fought duels over men at Epsom, Anne could never imagine herself doing such a thing. As a child, she had watched her father and later Edward, during a thousand hours of sword practice, but she had never so much as held a rapier in her hand, except in jest. Of course, she would absolutely refuse to behave in such a common manner.

Anne sat down in the chair by the fireplace, hands tightly folded, and waited for the sounds of John Gilbert approaching the cottage to force her to do his bidding. Because he *would* come for her; she was sure of it. As leader, he could not afford to ignore any act of defiance. She waited for some time. When he did not come, she felt a kind of impotent disappointment. Damn his eyes! He was too clever by half. If she did not appear with the other women, they would think her weak, and that would be more intolerable than the satisfaction she would give John Gilbert by appearing. Damn! Damn! Damn!

She threw open the chest at the foot of the bed and flung his clothes about, choosing his best pair of satin breeches, a ribboned Flemish linen shirt, and silk hose. So much the better if she got them dirty. Since this was his idea, her conscience would be easy.

Anne was halfway across the green before she realized that she had covered the distance in half the time it would have taken her in a gown. Her legs, although encased in breeches and hose, were free to stride as they would. It had never occurred to her that a gown and a lady's shift, not to mention bone corsets, had forced her to take small steps, and therefore, perhaps, forced her to think of small accomplishments. She began to take giant steps, aware that his eyes were following her.

He bowed low as she approached him, and saluted her with his sword. "You confirm me in my prejudice, Lady Anne. I have ever known that a woman's legs were more fit than a man's for the world's view."

She imitated his bow with an extra hand flourish. "If you thought to force a blush from me, sir, I must beg your forgiveness. I find your breeches quite agreeable on me."

His face didn't change as he brought his sword to a second salute, but she saw his dark eyes flash, and she could swear that his knuckles were white when he turned the sword and presented its hilt to her. "Would you like to observe the others first?"

"Nay, sir, I know very well what to do."

Near a dozen women in breeches stood in a line across the greensward, which was ringed with men nudging and shoving each other in various stages of helpless amusement. A sharp signal from John Gilbert sobered them.

He bowed to his students. "Ladies, take up your foot positions and follow me through the attack as I've taught you," he commanded.

With grave demeanor, they did. Anne was amazed. There was no simpering or giggling from these outlaw maids, just serious purpose on their ruddy faces.

John chose a new blade, tested its heft, and took a stance. "*En garde!* Lunge! Parry! Riposte! Faster now, and smoother. *En garde,* lunge, parry and riposte. No, not that way, Lady Anne."

She was hopelessly behind. It was one thing to watch her father or Edward at practice, and quite another to thrust a sword weighing several pounds to the full extent of her arm, while holding her body in a posture no woman should be called upon to display in public, even a woman in breeches.

He came up behind her and took hold of her sword arm. His other hand held her free arm in the air in a graceful arc. "You are too stiff," he said, jiggling her arms. "Let your body be supple, my lady. I can recommend it for most endeavors—especially swordplay."

She stiffened further. His entire body was pressed against her back, his right leg extended the length of hers, pressing his manly part against her thigh. This was too bold even for an outlaw! "I have no doubt you are acquainted with supple bodies, sir," she rasped fiercely. "Is that one of the lewd lines you speak to the mistress of the Theater Royal?"

She imagined his consternation, but when she looked up, he was grinning.

"No, my lady, to instruct Nellie in the lithesome uses of the body would be to belabor the obvious."

John blessed his wit, because he was achingly aroused. Still, walking away from Anne was out of the question. He would not cringe from his attraction to this woman. She was a penance for his life that he must pay Sir Samuel, and he would pay it until the debt was honorably discharged—no matter if the paying galled him in every part. And from the exquisite pain he was in, it was likely to do that and more.

It was only slight recompense that he'd thought he saw a flicker of jealousy at the mention of Nell Gwyn's name. He held Anne tighter to hide his discomposure.

She tried to pull away. "I cannot breathe, sir, if you hold me so tightly."

He loosed her only negligibly and whispered into her hair, "There will be no need to hold you so, if you will move freely. Allow your body the freedom it craves. It is not as arduous as you think. Pretend that you are dancing at the king's ball, only this is a deadly dance, Lady Anne, one that could save your life." He clucked his tongue. "I am saddened that the least of the women on this green have more skill in a gentle's art than you who were born to it." His too-sincere tone of voice grew wry. "Could it be that there is less that separates the common people than is thought at Whitehall?"

She wriggled within his ironlike arms. "That is traitorous thought, sir, if not blasphemy. You need not instruct me in the duties of my rank."

"It pleasures me to instruct you in all things, Lady Anne, though I have had better students." He brought her arm up. "*En garde.* Now lunge." He extended her arm straight in front with his own.

She could feel his big muscles moving along her small ones, and they seemed to add power to her thrust.

"Left leg absolutely straight," he said. He bent and straightened it; she was sure that his strong fingers left marks through the satin breeches on her calf. Her heart was pounding from the exertion. It was the unaccustomed exercise, she was certain.

Finally, he released and faced her, engaging her sword with his own. "Now, from the lunge position, you raise your blade thus, into the head cut. But you must be very fast, because I will parry—like this—and counterattack with the riposte."

Her blade flew from her hand and landed at some distance, quivering upright in the grass.

"Huzzah!" The shout went up from his men.

At that moment, she despised him and his wretched instruction, invented, she was sure, as a pretext for her further humiliation in front of this rabble.

His sword point danced around her throat. "You are at my mercy, my lady."

She stood absolutely still and unafraid. "Then thrust, sir. If you do not, then if I have to toil at practice from morn till eve, I warn you that I will give a better account of myself next time."

He barely suppressed the glint of approval in his eye as he picked up her blade and returned it to her. "You have a spirit of contest within you, my lady, that I find surprising in one of your birth. Perhaps you would care to instruct *me* in this regard."

He saluted her with his sword, and slowly at first, then more rapidly, led her through a practice.

She worked hard, but despite the growing heaviness of her arm and the stretching of her calf muscles until they ached, she knew without doubt that this highwayman had a strange intelligence. A notorious rakehell, still he had a peculiar regard for women's courage and abilities that she had never seen before in even the most philosophical of men. She had spoken with Mr. Pepys and Mr. Dryden at length in her father's house and at court, and they were not so well thought on the subject as this highwayman.

It occurred to Anne that whenever she looked for a good thing in John Gilbert, she found it. And then she remembered his kisses, two of them, and she grew overheated at the thought, despite the chill clouds that soon promised an afternoon shower.

Having circled her for some time, he sought to catch her off guard. He lunged, and she parried.

"Well done!" he shouted, and she felt inordinately pleased at his praise.

She noticed that his shirt was open and that a fine mat of dark hair curled beneath the red ribbon tie. She shivered as the first raindrops began to fall. The last thing in this world she wished was to want John Gilbert in the same accursed fashion that she'd wanted Edward. That part of a woman's life was closed to her. Love and trust had died for her that moment in the queen's closet when passion had been betrayed beyond forgiving or forgetting. After her uncle, the Bishop of Ely, had soothed the king and recalled her marriage banns to Lord Waverby, she would retire to her father's Essex manor and live a life of good works. And she would reorganize the dairy until it became a model for the shire, and perhaps teach the milkmaids the secrets of the sword.

She smiled at that woman-to-be. What an eccentric old crone she would become!

It was now raining in earnest, and still John Gilbert did not call an end to the sword practice. Anne noticed that Beth and the other women were slogging merrily through the soaking grass, back and forth in front of the men, the ring of their steel adding zest to their obvious enthusiasm.

"Are you tired?" he asked her.

"Are you?" she challenged, and lunged.

He parried and shook his head, amused and delighted. "In a fight, I'd rather have you at my back, Anne, than many a man."

She ignored his lack of formality. "Thank you, sir." She saluted him with her sword. He returned her salute, and they continued to stand before each other, their eyes unwavering, rain pelting their faces.

It had been a pretty compliment. Nay, more than pretty; a gallant and friendly statement. She searched his face for any mischief, concentrating on his eyes, dark as a forest pool, watching her from under straight black brows. Her oath on it, but that face held nothing of sham. It was open and honest, naught contrived. She could almost believe that he was a highwayman through no choice of his own, as Beth had told, that he had been just as betrayed by loved ones as she.

He was smiling now, blinking against the rain, and with the look of the earnest Oxford lad in place of the insolent highwayman. When he was like this, it was difficult to remember all his ill qualities, or, remembered, almost impossible not to forgive them.

She smiled, and then they were both laughing over nothing and everything, which made for the best laughter.

Two horseman exited the hidden tunnel, one blindfolded, the other a camp guard, leading. Both rode at a gallop toward the group on the greensward. Slipping the blindfold, the stranger dismounted and ran, drenched in the downpour, to John Gilbert.

"My master says that if you would continue to enjoy his protection, you are to come to Burwell Hall at once."

"But," Anne blurted, "that was your manor."

John looked at her, surprised at her knowledge. "Was to be, once, but no more." He nodded to the messenger. "Tell your master that I cannot come."

"Lord Waverby commands it. Tonight. And he must have the thousand pounds of tribute."

"Very well. Report that I will attend him at midnight."

John Gilbert did not look at Anne Gascoigne's face. He couldn't bear the loathing he knew that he would see there.

Anne stumbled backward, wanting desperately to distance herself from this monstrous treachery. And then she began to run.

Chapter Six

Troubled Hours

He caught her on the stone lintel of the cottage and pulled her, struggling, inside. "Anne, by God's wounds, it's not what you think!"

"Loose me, sir!" she rasped, her voice harsh with disbelief and something more: the intolerable sense that she had been on the verge of playing the fool with this man. She was indeed lost in the world if she could not trust her own emotions to ever be true.

His hands dropped from her arms, and he stepped away, badly shaken by what he saw in her eyes. They were dangerously wounded, crying out in pain. He knew that he had nearly made her at the least his friend, and now he had before him an implacable enemy.

With a great effort, he steadied himself. "My lady, you may not want to listen to me, but you will do so before I leave."

"Say on, sir," she said, and he hated the sound of loathing rising like an inexorable tide in her voice. "I have no doubt that a felon can excuse any vice, but you must graciously allow me the right to despise you for it."

Anger fell about him like a prickly woolen cloak. How dare this aristocrat condemn him with such want of compassion. Did she take him for that noble debauchee Waverby, or that royal fool at Whitehall?

He knew her heart was closed, but by heaven, she would not close her ears to him. In two long steps, he had her by the shoulders, shaking her. "By what moral authority do you condemn me without a hearing? Take care, my lady, that you do not allow Lord Waverby's betrayal to make you as heartless as he is."

"You are a fine one to speak of another man's betrayal."

There was irony in her tone, and he regretted it. Irony in a woman meant a final loss of innocence.

Gone was the lass who had grown more lithesome as she crossed swords with him on the green. Now she was unbending in his hands.

"Sir, you're hurting me!"

He reduced the pressure of his fingers but held her firm so that she could not turn away, which he knew she longed to do. And he must force her to look on his face, if she were ever to believe him. "I will say this but once, and you may do with it what you will." His tone was earnest but haughty. He was not a man to be content until his word was heard. "I did not lie to you or your father about my connection to Lord Waverby. You never asked, and it was a business that had naught to do with you." He rushed on before she could object. "For seven years, I have paid Lord Waverby an annual tribute of one thousand pounds. In return, he encourages the sheriff to stay hard by his prison in Oxford, or to patrol the wrong roads. Black Ben pays his protection to the sheriff, but I have preferred to deal with Waverby. It pleases me to further compromise the man who stole Burwell Hall from my brothers at cards."

Anne laughed bitterly. "Your brothers must be exceedingly poor players, Master Gilbert. Edward lost large sums almost nightly at Whitehall to my lady Castlemaine."

"I doubt even Waverby would cheat the king's mistress."

"As you plan to cheat my father by turning me over to

Edward. Tell me what value I have. What is to be my price?"
Her voice didn't quaver with fear, but was as hard as her
hope for vengeance could make it.

"Is that what you think?"

"Don't hide behind innocent pretense, sir. It ill becomes
your reputation. Tell me, what else would I think? You are a
land pirate of the first order, and ransom would be your
trade. My father made a grave mistake in you."

He stared deep into her green eyes, as old and hard now
as emeralds in amber; and yet, for him, still holding the
memory of the melting glances that had ignited his blood but
a short time earlier. "And you, my lady, did *you* make a mistake when we laughed together just now on the green?" For
a moment he thought he saw a hint of confusion in that too-
inflexible face, but it was gone so soon as to make him think
he'd seen false.

Then her words came, carefully considered and adamant,
dashing his hope for understanding. "No, Master Gilbert, I
made no mistake about you; I was right from the beginning.
You are a thorough rogue, sir, and therefore I can easily treat
with you. Whatever Edward offers you, my father will double."

"Your father has offered me my life and a rather agreeable life at that. I take the next fair wind for Jamaica. How
can he double that?"

"You are playing with words, sir. Just remember what
I've said. If you bargain me away, it will be a poor bargain
in the end."

He bent his head until his mouth was bare inches from
hers, his voice throbbing with intensity and an underlying
puzzlement. "Have I given you any injury, Anne, robbed you
of anything you came here with? There are few chaste
women who are not tired of their trade. Yet have I not held
myself away from you when any other man would have
taken you in your bed that first night? Why, then, would I lie
to you now?"

She turned her mouth away from his. "Even the devil has his devil's reasons."

He felt his control loosen and flow from him as if a river was at the flood. "Damn me, but you are an impossible wench! You use words like cudgels. Since you would have me a rogue, I will play the part with a mastery you will not soon forget."

He pulled her to him so quickly that the sudden impact she made with his hard body nearly took her equilibrium. His bruising kisses devoured her mouth, her throat, and her mouth again, completing the process. And then with the most insolent of bows, scraping his plumed hat across the floor, he left her shaking and gasping for air, as he slammed shut the cottage door.

Anne didn't know how long she stood staring after him, trembling with every strong emotion known to her, and some unknown that she could put no pious name to. But she knew one thing. She must flee from this man. He was more than flesh and blood and good sense together could repel.

Now she looked about wildly. How could she escape? Guards ringed the camp. Only Beth could guide her safely through them, but poor, misguided Beth would never betray John Gilbert. And what if she could gain the roads outside Whittlewood Forest? What poor cottager or passing tinker could resist the fortune for her return that Edward had probably offered by this time?

It was hours before she slept, supperless and depleted, as if by long illness. Horsemen rode past her door, and pitch-pine torches shone briefly through the mullioned window. Once she thought she heard Black Ben's voice echo from the green, but she couldn't be certain, and at last her eyelids grew too heavy to hold open.

She dreamed of fighting her way through the shadows of a long, murky tunnel, sword in hand, on and on, never reaching a distant, wavering light.

"Wake up," Beth said, pulling at the quilt. "Quickly, my lady. There be not much time."

Anne swam up from the depths of sleep toward Beth's voice. "What is it?"

"Ye be leaving, my lady. He's sent this disguise for ye to wear."

"But where—"

"Please, Lady Anne, Black Ben has returned, and Johnny dare not leave ye behind."

He was taking her to Burwell Hall, she knew. The betrayal had come faster than she'd expected. John Gilbert must think to strike an instant bargain with Edward.

Reluctantly, Beth handed Anne breeches and shirt, cloak and boots. "'Tis me own costume for the swordplay."

"But, Beth, why this disguise? Edward will expect a lady of the court."

Beth shook her head. "I know nothing, my lady, except that ye must be gone while Ben sleeps. He would have ye for himself." She shivered. "Hurry!"

The rain had stopped and a wild moon rode low in the night sky, casting an eerie light over the camp. The two women raced across the common to the smithy, its fires banked, and beyond to where two men waited. John Gilbert was already mounted; no heavy cloak could hide that cavalier air. His big chestnut stallion, named Sir Pegasus, nickered and stamped, impatient to be off.

"Get her a wig from the chest, Joseph. That reddish hair would be a beacon amongst us."

Beth grabbed Anne's hand and kissed it. "Farewell, my lady."

"Farewell, good Beth," Anne said, kissing her cheek in return.

Bewigged and mounted, Anne quieted her horse as John's danced alongside. He handed her a baldric and sword. "Pray you don't have to prove your newfound skill this night."

She tossed her head. "Do we go to plunder helpless travelers, sir, or will you be content to sell me quickly to the highest bidder?"

She could not see his face, but she heard the rage trembling in his voice. "I may do exactly as I please, Lady Anne. I have all power over you."

He spurred the big horse, and they made for the secret tunnel. Some minutes later, they were through the passage and into the forest, then splashing down the stream and on the track to Oxford Road, startling owls from their perches.

She considered making a dash for it, but caution warned her that she would be ridden down before she could go a furlong. Sir Peg, as John Gilbert affectionately called his powerful horse, could outstride her mare without raising a sweat. So then it had come down to this: Edward, John Gilbert or Black Ben, all men of no honor, out to use her body for their own gain. Of the three, Edward at least was born a gentleman, and might listen to her appeal for reason for the sake of whatever regard he might have for her father. It was ironic that the man whose base plans had caused her flight might, after all, be the one to save her from worse.

Although she had slept little, she was very alert. The heavy-scented forest, leaves dripping rain and shining with diffused moonlight, engaged her senses. On any other night, this would have been an adventure, a ride to recall in her mind, to bethink its earthy odor, and the shadows of light and dark cast by the tall man and the giant steed in front of her. As it was, she knew that she would remember this night as the night John Gilbert had proved himself the greatest villain in the world.

"Hold!" John shouted near the place where the Oxford Road crossed the forest track.

Anne reined, her mare between John and Joseph.

"I hear it," Joseph said, cupping his ear to the night sounds. "A lone carriage, no outriders."

John smiled. "Then we will do a bit of business if it does not delay us overlong."

They waited, well hidden, in a copse of woods.

Anne was furious. "Sir, you cannot force me to a felon's work."

He shrugged, handing her a black mask for her eyes and nose. "Cover your face or you will see it on a handbill ere you return to London. You would not be the first of your sex to work on the road and die for it."

John and Joseph donned masks just as a small carriage drawn by two horses slowed at the crossroads, seemingly uncertain of the way.

John spurred forward, Anne's horse following, his pistol aimed at the driver. "Halt! Hand over your weapons. Do not be foolish—I have a man in the woods." Joseph yelled a confirmation.

John's voice was loud and harsh, his words not open to dispute. The driver complied meekly.

"Open, I say," John commanded, knocking on the carriage door with his foot.

A pretty blond head leaned out, its eyes coquettish under a red silk-lined hood. "Sir, by your mask, I take you for a gentleman of the road. My life is at your mercy."

"Nay, madame," John said, bowing from his saddle as if he were riding of a Sunday morn in St. James Park, "'tis not your life I would have, but your fortune."

"Then, sir, you will collect no prize for this night's work. My husband died of a sudden, and I have come away, as you see me, without two pence to put in my purse."

John smiled and bowed again. "Do we not come into this world and leave it with nothing? We shall both survive your empty purse, madame."

He heard a deep cough from within the carriage, and was instantly alert. "Move aside, madame, so that I may see who is with you. Show yourself, with your hands up!" John demanded.

A bewigged head with several trembling chins appeared.

John stared at the man, a smile playing upon his lips. "Your name, sir."

"Sir Richard Mourton, brother to this lady, and dear friend of the sheriff of this shire."

"I am honored, sir, to be the occasion of much good conversation when next you meet with your dear friend the sheriff. In the meantime, hand over your purse!"

"Think you I am crazy enough to travel this road with gold?" came the sullen response.

John leaned out of the saddle and thrust his pistol into the man's green velvet doublet, trimmed with exquisite silver-and-gold lace, one row upon another. "Your purse, sir, or the sheriff will mourn a friend."

As if by magic, a fat purse was offered, but not without bluster. "I warn you, thief, that I will see you hang for this night's work."

John weighed the heavy purse in his hand. "Then I will die well paid, indeed."

Joseph sidled his horse alongside Anne and spoke to John. "The woman has a wedding ring with a fine stone."

The woman hastily withdrew her hand from the window. "Boy," she said, addressing Anne with passionate desperation, "think of your poor mother. Surely you would not take a widow's most sentimental possession."

Anne had watched the entire charade with wonder, and could only stammer a denial.

John interrupted. "The boy is of tender disposition, and I fear not suited for this profession. But he speaks for me. I filch no wedding rings." He quieted Sir Pegasus. "Madame, how far do you travel this night?"

"To the next turning," she said, "and thence to my brother's manse."

"Then we will provide escort." He laughed heartily. "There are truer rogues abroad than this lad here."

"Why did you not take her ring?" Anne asked when they had fallen in behind the coach. "She could have been lying."

John didn't answer, and Anne was forced for the next miles to contend with a troubled mind, which bent first one way and then another.

After parting from the coach, they soon reined in across from a three-story inn marked with the sign of two boars' heads. John waited for several minutes, studying the inn.

Joseph flapped his arms and drew his cloak close. "For mid-June month, it's colder than a witch's tit. I could use a tankard of strong ale." He started forward, but John grabbed his reins. "What's wrong, Johnny? It be quiet enough."

"That's what's wrong. It's too quiet. Look you, Joseph. Two large carriages, hard traveled by the look of them, drawn up in the yard, yet no pipes nor tabors play." He sniffed the air. "No smell of cookery, either. Wait here, and watch Lady Anne with both eyes."

John kicked his horse forward into a walk and slowly approached the inn yard, his hand on his sword. The moon was behind clouds as he reached the inn door. He got off his horse just as the moon came from behind a cloud and lit the front of the building, and just as quickly John Gilbert leaped into the saddle and spurred his horse back across the road and into the trees.

"What be wrong, Johnny?" Joseph asked.

"Plague! The red crucifix is upon the door. God have mercy upon them."

"Then what do we do with the lass if she can't keep safe there?"

Anne had overheard. "Why was I to stay at the inn?"

John looked at her, his mouth set in a troubled line. "Is it possible that you have wronged me?"

And then she realized what his purpose must be. "Oh, I see. You want to keep me out of sight until you haggle a higher price. Or did you fear that I might forgive Edward and escape to him of my free will?"

John looked at her, his dark face thunderous. "As you say! An earl can be forgiven anything. A bastard, nothing."

He spurred his horse to a gallop, and she and Joseph were forced to make haste to catch him.

They took Oxford Road west and turned north toward Burwell village, arriving near midnight at the long road through the deer park to Burwell Hall.

Joseph looked right and left. "Do ye know your way, Johnny?"

"Aye. I lived as a lad here. I could find the library with my eyes closed."

Anne's conscience flinched at the passion behind those words. The man might be the worst rakehell in England, but he loved his lost manor as a good son loved a dead mother. That part of Beth's story was true. She looked at John Gilbert, who was drinking in the moonlit scene, and felt a wrench of understanding. This man had been born disappointed, already wounded as a babe in his bastard's cradle; and for all his life he had been goaded by his lack of name and land.

She jerked her mount's reins in consternation. How could she sympathize with this highwayman's misfortune of birth? It must be the moon that addled her, or the midnight witching hour. She must keep tighter rein on her thoughts, which kept straying from her purpose.

They rode through the arch into the forecourt and around the side of the manor, which Anne could see was a jewel of a small country house built during King Harry's time, with graceful arched stone tracery windows and tall red brick chimneys. It would be impossible not to delight in such a place.

Anne reined in. "If your intent is indeed an honorable one, Master Gilbert, then leave me here."

He laughed. "And have you flee in the dark as soon as I'm out of sight?"

"Then leave Joseph to watch me."

"Nay, I have need of a friend's sword at my side." Taking her reins, he led her horse along until they stopped in a line of shrubs across from some candlelit windows. Anne could see a large book-lined room, and she had no trouble identifying Edward's tall, slender form, attended by a blue-and-silver-liveried servant.

She had wondered what her feelings might be on seeing Edward again. She had wondered if there might be some stirring of the ashes of love, some spark that could reignite her once most tender feelings for him. She stared through the windows and saw Edward bend close to a candle to light his tobacco pipe; she saw the long, tapered fingers, remembered the sensuous lips, but the ashes of love remained cold and dead.

Anne thought for a tiny moment to throw herself on John Gilbert's mercy, to beg him not to hand her over to Edward, to promise him her maidenhead, but just as quickly she knew that she could never forswear her chastity. It would have to be cruelly taken; it would never be freely given to any man, least of all to a rogue who had forsworn himself. She had felt some moments of weakness with this charlatan, but she would never repeat them, not in this life.

John Gilbert removed his wide-brimmed hat. "Put this on your head," he told her, "and keep your face down. Bide here, and speak not a word."

She looked at him, and her words were as icy as faithless love and betrayal had made them. "Why continue this charade, sir? Parade the goods, set my price and be done, you flesh merchant!"

John's face contorted. "Joseph, if she makes another sound, gag her!"

The three dismounted and walked their horses toward the library windows.

Joseph and Anne stopped in the shadows. John Gilbert handed his reins to Joseph. "Watch for the earl's men, Joseph. Treachery is his favorite dish. He might think to have my tribute and me, as well." John crossed the terrace and stepped through an open window. "Good evening, my lord," John said, bowing, but not nearly so low as custom decreed.

Edward whirled about, and Anne could see that he was dressed in silk breeches and a clinging silk shirt with brightly gartered sleeves, over which was draped a long purple velvet robe. " 'Pon my word, John, you're quiet as a cat."

"A cat bearing a thousand pounds," John said, and threw a saddlebag on the table. "Count it, my lord. You cannot trust a highwayman." He grinned, insolence marking his bearing.

Edward laughed and put aside his pipe. "What tomfool is this? Of course I trust you as I would the king." He tossed his head with a delighted smirk, and motioned to his servant. "The claret, man."

Edward handed John a full glass, and raised his own. "Eh, what?" He peered through his windows. "You have men lurking outside. I'd be more content to have them where I can watch their mischief."

"It's only my smith and a groom with the horses."

"My man will hold your horses." He waved the servant outside. "Indeed, Sir Highwayman, I do truly trust you as I would the king, which is to say not at all. Since His Majesty banished me from court for failure to deliver on a bargain, I would not present my back to you or your men—or the king." Waverby smiled at his own wit.

John felt alarm. Anne's disguise was a good one, but could it fool her former betrothed? "Leave the lad, my lord, and—"

Waverby stepped to the door and spoke harshly. "Inside, you two. I am master here."

Joseph walked the few steps to the library window, and Anne, head down, hat pulled low, followed.

"Wait!" Edward commanded, as Anne passed within arm's length and her heart leaped into her mouth. Whatever John Gilbert's plan, Anne was beginning to have a crazy hope that selling her to Edward was no part of it. Maybe he designed to sell her to the king for a pardon!

Edward tilted her face up with two fingers under her chin and studied her, but she could see in his eyes that he did not recognize this ruddy, smudge-faced, red-eyed, beardless country lad as the court lady he had romanced and pledged to love and marry.

"A comely youth for a groom." Lord Waverby winked at John Gilbert. "Have you heard the latest rhyme from the Drury Lane stews?" He repeated several lines about a whore who wronged a man, then with a suggestive leer at first John and then Anne, added. *"I storm and I roar, and I topple in a rage,/And missing my whore, I fall on my page!"*

The highwayman was at Anne's side and put his arm about her protectively. Waverby's eyes opened wider.

"I see that an occasional boy is agreeable even to John Gilbert." His laughter followed Anne, as John shoved her toward Joseph, who was standing beyond the firelight's reach.

"I am disinclined toward that fashion, my lord, of either whore or Greek boy," John drawled with a scarcely concealed scorn. "I find I love most a lass who would not jilt me."

Waverby had poured out two more glasses of wine, and his hand replaced the decanter very deliberately. For such an affront, he had called out and gutted nobler men.

Seething, but keeping a rein on his tongue for Anne's sake, John waved aside the wine. "If you will count the money, we can speedily conclude our business, Lord Waverby."

"Not so," Edward said, and Anne saw real malice in his eyes when he looked on John. She knew that he would remember this insult until he had satisfied it with blood.

Edward sipped his wine, twirling the stem of his glittering crystal glass, his style impeccable. "John Gilbert, I have another matter that will interest you very much indeed."

John bowed. "I am all attention, my lord." He paused and

smiled tauntingly. "Although I will be quite busy intercepting the increased carriage traffic from London to the Oxford crossroads."

Edward nodded, but was obviously eager to say on. "Nonetheless, hear me. I am searching for the Lady Anne Gascoigne, my betrothed, who was spirited out of Whitehall these many days past. I suspect her father, Sir Samuel, but I cannot prove it. She's not in her Essex manor and not in her father's London lodgings. I've had both places watched endlessly, and a generous reward posted. I have reason to think she might be in Oxfordshire, although the sheriff can learn no word of her. "

John kept his features relaxed when Anne's name came to the earl's lips, but Anne had no trouble reading the caution in John's eyes. "I am sorry for your troubles, my Lord Waverby, but how does your melancholy misfortune with this lady involve me?"

"It is all over London how you escaped from Sir Samuel, commandeered his carriage, wounded him in the arm, and left him beside the road. A bold piece of work, sir, if you'll allow me, and one that recommends you to me."

Anne listened hard at the sound of her father's name, and trembled when she heard of his injury. So that's what he'd meant to do all the time to cover John's escape. She was full of pride for her father's bravery.

John shrugged. "My lord, Sir Samuel was not my match in strength. I hope he is recovering, since I wished the gentleman no real harm."

Edward's mouth smiled, but his eyes did not. He smoothed the wide silver lace at his cuff with long, elegant fingers. "That particular wound no longer bothers the worthy justice, Master Gilbert. But two nights past, some scoundrels waylaid him in an alley near Covent Garden and clubbed him to death."

Chapter Seven

A Vow of Revenge

Anne would have cried out and swooned but for Joseph's iron-strong grip on her shoulder that caused enough sudden physical pain to interrupt despair. "Steady, lass," he whispered close to her ear.

But she could not steady herself. Her knees seemed to disintegrate; her strength flowed toward the parquet floor as a torrent of unshed tears. Finally, Joseph held her up literally by the scruff of her cloak.

Across the room, John blessed her for not crying out, although she had every right to. Without looking at her, he bowed very low toward the smirking man whose blood he longed to spill this very moment, then took up his wineglass, quickly stepping toward the fire, away from Anne and Joseph. John didn't know how long she could stay her mourning, but he did know that it couldn't possibly be for more than a few minutes' time.

Lord Waverby followed him into the bright firelight, his back to Joseph and Anne.

"My Lord Waverby," John said, taking a very large swallow of wine to drown his rage, "the streets of London are truly unsafe if a royal judge can be so cowardly murdered."

Waverby's elegant white face looked pensive. "It would

seem that when there's plague about, forcing good people to stay behind their doors, footpads and rogues are free to ply their trade. 'Tis a pity." He shrugged, a smile playing about his lips. "No doubt the good judge is now in those bright regions of eternal bliss we all so piously long for. Richly deserved, you'll agree, Master Gilbert."

For Anne's sake, John tried to hide his contempt for the man, with limited success. "I do indeed, my lord. I could wish no more than what is deserved, for the judge, or for you."

Edward laughed. "But not for some time, Master Gilbert, and certainly not before we have concluded our business. When you hear my proposal, you will be eager to drink to my very good health."

John managed a civil nod. His sword hand itched to kill the devil on the spot, for it was clear that Lord Waverby had foully disposed of Sir Samuel. John had grudgingly admired the judge when as a highwayman he had stood sentenced to death before him, more so when Sir Samuel had been willing to sacrifice all for his daughter. It had been an example of father love that resonated deep in his bastard's heart. Now Anne was near alone in the world, just where Waverby wanted her, and despite her haughty palace manner, John Gilbert felt pity for her, as one orphan to another.

"Then to business, my lord. I have a hard ride ahead, and the lad is asleep on his feet." He had seen Anne slump, and Joseph pull her against him, her face muffled in his cloak.

Lord Waverby looked at the smith and the boy, then curiously back at John. "You are indeed a democratical highwayman to worry so about your men's comfort."

"I have need of all loyal sword arms, my lord."

"You have greater need for your brain, John Gilbert. I want you to find the Lady Anne Gascoigne and bring her to me alive."

John felt a bone-deep chill. "Why me, my lord, when you can make inquiries and post rewards?"

"Nay, the commoners will tell you what they would never tell me or my agents. You know the people of this shire, every freeholder and squire, and they will have heard if the jade is about."

"You have the wrong man, my lord. I can hunt deer in the deepest copse, I can run a fox to ground, but I have never had to capture a lady who did not willingly come to me."

Lord Waverby frowned. "The jilt has damaged my reputation, told lies about me, and she will pay for it every minute of every day for the rest of her life."

John had to create a diversion. Anne was near collapse and should be away from this room, away from the haunting presence of a man who'd had her father killed so savagely. John threw his glass against the marble fireplace, where it shattered into a dozen pieces. "I do no such unmanly work, sir. No, damn me, not for a thousand pounds!"

Waverby smiled and spoke softly, flicking imaginary glass shards from his sleeve. "For Burwell Hall, then, Master Gilbert. If you find Anne Gascoigne and bring her to me with her virginity still ripe for the plucking, then I will deed Burwell Hall to you and your heirs forever, and get the king to pardon you, as well. A knighthood could very well follow after such service. Think on it, man. You could live the life you were born to live."

Waverby's face darkened at John's silence. "Or, Sir Highwayman, you can inevitably end swinging from Tyburn's deadly tree."

Anne had heard the shattering of John's glass through a great fog of pain, and then the voices, each word entering her mind raggedly until she was able to assemble them into a meaning. When she did, the cold cunning of Edward's plan drenched her scalding agony, and she drew away from Joseph, standing erect on her own two legs. Lord Waverby had offered John Gilbert the one reward he could never resist.

Anne stepped forward, some of her old boldness regained. If she was to be handed over to Edward, it would be with a show of courage. When the end came, it was her duty to equal her father's mettle. At the thought of his name, she faltered, but only for a moment, and then stood straight again. She would not be trussed and delivered like a lamb. She would doff the wig and toss it in Lord Waverby's face with the scorn he deserved. And hidden in the pocket tied under her smallclothes, comfortingly hard against her bare skin, the Italian steel lay waiting for the first man who thought to take her virginity, be he earl or king.

John was aware of her move toward them and divined its purpose. He spoke harshly. "You there, Joseph, take the boy and go to the horses. I would talk privately with his lordship. Get your arses out of here now!"

Joseph's hand propelled Anne through the open library window and out onto the terrace before she had time to respond.

A curious Lord Waverby watched them go until John distracted him with a dramatic wave of his arm. "All this could be mine, you say. My lord, you do play upon a man's weakness," he said, "but it seems a high price to pay for a virgin's blood."

"I have many manors, Master Gilbert, all a drain on my purse, but the Lady Anne is the one woman who can repair my fortunes for me."

"My lord, I would not have thought her so well dowered, although she does now come into her father's estate."

Waverby picked up his long-stemmed white clay pipe and relit it. "The estate is mine already. But her value to me far surpasses a few Essex acres and tenant cottagers. Yet enough! You do not need to know more. What concern is it to you?"

So it is true, then, John thought. This lord does plan to whore his own wife to the king for gain. "No concern, as you say, my lord, except that I do hear the lady is surpassingly beautiful."

"Handsome enough, I suppose, if you have a taste for the virtuous, but she is most willful." Waverby frowned, and pipe smoke swirled about his head. "A disadvantage in a wife, you'll agree, Master Gilbert, but one easily corrected in the marriage bed." He laughed.

John bowed. The cold-complexioned whoreson was trying the last shreds of his patience. "I must take my leave, my lord. Be assured that I will think of little else besides your generous offer." At least that answer was as true as could be.

"I must know the day, the very hour, you hear of her whereabouts."

"Rest easy, my lord. You will be the first to hear when the Lady Anne Gascoigne is discovered."

Without a bow, John crossed to the windows, stepped through and was quickly at his horse. Anne and Joseph were mounted, but her face was in shadow and he left her to her grief. "Let's away," he called, and they quickly retraced their path around the manor, down the wide lane and through the deer park.

But when they stopped at the turning to Oxford Road, Anne swayed, a sob choking past her pressed lips, and then another sob followed after, and another, until she was sobbing full tilt on her horse's neck, helpless to stop.

John encircled her waist with his powerful sword arm, lifted her bodily from the saddle and placed her in front of him on Sir Pegasus, not astride as they had come to Whittlewood Forest that first night, but across his body, cradled like a babe against his broad chest.

"Joseph," he said, "lead my lady's horse." And they started off at a slow trot.

At first, she struggled against that steel grip, but she had little heart for anything but her grief so inhumanly delayed, and now like to consume her with weeping.

Somewhere she had lost both wig and hat, and she was first aware of it when the breeze ruffled her hair, finding little passages between the curls, cooling her fevered anguish. She was next aware of her bare head when John Gilbert bent to touch his cheek against her hair, crooning her name again and again as you would to stop a babe's crying. The warmth of his body encircled her, comforted her, and for a long time she gave herself over to it because her need was so great.

This was the worst part of her character, she knew, this need for a man's tenderness, as if it would take the place of her dead father. What a fool she was to seek from men that which they did not have to give, except to further their own false designs. She must have a care always against this failing. But her cautionings were soon overtaken by memories of her father's barbarous end, and later still of her own predicament, a lone woman soon to be traded into whoredom for a small country manor.

Oh, she had no doubt of it. Edward's offer was too compelling for even a saint to resist; and John Gilbert, despite his feigned caring, was no saint. In a few days, as soon as ever it pleased his playacting heart, the highwayman would turn her over to Edward. He was no longer bound by his vow to her father and could never expect the promised reward. Death canceled all vows. At the thought of her father, that learned and kindly man who'd suffered death for her sake, she succumbed anew to hot, desperate tears.

John reined in. "Joseph, the Lady Anne needs shelter for the rest of this night, a bed and some food."

"Aye, Johnny. Squire Taunton is nearby, and he be in your debt."

They turned their horses into a rutted carriage track and in a mile or so came to a small two-story house, half-timbered in the style of the old queen's time. Clattering into the cobbled courtyard, they were met with flaring lanterns and the squire in his nightshirt.

"Welcome, John Gilbert," the squire said when a lantern shone on John's face. "Enter and bring thy men with ye. What's come over the lad?"

John carried Anne into the great hall, the cowl once again covering her hair. "A great loss, squire. And if you please, a room for the night."

The squire pointed to stairs. "Up to the gallery and 'tis the room on thy left."

Anne felt herself rising step by step, a door being kicked open, and a soft eider mattress replacing John's solid arms. He sat on the bed's edge, staring down at her.

"Where are we?" she whispered.

"Safe enough for now, Anne." His hand reached out and pushed the tangle of auburn curls out of her eyes. "I like you not as a boy," he whispered gruffly, and then cleared his throat, "but you're not the prettiest girl I ever saw, either."

"I'm not?"

"But you do have the prettiest eyes. Yes, they're quite unmatched, like emeralds floating in cream. Damn me if I ever saw a woman's eyes until I saw yours. Even Nell Gwyn's eyes are not close to their equal"—he traced her mouth with his forefinger—"although Nell's lips are somewhat more pleasing, as I remember."

He winked, and she looked away. "Why do you always jest at my expense?"

He turned her head and bent until his eyes were level with hers. "So that you will know that you still live, Lady Anne Gascoigne. This grieving for your father will quiet after a time. I know that, Anne, because I, too, lost my father—a father I loved deeply, despite he made me a bastard."

She stared up at him. "I have family name but not the loyalty and good friends you have."

He blinked. "Yet would I trade all I have for legitimacy."

"You would strike a poor bargain."

Anger shone in his face. "What would such as you know of my needs?"

She bit her lip.

The cloud passed from him as suddenly as it had appeared. "Now rest you, and I will return with food and ale. The spirit will heal sooner if the body is fed." His eyes glinted with amusement. "Besides, I must fatten you for the marriage market, mustn't I?"

"How can you laugh about such as that?"

"Because I must laugh. I am caught in a ticklish web the like no man has ever laughed at before." And indeed he was. For his life and safe passage to the colonies, he had pledged to Anne's father the safety of his virtuous daughter. Now the father was dead and his killer had offered him life, pardon and Burwell Hall, as well, more than he'd ever dreamed of having in this mad life. That was jest enough. But funnier was to follow. He, John Gilbert, scourge of His Majesty's highroads for the past seven years, had rejected his life's dream to help a woman save the chastity that had formerly meant so little to him. He laughed aloud again, touched her cheek with a warm finger, and stood. "Come, sweet Anne, close your eyes until I return."

She disobeyed and watched until his broad shoulders disappeared through the door and it closed behind him. Then a desperate plan took form. She could not trust John Gilbert, no matter how much . . . well, no matter. And the more she wanted to, the more on her guard she needed to be. She must away to London to gain the protection of her uncle, the Bishop of Ely. He was still in residence for the spring court, but for how long with plague driving everyone outside the city?

Quickly, she stood and caught sight of herself in the mirror. There, that ribbon would be just the thing to tie back her hair into a boyish pigtail. She roamed the room looking for some escape route. There was no other door; only a window overlooking the stables. In the dim light of the setting moon, she could see Sir Pegasus munching hay.

Going to the bed, she removed the strong linen sheets, knotted them together, then carefully opened the casement window and lowered the sheets to the ground, after securing one end to the heavy, carved bedstead.

Carefully, she climbed out, and without looking down lest she lose her nerve, slid and clutched her way down the sheets, then, out of control, swung around, her sword hitting the side of the house, skittering off the wall, making a fearful racket. Hanging on to the rope, she waited, but miraculously, no one was roused to cry the alarm, and she dropped to the ground.

The big horse recognized her scent and nickered as she approached, waking a stable boy.

Anne's voice, hoarse from crying, cracked an order. "Saddle the chestnut for my master, boy."

"Aye," the boy grumbled, rubbing his eyes sleepily. "Like to keep me awake all night with comings and goings."

"Quickly," Anne said. John Gilbert would discover her gone any minute.

At last, after what seemed like hours, but could only have been two minutes, the cinch was tightened. "Now give me a hand up," she commanded, "and give me your stocking cap." If the boy had been thinking of aught else but returning to his warm straw pallet in the corner, Anne reasoned that he'd have been more suspicious. And if she'd had time, she would have liked to wrap Sir Peg's hooves for silence, but there was no time and perhaps, after all, no need.

By now, she was surely only seconds away from discovery. She could see John Gilbert mounting the stairs with a platter of steaming meats and a tankard of ale, and her growling stomach longed for the sustenance. She tried not to think at all of John's face when he saw the empty bed and found her escape route.

With a kick of her booted heels, she clattered through the cobbled courtyard and out onto the carriage track, briefly blessing the rough stablemen of her childhood for teaching her how to handle a spirited stallion. When she reached Oxford Road and turned toward London, she heard distant, pursuing hoofbeats and what she thought was the sound of her name carried on the night breeze, but she could not be sure. For the first few miles, she prayed that there was no match for Sir Peg in the squire's stables.

Once on the highroad, John's big steed stretched out his

effortless stride, putting ever more distance between her and the highwayman. But she knew that before morn he would be after her in earnest. She was too big a prize to let slip through his fingers.

But one thing bothered her. If there was some larcenous trick in the highwayman's heart, she couldn't think what it could be. He could have given her over to Lord Waverby back at Burwell Hall, and he hadn't. He could have allowed Black Ben liberties with her person at the camp, if peace between the thieves was as important as he'd said. And he could have, as he'd so indelicately reminded her, taken her body for himself at any time.

In bed that first night in the cottage, momentarily crazed to be sure, she had even given him some indication that his attentions were not entirely rejected. Her face flushed hot at the thought.

There was more that she felt, but she didn't know what the more was—a kind of wish, perhaps, that John Gilbert had caught her out here on the night road, cozened her in some manly but suitable way to set aside her vow of chastity.

Oh, she was so confused. She'd not grown weary of guarding her precious maidenhead; she just hadn't known how much energy it would take to forestall the seemingly natural inclination to surrender it to John Gilbert.

She gave the big chestnut a pat on the neck and shouted in his ear, "But this is crazy, Sir Peg; I'll just not think more along these lines." Yet a jumble of thoughts filled her mind, and snatches of a sonnet surfaced that she had once loved and committed to memory:

> *Since there's no help, come, let us kiss and part.*
> *Nay, I have done. You get no more of me.*
> *And I am glad, yea, glad with all my heart,*
> *That thus so cleanly I myself can free.*

The night was now cold on her face, and she must think no more of a highwayman she would never see again. Patches of ground fog swirled under the trees as she rode on, the swift passage snatching her tears of grief and flinging them behind her. Her heart pounded in time to the hooves of the great horse, its flank muscles flowing smoothly beneath her legs, and with each passing mile she vowed anew to punish Edward Ashley Carter, the Earl of Waverby, with her own hands, for he had surely killed her father as much as the street ruffians he had hired to do the bloody work.

The sun was high when she reached Reading. It was market day in the square, and the odor of hot, spiced seedcakes nearly drove Anne mad. She hadn't eaten for a day, but she didn't have a penny. She got off Sir Peg and led him among the cheek-by-jowl stalls of fresh vegetables and meat pies, hoping to see a kind face, one that looked like it would give a hungry lad some breakfast. She saw no such face.

Without warning, a heavy hand fell on her shoulder, and she jumped in fright.

"What have we here?" a male voice boomed out behind her. "And what's a dirty-faced country boy like ye doing with a horse worth fifty pounds, if it be worth a farthing?"

The hand was joined by another, and she was twirled around. She encountered a big, bearded man in patched breeches, a scowl on his face and a brace of pistols in his belt, and by his badge, a member of the town watch. He was more than a little the worse for drink, whether from a night's carouse or a morning's early start, she couldn't tell.

"I am to London, sir," she answered in her boy's voice, trying to look the man in his eye.

"And who might ye serve, my young cock?"

She said the first name that came to mind. "Lord Waverby of Burwell Hall, gentleman of the bedchamber to His Majesty, King Charles, being the second of that name, sir." She wriggled in his grip, but he only held her the tighter.

"Your accent be not of these parts, boy. I think ye be not who ye say. I think ye be a scholar out of thy gown from Eton or Oxford town, and this be some jape with a master's horse. Now hand me thy sword." He took the sword and the horse's reins from Anne and grabbed her cloak with the other. "Come along, boy, and we'll soon get the real story out of ye, or I'll send to Lord Waverby by the next post."

The thought of Edward capturing her so easily after all that she'd been through gave her a desperate energy. With a wrench, she slipped the knot on the cloak and dashed between the stalls. "Stop, thief!" The watchman raised the hue and cry behind her, but she twisted and turned until she was away from the market stalls and running through crooked side streets. Breathless, she hid in a stinking garden privy until she was certain that she'd not been followed. But what now? She had no money and, as well, no horse. She missed Sir Peg, and vowed to have her uncle send for him. But how would she get to her uncle, the bishop, in London?

Cautiously, she stepped from cover and followed the winding alley until she came to the town common clogged with carriages, one of them with the curtains drawn. Townspeople pelted it with mud and dung. At first she drew back from the holler sent up by so many angry people. Surely it would draw the watch.

"Begone!" shouted a chandler, loosing a missile at the driverless curtained carriage, his candles swaying by their wicks from his leathern jerkin. "Ye bring the plague with thee. I see the death's head smiling—there!"

The crowd drew back farther as the curtains parted. A matron stuck her head out the window. "We carry no plague, good sirs, although our servants have run away in fear. My husband, it is, who is in want of heart physic. I pay in silver the man who drives us to the nearest leech."

As one, the crowd drew away in disbelief. Anne stepped forward, her stomach grumbling its hunger. She had often driven a coach-and-two on her father's estate in Essex, from the time she was a child seated on the driver's lap.

"Madame," she said with a bow and as husky a boy's voice as she could manage, "I will drive for you."

"I am grateful for your kindness, lad."

Anne turned to the chandler. "Where would I find a doctor?"

"You'll find the plague, boy, for thy trouble."

"A doctor," Anne insisted.

"Down by the river on his barge. Dr. Wyndham will treat the plague or the devil himself, for a fee."

Chapter Eight

Dr. Wyndham, Physician or Mountebank?

Anne scrambled atop the carriage driver's seat and hastily turned the horses toward the river. The crowd shouted angrily, throwing more street refuse, and as she left the town square behind her, she heard the chandler railing at top voice against rich Londoners who brought plague to honest country folk.

At the river Thames, she reined in next to a man bundling reeds. "We seek Dr. Wyndham, good thatcher," she said in her low voice.

The man looked up from his work and pointed downriver. "Ye seek a mountebank, then. But if ye must, try the second barge by the aspen grove."

"Hurry, lad, my poor husband worsens," madame called from inside the coach, where a man's groans grew ever louder.

Anne halted the horses by a small barge in front of which a posted handbill announced that Dr. Josiah Wyndham, member of the Royal College of Physicians, also trained in chirurgery, practiced physic within. In smaller letters, the sign added that the doctor's special training, acquired at the University of Padua in Italy, was in the diseases of women, in particular the green sickness associated with a woman's periodical flux. At the bottom of the sign in slightly bolder letters, the doctor noted that he was renowned in London, Paris and Rome for the art of preserving a woman's beauty and complexion.

At Anne's call, a very short man emerged from the barge cabin. His face, florid and round, was topped by a towering periwig, which made Anne wonder how he kept his balance on the moving deck beneath him.

"Yes, lad, you have need of my healing services?"

Anne was startled. For a man so small, the doctor had an exceedingly deep voice, even deeper than John Gilbert's.

Madame stuck her head from the window. "My husband is bad taken with the heart sickness, sir."

The doctor bowed. "My specialty, madame." He boomed over his shoulder, "Philibert, come you here and help with a patient."

A young man Anne took to be the doctor's son, because of a startling resemblance up to and including a matching wig, appeared on deck. The two men then heaved a very fat patient from the coach. "Give a hand with his legs, lad," the doctor commanded, puffing the words.

Anne approached the sick man's feet and grabbed his muddy boots, lifting them clear of the ground, staggering after the rest of him onto the deck and into the cabin. Madame came right behind, urging all three to have a care.

They laid him on a table, and his wife fell over his chest, sobbing. "Oh, I am to be a poor widow, and what will become of me?"

The doctor removed her to a chair, where she continued crying piteously. Anne wanted to comfort her but stayed the urge, since it was inappropriate to her assumed sex and station.

Dr. Josiah Wyndham motioned Anne closer. "Take off his

boots, boy. You, Philibert, loose everything binding—sword belt, smallclothes, all."

Anne spoke up. "I'll just have my silver, madame, and be gone." But in her worry, the woman didn't answer or even notice Anne.

Dr. Wyndham glared hard at Anne, rumbling in his deep voice, "Be quick! The boots, lad."

She began to pull on the fat man's boots, and then removed his hose. He was groaning mightily.

The doctor felt the bare feet. "Heat in the feet makes cold in the heart," he said, musing aloud. "Madame, did your husband complain of pain?"

Anne saw madame start up from her chair and approach the table. "Oh yes, Doctor, all the time."

"Where, pray?"

She touched the right side of her husband's enormous stomach.

"Not here?" the doctor asked, his hand resting on the patient's chest. "Or here?" His hand moved to the left shoulder and down the arm.

At a great moan from her husband, the wife renewed her crying and piteous questioning concerning her dismal prospects, and was unable to answer the doctor's further questions.

"Where do you hurt, sir?" the doctor said aloud, close to the patient's ear.

The words came from behind clenched teeth. "Everywhere! Give me some poppy to kill the pain. Hurry!"

The doctor lifted the man's eyelids, then put his ear to his patient's chest. "Madame, did your husband dine and drink well within the morning hours?"

"Why, yes."

The doctor bowed. "Just as I thought." He held a spoon of liquid to the man's mouth and tipped it in. Then he contemplatively twirled a finger through a curl on his long wig. "I do not think he has trouble of the heart, dear madame. Stone is his problem; an uncommonly high-placed stone."

Madame stopped crying. "How can this be? He has had treatment for the heart of the best physicians in London."

The deep voice rumbled imperiously, "Then he has been ill treated, madame. I have given him a potion to dull his pain. Now you must take him to an inn for rest, and allow him no spiced ale or heavy meats of any kind. And each morning, he must hang himself upside down to keep the stone from bringing on the bloody piss."

Madame sputtered, "But, Doctor, this is no cure. We are accustomed to paying the highest fee for the best medicines." Her face grew almost as red as her husband's. "I *demand* that you give us your costliest heart potion. . . . Your gold pills!"

Dr. Josiah Wyndham looked grave and appeared to deliberate. "I hesitate, since the price is one pound, plus my reasonable examination fee—"

Madame stood, rather menacingly, Anne thought, for someone of her modest courage. "Your *best,* sir, and at once!"

"Of course, madame. For your husband, two medicines at once, as you say," the doctor declared, bowing to her demand. From a small carrying chest he withdrew a stoppered green bottle and handed it over, along with a paper packet. "One spoon after meals," he instructed, "but never during the new moon. As ancient Galen taught, it disturbs the ebb and flow of the blood. As for the gold pills, he must have one each night."

Anne was too astonished to hold her tongue. "But your fellow at the Royal College of Physicians, Dr. Harvey, proved that the heart contracts to propel the blood through the body."

Wyndham whirled about, eyeing her sharply. "You seek to instruct a graduate of the University of Padua in physic, lad?"

Anne shook her head, wishing she could recall the hasty words, which showed a bit too much knowledge for a lowly farm lad. "No, sir, I seek just my penny for driving madame and her husband to you."

The doctor frowned, then shrugged up into his full wig. "You see, madame, how uncivil this generation becomes. It is all Cromwell's doing, all that talk about liberty and handshakes and equality. Infects even the lowliest boy, eh?" He exchanged a knowing look with madame. "Now, you *will* remember my instructions, won't you, dear lady?"

"*Not* in the new moon," she repeated, nodding vigorously.

"Quite so. I pray you be most especially careful about the phases of the moon, madame, for on your care, your husband's health, *nay*, his very life, depends."

"I will take great care, good doctor," she said, beaming, obviously satisfied with the prescription.

Dr. Wyndham smiled, and standing on tiptoes, looked very close into her face, backed off and looked again, squinting his eyes as if in deep study.

"What?" she asked, her hands skittering to her face, her hair, her hood. "What do you see?"

The doctor heaved a great sigh. "Alas, I see a great crime, madame, a beauty that has been spent in the care of others."

Madame looked pained and pleased at once, but rallied to a correct answer. "Such is a wife's duty, sir."

"How true," Dr. Wyndham said, and Anne, scarcely able to hide her amusement, wondered what the rascal was after. She almost wished John Gilbert were here to observe this performance, since the two men were of a kind. She watched as the bantam doctor bowed very low but looked up at madame as if he couldn't bear to remove his gaze. "Oh, how I wish"—he bent his head in deep thought—"but no—"

"What? What is it that you do wish?" madame urged, her curiosity provoked beyond bearing. "If you see something in my visage, then you must tell me. It is the duty of your calling."

"True again, mistress."

"Father," Philibert injected earnestly, "this lady deserves the same assistance that you gave the Countess Castlemaine. She should not be penalized for her very faithfulness to her husband when His Majesty's mistress was rewarded for less. Did you not help the wanton to steal the affections of the king?"

The doctor nodded, giving in to the weight of their separate arguments. "How very right you both are. I have an obligation to provide cures for more than the scurvy or obstructions of the liver and spleen, dear lady. That I cannot deny, for I have studied in Italy and learned the miracle art of how women of forty or beyond can bear the same countenance as a lass of fifteen."

Madame's breathing grew labored, and the doctor withdrew a step, raising his hand in an eloquent dismissal of his own words. "But I will mention my miracle salve no further, dear madame, because you could not possibly consider such treatment now at the time of your great worry. A woman of your nature would not contemplate the application of a simple aging remedy when her husband is in his sickbed."

"No, I suppose not," madame responded, sad, but a willing martyr to her task.

Dr. Wyndham bowed, half turned away, then turned back to gaze longingly once again into her face, which Anne could not believe had ever been close to beauty. The doctor smacked one hand resoundingly against the other. "Although, I must say if I am damned for it, mistress, that I would take more glory in preserving your beauty than in bringing most patients back to life."

Madame flushed with a pleasure Anne was sure she had not felt since she was fifteen, if then.

Her husband, in the meantime, had stopped groaning and was looking about him, trying to sit up.

"Give us a hand, my know-all lad," the doctor rumbled to Anne, and she and Philibert helped heave the patient into a sitting position on the table.

"Madame," Anne repeated, "my silver, and I'll be gone."

Madame frowned. "What impudence! You'll have your penny when you drive us to the nearest inn."

The doctor bowed with a shake of his head. "My deepest apologies, but I must insist that my son, Philibert Wyndham, drive you. He is my apprentice, and he will arrange accommodation at the White Hart and order the proper diet with the landlord. And you will need his strong arms over this puny lad's."

Anne stuck out her grimy hand. "My penny, if you please." She was faint for lack of food.

"Very well." The woman tossed a coin, and Anne caught it, bringing it to her mouth and testing its metal as she had seen so many hostlers do.

"And doctor," madame said, as soon as her husband was on the gangplank, leaning hard on Philibert, "I'll have that salve of which you spoke. It is also a wife's marital and Christian duty to preserve that image which God has granted her for the pleasure of her husband."

"Again, mistress, you are wise above most women." He bowed and produced a small lacquered box of salve and a vial.

"What is this?" she said, holding the vial to the window light. "You spoke only of a salve."

Dr. Wyndham's voice lowered to a conspiratorial whisper. "The oil is nothing of mine, but I wish to give it to you, without fee, for your protection, dear lady. It comes from an old gypsy woman, and its spell will most assuredly ward off unwelcome attentions from lecherous men. Madame, I pray you keep it close, for when you begin to apply my salve, you will most immediately attract the lust of many men—" His voice ebbed into nothing as madame gasped at such future possibilities.

"In that case, I am truly in your debt, good physician."

The doctor bowed low. "That will be an extra two pounds

for the miracle salve." He kissed the fingers that handed him the money, and waved her merrily off the barge.

Anne tried to slide past him at the door. She must away, and quickly to find some food and then to London town. John Gilbert could not be far behind her after this delay.

An arm blocked her exit, and Dr. Josiah Wyndham looked up at her, for he was a full six inches shorter. "Stay, my lady, and tell me why you hide that faultless complexion and such obvious quality behind such a dirty costume."

Anne gasped, for she had gone unquestioned for so long that she had ceased to question herself. Now she was well captured, and would probably spend this night in a Reading gaol. "What do you intend to do with me?" Her voice quivered in spite of the brave tilt to her chin.

He smiled. "It greatly depends on how entertaining your story is, my lady."

"In truth, I have been a great fool."

"Do not blame yourself, lass. The counterfeit is quite good, but I am a physician and experienced in looking behind false guises. Most people, even those gravely ill, try to fool a prying doctor. The drunkard swears that he has only an occasional watered wine, the French-pox-afflicted vow that they have never lain with a whore, and so on."

Anne regained her composure. "A base mountebank, sir, is a strange one to talk of false guises."

"Oh, indeed," he said, crossing the room, "mountebank be true, but not base, lass. I have the honor to be the very best mountebank in the business of physic." He poured two tankards of ale, handing one to Anne.

She took it, but faint, leaned against the cabin wall. "I'm very hungry, good physician," she said in a suddenly polite voice.

He nodded, and from under a cloth took a three-for-a-penny white bread, cutting her a generous slice.

She took a huge bite of the delicious bread in her mouth, and promptly gagged.

"Quiet yourself," he boomed. "Small bites and slow, or you will not keep food in your stomach long." He cut a piece from a cheese that proved to be her favorite Wensleydale flavored with alder charcoal.

He drew two chairs to the surgery table, courteously brushing it off for her with his handkerchief. A bowl of fruit appeared, and she sighed happily. "You are indeed a most well-supplied mountebank, sir."

"Eat your fill, while I further your education, lass. You call me sham physician, but did you not see madame reject my best diagnosis? She wished to be deluded; nay, she insisted upon it. If I had not produced the mock heart medicine, which promised a future cure, she would most likely not have urged present moderation on her husband, which is his only hope to live with the stone, short of the knife."

Anne interrupted her meal to scoff. "And what future cure does your *miracle* complexion cream offer?"

He shrugged and smiled. "You are young and scorn the foolish fancies of your elders, but I have seen my cream work its miracle—lines of care fall away, lips redden, eyes become clear and confident." He smiled slyly. "If a woman expects lust from men, she usually finds it."

"But surely these visage changes are not permanent."

Dr. Josiah Wyndham smiled, twirling a curl of his wig. "Ah, but lass, in life no change is permanent."

She prepared to show him the philosophical immorality of his thinking, but something heavy hit the side of the barge, and then several somethings, even heavier.

"Come out, physician," a man's voice cried from the shore. "Come out, I say, and we'll burn that plague barge to the waterline." Anne recognized the rasp of the chandler from the square, and his cry was succeeded by a holler of bloodthirsty whoops.

Wyndham was immediately at the window. "I'll go out and engage them while you slip the anchor rope on the other side. Can you do that, lass?"

"But your son?"

"He will know what to do," the doctor replied, his eyes alight with excitement. "We do leave a town in haste now and again. Quickly, girl, do as I ask."

Anne was frightened but she had little choice, and went out the far-side window. Slowly, she crawled the splintered planks along a narrow walkway, around barrels and gear to a rope anchored to an aspen tree. She wanted desperately to get away, but she could not swim, and even if she could swim, the world seemed somewhat less dangerous in the company of Dr. Wyndham. She could hear him trying to mollify the plague-frightened mob, but to little avail.

As she crawled, she muttered curses against John Gilbert under her breath. If not for him, all this would not be happening. She was sure of it. Somehow, he was the source for every hard thing that had befallen her. Why, she had almost lived the frights of a lifetime in the last week!

A pitch-tar brand came over the cabin roof and dropped on a heap of tarred rope just as she sliced the anchor cable through with her Italian blade. The rope began to burn immediately, and she pounded the blaze with her hands, putting it out but scorching her skin in the doing.

The barge swung into the gentle current midstream and drifted away from the disappointed crowd, now shouting angrily on the bank. Dr. Wyndham rounded the deck cabin and found her blowing on her hands.

"Ah, what's this? My brave lass is hurt."

"There was a fire," she explained.

He led her inside and removed a box of his miracle complexion salve from his medical chest.

Seated once again at the surgery table, Anne watched as he spread the pinkish-white concoction liberally on her hands, a smile playing on her face.

Anticipating her scorn, the doctor declared, "It is also excellent for burns."

Anne smiled. "And a good thing, too," she said, raising

her hands close to her face, "because I don't have wrinkled hands."

"You see, lass," he rumbled, "it works its wonders already."

Anne laughed aloud, and was soon joined by Dr. Josiah Wyndham. They laughed until they cried of laughter. The sound of such merriment carried to the bank and drove the frustrated mob into a frenzy of righteous indignation.

John Gilbert sat atop a little knoll overlooking the Thames and the mob below. He was disguised as a tinker in a two-wheeled cart hung around with pots and pans. Clearly, the sound of laughter from within the barge reached him, and an answering smile crossed his lips. He had heard that sweet, feminine laugh before on the sword practice green at the camp.

Anne had left an unmistakable trail through Reading town, but had somehow—miraculously, he was certain—come to a safe rest for the present, if her humor be any indication.

A very short young man in an extremely high periwig stopped near the cart.

"By Christ's wounds," the young man muttered, looking down on the scene, "I leave but an hour, and this is what I find on my return. Damn!" His anger escaped full-blown. "Now I must walk me shanks mare to Windsor."

John, smiling at his uncommon good fortune, gave the youth a friendly salute, which was returned with a black scowl.

"But 'tis a fair day for a stroll, lad."

"An easy sentiment, tinker, when you do ride in a fine cart."

John grinned after the youth, who had immediately started on his dusty way. So Anne would stop in Windsor, would she? He drove back through Reading town and off Oxford Road into a woods where Joseph was to meet him.

"Johnny." Joseph greeted John with a clap on his shoulder. "Look what I be finding at the horse trader's, and me now thirty guineas the poorer for it." Sir Pegasus whinnied a welcome. "I vow the Lady Anne be in trouble e'en now, hiding from the watch."

John laughed. "Do not fear for her, Joseph. She is one of those prodigious phoenix creatures that seem to rise out of the ashes of every disaster."

"If that be true, why do ye plan to ride after the lass, when ye get closer to Tyburn's ugly hill with each mile? Can ye explain it so that a poor smith like me understand it?"

John Gilbert couldn't account for his behavior to Joseph or to himself, because the answer was too disturbing and too obvious. He was a little mad, of course. How else to explain that even now he could remember the taste of her lips, even the taste of the butter that she had churned, and her emerald eyes flashing defiance as she lay on the greensward, looking up at him after the churning. Yes, he was definitely mad enough for Bedlam.

Chapter Nine

Cozened by a Mountebank

Anne woke the next morning, curled on a pallet on the deck of the barge with the June sun warming her, scarcely remembering where she was until she saw Dr. Josiah Wyndham's round face peeping from under his wig. His hand was on the sweep tiller, but his eyes were studying her.

She stretched, feeling wonderfully rested. "Good morning, Doctor. I have never slept so well. If my bed were always on water, I would live to a hundred years"—she smiled up at him—"and have great need of your miracle salve."

The doctor half bowed. "It is impossible to think, my lady, if one does believe in the stars, that your beauty would ever wither."

She applauded lightly, for her hands were tender although they had not blistered. In fact, they were well along toward healing. She held up her hands to show him, smiling, for after madame's leave-taking, Anne had liked him almost instantly, and the feeling was still upon her. "You have pretty compliments enough for the court, sir."

He bowed again. "It is not flattery in your case, but astrological prediction. The heavens smile upon you, lass. I read it in your palm and most assuredly in your physiognomy."

She stood and wondered if she dare ask again to break her fast, for the river air had renewed her hunger mightily. "I do naturally hope your prediction is correct, Doctor, and I ask pardon for my doubt. I fear, though, that the direction of my future life is uncertain."

"Who is this John who troubles you so?"

She was startled. "How do you know that name?"

"You called it out in your sleep—not once, but several times," he said, openly curious. "If I knew your dreams, I might better divine your future."

She laughed, somewhat embarrassed, because she had suddenly remembered her dream of John Gilbert, and had no wish to tell it, especially to a man, even though he be a doctor of women's complaints. For she had been back in the highwayman's hidden village, bathing in the stream, and John had been with her, touching her, and—and they'd both somehow misplaced their clothes, and—

"What is it, lass?" the doctor asked. "You are suddenly pink in the face. You do not suffer from the falling sickness, I hope."

Anne took a deep breath of clean river air, blessing its cooling effects. "No, good doctor, it is just that I do not wish to impose on your generous hospitality, and, alas, I am hungry again."

The doctor smiled. "It is astounding to me that the young can eat at will and keep their bodies without fat." He lowered his head and looked slyly out from under his wig, a look she had already come to know meant that something outrageous was apt to follow. "Although, dear lady, my precious miracle salve takes away fatness from those who have overmuch, *or* adds flesh to those who have little, without the least disadvantage to their dispositions."

Anne laughed, delighted. "It would appear, sir, that your

miraculous discovery is indispensable to every aspect of a woman's long and happy life."

"Thoughtfully stated," he said, moving the tiller to take advantage of the current. "You'll find a morning draft of ale and some bread and butter in the cabin, and if that son of mine has not found and made free with it, a crockery pot of plum jam in the chest. We will break our fast here on deck while you tell me your story. I am all eager attention."

After eating, Anne rinsed the pewter mugs in the river water. "I have need of your good counsel, Doctor," she said when she returned to sit beside him at the tiller, "but I dare not tell you how I came to this pass."

"I see," he said, frowning in concentration. "There must be a father, a husband or a betrothed somewhere, perhaps even a great reward. You think not to trust me, is that it?"

She looked at him. "You have been good-hearted, I grant, but I am not a fool."

"Careful, my lady," he said, "for there is such a small distinction between the wise woman and the foolish one. You are alone without money or protector. Is it wise or foolish to trust no one, especially one who has given you no reason to doubt his sincerity?"

"You are skilled in argument, good doctor, but I need only passage to London. There I will see that you are handsomely rewarded by my uncle for bringing me to him."

Dr. Wyndham removed his wig, thoughtfully scratching his exposed pate, meagerly covered with short brown hair. She was relieved when he put the wig back on and became himself once again. He waved off a rowboat making the passage from one bank to the other.

"I want no reward, my lady," he said finally. "Think you that there is great pleasure in having money; nay, only in the way it is acquired. I would rather convince one doubting Bess or Mary to buy my miracle salve than turn a dispossessed young woman over to magistrate or to uncle for reward."

After such reassurance, the tale of her adventures since fleeing the palace was on her tongue before she could stop herself. She wanted to trust him. She needed to trust him because she had never felt so alone in her life, loneliness, she realized with an emotional start, that she had not experienced with the highwayman.

Although the doctor laughed, to her annoyance, at the part about John Gilbert's lovemaking lesson that had fooled Black Ben, and even harder at her experiences as a milkmaid, he was quite sober as she drew her story to a close with a description of her father's death and Lord Waverby's perfidy, her escape from the highwayman and her near recapture by the watch at Reading market.

"My dear Lady Gascoigne," he said, bending to gently kiss her hand, "you have my solemn oath of protection, humble as it is, since I could not hope to match your highwayman for courage or swordplay."

Her mind eased instantly at the promise, but not at mention of John Gilbert. "He is not *my* highwayman, sir. I shall nevermore see him, and good riddance." There was an unseemly quaver in her voice that came too quickly to correct. She covered it with a more measured request. "Then you will truly take me to my uncle, the Bishop of Ely, in London?"

"Of course, Lady Anne, after we stop at Windsor this afternoon."

"But I must make haste to London town, sir."

"And you will. It is but twenty-three miles by river from Windsor. We should arrive tomorrow late."

"Now! Today, sir. I must insist."

"My dear Lady Anne, it is true that I wish no reward for your safekeeping, but you will need to pay your passage."

Anne was indignant. "You know, sir, that I have only the one penny. Here"—she opened the kerchief tucked in her shirt—"you are welcome to it!"

"My thanks, but no. You have something far more valuable to me—the face of an angel, and the complexion of a babe. The merry maids and wives of Windsor village will stampede to my miracle salve when they look on your face." His short legs fairly danced with glee at the tiller.

"I will not be a counterfeit, sir, not even to repay your kindness, most certainly not for passage on this rude barge."

Dr. Josiah Wyndham put the tiller hard over and headed for a bank of giant poplars.

"What do you?" Anne cried in alarm.

"I am discharging a nonpaying passenger, a member of the privileged gentry who desires to eat a commoner's food and use his barge without recompense. These are the rules of the river."

"You men," Anne said angrily, "you have a rule for everything that you want a woman to do."

"True, my lady," the doctor agreed, "if it is the only way we can get the ladies to see our reason."

Anne kicked the railing in frustration, while the barge was moving very fast toward the shore, too fast. Quickly, she put a placating hand on his arm and introduced some maidenly sweetness into her words. "Pray, come about, good doctor, and I will do as you want."

Dr. Wyndham reversed the tiller with only a few feet of turning room left. "So you see, Lady Anne," he said, poling slowly back into the current, his eyes bright with male triumph, "your young highwayman, John Gilbert, did not ill treat you. Beyond the palace and the world of birthright that you know, all men and women must earn their way. The world is an agreeable place for those who accept this; quite unpleasant for those who don't."

She was angry again and didn't hide it. "What unlawful scheme would you cozen me to join?"

"No scheme at all, my Lady Anne, but a small business venture certainly not beyond the powers of the actress who played at chaste lovemaking in a highwayman's bed, or turned a court lady into a sturdy country lad crying for his penny."

"Hunger did lend me skill," she sniffed.

He smiled at her. "And so it shall again. You perform, my lady, or you do not sup this day."

"You have yet to tell me my part," she replied impatiently, although smoothing her hair at the thought.

He laughed so heartily that swans swimming against the far bank flew away. "My mother," he said. "You will play Mistress Jane Wyndham, a dear lady of sixty full years, most uniquely preserved." And the doctor laughed again even louder.

John Gilbert reached Windsor village, rounded the old motte and double-bailey castle atop its chalk cliff and took wide Thames Street down to the river docks. He was superbly mounted for a Puritan divine, but dressed appropriately in severe black and white with an exceedingly wide-brimmed, high-crowned hat shading his face. A huge Bible was slung to the rear of his saddle with his sword, and he prayed loudly as he rode, calling all who passed to repent their godless lives. As a result, people with sin, that is to say, everyone, gave him plenty of room, hurrying by without looking up, for fear of engaging his accusing eyes.

If they had returned his gaze, they would have seen eyes that glinted with sport. He had learned something from this masquerade and would ever cherish the lesson. Sometimes the best place to hide oneself was in plain sight.

There seemed to be an unusual number of townspeople hurrying toward the landing. He stopped a beldam leaning heavily on her cane, too slow to avoid him. "Goodwife, where do all these people go?"

"To see the great physician at the docks, good preacher. It is said that he has a miracle salve—"

John frowned, though his voice was gentle. "Miracles come from the Almighty, old dame."

She nodded, fairly jiggling her cane in a desire to be off. "Aye, sir, but there are some as do say that this doctor can make an old woman turn into a maid again. I would see this for myself."

"You question the laws of God and nature, goodwife."

"Nay, sir, my soul is safe, for I could never afford such a precious salve, but I would see its mystery."

"So would I, good mother," John said, laughing privately, and trotted Sir Pegasus down the hill, reining in behind the crowd formed around the narrow gangway to a small barge.

He immediately recognized the young man playing a large Spanish guitar and singing as the one who had been forced by the mob to walk from Reading to Windsor. Since there was no way he could have walked the near thirty miles in one day and a night, John assumed that the old sway-backed horse tied to the tree next to the barge was getting a rest from some cottager's plow. He tied Sir Peg alongside.

A short, very bowlegged man in a dizzying periwig stepped out of the cabin and began to address the crowd. John smiled at the long list of misty credentials Dr. Josiah Wyndham announced, especially his claim to regress the age of women. If true, he would have been the most celebrated and wealthiest physician in all England, nay, the world. But John admired the man's effrontery and drew closer so as not to miss a word, although the doctor had a voice to carry past London.

At the same time, the highwayman eagerly watched the windows of the cabin, hoping to catch a glimpse of Anne, if she were still aboard. The thought that she might not be, that she could be dead or ravaged in some foul place, in short, that his careful calculations had been wrong, caused him to shoulder his way closer still to the gangway.

Dr. Wyndham bowed. "Ladies and lords, goodwives and good husbandmen, I will today give you such a miracle remedy that you will throw aside the paints and daubings that hide your spots, freckles, pimples, the pits of the smallpox that have scarred and seamed your faces, aye, even the wrinkles and care of a life of hard work. It is said that my remedy works faster than the king's touch for scrofula."

The crowd began to move against the gangplank, some sinking to their ankles in churned mud.

The doctor held high a black lacquered box, opened it, dipped in a forefinger and withdrew pinkish salve that he rolled about with lascivious relish on his fingertips. "My salve is full of precious ingredients from the northern hills of Italy, where nature does preserve the beauty of women nigh onto their deathbeds, and some do say beyond. Ladies and goodwives in that far country e'en use it to keep their lips as red as coral; to make those lips softer than a husband might wish, lest his wife fly from him to some young cod half his age."

Women of all ages pressed eagerly forward once again, taking John with them.

Dr. Wyndham had spied the tall divine earlier and cursed his presence. Such ranters were always trouble, because they would not leave off their industry of seeking souls, not for one minute. All appeals to beauty and pleasure were lost on such men, who saw grim hellfire as enjoyment's reward. The address must move faster than he would like, before the reverend was roused to pious outrage.

"If I appear to anyone here a counterfeit"—Dr. Josiah Wyndham looked confidently about him as if to belie the thought—"then it is a point of honor that I present my aged mother, of some sixty years, to attest my word. She was my first patient, and not only is her skin cleansed and preserved with my miracle salve, but her teeth are white and fastened tight with its further use."

John looked on with interest. The mountebank was a bold one at that. Not a few in this crowd had most of their teeth loosened by the scurvy.

Majestically, Dr. Josiah Wyndham walked to the cabin door and carefully extracted an elderly lady in a prim black dress, her hair white although showing here and there traces of a youthful auburn, her rounding shoulders covered in a plain gray shawl. The doctor helped this worthy dame over the threshold as if she were made of a fragile bone china. It took her forever to make her way to the gangway and into the full sun.

When she did, Dr. Wyndham tipped up her face, and the crowd gasped, then broke into excited exclamations one to the other.

It was Anne, of course, as John had known it would be. No masquerade could hide her roses-in-the-snow complexion nor her sea-green eyes that held such unfilled promise in their depths, although accursed Waverby had forced her to bury her true loving nature.

Yes, despite her halting walk and that very clever little stumble that made her cling the harder to the doctor's arm, it was Anne, without doubt, but with a widow's hump, and her hair covered with white powder.

A grin formed that he did not allow to reach his mouth. Well, he would see just what kind of actress she could be. He would not challenge the good doctor's miracle salve; he knew better than to get between the stout women on the dock and their dreams. But he would challenge Anne.

"Vanity of vanities," he intoned in a voice that seemed come down from heaven. "Are we not all beautiful in God's sight? Have a care, old woman, that you do not try to change his plan and thereby lose his grace with you so near to heaven's gate."

It pleased John to see Anne jump at the sound of his voice, and she met his eyes with a mixture of rage and—what! Could it be welcome? But no, he must have misread the fire there.

He approached the gangway, stepped upon it, and stopped before the two. "Good doctor," John said, loud enough for his words to carry to the far edge of the crowd, "I would see this miracle salve to determine that it derives not from the devil: For it is writ that the dark man comes in many guises."

Anne was suddenly ashiver, even though it was a warm afternoon. She had forgotten how handsome he was, how the tips of his dark brows and narrow mustache sometimes moved together when he spoke, as if to underscore the importance of his every word. Such pride in a thief was intolerable!

"Leave me be, you rogue," she pleaded in a hoarse whisper for his ears alone. "Why can you not just leave be?"

"I ask myself that question, my lady," the divine replied, his own voice low and ironic. He looked at her, aged beyond the Anne of his dreams, but an Anne with a beauty even more whole, and he felt, not for the first time, a savage loss. He sickened at the wanting of her and at the denying of it, and yet he knew she could be the worst mistake of his life. A woman determined not to love would be a waking nightmare for a man of his hot blood.

"But all questions aside," he continued in a voice low but thickened by too much thought of her, "you *will* come with me."

She grew dizzy from the sound of him, and, oh, the smell of him, of forest and horse and sun and a man scent of mysterious origin. She wondered in shame if he could see all on her face. And, more astonishingly, in the secret places beneath her old woman's dress, she felt him touch that which she had never allowed anyone to handle.

The doctor looked at the two of them with astonishment, and to cover it, announced to the restive crowd in his own professional voice: "You must agree, good reverend, that it is no sin to preserve God's gifts, as long as it be done by day and not as some fearsome night witchery act." He handed over the box of salve. "You are free to look, and to give us your favor."

The divine lifted the box to his nose and sniffed, and to

Dr. Wyndham's further astonishment, winked at the Lady Anne.

"Who are you?" the doctor demanded softly, maintaining his smile.

"A simple divine doing God's work," John whispered.

Anne hissed a denial. "He's John Gilbert, the highwayman, the man I told you of, and a thoroughgoing rakehell."

"I have the honor to be all that and more," John said sardonically, "and also to take the Lady Anne back under my sworn protection."

He put his hand on her arm, and she dared not pull away with the crowd onlooking. By God's bowels, she did not even want to loose herself. Indeed, that unwelcome touch set her ashiver again, though perspiration dotted her nose. There was as ever a strange, fiery power in John Gilbert that affected her higher sensibilities. The man did threaten her maidenhead even in a Puritan preacher's garb!

The doctor smiled at John from behind a covering hand. "John Gilbert, the famous Gentleman Johnny, eh? Then who, sir, could be exposed this day?"

"We will see," John said in a low voice, sniffing the salve again. "The Lady Anne will walk down this gangway with me of her own choice, and I will call heaven's blessings upon your miracle salve, swearing that I know this beauteous old hag to be a true six decades."

"No, I will not come with you," Anne whispered, although some need blazoned in her small voice that belied the meaning of her words. "Leave me, or as God is my witness, you will betray me, John Gilbert, or cause me to betray myself." With a choking sound of great bafflement, but with the strength of a much younger woman than her white hair would admit, she caught him off balance, leaning toward her; planting her hands on his chest, she gave him a mighty heave backward. The divine went off the gangway and into the water, with black hat and lacquered box.

"Oh!" Anne cried, looking at her hands, and with the

look, disowning them. "Doctor, help him. Don't let him drown!"

The crowd pressed back up the small rise, as if expecting lightning to strike at the barge.

"We must away, Philibert," Wyndham yelled to his son.

"No," Anne said, leaning a hand far out for John, without a hope of reaching him. "Do something, Doctor."

"Careful, you'll fall in yourself. Now stop your mewling after that rogue and help with the tiller. This could turn into a bloody business if the crowd be riled."

The anchor rope was slipped and the gangway pulled aboard before he finished speaking and Philibert frantically poled away from the shore.

John sputtered to the surface, river water sluicing down his face, his hat bobbing toward London. "Anne," he called, as she watched from the receding stern, "I made a vow to your father."

"I release you from your vow," she yelled, utterly relieved to see him able to stand, shoulder deep, in the water.

"You can't release me! I won't allow you to release me!"

"You have no choice," Anne yelled. The distance between them was widening, and now that she saw he would live and that his strange power over her privy parts was somewhat dampened, she regained her determination. "Wasn't it you, sir, who taught me the reality of this world? May I remind you that you are in the water, and I am dry on this barge."

He sputtered and slung his long, wet hair out of his eyes, the sultry June sun glistening off water droplets on his proud nose. "Know you that I gave up Burwell Hall for you."

"Then you made a poor bargain," she replied, "although you are not such a fool that you think Edward would ever keep his word."

"No more, it seems, would you," he said, throwing the angry words at the barge, and flailing toward the bank.

The crowd was following this exchange, back and forth,

as they would follow a cockfight between two evenly matched birds.

She could see that John was wet and furious, a dangerous combination in such a man. His enraged voice assaulted her ears. "Do you think to stop me so easily?"

"It has not been easy at all," she assured him, "but stop you I have." She spoke more, but under her breath and not for his ears. "Good-bye, highwayman, and may God keep you from harm as he keeps me from desire."

She turned away after she saw him safely climb onto the dock, then sweep a low and taunting bow in her direction. She could not bear to look at him longer. Now he was truly and for all out of her life.

Anne caught Dr. Wyndham's inquisitive stare and lifted her chin. "Well," she said in a voice too loud, too frustrated and too hot by some degrees, "it is not my doing that you did not sell your pots and bottles."

"Is it not, my lady?" He pursed his small round mouth in consideration.

"No, of course it was no fault of mine. You saw what he did with your own eyes."

"And what you did, my lady, and a fascinating display it was," the doctor said, and motioned an interested Philibert to resume his poling.

Anne was surprised at what she'd seen flit for just a brief moment across the little doctor's face. It seemed that Josiah Wyndham, Fellow of the Royal College of Physicians and possessor of the beauty secrets of Northern Italy, had formed a true affection for her.

John watched from the dock, wringing water from his thick black doublet and, with effort, his breeches as well he could, while the barge caught the downriver current flowing toward London town.

Oh, that was where Anne was going, all right, without the slightest idea of the perils that might await. He had offered her protection at great sacrifice to his own ambition, and she had rejected it. Then to hell with the Lady Anne Gascoigne! She had chosen her champion in that mountebank doctor, and she could have him and be done with it. He was sick unto death of his oath to her father, anyway, an oath that no one honored but himself.

John Gilbert started to climb aboard Sir Peg, and realized that he still held the lacquered box of miracle salve in his hand. He pulled back his arm to throw it into the river, then changed his mind and put it in his doublet pocket.

He made his way back up Thames Street to find an inn. He needed sleep, food, dry clothes, and time to cool his temper with some good spiced ale before starting for Whittlewood Forest. Black Ben would be up to his old mischief by now, and he dare not be gone from his men longer.

"Our Lord Christ was baptized in a river, preacher, albeit not by a woman," cackled the beldam he'd met earlier. She was grinning at him slyly from her cottage door, her cane quivering with her scarcely containable mirth.

He wasn't in the mood for the old woman's idea of jest, and he passed without speaking.

Shortly, he reined in the big chestnut and came back. "Here, goodwife," he said, and handed her the lacquered box. "Mind you that when next I pass this way, I'll want a kiss or two from your coral lips in payment."

He looked back once when he turned into Castle Street, and she was doing a bit of a jig on her door stoop, her cane nowhere to be seen.

Chapter Ten

The Bishop of Ely

The hot, thick odor of London town reached Anne's nose as the barge passed Hampton Court, and grew into an almost unbearable summer-evening stench by the time Dr. Wyndham tied up just below the Tower's Traitor's Gate beyond London Bridge.

"I beg you, Lady Anne," the doctor said, his big voice rising with urgency, "at least wait until morn. It will soon be dark as pitch, and you must not venture into the city streets by night."

She did not answer him. She did not hear. Anne had been unnaturally quiet since leaving Windsor, standing by the cabin window for hours, staring at the slowly moving landscape without really seeing, except for the daft times when she fancied that she saw John's dark figure riding Sir Pegasus in the dusky moonlight amongst the poplar trees.

She'd squeeze her eyes in disbelief, and when she opened them again, he'd be gone from imagination but not from her mind.

The closer she came to reaching her uncle's protection and ending this incredible adventure, the more she felt that she had little to be proud of in her behavior toward John Gilbert.

Mile after mile, as she distanced herself from him, she remembered small things: a way with a word, a slantwise look
from his dark eyes, a cock of his head. All had held such
hazard for her at the time, but now inexplicably seemed be-
nign, if not charming. Yes, definitely warm and charming.

She remembered the lazy insolence that she now knew
disguised his regard for her welfare, and she was ashamed
that she had discerned only the insolence and had not recognized the regard that was now so plain in memory and em-
bedded there forever, she feared, to taunt her future sleepless
nights. She believed without doubt that John would never
have handed her over to Lord Waverby; she had deliberately
clung to that falsity to protect herself from her own feelings
for a highwayman. Intent as she was on punishing Edward,
Lord Waverby, for so foully betraying her love, she had foolishly denied her attraction to any man, especially to John
Gilbert.

Even now her admission of his appeal rankled, as super-
ficial as that appeal surely *must* be, and as doomed. His destiny was to hang on Tyburn Hill, and hers—perhaps she had
no destiny beyond a discreet withdrawal to the country once
she gained release from the vindictive anger of both the Earl
of Waverby and the king.

Anne had no doubt the Bishop of Ely, her uncle, would
obtain that release once she made known to him that Edward
had hired her father's murderers. The dastardly act would set
the Earl of Waverby outside the esteem of most men; and
then perhaps a trial, but surely an exile, would follow. Once
her father's dying was avenged, she would be free at last to
fill her empty life with good works, until the end of it.

Dreamily, she thought of the lifetime of sacrifice that lay
ahead of her. It had its allure and its aversion. In truth, and
she had more than an inkling of the truth, she sought to be
safe from John Gilbert, a lowborn bastard who seemed to
have the power to tempt her from any purpose to his own,
even make her break her vow of chastity; a man who could

insist she become that other Anne she felt lurking inside her just below the surface, the Anne who wanted passion and danger and sweet forgetting.

She laughed bitterly and leaned out the cabin window, watching the dockside sights of London town, crowded carriages, sellers of trinkets, apprentices braving the brawling streets. She knew that she would not find happiness here, but she would at last be secure from her own desires.

"A laugh is no answer, my lady," Dr. Josiah Wyndham said softly behind her. "I insist that you wait until morning to seek your uncle."

She turned and looked down at him, and he bowed in homage to her notable beauty, for she was now dressed in a fine gown, once a widow's barter for a year's supply of his miracle salve. Anne's hair was clean and fashionable; auburn ringlets hung behind her ears; and her face and form glowed with careless, easy youth.

If he had harbored any hope, when she had been disguised as an ill-clothed, grimy country lad, that someday Anne Gascoigne might return his growing affection, he gave it up on the spot. He allowed himself a momentary pang of regret before tucking the feeling away forever. A small man's affections often overreached his attractiveness to women. " 'Twas ever so," he murmured.

"What was ever so?" Anne asked, smiling affectionately.

"Nothing, my lady," he replied, clearing his throat.

She smoothed her gown as if to satisfy herself that she was once again a full woman, although she missed the comfort that a lad's sword at her side had given her. She smiled at the thought of a baldric crossing the satin bodice of her stylish gown, a daring fashion not even the Countess Castlemaine herself would hazard.

"You are in good spirits," the doctor said, relieved to see her light heart.

Anne brought her straying mind under control. "It is because I am almost at my destination, good doctor, but I must make my way to my uncle this night. It is too dangerous to wait. You do not know Edward as I now do. You and your son are imperiled by your Christian charity."

Dr. Wyndham did not dispute with her, although there was little Christianity or charity in him where she was concerned. Now that it was time for her to go, he simply could not bear to think of parting from her any sooner than absolutely necessary. The ideal of female beauty that he had spent half a lifetime so cheerfully ridiculing had now enslaved him. The irony of his feelings was not lost on him.

"At least, my lady," he said, spreading his hands in a pleading gesture, "allow me to accompany you to your uncle's house. It would be folly for you to go abroad alone. They say that there are now near a half-million souls in London, most of them, I wager, headed for the lowest level of hell."

"I accept your kind protection, and gladly, good doctor." She curtsied deeply, as she would have to the king, and he knew it was the prettiest thing that he would ever see in this life.

The watch was passing as they disembarked. "Nine of the clock and all's well," the man called, a flaring torch held high in one hand. His voice followed them as he announced the parish deaths. "Buried today fourteen persons, one dead of worms, one of griping in the guts and twelve of the plague. May God have mercy on them all."

And on us, Anne thought.

Beyond the light of the watch's flare, they groped their way along narrow, filthy alleys and into Cheapside, with its running sewer, past Milk Lane, toward old St. Paul's with the dim illumination cast from the doctor's ship's lantern containing a single beeswax candle.

"I thought the tales of plague exaggerated," Anne said, "but look you, doctor, at all the doors with bloody red crucifixes." She began to count them, but gave it up when the total became distressing.

They met constables with bread, leaving one loaf at every marked house. At one door, a dead man, his white face frozen in a final scream against the dark, sat propped by the wall, awaiting the cart to take him away to a common plague grave, to remain ever unknown and unremembered. It was all the living inside—maybe sickened themselves—could do for him before they shared his anonymous fate.

Anne stared at the body in horror until the doctor tugged at her arm and they hurried on.

"Death is not evil, but a natural occurrence," the doctor said. "Even my dear Mrs. Wyndham went to her grave within an hour of her expiration from childbirth."

Anne tried to clear her mind of the sight and to concentrate on Dr. Wyndham's words. "I am sorry to hear of it."

The doctor shrugged, being a doctor and so long a widower.

"It is the living who can be evil, Lady Anne. I was in Amsterdam last year when twenty and more thousands were carried off by the black plague. It shames me to say it, but physicians fled the city, as they will here." His small mouth was set into a grim pucker.

"What will *you* do?" she wondered aloud.

"There is little that any doctor can do for the plague, but I will not run away from it, nor blame the eating of radishes, the drinking of heady beer or the keeping of tame pigeons." His voice was scornful.

She stopped to catch her breath, clutching up her skirts, for they had walked very fast. "You are not the mountebank you pretend yourself to be."

He smiled. "Perhaps not entirely, but I will charge a good fee for my service, you may be sure. I have a few remedies that reduce suffering, and believe me, Lady Anne, there comes a time when that is all they cry out for."

She walked on in silence for a time, her hand on the pommel of her Italian knife, alert for footpads, even though the streets were now near empty except for the skittering of rats in the dark.

"You do not fool me, Dr. Josiah Wyndham," she said finally, and he heard the affection in her voice filtered through the ache in his own heart. "I'll remember you always as a good and courageous man."

She directed a turn into a lane beyond St. Paul's, and stopped across from her uncle's imposing London house. Servants were moving from the front door in a continuous line, loading boxes into a large wagon.

"It seems," the doctor said wryly, "that the clergy is not far behind physicians in their haste to leave the plague behind."

Anne was indignant. "My uncle never abides in London of a summer"—she wrinkled her nose at the street smells—"for obvious reasons."

He bowed. "Send me word of your happy homecoming, my lady," he said. "I will remain below London Bridge for some few days."

"I shall send word to you, and gladly. Thank you for everything, dear friend," she replied, pressing his hand, which he politely brushed with a kiss. "You will be amply rewarded for your kindness to me"—she smiled at him in the lantern light—"and remembered for your lessons in life's verities."

Then she walked across the street, leaving him in the shadows.

Halfway to her uncle's door, she stopped in the light cast by the workers' torches and waved once; then lifting her skirts, she mounted the stone steps and disappeared inside.

A rheumy-eyed old servant in the bishop's livery stopped her in the hall. "Why, my Lady Anne, is it truly you? We had feared for your life."

"In truth, I have never been more alive, William. Now ask my uncle to receive me."

He bowed and disappeared through two large, elaborately

carved doors, which almost immediately reopened to admit her.

Her uncle stood by the unlit fireplace, papers and books on a table beside him, wearing the black silk gown trimmed in gold lace of a Doctor of Sacred Theology. She hurried across the candlelit room to him, and bowed her head for his blessing.

"My dear child," he said, touching her hair, "God has answered our prayers and brought you safe again to our side."

Oh, Uncle, she thought, if you only knew how much help God has had. But she couldn't speak. Her throat was too full and her eyes were brimming with tears, for her uncle's voice held an echo of her dead father's; and when she looked into the bishop's eyes, she remembered when last her father had looked on her with his gentle love.

True, her uncle's eyes did not crinkle at the corners and squint into a tracery of laughing lines; rather, a deep vertical line of care and responsibility formed between the brows. Still, she could understand the difference between brothers: Her father's authority had come from the king, but her uncle's came from God.

He poured her a glass of claret and invited her to sit. "Another day, and you would have missed me, Niece."

"My father," she choked the words.

"He was buried three days gone, my child. I officiated myself." He folded his hands as if in prayer. "And now his soul is at peace with his maker, and his body rests in Essex beside your mother, in full and certain hope of the Second Coming of our Lord."

She nodded helplessly and longed to wring comfort from his words, but she could not. Instead, she lifted to him a face grown suddenly harsh with loss and rage. "Edward did it, Uncle, or hired it done. He killed my father, your brother, and I live only to see him punished."

Her uncle started where he stood. One hand bunched the silk of his gown and wrinkled it badly. "I do know you bear my Lord Waverby a deep grudge, Niece, but to accuse a peer of such base cowardice—"

"Then my father came to you, he told you what schemes Edward planned for after our marriage."

"Yes, yes, he told me what you overheard passing between Lord Waverby and the king."

"Then he *was* here—" She stopped, looking around the room as if to see some lingering trace of her father's presence.

"Yes, my brother was here before—just before, indeed on the very evening he was set upon by nameless rogues."

"They are *not* nameless to Lord Waverby." Her voice held so much loathing it filled and circled the room and came to rest in the anguish on her uncle's face.

"Quiet, child, the walls in London hear, and spies are everywhere."

"Whose spies? Edward wouldn't dare spy on you."

"That is not your worry, my child." He smiled reassuringly down at her. "Come, now, tell me what has transpired since you left London. I could not believe that my brother had placed you in the hands of a felon, no matter how much the new Robin Hood. You are not—not compromised, are you?"

"Yes," she said, and watched the line between his eyes deepen. "Oh, my maidenhead is safe enough, Uncle, but my innocence is gone forever. I no longer believe that king and peers are superior to milkmaids and smiths. I do know now that highwaymen and charlatans can have more true honor than men of high station. If that be compromised, then so be it."

The bishop drew back. "Are you feverish, Anne? The plague is everywhere."

"No, Uncle, I am as well as my hope to avenge my father's death"—her grim voice momentarily choked—"preferably by my own hand."

He started anew, and his voice was stern. "You must ask

God's forgiveness for such unwomanly thoughts, Niece. Now, tell me how you came to this pernicious resolution."

She told him then of John Gilbert, of how, disguised as a groom, she had seen the truth of her father's murder on Edward's bragging face at Burwell Hall. Her voice shivered with disgust when she said her betrothed's name.

"But, dear niece, that is no legal confession. Could your opinion of the scene not be jaundiced by your anger at him?"

"No." The single word rang about the huge reception room.

"I see," he replied. "I had planned to return to Ely tomorrow, but this changes things. If wrong has been done, wrongdoers must be confronted."

"Then you will set aside my betrothal, and tell the king—"

"We must be cautious, child. You must place yourself in my hands, allow me to assume this heavy burden from your weak and tender shoulders." Smiling, he touched her cheek. "You must once again become the beautiful young treasure who brought such glory to our family name. I do know that Queen Catharine longs for your return, and the king's pique is easily assuaged. He is really a most agreeable and merry monarch."

"Never, Uncle," Anne said. "I will *never* return to the palace." For a moment, staring into those eyes so like her father's, she wondered if her uncle had heard a word she'd said.

He offered his arm, and she took it wearily. "Now to bed, dear Anne, for you do look half exhausted from your wild adventures. Trust me that their unpleasantness will fade with time."

She nodded, but she doubted that even a bishop could promise her total forgetfulness; she wondered further if she even wanted it. When her hair was white with age, she would sit in a warm primrose garden in Essex and think of John Gilbert. By then, her memory would be truly harmless, as it certainly was not now.

The bishop escorted her upstairs to a bedroom where she had stayed many times before as a young girl. At sight of the familiar carved furniture and the brilliantly colored turkey carpets and bed hangings, it was almost like coming home, and she squeezed her uncle's arm affectionately.

"Sleep well, Anne. All will soon be as it should," the bishop said, and kissed her forehead.

"Thank you, Uncle," Anne replied, looking with longing at the thick featherbed and satin-covered pillows.

The door closed behind her as she crossed to the bed to remove her dress. She had undone the bodice ribbons when she heard the door lock grate into its catch behind her.

Anne ran to the door, rattling the knob, which would not give; then she pounded on the heavy paneling. "Uncle! Unlock this door!"

She heard his voice clearly. "It is my right as your next-of-kin to protect you from your own youthful folly. Remember, Niece, that your duty in life is to be obedient to your guardian and then to your husband."

The words of betrayal nearly choked her, but she managed to shout, "I will escape."

Her uncle's voice receded down the hall. "Pray for guidance, Anne. There is no escape in this world from a woman's duty."

The next night, a short, shadowy figure watched the bishop's tightly shuttered house, while another very much taller shadow detached itself from a doorway and crept behind the first.

"Good evening, Dr. Wyndham," John Gilbert said. "We meet for a second time, but for the same reason. The Lady Anne Gascoigne is becoming quite a botheration, wouldn't you say?"

Dr. Josiah Wyndham laughed softly. "And what decided you upon this course, good reverend? You do not seem the man, by reputation at least, to follow a lass who gave you such a rare ducking."

John thought a moment. "A good question, Doctor, and when I have an answer beyond my present amusement, you will be the second person to know it."

"Perhaps I know the answer now."

"Do you think so?" John said, his voice irritable. "You remember the affair at Windsor and think you understand it."

There was a pause. "And I don't?" the doctor asked.

John could plainly hear the doctor's amusement, and didn't like it. "Don't forget, Doctor, that in my business, I could lift your purse where you stand."

"You could, but you are not here on business."

John stared at the windows of the bishop's fortresslike stone house, only faint light filtering between shutters. "Have you seen her?"

"No," the doctor answered, "but that is not what worries me. I asked her to send me word, and she has not."

John shrugged, and his voice was bitter. "She has returned to her highborn place and forgotten everyone who helped her to get there."

"That is not the Lady Anne I know," Josiah Wyndham said softly.

John was silent, defensive and a bit ashamed. He had been speaking out of some deep pride that tried to explain his presence in that dark London lane by lashing out against the doctor, against Anne, against everything, including the truth.

He was there because he could not be content in any other place until he knew her to be safe and protected. Then he could walk away and leave her to her gentlewoman's life; only then could he be done with her, and be glad of it.

"I beg pardon for my ill humor, Doctor," John said calmly. "I am not quite myself. Little sleep, and"—he laughed heartily—"that unexpected wetting in the Thames."

"Of course," the doctor said, no more amusement in his

tone. "What say you, John Gilbert? If I do not hear from the Lady Anne tomorrow, should I present myself with my doctor's chest at the bishop's door and inquire after her health?"

"You could," John said, "but I don't like the look of this. I don't like this inactivity. A bishop has vast affairs, callers, petitioners, and yet the house is shuttered and closed as if empty. Why?"

A gilded carriage preceded by linkboys running ahead with flares turned into the lane and stopped.

"Well," the doctor said, relief in his piercing whisper, "here is activity for you."

An armed driver bounded from his high perch to the street and opened the carriage door, and Edward Ashley Carter, Lord Waverby, stepped out, victory blazing on his face.

Chapter Eleven

The Darling Strumpet

The Bishop of Ely paced his reception room, keeping a wary eye on the Earl of Waverby. "Anne refuses to discuss the marriage, my lord." He raised his hands palms up placatingly. "If this were a hundred years ago, I could throw her into a dungeon on bread and water, but these are modern days." He smiled hopefully. "You must give me time to bring her to reason."

"There is no more time," the earl said, his clipped voice casting a chill on the room, sultry after an intense summer downpour. "I am now more than a week beyond my announced wedding date. I cannot suffer this public humiliation further without demanding redress from the nearest male relative, plus the immediate payment of double her portion as written in our nuptial agreement."

The bishop's mouth dropped open and a flush of dismay spread over his face. "My lord, you are not proposing—nay, it is some jest. A bishop does not fight duels. As for money, I have only my clergyman's living." He forced a laugh and then put a hand on each hip in a painfully poor effort at bravado, something that had not worked for him even as a much younger man with the bully boys at Oxford. He had won his high church preferment not through courage but through diligence and bargain, two skills that now failed him utterly.

Lord Waverby sat absolutely still in his high-backed chair and watched the bishop the way a hawk would watch a disabled mouse, waiting for one small, revealing twitch that would be a signal to pounce.

"My dear bishop," he said, and his tone was as cool and as assured as his white aristocratic face, "I would challenge Christ himself to sabers at Epsom if it would bring me my due. As it happens, there are even easier ways of satisfying my honor."

A charge of blasphemy remained unspoken. The meaning of the threat hung between them in the heavy storm-laden air, and the bishop, remembering his brother's premature death, chewed at his upper lip, trying desperately to think of something that would persuade the angry earl to reasonableness.

Waverby played with the costly silver lace on his cuffs, his long, slender fingers shredding the delicate material most cruelly.

Anne's uncle saw and scarcely controlled an ague that threatened to shiver its way through his backbone. The savagely handsome man in front of him was hard, seemingly beyond appeal, but a loving uncle could not so abandon his niece without one last entreaty to the man's more delicate nature, delivered, of course, in high-pulpit tones.

"Anne is young, my lord, and willful, e'en for her sex. But with just a little patience, you would be rewarded greatly in time, when, with continued demonstrations of your regard, you could easily return her to love and passion for your person. A woman of her temperament, if you'll allow me to say so, my lord, needs a soft captivity."

"I will allow nothing to thwart my aims," Waverby said, ripping off the final shreds of silver lace at his cuff and throwing them on the polished parquet floor. His tone was made of dripping ice. "First your brother, and now you. Are all your family of such indifferent intelligence that you do not see what you have?"

The bishop's shoulders sagged with the weight of his guardian's responsibility. "I would not have her a strumpet, my lord."

"A king's strumpet! A darling strumpet!" The earl's voice was filled with naked rage. "The Lady Anne's chastity has such charms for our king that a dukedom and rich colonial plantations are sure to be my lot, while the seat of Canterbury could be yours if you make me your friend. But think you that this royal itch will last forever? I hear the king is already looking with favor on the actress Nell Gwyn. That's right, Orange Nell, who once sold oranges in the pit of the Theater Royal, and now could fill the bed royal, to my great loss and your own if you do but think on't."

The bishop looked dazed, staring vacantly at the ceiling. "Me, Archbishop of Canterbury, primate of all England," he said, his voice full of wonder and desperate yearning.

Lord Waverby stood and confronted the man with scarcely contained disdain. "I will take your niece to my house in St. James this night for safety's sake—you would not believe how very hotheaded our Anne is—and then you will wed us tomorrow evening at St. Paul's."

The Bishop of Ely sighed. "Of course, I have always been convinced that her marriage to you was for her best." He called a servant, removing a large key from the depth of his robes. "I will ask her to join us as soon as possible."

"I would see her now," Waverby said, striding for the huge carved doors.

"But she is in her bath," replied the bishop.

"Even better," Lord Waverby said, a smile suddenly on his thin lips, and he grabbed the key and was out of the room and mounting the stairs before the bishop could issue another feeble and useless protest.

* * *

Anne lay submerged in her bath laced with the heavy, sweet scent of lilac and rose petals, rising from the warm water to tickle her nose and trigger her memory. She found the water even more soothing without a bathing gown, and determined never to wear one again. For a moment all care vanished as she was seduced by the floral and woodsy undertones so reminiscent of the pool at Whittlewood Forest.

She closed her eyes on her locked prison-room and inhaled deeply, trying to bring back the scene of her dream, the one she had nearly every night, a dream of being naked in the flowing water, held tight in John Gilbert's total embrace.

A key turned in the lock behind her, and the door opened. She twisted about to speak to the maid, and saw a male figure outlined in the dim candlelight. She knew at once that it was not her uncle. It took but a moment more to recognize the ominous stride of the man who stepped toward her. She crossed both arms to hide her breasts from his hateful gaze.

He picked up a stool and placed it beside the large brass bathing tub near the fireplace, then sat down, stretching his long, slender legs, at total languorous ease, his amused glance seeming to penetrate the milky fluid that surrounded her body.

She calculated the distance to her Italian knife, lying hidden under her dress on the huge four-poster bed across the room, and knew she could never reach it. "Leave at once, Edward, or I will call my uncle." It was a futile bluff, but the only one she had to make.

He poured himself a cup of tea from the side table, and she watched, fascinated, as his long white fingers curled about the delicate china drinking bowl. Once, she had thought those fingers so fine, had longed for them to touch her; now she despised that longing, knowing that it had been founded on the most despicable deceit.

"I see that you follow the tastes of our Portuguese queen," he said, sipping the tea, as if he were making polite conversation at a reception. "As for me, I prefer good English ale, or better, Spanish wine. And *do* remove your arms so that your future husband can see the goods he has gone to so much trouble to acquire."

"Never!" she said. "I will never be wife to the cowardly murderer of my father."

He drew back in mock horror, an elegant hand waving lazily in the air. "You are cruel beyond most of your sex, my dear Anne. Whatever I did, I did for your future. It is so like a woman to blame a man for what she gives him no choice but to do."

He smiled at her and she shuddered, realizing that, if possible, every smile of his made her loathe him more.

"Perhaps," he said, and he dipped the long fingers of one hand into the bathwater, "you should have remained a dirty little groom at Burwell Hall—so much more congenial, eh?"

She gasped. "If you knew—"

"Oh, but I didn't, not at first. I was distracted by your excellent masquerade—'twould have done any actress proud." His smile flickered. "But when my groundsman found a wig and hat, and the watch at Reading sent an inquiry about a red-haired lad said to be in my service, it was not difficult to see through the ruse."

Edward shrugged. "I must admit, dear Anne, that yours was a particularly entertaining trail to follow." He shook his head in sham good humor. "I'm astonished; I really am. You seem to cause trouble wherever you go. But not for long, my sweet. Soon you will be my adoring and very obedient wife."

She was watching, fascinated, as his fingers moved through the water toward her. When they touched her stomach and moved with terrible leisure toward her hidden breasts, she shrank into herself, stifling her revulsion, determined not to give him the pleasure of her scream for help. Somehow she knew that he wanted her to beg, that her scream would arouse him mightily.

Lord Waverby felt increasingly frustrated. The Lady Anne Gascoigne wasn't trembling or weeping. The slut denied him every enjoyment, even the momentary diversion of a stiffened cod. She had no heat in her that he could find; the king would not be pleased that the virtuous runaway returned a burnt-out cinder. He bent over her mouth and kissed it hard, brushing his tongue back and forth against her lips, then drew back to appraise the result.

She stared at him, her eyes dead and still, like green agate. "Not a thousand kisses of yours would make me love you, or willingly whore for the king."

"Then you will do it to save your uncle, because you *will* marry me and be the king's slut, I promise you that you will, or wish to heaven that you had."

"You would not dare kill a bishop."

"As easily as I will certainly watch John Gilbert slowly strangle in his noose."

She drew in her breath sharply and tried to cover the fact by turning her face from him, but not before he had seen her eyes change, mist and cast a despairing, desperate glance toward heaven.

"So," Edward said, "the highwayman has melted the maidenhead and ruined the purchase."

"No," she cried, "he never—we never. An oath for him is not lightly given or lightly broken. You would not understand. I did not myself."

A laugh rattled in Lord Waverby's throat, and his tone once more was the bored courtier's who thought every form of virtue some disguised hypocrisy. "If he did not have you, then that Lakeland bastard is a bigger fool than ever I thought." Waverby spoke rancorously. "He owes his life to the gallows a hundred times over, but it will please me more to see him hang for a crime he did not commit. I will put such a reward on his head that his own mother would give him over to the nearest constable."

Abruptly, Waverby put both hands on Anne's wrists and

forced them apart, exposing her breasts. He was not quite prepared for what he saw: two perfectly formed flesh-pale orbs that pulsed with a rapidly beating heart, and piercing the air above them, two wine-red nipples that, while he hungrily watched, came thrustingly erect, denying her feigned frigidity.

She loathed seeing his eyes on her and the elementary fear that had betrayed her nipples, but her voice was steady. "You will have no pleasure if you force me, only shame."

He laughed and dropped her wrists, reddened from his grip, into the rapidly cooling water. "You are such a little Puritan, after all, much like your mother. For me, force is the greatest aphrodisiac, my lady, with shame running a close second. Soon you will know these truths very well indeed."

He laughed again, and she understood that this was the first genuine mirth that she had ever heard from his mouth, and she shuddered.

He rose and sauntered to the window, unlocked the shutters and called through the iron bars to his footman below. "You there! We leave with the half hour."

He stepped back to the tub, and she made no further move to cover herself. "Good," he said, taking the act as one of submission, although if he had known her as well as he thought, he would have recognized a new determination. "Dress yourself. I am removing you to Waverby House in St. James. Your uncle will perform the wedding ceremony tomorrow."

He left her then, closing the door behind him. She heard the lock turn as, dripping bathwater, she dashed to the Italian knife under her dress on the bed. With all her might, she flung it at the place where Edward had been a moment before, and it stuck, quivering, heart high in the door.

It was a fruitless defiance, she knew. Edward had won in a way. Oh, he would never have her or hand her to the king—she would die by her own hand first—but she would lose, too, never to be free to choose a love or a life. She smiled bitterly. Unlike Beth, the milkmaid, she had no vote in her affairs.

Slowly, she donned clean smallclothes and hose; very slowly, her mind trying to find an escape hole to crawl through, but finding none.

Drunken roisterers on the street below were singing, and for a moment the song sounded familiar, very much like the country tune that Beth had sung to her lute at the highwayman's camp. A vision of John's dark face on the greensward came to her, his eyebrows and trim mustache curved in delight as she parried his sword thrust with the skill he'd shared with her.

She clenched her fists at the memory, until her nails dug into her skin. Fate was indeed cruel; at the darkest of life's moments, it constantly reminded of wonderful moments lost forever.

She crossed to the window, looked down, and seeing nothing but Edward's waiting carriage, closed the shutters against the song.

A blinding downpour had started again. Anne, in the strong grip of Lord Waverby, was half carried, half dragged, the few steps from the bishop's door to the street and into the carriage.

The earl knocked against the covered peephole, which was opened by the footman. "Home to St. James," he yelled above the noise of rain pelting the coach's roof.

"Aye, my lord," the driver answered.

"You are wet, Anne." Waverby sat opposite her, flapping the raindrops from his own cloak. He smiled. "When you are safe in my home, we will have a frisk to dry our bare bodies before a fire."

She was silent and very aware of hard steel, which she had tied by a ribbon against her calf, the quicker to use it, if needs be.

Waverby shrugged. "I see that I am not to be accorded the

pleasure of your nimble tongue. In truth, it is just as well, since you have led me such a chase these past days that I am fatigued beyond belief." He eyed her slyly. "I must be rested for my wedding tomorrow. It will take far more of my strength than I thought to give up your maidenhead to the king."

He promptly pulled his cloak about him and lowered his eyelids, although Anne was sure that he watched her as the carriage swayed and creaked on through the rainy night.

She calculated the chance that she could wrench the door open and jump out. If she landed without breaking a leg, could she hide in the dark streets of plague-ridden London? And for how long? She had no money, and her uncle, although choked with disgrace even in his own eyes, did not have the courage to stand up to his own ambition or to Edward's will.

There was her friend the doctor on his barge below the Tower, but she would not return his great kindness with such trouble as she would surely bring him.

The man who could help her, the one man who feared no earl, bishop or king, was gone. She had sent him away with a finality that, now she remembered it, left her in total, tumbling despair.

"My dear Anne," Edward said, reclining in the dim light across from her, his thin lips pursed in thought, "you look so troubled that I am urged by every manly feeling to comfort you."

"Do not trouble your poor sensibilities, my lord earl," she replied stiffly and with irony. "Allow them to slumber on."

Taking hold in the swaying coach, he crossed to her awkwardly and sat close beside her. "When I look at you thus," he said, "I remember my beauteous nymph in her bath." She felt his hot breath on her cheek. "I remember, too, the time when you wanted me, when it was me that you adored. "By God's tears, I want to keep you for my own exclusive pleasure!"

He pinioned her arms against her sides and kissed her wolfishly, so intent upon possession that he was unaware the carriage had halted until the door opened.

"Why have we stopped, my man?"

A hand with a cocked pistol came through the door, followed by John Gilbert's wet but smiling face.

"Johnny," Anne breathed, as if the affectionate name had been forever sitting on the tip of her tongue, waiting for the one moment when no other name would serve.

Chapter Twelve

Sealed with a Kiss

"Johnny," she said the name again, as if she could not get enough of the sound of it, the feel of it on her tongue.

"I thought you'd be happy to see me, my lady," he said with a grin on his wide and sensuous mouth, "although I'm no drier than I was the last time we met." He lifted her hand to kiss, his gaze never leaving the earl.

She was quite delirious with the pleasure of hearing his voice again, although she tried, unsuccessfully, to drain all delirium from her words. "Sir Highwayman, wet or dry, you are most heartily welcome in my sight." She barely suppressed a delighted smile. "Wouldn't you agree, Edward?"

The Earl of Waverby, far from agreeing, stole his hand under his cloak.

John's easy grin did not change as he lifted the earl's cloak and relieved him of a loaded pistol. Then he shoved the muzzle of his own primed flintlock between the satin breeches and into the earl's groin. "I wouldn't move, my lord, or I will leave you without that which signifies your manhood. You have nothing else, I think, to recommend it."

"What have you done with my footman?" Waverby said, his voice shaking with anger.

"He is sleeping off a draft of poppy prepared by a friend

of mine. You will find your servant in the alley across from
the bishop's house, soaked to the skin, probably, but very
content, I'll wager."

"You will die for this dabbling in my affairs, John
Gilbert."

"How many times can one man kill another, my lord of
Waverby? You have already condemned me twice, once for
hiding Anne, and again for making a fool of you. I would
happily die yet once more to rescue her from the whore's
role you would have her play to fill your purse."

"Righteous words from a low felon!" Waverby tenta-
tively extended his hand. "In truth, this is not a commoner's
business. Give me your pistol and I could be persuaded to le-
niency. Obviously, the Lady Anne has bewitched you."

John bowed slightly. "Possibly, my lord. I do admit that
my behavior has been strange in my own eyes of late."

The earl shifted unexpectedly, and John shoved the muzzle of his weapon deeper into the earl's breeches, smiling
grimly as Waverby's arrogant, still-unbelieving mouth
thinned to a tight line.

The earl spit out his next words. "You will not laugh
when I have you drawn and quartered for the rabble's
amusement."

John clicked his tongue mockingly. "My lord, you do
give our English aristocracy, known for their gentle thieving
taxes and kindly enclosure of common grazing lands, a very
bad name indeed."

Waverby swallowed but sat rigidly still, his eyes flicking
from Anne to John and back again. "You may have my
purse, my rings and my carriage, John Gilbert, but the
woman will bring you nothing but troubles."

John nodded, his smile broader. "For once, you speak
truth, Waverby, but it is the kind of trouble for which a real
man lives."

Anne watched the highwayman in wonder, her eyes wide,
her flushed skin glowing, her mouth prettily agape. She had

never seen him as she saw him now. Indeed, she had never seen any man more easily courageous, more easily gallant or with such wit in the face of desperate acts. It was amazing to her that she had failed to recognize these qualities in him, for they were ones that she had always looked for in a man, and until this moment had needed to manufacture.

Once more, her marveling lips formed the two syllables of his name, and, hearing its soft expression, he smiled on her.

"Anne, my sweet, if you now believe your beautiful green eyes, I would have you close them. I'm afraid Lord Waverby will have to disrobe."

A steely look in John's dark eyes and a twist of the pistol barrel silenced the earl's instant objections.

"Off with them, my lord. I would almost give you another of my lives to see how you explain a naked stroll in Hyde Park to the dandies at Whitehall."

Waverby untied his cloak and doublet.

"Faster, my lord. The lady Anne and I have a long ride."

The earl removed his shirt. "Whittlewood Forest will not hold you now, highwayman. There will be no safety for you anywhere in the realm. I promise you that I will hunt you down like a cur."

John withdrew the pistol from Waverby's groin and pointed it at his head. "Now the breeches and the boots, if you'll be so good, my lord."

Anne did not turn away, but coolly watched Edward's humiliation. Now let him feel scornful eyes upon *his* helpless, naked flesh!

Again, as she looked, she felt astonishment at herself, or at least that Anne Gascoigne that had so recently existed. As her betrothed's pale, slender body emerged from under its costly cloth, she wondered that she could ever have found him so aesthetically handsome and desirable.

She much preferred the dark visage, the bronzed flesh, the wider shoulders and harder muscles of John Gilbert, even though such were thought at court to be the marks of a commoner. There was much the court obviously did not know. It pleased her mightily to think that she might teach Castlemaine a thing or two about a man.

"Hold this on him, Anne," John said, handing her Waverby's cocked pistol.

She took it without hesitation and pointed it at Edward's heart.

"Are you mad, Anne?" the earl cried. "Do you want to hang with him?"

She looked at Edward and then she laughed. "It is you who are mad to think that I would consider life with you, Edward, to be better than death with him."

John threw her a glance that might have been admiring, but it had more fire in it than mere esteem, much more fire. He tucked his own pistol into his belt and backed out of the carriage into the rain.

"Come out, my lord," John said, shivering briefly. "Now the smallclothes," he added, once the earl had scrambled past an alert Anne and his bare feet were on the ground. Slowly, he undid the ties and dropped his flimsy silk undergarments to the muddy Ring Drive.

John drew his sword, pricked the clothes, and tossed them high into a tree, where the driver of some fashionable lady or noble coxcomb would discover them early the next morning.

John bowed politely. "Have a fine walk, my lord earl."

Then the highwayman slapped his sword across Waverby's rump, sending him stumbling, climbed onto the driver's box and urged the horses into a gallop.

Anne held the pistol on Edward until he was out of sight, but she would never forget the look on his face, his mouth like a white gash receding into the night. Although he was pale as death, it was not his own demise that he contemplated, but her painful death and John's.

She shivered, but not from the summer downpour. Where

once Edward had been determined to use her for his own evil ends, now she knew that he wanted her obliteration; and he wanted it to hurt.

Oh, it wasn't her defiance that he hated. That, she was sure, was only a nuisance, and had always somewhat amused him. But he would not forgive what he had seen in her eyes when she had looked at the highwayman, what she would never again be able to hide from anyone's inquiring eyes.

Beyond Hyde Park, John doubled back and finally turned the horses into a side street off the Strand and stopped at an imposing stone house near Drury Lane. He was chilled through to his bones as he climbed down from the driver's box and got into the carriage.

He sat down across from Anne and reached for her two hands, which she willingly gave to him. "My lady," he said, his eyes searching her face, "we must bide here."

"But I thought we were returning to Whittlewood Forest."

"Nay," John said, his voice urgent, "at least not until the hue and cry dies down. Waverby will have an army watching the Oxford road." He closed his eyes in thought and then slowly opened them again. "We have need of a friend who will hide us for a few days. Think you well. Before it is too late, you may want to change your mind; you may want to know better of the dangers you face."

She interrupted him. "I know. I know all that I need to know. I am here with you now, and that is all there is of importance to me in this world."

"But, my lady," he said, and she saw his laughing eyes searching her face, "have you forgotten your vow of unremitting chastity?"

Before she could form an answer, the driverless horses shifted their feet, and the carriage jerked forward, throwing her to her knees before him.

He tugged at her hands to pull her up, but she resisted.

"No," she cried, her voice a mix of joy and earnestness.

"Let me remain on my knees, humbled before your courage."

"Nonsense," he said, lifting her up, his voice and closeness spreading warmth through her. "Come sit by my side. That is where I would have you remain always, if only it could be."

She leaned against him and sighed, thinking only of the words and thoughts tumbling from her mouth without once having passed through the censor of prudence. "Oh, Johnny, I may regret these words, but I would like to be an earnest Anne with you, a supplicating Anne with you."

"No, my sweet," John said, and there was a marvelous quality in his voice that thrilled her through, "you will *not* regret those words."

He leaned back against the seat rest, still smiling the boldly quizzical smile she remembered, the one that lifted together the tip of his dark, curving mustache and brow—once an image so totally infuriating, now one utterly charming to her. At sight of that smile once again, so near in the narrow carriage, she was overcome with a desire to bend just slightly toward him and touch it with her lips, to taste it and seal it forever as it appeared now, nevermore to change.

Afterward, she could not remember how much time elapsed between the desire and the kiss; there must surely have been a proper delay, since she had been well bred, and a lady of breeding did not fall upon a man in the dark seat of a carriage parked on the public street, no matter how heated her lower limbs.

When her lips finally met his warm, full mouth, he did not seem surprised—pleased, rather—and he allowed her to explore at will; but she was almost immediately unable to realize her wish to seal his smile forever with her kiss. The kiss grew somewhat beyond her control, until her pointed tongue invaded his mouth, only to find the most determined parry and thrust. Then his hands found entrance beneath her cloak and cupped her welcoming bosom.

Her own hands answered, parting his wet doublet and eagerly sliding along skin barely covered with a thin summer shirt now almost dry.

Startled, she drew back, breathing unevenly. "But, Johnny, are you feverish?" she asked, and like a mother rubbed his cheek with the back of her hand to confirm her diagnosis.

"A fever of desire, Anne. Now say my name again. I like the sound of it on your tongue."

She obliged happily, not once, but several times, helped along by his inquiring hands.

With great effort, John Gilbert stopped and looked through the side curtains. He must be mad, on the verge of making love to Anne in Waverby's carriage with his crest bright on the door. The watch and every parish constable would be looking for them.

He opened the door and lowered the steps. "Anne, this is the one place in all London we can safely stay until the hue and cry dies down, other than some low Southwark den of thieves, and I would not take you to such a rude place."

"What is this house?"

"Nell Gwyn's. She will hide us and think it great sport."

"Your mistress?"

"My friend."

"An amorous friend, you'll not deny it."

"No, I'll not deny it was once true." He jumped out and then helped Anne to the cobbles—more than helped; overcame her resistance. The downpour continued unabated.

John pounded on Nell Gwyn's front door until a muffled voice asked his business at this late hour. "A friend awaits outside," he said.

"What friend?"

"The master of Whittlewood."

The door opened on an elderly manservant, holding a lantern. "John Gilbert, sir, it be good to see ye alive. Mistress Gwyn did tell me how ye escaped Tyburn's noose."

"Now that my neck is safe, I and this good lady need lodging, William. Tell Nell I am drowning at her door."

"But my mistress is not here. She be gone to the country with others from the Theater Royal, to escape the plague. I cannot offer her hospitality."

John didn't like to bully servants, but the need was exceptional. "What would your mistress say if she knew you closed her house to friends in need?"

The old retainer muttered but threw the door wide, and holding a lantern high, lit the stairs to the gallery. "Ye remember your way, Master John," he said slyly, eyeing Anne.

John answered with a nod, aware of Anne standing stiff and in ill humor at being in Nell's house. "Good William, have the groom take the carriage around to the stable, and bed the horses." He slipped William a gold coin that insured good treatment for both horses and people. "And William, some wine and mulling spices, some bread and fruit, if the strawberry woman passed today."

John led a reluctant Anne up the stairs and into Nell's bedroom, paneled in linenfold with jewel-colored tapestry bed hangings and turkey carpets everywhere, giving the room something of the appearance of a sultan's seraglio, no doubt by design. Gowns flung over chairs and bed in disarray attested to the haste of the departing Nell. Still, she had left her orange blossom scent everywhere.

Anne's gaze slowly circled the room and then circled it again, as she felt her righteous anger rising. "I cannot stay here. What manner of man are you to expect this humiliation of me?"

"As you see before you, a tired thief. You greatly disturb a man's sleep, Anne. I have not had one good night since we met more than a fortnight past."

"I would rather sleep in the stable than in your mistress's bedroom."

John's anger swelled. "As you will." He turned his back, knelt on one knee at the ornate fireplace covered in Delft tiles, struck a flint to tinder, blew mightily on the spark, and fanned a leaping fire in the grate.

Anne regretted her sharp tongue, as she quite often did. "After I warm myself and dry my clothes."

"That's surprisingly sensible for a woman who prefers stable straw to goose down," he said, not resisting his need to show the anger she'd aroused. Damn the woman! She was as changeable as the English weather. He would not beg her to come to him. He had obviously overcoddled her, and if he was ever to assume mastery . . . his mind stumbled in midthought. Oh, God, the lunacy that attacked a man who reached for the unattainable woman, the lunacy that he had so feared, had struck him, and was like to strike him down. He could offer her nothing but a thief's death, but he could take the one thing she would need for a good marriage, and thereby lose all honor. And he would need his bastard's honor to survive in a world that denied him a rightful place or a death with his head high. But his cod ached with what he had almost had.

He began to strip off his wet doublet and breeches, until he was standing in smallclothes. He hung the soggy lot over the brass firedogs.

Anne averted her eyes, but not before she'd seen a form she thought the most manly she had ever known. It was on her lips to apologize when William knocked and entered with a tray of food and a wine bottle with two tankards.

"Put it there, William," John said, motioning to a table near the fire, "and then go back to your warm bed, with my thanks. I will tell Nell what good care you gave us."

William bobbed and pulled his forelock. "Thankee, Master John. Enjoy thy . . . supper," he said, broadly winking.

Anne tried to look at nothing but the warm, beckoning fire. She moved as close as was safe, attempting to dry her gown, which had left a puddle where she stood.

John's anger softened at the sight. "You need dry clothes, Anne, and there are a half-dozen gowns in this room."

"None that I shall ever wear, sir." Her hauteur was all she had left, standing here with a near-naked John Gilbert in the room, a room so full of the memory and scent of his absent lover.

He rummaged in a chest and pulled out a rather plain dressing gown, its linen wrapping folded underneath. "I vow this has not been worn," he said. "Put it on before you catch an ague. Or would you rather I put it on for you?"

His voice was low and soft, therefore, the more to be believed. She doubted not that he would undress her himself, and then of a certain she would be lost, as she had almost been in the carriage. But she did not move fast enough, and appeared to defy him.

He clasped her arm roughly and removed her lace cap, tossing it to the floor, then unable to stop himself, kissed her hair. "Anne." He said her name with a kind of amazement. "Anne." He whispered it again softly, and the sound of it, so much more than a name, jangled within her.

"Curse you, John Gilbert," she said, although it didn't sound like a curse at all. "Do you have no sensibility? How could you bring me to your paramour's . . ." Suddenly, her feet left the floor, and she was being held against his hard body, legs dangling, his warm mouth sliding toward hers.

Still unforgiving, she swung her head to one side and then to the other, but not fast enough. He caught her parted lips with his own before she could press her mouth shut. For a moment, she fought him, but he was as granite and she was a zephyr.

His breath came hot and gasping into her mouth, sending tremors through her of such intensity that her woman's parts seemed to leap into intense flame. She felt at once empty and full, prisoner and free, chaste and whore. Her surging pulse seemed poised to leap through her skin at a dozen places. At some point, her strength left her, and in its place came a desire to stay where she was at least a bit longer. Fleetingly, she wondered, Where was her mother's teaching? Where was guilt? Those twin protections of chaste womankind against lustful men.

Encouraged, John pressed Anne closer to the length of him, and she felt the manliness of his fierce cod for the second time in one evening. God's bowels! There was no avoiding it. She was well shaken now, for she had discovered not for the first time how little a woman, no matter how determined, could trust her own body.

And then his lips left hers, and with a look from those half-closed, hungry eyes that must have melted more than one woman's determination, and nearly thawed hers, he carried her toward the bed. It was clear that he meant to take her, and that she clung to him with an overwhelming desire to assist him, her anger at being in his mistress's bedroom all but evaporated in the heat of an urgent need.

He stopped abruptly and put her feet on the floor, holding himself rigidly away from her. "Oh, my God, forgive me, Anne," he said, the words near choking him. "In honor, I cannot take that which your future husband would want for his own."

She scarcely stood without his support, her knees shaking. "You are no true scoundrel, as the alehouse songs say."

He grinned, but his lips stayed in a straight line, as if the smile hurt. "I am found out, Lady Anne, but if all the world knows it for truth, I will not take you when I cannot be husband to you."

Her chin went up and her eyes flashed a wounded look. "I will go to another room."

"This is the only bedroom, save the servants'."

"You would know that."

He bowed mockingly. "Take the bed," he said.

"No, you take Nell's bed. I will sleep on this chair near the fire."

John poured a tankard of wine, took a great drink, wiped his mouth on the back of his hand and flopped onto the bed, his damp, dark hair shining against white linen. He closed his eyes, and his fists, digging in his nails, exchanged a little hurt for the bigger one.

Anne stood, uncertain, in the middle of the room, feeling foolish and angry and frustrated at once. Finally, she crossed to the chair and sat down and almost immediately rose, her wet gown clinging, a chill traveling through her. She studied John for a full minute, but he did not move and his eyes did not open. Quickly, she removed her gown, and holding it awkwardly in front of her, took off her sodden undershift, draping them over the back of her chair, using a pillow to hide her nakedness.

Anne was not positive that John slept, but he did not move for the long minutes she watched him, and she finally thought he must be sleeping. It was baffling to her how a man could sleep in a room filled with such strong sentiments. Now, a woman would be wakeful until all matters were examined and resolved.

Soon, she grew more chill, and pulled Nell's shift over her—that would not count as wearing it—and thus, eventually fell into a troubled sleep.

Some hours later, in the full dark, she awoke stiff and aching. She stretched again and swore under her breath, half convinced that the chair would turn her into a bent old woman by morn. With one eye on John's still form, she tiptoed to the opposite side of the bed, stealthily parted the hangings and slowly stretched herself under the warm coverlet, lying at the very outer edge. For what seemed hours but could not have been, she waited for him to seize her. When he didn't, she moved closer.

Chapter Thirteen

You and No Other

"Anne," he said, and she knew that no man would ever say her name quite like that again, half exasperation, half choked desire. "Do you think me a monk from the old days that I can bear to have you so close and keep to my course?"

Anne moaned, a tremor shaking her. "I was hoping you could not, Johnny."

With a groan that expelled most of his frustration and all of his resolve, he drew her into an embrace, his mouth finding her eager lips. He had tried mightily to resist her, but he was only a man, and withstanding Anne Gascoigne would take a great sorcerer.

Once again, Anne was in the power of her own passions. She cared not one jot if this were Nell's house and her bed. It could have been the devil's and it would not have mattered. Her hand brushed his upright cod, surely by accident. "You think me brazen, don't you?"

"For a lady," he teased, his hands moving quickly to undo the ties to his smallclothes, kicking them from under the coverlet to the floor, until he lay naked before her.

Anne looked long and he allowed it, indeed smiling. She took a deep breath and slowly expelled it, her eyes gorging upon his body. She was aware that she felt no surprise at seeing a man in full passion for the first time. There was something about him she recognized, something of the brown earth of Whittlewood, something as old as man and woman, pulling her with a compelling mystery to fling herself upon his stiff cock.

John was looking at her naked body, and she feared his disapproval. Her Puritan mother had been a poor teacher of allurement, and she had ever been on her guard at court.

"Anne," he whispered urgently, "open your eyes."

She did, and saw his dark eyes reflecting the firelight, his face losing its emotion softened with wanting and flushed hot with desire.

John Gilbert had never seen such loveliness in one woman, nay not ten women together. Although her form was not yet rounded by childbearing, her pure white skin and perfect, pointed breasts tipped with opening red buds, glowed with the kind of warm pink light that he had only seen as a lad in the very early morn at Burwell Hall. And he was that boy again, and this was his first maid, her tender breasts sweet against his boy's skin.

Abruptly, he rolled to the edge of the bed and stood up.

Anne was devastated. "Am I not pleasing to you?"

"My sweet, you please me most exceeding well," he said quickly, rummaging in a purse concealed in his doublet, and a little astonished that she, unlike most of the women he had known, would not be aware of her own obvious charms.

He returned to the bed to find Anne sitting up, her lovely eyes wide and injured.

"This is for you," John said softly, taking her hand and dropping a wide golden ring with entwined letters into her palm. "My father gave it to my mother as a pledge of his love though he could not marry her, and now it is yours."

She twisted the ring about and leaned to catch the firelight, slowly reading the words inscribed there. "You and no other," she said aloud, with a catch of deep emotion in her voice.

Gently, he slipped it on her wedding finger, and it settled there as if made for her alone.

"Oh, Johnny, I want to be your wife, but if you will not have me, then I will be mistress or road doxy, or what you will." She knew that she was forsaking all pride, a thing she had never done before, and she didn't care, seeing now that pride was less than love.

He lay down, his head against the pillow, his hands behind his head, looking at her and sensing the end of his long struggle. "I have wanted you, Anne, since I first took you on that long night ride into Whittlewood, and most desperately once I saw the tired milkmaid on the greensward, butter glistening on her lips in the sun."

Anne moved to lay atop him, imprisoning his arms, feeling like a hoyden and loving it. She kissed his eyes, each in turn, and laughed with delight, sensing his cod stiffen further, if such a thing were possible even for John Gilbert. She teased his lips with her tongue, and his, hungering, came out to meet hers.

With a great groan, he tumbled her over and fell to sucking each breast like a starved babe, winding a finger in the silky muff between her legs, pushing it past softness to the velvety entrance of her womanhood, then pressed his hand there as if to capture her whole drenched passion. And when he thought that he could no more bear either his pain or her pleading, he mounted her.

"This will hurt you, Anne," he whispered, wondering if he could truly stop himself if she begged to be spared the pain of a sundered maidenhead.

But she did not beg for him to stop. "Oh, hurry Johnny," she cried, arching her fevered body against him, so needy that he felt it vibrate under him. "I will die if you do not."

"Then I will save your life again, my Anne," he said, and to her jubilant ears there was a trace of the sardonic voice of the highwayman in the night, determined to have his plunder.

Nothing in her childhood or her days at court had prepared her for what happened next. She had always had a good idea of what befell men and women in the marriage bed, but she had not known that joy would surge through her and reach through pain to such astounding heights.

"Johnny! Johnny," she cried, raising her hips to meet his satiny smooth cock and his thrusts that moved faster and faster until he drove into her deepest part and she was writhing inside in the most exquisite agony.

He had expected that her chastity, cherished for so many years, would be as stubborn as she was. Taking any woman's maidenhead was hard work; taking this woman's maidenhead, so long protected by her fierce oath, might prove to be arduous in the extreme. Finally, he had to admit his deepest fear. He had lusted after Anne for so many days and nights that fulfillment might not match anticipation.

But Anne's maidenhead proved not to be as formidable as John had feared; indeed, it breached as if it had been waiting forever to surrender, and he plunged on into a deep, shuddering, collapsing ecstasy. Fleetingly, he wondered if loving had been all that Anne had expected, but bliss overwhelmed him and he could think rationally no longer, nor remember any time but this one, nor any other woman. It was as if all love's history were written from this night.

He could not bring himself to leave her, but remained locked in her tight warmth. She embraced his cod as if to never let him go.

Later, they entwined face to face, warm and wet, drowsing for brief moments in love-scented lassitude, only to awaken again and yet again with a kind of wonder upon them. John Gilbert had not expected the surge of feeling that made him hold tight to her, that quieted the torment in his lonely heart for the first time and that blocked any thoughts of their inevitable parting. Anne, sighing, lay within his arms, conquered yet powerful, savoring the fragile but complex secret of a woman well loved.

Later, he brushed his lips against hers, and when she would have responded with fervor, he playfully nipped the lobe of her ear. "We must eat," he said, reclaiming his cod and dropping to her side, wonderfully tired. "You are hungry work for a man."

She pouted prettily and drew away so that he reached for her, and they frisked upon the bed until they were out of breath again, and then lay with green gaze searching black gaze as their passion ignited twice more, and it was morn's first light before John Gilbert thought of food again.

He rose and pulled on his dried breeches, fastened the horn button, and handed her the undershift she'd left drying on the chair. "We mustn't fright the servants," he said, grinning.

Anne put it on with a show of reluctance. "Is that all?" she asked, feeling hungry again, but not for bread and wine.

He plucked her from the bed and sat her in the chair by the fire, stoked the sea coal and added more. "Ha, a greedy little bed baggage you are," he said, replacing the poker. "There is more, much more to loving, as you will learn, my sweet, but first . . ." He handed her a tankard of wine and tore a piece of bread from the loaf for her. He placed the tray on the floor, dropped down beside it and stretched himself along the tiles and onto the turkey carpet, up on one elbow, watching her as she ate each bite.

"Do you plan to have all those strawberries for yourself?" she asked, finally hungry for food, and a bit bereft without his touch.

He took a berry by its stem and dangled it back and forth before her until she came out of her pique and dropped down beside him, the firelight causing her hair to shine as red as the fruit he pressed to her lips.

So they idled away the morning by the fireplace, feeding their stomachs and their thirst, pledging their love, asking love's timeless questions until she closed her eyes, contented, and slept in his arms, while he memorized every curve of cheek and shoulder and every curling tendril falling about her lovely face, against the time when they would no longer be his.

When she woke, John Gilbert rose stiffly and stepped to the gallery railing, calling for William. "Bring hot water, bowl and razor."

"Oh, allow me, Johnny," she said, when William had delivered a bowl of steaming water and some scented shaving soap.

He laughed, rubbing his stubbled chin. "You forever surprise me, Anne. First a lady of the court, then milkmaid, swordswoman and now barber! What can you not accomplish with such vast talents?"

"Nothing," she said, head high but smiling, happy to be doing anything that allowed her to touch him. "Now, sit you down here. I have seen my father shaved many a time."

She lathered him, rather too generously, but he swallowed the soap rather than disappoint since she was so in earnest, her pink tongue between her teeth in concentration. The blade was sharp, and as she brought it close to his cheek, her hand wavered.

He grinned up at her. "There was a time when I would not have trusted you with a blade so close to my throat."

She sniffed, taunting him with a breast that had escaped her shift. "What makes you think you can trust me now?"

He buried his face in her breast, the scent of shaving soap rising to her nostrils, and she dropped the razor. "Johnny," she said, pretending to be exasperated, "how can I . . ."

But John Gilbert was no longer interested in being shaved. He pulled her down to straddle his legs, facing him, and soon all the shaving soap was transferred to Anne's undershift as he explored her breasts and neck and arms, and she, without bidding, unbuttoned his breeches and took his smooth cock into her hand, feeling it swell as if to burst free.

Suddenly shy, she put her head on his shoulder. "You must think me a terrible wanton. I do not understand why I have such a need for you. . . . I mean, I do . . . but . . ."

"Sweeting, you are not wanton. You are a woman who has denied her own needs for too long, and now they must be fed." He grinned down at her. "And, most fortunate woman that you are, you have within your grasp the man who can feed them." Before her temper could rise, he gently parted her hot, swollen womanhood and slowly, gently slid himself deep into her, rocking Anne back and forth as if a babe, showering her with kisses, while she shed tears of joy and wonderment, her head thrown back as if she were riding Sir Pegasus up a long, dewy hill. The sands would have run through the glass before they rose, if they had given any thought at all to turning the glass.

John laid Anne gently on the bed. "We must talk and plan, Anne. We cannot remain here for long. Waverby's reward will tempt the best of servants. And I dare not take you back to Whittlewood just yet, but in some way I must keep you safe from Waverby."

He got no answer, for Anne once again was asleep in love's exhaustion. Feeling a chill, he stoked the fire, and donning his dry doublet, sat down to watch Anne, to store up more memories against the days and nights when he would desperately need them.

When Anne woke, she called his name, but for answer heard a stifled moan.

John sat slumped in the chair by the fire, his hand to his forehead, squeezing hard, and then as she watched, he was taken with a violent ague.

"What is it?" she asked, scrambling from the bed, fear forming, which she refused to name. He groaned again.

She ran to the door and shouted over the railing. "William! William!" The servant appeared in the hall below. "Attend me at once," she called down, and then ran back to John, who had not moved.

"What be the trouble, my lady?" William said, carrying a candle against the failing light.

"He has an ague. You must help him."

"Master Gilbert," William said, shining the candle before him. Then he backed away in horror. "He cannot stay here! Take him away or put him in the street for the constables."

"Listen well, William! I must get him to a doctor. Have the carriage brought 'round, if you do not wish the house and all in it to be condemned."

William stumbled out.

Anne looked into John's face. The truth was almost a release. After the denials that she had spun through her head she could no longer mistake the signs. Everybody knew them, if not from experience, then from tales told to them as children to frighten them into good behavior.

"Leave be, Anne," John said, closing his eyes. "Save yourself."

"No," she said, and for his sake, she lied. "It's not the plague. You are but exhausted, and that my own fault for keeping you at lovemaking when you needed rest." Her determined voice shook. "Listen to me, John! It's *not* the plague."

His voice rasped at her, his face florid with fever. "Leave," he ordered. "I do not need you or want you." And then with a groan of pain, he dropped his hand from his neck, and she saw the telltale swelling, the bubo, the plague boil that would soon burst open.

She dressed quickly, never taking her eyes from him. "John, hear me. You must stand and lean on me. You can walk down the stairs. You *must,* as you love me!"

With a great effort, he heaved himself from the chair, swaying and holding on to her shoulders. Later, she could not remember how long or how much of her strength it took to get down the stairs, out the door and into the carriage, where John collapsed in a heap on the floor.

Anne grasped the whip and climbed quickly into the driver's box.

It was one thing to drive dressed as a boy in daylight along wide, pleasant paths; quite another to careen through narrow London streets in the dark, a woman in a soiled satin gown, her curls tangling wildly about her. But if she thought of this, it was briefly noted and quickly dismissed. He had risked all for her; she could do no less for him. Indeed, there was a heartful of resolve in her that approached a soldier's going to battle. She would save him. She *must* save him. . . . Yes, even at risk of her own life.

Anne circled to the Strand and headed toward Cheapside, the Tower and London Bridge below. Several times she passed knots of threatening men, footpads likely to be intrigued by the gilded carriage driven by what appeared to be a lone woman, perhaps a night witch, but an attractive target nonetheless. At each group she flung the cry, "Plague inside," and they shrank back into the filth and shadow.

And so at last, after several false turns, she came to Dr. Josiah Wyndham's barge, and found herself beating upon his closed door. "Doctor, it is Anne Gascoigne. For the love of God, open to me!"

The door opened a crack, then full wide. The doctor stood in his nightshirt and cap, shock writ plain upon his face. "By Christ's wounds, my lady, what—"

"I'll tell you everything later," she interrupted, words tumbling in a torrent from her mouth. "It's John Gilbert in the carriage. You must help me. You are the only man in London I can trust. Do not turn me away."

"Ssshh, now," he said. "Take a deep breath, ere you have the vapors and swoon, and tell me slowly what has happened."

"He is very ill," she said, complying. "You must give him those medicines of which you spoke—the ones to ease pain."

"Philibert," the doctor called behind him to his bleary-

eyed son, and the two small men removed, with some difficulty, an inert John Gilbert from the Lord of Waverby's carriage, and brought him to a corner pallet within the cabin.

Anne knelt beside her highwayman. "It may not be what
it seems," she said, looking up at the doctor, hope winning
once more over facts.

The doctor put his hand on her shoulder. "It is plague, my
lady. There is no doubt, and very little hope."

"Help him, I pray you, good doctor."

The doctor's hand tightened on her shoulder. "I will do
what I can, but you must leave at once. You have already
been too much with him, I'll wager."

She was speaking. She must have been, because she
could hear the sound of her own voice and feel her mouth
open and close, and her throat contract upon words.

"But you must leave," the doctor said, his deep voice
breaking through to her. "I do not wish to be brutal, my lady,
but he will surely die. Not three in ten survive."

"No," she answered, and heard herself full well this time.
"Johnny will not die. I will not let him die, if I must fight
God himself for his soul."

Dr. Wyndham scowled. "I have seen enough of John
Gilbert's pride to know that he would view your sacrifice
with repugnance."

"Damn his pride!" she said, her voice rising, close to hys-
teria, but still in her control. "I care naught for his pride—it
is his life that I owe him. Don't you see, Doctor? Were it not
for me, he would not have come to London. I put him in danger of his life, and I must save him, if I die trying."

"Quiet yourself, Anne. You will save no one at the top of
your voice."

"Then you will instruct me in the medical arts before you
leave so that I can care for him?"

"If that is what you will, my lady. Although I swear that
before another day passes, you will beg me to mix a potion
that will grant him eternal sleep."

Chapter Fourteen

Sealed Together

Naked, John lay on the cabin pallet, Anne sitting beside him. Although she was exhausted from worry and lack of sleep, she constantly sponged his fevered body with cool vinegar and rosewater. His face, except for ashy smudges under his closed eyes, looked in repose, as if he were merely sleeping and would soon wake to caress her again.

Sometime in the early morn, a constable had noticed the red crucifix on the cabin and officially sealed the door and windows; this meant that no one could come in or out, under penalty of death. It was the law. Once plague was present, all in a room or building were imprisoned until they either died or recovered. It was the only way known; the law itself had been urged on the city justices by the Royal College of Physicians some twenty years earlier.

Behind her in the dim cabin, scented candles gave a feeble glow, which nonetheless clearly illuminated her own fear, the ancient fear that she tried to push away, but which came back upon her when she allowed herself to think what she had done, what she was doing now. Without doubt, she knew that she invited her own swift and painful death with no one to care for her.

She tried to chide herself, to scorn the old wives' tales—

stories of the horrible fate of plague nurses, most of them convicted felons—but she could not erase the stories for long because such grisly tales had been part of the air she breathed since she had first understood anything.

The same, she knew, had been true for John Gilbert. The fear of plague meant not only an almost certain death, but also abandonment in the last bitter hour. Husbands flew from wives, mothers from children, priests from flocks and doctors from patients.

All that was true, and yet just as true, Anne knew that she would never abandon John Gilbert as long as life remained in him, and mayhap not after. In the cabin's silence, broken only by his hoarse breathing and low moans, she knew that she would rather share his fate than leave him. Not that she would ever, ever tell him this, and hurt his man's pride, or tell him that in her deepest self, she had longed to shed modesty, chastity—shed all for him—almost from the first moment of meeting, if she had but understood the signs.

It could never be in a woman's best interest to allow a man such devastatingly intimate knowledge of her heart, and yet she, like every woman, longed to reveal her soul to the man she loved.

The three huge boils on John's neck, armpit and groin had not broken into open sores. They were badly swollen but not yet ruptured. Dr. Wyndham, who went bravely about the city, tending patients, had insisted that she send Philibert, who waited on the dock, for him at the first sign the boils were ripening.

Anne sponged John's face again and brushed back the dark hair plastered against his forehead. He was ill unto death, pale and delirious, but yet the very image of a strongly built man.

She marveled that she had not from the first appreciated his body, even when she'd glimpsed the defined muscle under his shirt during the fencing lesson; for that matter, even that night in the cottage bed, when he'd lain full length

on her body, pretending to be her lover to fool Black Ben.
Nothing had given her full knowledge of his glorious person
until they'd made such adoring love in Nell's house. Now if
they lived hours or a century, she would never be able to forget what she saw in him or felt.

His form fascinated her now in sickness as much as in
lovemaking. Sinewy muscles in his arms and legs bulged
symmetrically at shoulder and thigh, and the broad, deep
chest tapered to a narrow waist, reminding her of the Ara-
bian stallion King Charles had imported to improve the English breed. That sleek magnificence of feature was so much
the same that it caused her to lose concentration and suspend
the cooling cloth above John's body while she drank in the
image of him.

It was a cruel sweetness to so recently discover such male
beauty only to have it snatched away. Surely God in his
heaven could not be responsible for destroying such an astounding and manly creation.

"Anne," John said, but it was his dream that he addressed,
because his eyes remained closed.

"Yes, John, I'm here," she replied.

He croaked her name over and over, and every time she
reassured him with her answer or the pressure of her hand,
always dipping her forefinger in fresh water and laving it on
his lips. Sometimes he sucked the droplets in greedily; other
times they ran unlicked from his parched lips.

As soon as needed, she changed the poultices on the
boils, which Dr. Wyndham said might draw out the putrid
humors. There was little more that she could do but wait and
pray and watch for signs of her own sickening. And thus
passed the long hours. Finally, as full dark again approached, she dozed off and on, unable to face both horror
and fatigue together.

She awoke to the heavy sound of footsteps on the deck
outside. "My Lady Anne, how does our highwayman?"

It was Dr. Josiah Wyndham at the door, and she scrambled to her feet, grateful to hear his loud voice. "He is very fevered," she called out.

"Have the buboes opened?"

"No."

"Are they reddened and hot to your touch?" he said.

She bent and removed the poultice on John's neck, and gently so as not to cause the smallest additional pain, she touched the boil. "Yes," she said, her voice breaking low, "it is fiery hot, and of red color."

"I cannot breach the door's seal. You understand, my lady, that I have other patients who are yet unsealed and nigh unto death. It is my duty to remain free to ease those who do not have an angel to tend them. As I thought 'twould be, many physicians have fled the city."

"Yes, I do understand," she answered, although she wished that she didn't, especially since there was something in his voice that increased her apprehension. "How long before the crisis is over?" she asked anxiously.

He answered her question with a question. "Has he coughed or sneezed?"

"No."

"Christ bless! 'Tis a good sign if the plague has not seized his lungs."

She sagged a bit from relief at the good news.

Dr. Wyndham's voice came again, and it held more than the concern of a physician. "And you, Lady Anne, have you any signs of sickening?"

"None, good doctor, and I thank you for your regard."

"Still, I want you to eat one of those figs in the bowl on my surgery table. The French do think it a preventive for the plague. Won't do to have my assistant collapse. Where would your lover be then, eh? And don't deny it, my lady. It is writ entire upon your beautiful face."

She didn't argue with him, but with one last look at John, who was unmoving, she retrieved a fig and sat down to eat it on her side of the door, where she could see out.

The door was badly warped at the top, leaving a viewing space the size of three fingers low along the side.

There was a fresh north breeze sweeping the deck, filtering through her narrow opening, and for a moment her careworn tiredness was blown away. But only for a moment. She could hear the funeral bells in some nearby parish church.

"There to the north, good doctor, what is it that lights the summer darkness?"

"Burial torches, my lady," the doctor said, kneeling in her view. "The dead are being taken to the plague pits at night to spare the populace more panic."

She shivered. John would never rest for eternity in one of those. Never!

She vaguely saw the outline of Philibert standing at the rail behind his father, staring at the distant torches, and she could smell the scent of the strong tobacco he was chewing to ward off the plague.

She called to him. "Thank you, Philibert, for disposing of my Lord Waverby's carriage."

He spoke harshly without facing her. "I didn't do it for you."

She had sensed that the doctor's quiet son hadn't liked her from the first, but this night she heard real enmity. "My thanks to you, anyway, Philibert. I regret that I—"

"Save your regrets for men as believes them, Lady Gascoigne."

She saw the doctor pivot about. "Philibert! You will apologize to her ladyship at once."

"Huzzah, Father! You would make me a young fool to match your old fool, cozened by her beauty and saucy ways. You know well that gentles are all alike, expecting the commons to serve at their pleasure, even to the very death of us." And Philibert stomped ashore, refusing to answer his father's beckoning cries.

Dr. Wyndham looked after him helplessly, his head bowed. "'How sharper than a serpent's tooth,'" he said ironically,

quoting the passage from *King Lear* that offered understanding to misused parents. "Lady Anne, my son suffers because his father is imperfect in his eyes. Please do forgive
him his impertinence, and me for failing to teach him proper
deportment."

She rested her forehead against the door and spoke in a
resigned voice. "It is I who must apologize to Philibert and
to you, good friend," she said. "I have interrupted your lives
and livelihood, and have now put both of you at even greater
risk for hiding us."

Dr. Wyndham moved closer to the cabin door. "My lady,
do not worry over us, for I must now ask you to do a hard
thing."

"Of course. What is it?"

"You must cut the buboes, my lady."

She was suddenly shaking as if the palsy had attacked her
full force on the instant. "No!" she cried. "I could not. I
sicken at the very thought."

The doctor's loud, deep voice, undiminished by the plank
door, penetrated her soul. "The buboes *must* be opened, or
he will surely die most painfully this night."

She thought to defy him. "Doctor, you are very sure of
yourself."

"I would not be a physician were I not so. I repeat again,
my lady, you must cut. Do you hear?"

She choked on the words. "I hear."

"Many physicians think the poison does not collect until
the fourth day, but I think poison is present now and killing
him. Do not fear the knife for John Gilbert; he is a strong
young cock, and I will stay here to guide your hand in surgery. Now, quickly go to him and tell me his color."

She crossed the small cabin on shaky legs and knelt again
beside John, brushing the damp dark hair from his fevered
forehead. "He is ghostly pale," she called, "but still very
hot."

"His breath. Is it rapid or slow?"

"Rapid and shallow," she said, watching John's bare chest rise and fall.

"My lady, look in the small coffer at the foot of the bed. Do you see it? Now remove my pocket set of surgical instruments. Do you have them?"

"Yes," she said, staring at the small, elaborately scrolled case in her hand.

"Do you see the scalpels?"

She undid the clasp on the intricate lid and looked inside. "I see several things forged of metal. A scissors is all that I recognize."

"There are three knives folded into bone handles."

"Yes," she said, looking at them in horror, "but for God's sweet sake, I *must* give him syrup of poppy before I do this thing."

"Nay, if he takes drink, he would choke on his own vomitus."

Inside the cabin, Anne drooped despondently, shivering in dispair.

"Are you listening, my lady?"

"Yes."

"Speed is of the essence. You must free his blood by cutting fast, for he will feel great pain."

She grasped eagerly at a thought. "Then let me bleed him. I can put the leeches to him; I did that for my father's gout."

"If you have not the stomach for this surgery, Lady Anne, then I do advise you to go back to your prayers for his soul, and I will return to my eager patients."

"Wait, Doctor!"

"I wait to hear that you have the courage to give him a chance for his life, but I pray you, do not delay."

She answered him in a voice as calm as she could make it. "I will not delay."

"Open the bubo on his neck first, my lady, but with great

haste. You must withdraw the knife before he begins to
thrash about."

Her breath quavered in her throat. The thought of cutting
John Gilbert's body was intolerable. Everything in her nature told her that she could not do such a thing to the man
she loved. Yet everything before her eyes told her that she
had no choice.

Anne stretched out her left hand, barely under her control, to John's cheek, her thumb pressing along the curve of
his cheekbone, tilting his head to expose the boil on his
neck.

He moaned softly when he felt the pressure, and called
her name. She bent her lips to his ear. "I am here, Johnny."

Dr. Wyndham called anxiously, "What is the dillydally?
Are you ready, my lady?"

She took a long, deep breath. "Yes."

"Then cut!"

"God, guide my hand," she prayed, and forced that hand
to descend quickly. She flinched as she felt his flesh give
way under the knife, then watched in horror as the huge boil
gaped open like a grotesque red mouth. She pulled the knife
out so quickly that it fell from her hand, the tip breaking
against the plank deck.

A high-pitched animal shriek broke from John's lips, his
eyes stared wide, and he tried to jerk his head from her
grasp, but she leaned her weight on him, sobbing, holding
his head in a vise as tight as she could make.

A second cry nearly broke her grip on him, and certainly
broke her heart. Tears blinded her while she held fast, until
his body slumped and he was still.

"I've killed him!" she screamed.

"Nay, he's not dead, I vow," called the doctor, "but surely
fainted. 'Tis a mercy. Quickly, now, what color is the
blood?"

Thick black blood oozed from the wound.

"Black, followed by red."

"Good," he said. "There is no sign of the green corruption that means certain death. You are very brave, my lady, but now with all speed, you must open the other two buboes."

She opened the second bone-handled knife, and somehow she could cut, each time faster and with more perfection than the last. When she reached his groin, she marveled that she could do what she did so near his privy parts that she had so recently caressed in love. After this night, she would cherish his manhood more than ever.

Then before John stirred, the doctor directed Anne to cauterize each wound with a fresh poultice of gum resin.

"I must leave you now, my lady, and make my way to the stews," Dr. Wyndham said, his voice weary but determined. "Some harebrained zany started the rumor that the French pox would protect against the plague, and the men of London are storming the city's brothels. I will save as many from this lesser plague as I can, although it is difficult to dissuade a man from so pleasant a cure."

She called out her gratitude to him and then took up her sponge again, dipping it into the cooling vinegar-and-rosewater mixture, cleaning John's body and his pallet of all corruption.

Over the next hours, John's fever seemed to diminish.

For the first time in days, Anne was easier in her mind and able to reflect on the strange turn her life had taken since her father had left her with John Gilbert. She had learned more of life and death than she had ever known, and more of love, much more. It was passing strange, this passion of love. She had thought it a thing of soft words, scents and jewels, of witty conversation over a game of cards, and a life of ease, protected from every harsh and common reality.

And yet she had discovered it to be equally made of troubles and tears, of doubt and surprise. And more, she had found that her love had nothing to do with what a man gave her, but of what she offered him, and of what they shared together.

These last desperate hours that had demanded so much more giving than she had ever known before had doubled, nay, tripled, her love for the man who lay before her. If she had never known aught but lovemaking with John Gilbert, she would have survived his death, but to give him life now tied her to him forever and beyond.

Outside the cabin door and the gently swaying deck, she could hear gull cries and the sound of oars scraping in their oarlocks as a small boat moored to the quay nearby.

Anne was determined to remain awake until the day broke and the sun rose, and then, only then, if John remained cool in his body, would she sleep.

She clasped her hands around her knees and stared at him. It was a long vigil, but one she did not regret because there was nowhere else in England that she wanted to be.

It seemed to her, as she watched him breathing, slowly and, in time, deeply, that she could hear the trees of Whittlewood Forest rustling nearby and the sounds of the hidden village slowly coming awake. She could stare at him and see the thick woods stopping at the stream's edge, and two white bodies, a man and a woman, pressed tight together in the water's gentle flow. And the man was John Gilbert. And the woman was Anne Gascoigne.

Someone, somewhere, long ago, had ordained that this love between them should take shape as it had. Everything that she had done to escape it had been of no account, and now it seemed that she was completely undone by John Gilbert; and he, if she was right in her mind, was as undone by her.

Anne bent and laid a hand on his dark-stubbled cheek, now in more need of the razor, and it felt cool to her touch. A slight shiver started in him, and with scarce a thought, she disrobed and lay down beside him, clasping his naked body in her warm arms. "I do so love you, Johnny," she whispered into his unhearing ear.

Chapter Fifteen

A Fire in His Blood

"I've decided," Anne announced a few days later on the deck of the barge, watching John closely for his reaction, and frankly just a bit uncomfortably, "that now I've set aside my vow of chastity, I will also renounce my rank so that we may marry." Gathering courage, she rushed on before he could respond. "If that is what separates us, I will remove it."

She waited a moment, then two moments, but he did not look at her. God's bowels! Was he deaf? Anne stepped closer and strengthened her reasoning. "There is, I think, ample precedent. Remember, Eleanor Plantagenet, sister to King Henry, did the same for the sake of Simon De Montfort."

Her words pierced through to his heart. Once, he would have laughed aloud in victory, confirmed in his own seductive powers and the relative ease with which Gentleman Johnny could penetrate any woman's reluctance. But not now, and he gripped the rail, breathing deep of the healing air washed fresh by morning showers. Still pale and weak but gaining astounding strength each day, he looked away from the man-'o-war passing in midchannel, no doubt headed for the Medway and a naval battle with the Hollanders, and smiled wryly into her eyes.

"And as I recall," he said, "King Henry eventually had Simon hacked into quite small bits at Evesham for a reward."

She nodded, her eyes bright. This was the Johnny of old. "Now that I do think on it, sir, I remember reading about some such unpleasantness."

"Have you also thought that perhaps four-hundred-year-old precedent between royalty and nobility doesn't quite apply to a lady of the court and a modern knight of the high-road?"

"You're laughing at me," she said, pouting, "and I thought you would be, well"—"happy" was the word that almost came from her tongue, but she caught it in time and substituted—"interested."

"Oh, I *am* interested, *quite* interested," he replied, his brow wrinkled as if he seriously studied her words. "You took the vow of chastity hastily, based on the deceit of one man who forced you to bury your loving nature without any real knowledge of life. Now you are just as hastily renouncing your proper place in the world. Someday, Anne, you will want a husband to match your name, and his children; you will want to be the lady you were born to be. I could not take that from you and offer you nothing."

Her chin rose. She didn't much like the formal, even brotherly, tone he was assuming, so she answered in kind. "Sir, I took the vow to keep my body my own, and now I take a vow to give it to whom I please, to the man of my own choosing. I will never be hauled like a prize sheep to the auction block."

He smiled ruefully. "In truth, I have cause to believe you, as does Black Ben and the Earl of Waverby, if I remember aright."

"You do remember most excellent well," she said, fingering the Italian steel that she hid at her waist under her bodice. But she smiled in her turn, suddenly feeling very much the coquette. "Sir Highwayman," she said, playfully tapping his arm with an imaginary fan, "I am truly baffled by your responses. I had written your answering lines in my head somewhat more in keeping with your occupation."

"And what did I say—all in your head, of course?"

"Something akin to, 'Stand and deliver, maiden!' "

"You have been listening to servant's gossip. I would almost certainly take your jewels, but I would never so address a beautiful aristocratic lady in any carriage I robbed, as well you know, especially a lady who had just made such a startling declaration of intent to quit her virtue and station in life, both in a fortnight. Instead, I would strongly counsel her, as would a concerned friend, to consider the future and retain her marriage value."

He turned again to watch the passing warship, the ship's sailors towing her toward Deptford, bending double to their oars.

Anne flushed hotly at the seeming rebuff. She had thought to put aside his objection to their marriage by denouncing her quality, and that on hearing her decision, John Gilbert would drop his objections to their union, sweep her into his arms and ravish her in the cabin, if not impetuously right where she stood on the deck.

He was capable. She knew that full well and had seen the hard evidence at Nell's, even the morning he awoke in her arms, and he just returned from a brush with eternity. Could it be that she had misjudged his feelings for her and the ring that she now wore on her marriage finger? Could he have a trunkful of such rings to cozen women into his bed and away from matrimony? This practice of following her about England, of making love to her until she was mindless, was just some low jape, after all?

"Forget that I mentioned my new vow, sir, since the subject seems to hold so little appeal for you. Indeed, it seems to make you churlish." She laughed aloud, but try as she might, she could not keep the bitter undertone at bay.

It seemed an age that his dark eyes clung to hers, and

when he spoke, his tone was not to be mistaken. "Do not be angry, Anne. You were not wrong about me."

But now she did not dare to believe him, having been so amiss in her judgement before. Each woman in love was like the dancing Salome, removing one veil at a time, ready to expose her deepest heart, but cautious, too, prepared to snatch back the veil and conceal her love at the first sign of refusal, or else all respect for self was lost and never regained.

Anne drew back from John, and her voice shook with humiliation. "On the contrary, sir, I have been very wrong about you. Do not now fancy yourself the fortune-teller, able to read what is in my mind." The green eyes flashed anger, unable to bear their disappointment, and she whirled about to leave him.

Just as quickly, two large, strong hands whirled her back and pulled her tight into his chest, but with a noticeable blanch when the wounds she'd cut set to throbbing. "Enough, Anne! You risked yourself, and I will always be in your debt. I owe you my life."

"Then I make you a gift of it, and gladly, to be rid of it." Flailing at him, she broke away and fled to the cabin door, and there she lingered, longing to call back everything.

And it was there that he caught her. "Sweetest Anne— Anne." Her name was not a long word to express so much, but she heard in it everything that she had hoped would be in his heart and on his lips. Behind her, he breathed her name over and over into her hair.

"Have I ever told you that your hair is the color of autumn leaves?" he said.

"Tell me now," she begged, leaning back into him.

He pushed open the door with his foot, and they moved across the threshold and toward the pallet as one person, a drowning person who swims through turbulent water to a wilder shore.

In the dim light of the barge cabin, his body, which she

had tended to near death, his and hers, appeared now as the lover she had known before plague struck. She had to bite her lip to keep from beseeching him to touch her every part, especially those normally hidden from a man's view. Her maidenly reserve was completely gone. She had left it in Nell's room and would never again recover it.

John was already aroused to the limit that he could endure, of that he was sure. He could not hold himself this side of the flame, nor halt his own quick, deep breathing that only added fuel to the fire in his loins.

In his deepest heart, he knew that he must keep his breeches on now and not further compromise this woman, but once, just once more, he wanted to feel that she could have been his had he not been born of a dairymaid on the wrong side of the blanket. Anne Gascoigne and John Gilbert. He felt an intense satisfaction at the linking of those two names, and it would have been possible had he been the Duke of Lakeland's legal son.

He had only to look at her to see that she loved and wanted him. It was knowledge that he would have to subsist on for the rest of life without her.

Anne knelt on the pallet with John in front of her. She would have willingly stretched herself full length, but he prevented it, although it cost him some of the resoluteness that he desperately needed.

He bent his mouth to hers and felt her trembling lips beneath his own, and he experienced an eager surge of craving that had nothing to do with what his brain had so lately reasoned. He broke off and sat down heavily on his heels.

"I did it wrong?" she asked, her lips still atremble. "I am still not as practiced as . . ."

"No, Anne, *I* did it wrong. I thought that I could—"

"But you can. I want you to do with me what you will, what we did at Nell Gwyn's. . . . What you did to Nell Gwyn."

"That is different," he said hoarsely. Indeed, it was. He

did not deny that Nellie was a voluptuous woman, and that he had had much pleasure of her and she of him. Not a line of her, from her cupid's mouth to her arched feet, failed to softly curve and tempt a man. And Nell had saucy speech in bed that aroused a swain grown weary of simple country maids. Truly, he had enjoyed the favor of the greatest actress of the age, but he had not loved her, nor ever could. He loved Anne, hopelessly loved her. It was Anne, troublesome, stubborn, dangerous, beauteous and now courageous Anne, who was distinguished in his mind above all womankind.

Unlucky chance that Sir Samuel had not let him hang! He was trapped tighter in love's noose, and he didn't even want to be free. "That is the difference," he said aloud without meaning to speak the words.

"What is the difference?" she asked, clinging to his hand. "Am I not the woman I was just days ago? Don't you want me as a man wants any congenial woman?"

He groaned. "You certainly have as many questions as any woman."

"More," she said, snuggling down beside him, forcing him to wrap an arm around her shoulder. "When did you first know that you—well, that you—" She struggled to say the word, looking up at him, her liquid green eyes fastened to his.

"That I wanted to bed you?" He finished her question. "You have asked me that already, sweeting."

"But I have not tired of your answer. I want you now, John, as we were when we made love for the first time, cold and wet and . . ."

The image of it that first night was too much for his shaky control. He kissed her lifted lips again, and she parted them so that he could feel her hot, quick breaths beating against his tongue. And much against his severely strained better judgement, he laid her upon the pallet, opened her bodice and cupped her breasts, though he realized instantly that touching her womanly flesh would shred the last of his sanity.

Anne felt as if she floated into him, as if someone continually poured blissful fire into her hollow limbs. She did not know when, but she became aware that her tongue had reached inside his mouth and tempted his to come out to play. At the same time, his hands were sending spears of lightning through her breasts, and with a little animal sound in the back of her throat, she eagerly let them loose to overflow his hands.

John drew in a quick, sharp breath. It was as if she had lashed him unawares.

"Oh, God, Anne!" He was breathing hard, every breath reminding him that he had almost died but for her, and owed her everything but his honor now. Yet his cod was a hot, hard cinder with its own pulsing demands, and everyone knew that a man's privates had no honor. Who could blame him if he let his cod have its way just this once more?

"You are even more beautiful than I remembered," he murmured, his voice frayed by stabs of need. He lowered his mouth to suckle her nipple, while one free hand roamed down her arching body, along her leg, searching for the bottom of her gown, which he raised until her woman's parts were exposed to him. He would have liked to show her how he could bring her delight without his cock, but early loving is too demanding, and he ripped at his breeches button because he could not bear to dally more. There, on the pallet, still clothed but unable to deny her or himself, he drove deep into her well of love.

Anne had thought that she wanted John's lovemaking to last forever, but once they started, her passion climbed higher and ever higher until she thought she would die from hot, shuddering need and want of breath. "Now, Johnny! NOW!" And he obliged, pouring his love into her as she reached mountainous ecstasy, their bodies collapsing together, touching everywhere.

Below him, Anne's eyes swam with tears.

John felt a drop on his hand and raised his head from

where it lay pillowed on her breasts, to look at her uncertainly. "Anne, my love, have I hurt you in some fashion?"

She shook her head.

"What is it, then, that makes you weep?"

With a great effort, she looked into the dark, wild depths of his face. "Joy," she said, and her voice was very soft and blurred. "It is because I am happy, my Johnny. I never imagined that I could so love a man now more than a week gone, more than yesterday, and surely more tomorrow." She sighed and her entire body vibrated with it. "We will go to Whittlewood. I could be content for my life long with you in the forest."

John froze. She spoke the words in his own heart, and he longed to do her bidding in this, but he would do her more harm than to take her body. If he wedded her, as every part of him urged him to do, he would be condemning her to share his doom. Eventually, and probably very soon, they would be caught, strangled at the end of a rope, then cut down while yet living, and torn asunder by four horses tied to their limbs. Her beauty and sex would not save her, just as all his schemes and wit, even his love for her, would not save him.

Waverby would never stop until he had revenged himself on a base-born highwayman who had held him up as a fool, and a woman who had betrayed him and her class and, thus, destroyed his dream of a king's high preferment.

Determined on a course of action he had hoped to avoid, John stared at her, her radiant eyes smiling at him, still shy. It reminded him of those rare days when a rainbow—nay, two rainbows—accompanied a soft spring shower.

"Anne, look at me," he said. His finger wiped away a sliding tear on her cheek, and came to rest under her lovely rounded chin, tilting her face to his.

Her hand slipped inside his doublet, coming to rest over his still-pounding heart. He suppressed a long, deep sigh, and proceeded with what he had, for her sake, to say. "Anne, do you have friends at court—anyone who could take my case before the king?"

"No one has more influence than Edward. Oh, the king may exile him from the court for disappointing his royal desires, but Edward, when he wants, is too amusing to be banished permanently." Her voice turned bitter. "His Majesty will pay a high price for a moment's pleasure."

"Barbara Castlemaine, then."

"Think you, John, that the king's mistress would look favorably upon my request, and I a potential rival for the king's affections?"

"She might if it was to her interest. I hear that she has great debts. What if my band in Whittlewood Forest paid *her* Lord Waverby's thousand guineas a year? She might offer me the protection from royal warrant that Waverby has most certainly now withdrawn. I find that the roads of Oxfordshire provide too lucrative an employment to be let go so lightly, my lady." He deliberately made his voice very businesslike.

Her fingers went rigid against his flesh, and slowly she withdrew her hand from over his heart. She stared at him for a very long moment, and it was obvious that she was more curious than outraged. "Why these questions?"

"Sink me, woman, if I must explain the obvious! I want you to go to Whitehall, play the king's slut if you would save me," he shouted, drawing angrily away from her to the safety of the far end of the pallet.

Then she smiled and looked far wiser than her beauty or her years. "Johnny, you do not bluff me for a minute. I know that you would not have me whore for the king for your own protection. Why would you want me to believe such a thing?"

He was really angry now. In truth, it had taken every bit of unfamiliar artifice in his ken to say such hated things, and still she had not believed them.

He bolted from the pallet. "May I be damned if I ever love such a one as you again!"

She smiled at him in some delight; these pitiful denials sounded so like towering affirmations to her ears. "I assure you, John Gilbert, that you never will love another as you love me. I will see to that. At this moment, I keep a lustful warm place for you"—she lowered her voice to seduce as she now knew she could—"Gentleman Johnny, if you but come to me."

The words sounded terribly bold even to her ears, and she was thrilled to know that she could say them so. . . . And mean them.

He passed a hand before his eyes, and the hand shook.

She could see that he was still weakened from the plague or from their lovemaking, perhaps weaker than he knew. She scrambled to her feet to help him, her nurse's instinct still strong.

"Stay there," he ordered, gripping the surgery table. "If you come closer, I will not be able to say what must be said."

Anne edged closer to him, unable and unwilling to stop her feet, no longer even surprised at her audacity. "Pray, John, if it is a matter so easily challenged, then it can be of little consequence. Wouldn't you agree?"

"Stop right there! You have the charming contrivance of a saucy minx, my lady, behind the reputation of a recent virgin. Perhaps you *have* missed a bawd's calling, after all."

She laughed at his obvious attempt to insult her, continuing her way toward him in tiny but not hesitant steps. She didn't want to frighten him, and she knew that he was cornered like a bachelor animal with absolutely no mode of escape. "Perhaps you would like to test your theory, sir, and determine for yourself if I am minx, near virgin or bawd."

Her voice was throaty and so full of amusement that in most other matters he would ordinarily have surrendered any objections with great good grace. But he could not.

What he could do, in one long step, was to take her adorable self inside his arms, and he did.

"Devil take you and your clever words, my Anne. Listen well to me. We can never live in Whittlewood Forest together. If we escaped London, what could I offer you but a life of danger and a death that did not creep into your bed in life's good time, but death that tore you limb from limb on Tyburn's bloody hill while you were yet young and beautiful? Think you, my heart, that I could live with such certain knowledge?"

"I don't care," she cried, echoing lovers through the ages. "We could marry and be together for as long as God wills, even if that be but a year."

"You believe that now, but would you believe it on the gibbet? You would end cursing my name. I cannot risk that by marrying you."

"Then to hell with marriage!" She tightened her arms about his neck.

"Think you that I could take you without name or wedding, like any chance maid, watch you grow old and bitter bearing nameless bastards, to be scorned their lives-long, to be the butt of low jibes as I have been since a lad?"

"None of what you say matters one whit to me," she said firmly, her voice against his chest, warm again with desire.

"It matters, my Anne. Nothing matters more to my honor than that I not bring you down with me," he replied, his tone matching hers in every determined nuance. "It is near all I have to my name."

"Halloo the barge!"

They looked at each other, startled, questioningly.

"It is not the sound of the doctor or his son," Anne said. "Wait here, John, out of sight."

She stepped to the cabin door and opened it. "Who hails?" she asked.

"The constable of the parish," the man on the quay

shouted. "Your seal is broken. Have you any dead of the plague to be taken away?"

"No," she answered. "The afflicted are now well."

"God be praised!" The man doffed his hat, as John moved behind her, staying well inside the cabin's inner shadows.

She sensed something amiss. "Do not turn about, Anne," John said, and she could hear him slipping on his baldric and sword. "Where are the pistols?"

"I left them in Edward's carriage. Why? What is wrong? Tell me!"

"That is no constable. He is Waverby's footman, the one I drugged when I stole the carriage. We've been discovered, but they will not have you."

Her mind worked frantically. He was still too weak to fight several men, and if there was one of Edward's men, there must be others close by.

As if to confirm her thinking, several men in Edward's blue-and-silver livery swarmed onto the quay, swords and pistols drawn. A slant of sunlight on gilt caught a carriage as it turned from Tower Street toward the barge.

"Hide yourself!" she implored. "Do it now, Johnny." As she spoke, she stepped onto the deck, blinking in the sunlight, and quickly walked down the gangplank onto the quay. Waverby's men formed a double line of polite escort.

The familiar carriage stopped a few feet in front of her, and she looked into the exultant pale blue eyes of Edward Ashley Carter, the Lord of Waverby. "My lord," she said, her voice surprising her in its firmness, "I am ready to do your will. Let us begone quickly."

He opened the door and bowed her inside. When she was seated, he stared at her with the most malignant gaze that she had ever witnessed. It took all her will not to beggar herself with entreaties.

"Search the barge," he shouted at his men, smiling all the time into her eyes.

"There is no need, Edward," she protested. "You see that I am quite alone."

But his men were swarming aboard, and after the sharp sounds of scuffle and the brief ring of sword on sword, they emerged, four of them holding a struggling John Gilbert.

"Bring him to the stables at St. James Street," Waverby shouted, "and upon my wedding night—GELD HIM!"

Anne's scream rang in John's ears long after the carriage disappeared back into the narrow city streets.

Chapter Sixteen

The New Anne Gascoigne

An unearthly howl bridged the gap from one nightmare to another, and Anne Gascoigne sat bolt upright in her bed at Waverby House in St. James Place.

A young maid, her pox-pitted face screwed with worry, threw back the bed curtains. "My lady, thee be dreaming, and taken with terrible fright."

Anne nodded, not trusting her voice, which seemed unable to pass her throat still taut with the memory of the fearful scream she'd recently sent through it. Today was her wedding day, and on this night she would be defiled by Edward. He'd cynically promised her that in the carriage from Tower Wharf. Her mind's image of Edward's white, thin, hated body slowly erasing the memory of John's long-muscled brown limbs tight about her was almost more than she could bear, and yet the picture crossed her mind without her bidding.

Edward's exact words were emblazoned in her memory: "And when I've been satisfied as a husband expects, you will take a vial of sheep's blood to the king's bed. You would not be the first minx to so prove her chastity, nor, I warrant, the last." It pleasured her little that Edward did not know she needed such a vial for him, having given her virgin's blood to John on Nell's bed.

And Johnny, what of him? His very name brought a flood of images, and one which she could scarce imagine. He would suffer the most brutal indignity to his body that any man could endure: his unmanning. And it would be her fault, solely hers.

For too long, she had denied John Gilbert's worthiness and gone her own headstrong way. And John, honor-bound to her father even after his brutal death, had followed her to London, putting himself in jeopardy to the noose and now e'en his proud manhood. She would go to her grave bearing full guilt for what was about to happen to him.

She quaked beneath the coverlet at the grotesque image that now leaped unbidden to her mind: John being held fast by Edward's hired brutes, a honed knife flashing in the stable lamplight, poised to descend, defiling his glorious male body that had so recently given her such lasting pleasure. She covered her mouth to hold in a second scream swelling in her throat.

The maid bustled about her, smoothing the eiderdown cover and fluffing the stacked pillows all trimmed in wide Flemish lace point. She left for a minute and returned with a bowl and clean washing towels. "My Lady Anne," the maid said sympathetically, "thine eyes are most piteously swollen."

"I care not," Anne said, sinking heavily back into the pillows, trying to shield her spent eyes from the sun streaming through the windows opposite. They were open to an already sultry breeze, and below on the street she could hear a peddler shouting her wares. "Thread laces, long and strong." And a man's louder voice crying, "Mothers, I bring fresh ass's milk, best for babes."

The maid sighed. "But my lady, thee must stop this crying. My Lord Waverby has requested thy presence at a nuptial supper—"

"I will not attend."

"Oh, my lady—"

The plain little maid looked so distraught that Anne felt sorry for the girl. And a refusal would do no good. Edward didn't brook contradiction of his will. Anne had ample reason to know that.

Bitterly, Anne knew that today would be a test of her strength, and she must not fail it if John was to have any chance to live. "Then do what you must, woman."

"Allow me to bathe thy poor face, my lady." The maid wrung a fresh cloth in the cool rosewater and apple cider and applied it gently to Anne's eyes, cooing softly as if to a babe.

Somehow the tenderness of her touch reminded Anne of her own mother soothing away childhood illnesses; the memory of her mother then reminded Anne of her father, and that last memory of her father reminded her of the first time she'd seen John Gilbert in the firelight of an inn's upper room on Oxford Road. Scarce three weeks had passed, and yet a lifetime.

"My lady," the maid said soothingly, "I cannot restore thy beauty if thee do not stop crying. What could trouble thee so? The earl is a handsome man, some say hard, but they do also say that he is generous with women." The maid blushed. "I beg thy pardon, my lady. I do forget myself in my desire to help thee."

Anne's eyes were closed. Indeed, the cool water was healing the ache and swelling about her eyes. "You are a Quaker?"

"Yes, my lady, I am." The words were quiet but proud.

"Then you know much of persecution."

The maid nodded. "I do."

Anne felt pity for the girl. The Quakers were hated and feared for their belief that they needed no ecclesiastic but could each go directly to God, even women, which offended High Church and Puritan alike. Even now they were being blamed for the plague. "What is your name?" Anne asked.

"Kate, my lady."

"Well, Kate, we are both women no matter our station in life, and you must know what it is like to lose the man you love, and lose him most inhumanely." Anne opened her eyes to look at the maid, who sat with a wet cloth suspended in air.

Kate bowed her head shyly. "No, my lady, I do not have a love beyond bread and meat, a warm place to sleep and a meeting house." She looked up at Anne. "But I would like to know more of such things as thee speaks."

Anne expelled a long, shuddering sigh. "Do not wish for what you don't know, Kate."

Kate smiled, her brown eyes soft. "Aye, my lady," she said, finishing the ablution. She gently squeezed Anne's shoulder to get her wandering attention. "Do thee want to dress now?"

Anne caught at Kate's hand and clasped it within both of hers. "I want you to take a message to him!" From the startled look on Kate's face, Anne knew that Kate had heard of the man shackled in the stables.

Kate tried to pull away, but Anne tightened her grasp. "Please, for love of God!" Her tone was fierce.

"I cannot!" Kate's tone was a match for Anne's. "It's Newgate or the Fleet prison for them as ever goes against his lordship. And thee don't come out of that purgatory, my lady, at least not the same." She cringed away. "I'm most truly sorry. Please don't have me whipped, mistress."

"It's all right, Kate. Don't fear me, for I do understand," Anne said.

Indeed, she had expected the young maid's answer, and now that she had it, the morning was somehow complete. Instinct had told her that what she asked was far more than for a servant to deliver a message; she'd asked the woman to betray her master, a capital offense or easily made one. "I will dress myself, Kate. What hour is the nuptial supper?"

"Six of the evening, my lady."

Anne took a deep breath, aware of the faint scent of blue-bells in a vase by the bed. The kind little maid must have put them there. "I will be ready by six. You're dismissed, Kate."

"I thank thee, my lady. Anything else, my lady, anything at all—"

"No, nothing, Kate. There is nothing else that I want in this world."

The maid left the room, closing the door silently behind her, and almost immediately opened it again. She chewed at her lower lip, and then the words tumbled out. "I will take thy message, my lady. What must I say?"

Anne scrambled from the huge bed. "I will write it," she said, looking hastily about for writing materials.

"No, my lady. I will learn it. If I be caught, they will only suspect—they will not know."

Anne nodded, taking both Kate's hands in her own. "Tell him that I love him with all my heart and body, and will love him forever. Tell him that somehow I will gain his release. Tell him not to despair. Can you remember all that?"

Kate repeated it several times, blushing, and stumbling each time she came to the words of love.

"Now go, and Godspeed, Kate." On impulse, Anne slipped an emerald ring from its string around her neck. It had belonged to her father, and had been a guilty gift from her uncle the bishop. "Give him this."

Kate stared openmouthed at the flashing gem in her palm, and Anne felt a moment of alarm. Such a ring could bring more riches than a servant maid would ever see in two lifetimes. But the moment passed, and Anne's alarm was forgotten. She and Kate had an unspoken pact as only two women could. Once, Anne would not have trusted the girl, but that seemed long ago, and another Anne Gascoigne entirely. Since John Gilbert came into her life, she had begun to live and think differently.

"I trust you, Kate," Anne whispered.

Kate nodded, slipped the ring inside her bosom and left

the room. Anne heard her heavy leathern shoes on the narrow back stairs.

As six struck on the enameled French clock above the fireplace in her room, Anne brushed past the guard come to escort her and descended the staircase into the main hall of Waverby House. Huge candelabra, swaying above on their ropes, cast brilliant light on the long wood-paneled banquet table covered with fine damask cloth, and she counted two standing salts, and gilt-edged Staffordshire plates set for fourteen. Heavy silver utensils with carved ivory figures for handles, including the new and fashionable forks, gleamed in front of every chair, each attended by a liveried serving man.

Edward Ashley Carter, the Lord of Waverby, sat at the head of the table, alone.

Edward had never seen Anne look more seductive, although he had always thought her provocative under those virginal airs of hers. It had been that combination of allure and innocence that had driven the king mad for her, and, Edward had to admit, left his own normal suspicions of such virtue deferred until it was almost too late to accomplish his aims.

But all that was in the past. She had proved herself a slut by denying him. Now he would bend her to his will or break her; indeed, maybe both, first one then the other. But he was forced to delay those pleasures until the king had rewarded him for the use of her person, and such rewards could not come too soon. He was on the brink of insolvency; even his basest creditors, his booter, his wigmaker and tailor were beating at his door. Old Cromwell had a lot to answer for in the current effrontery of such common people to demand payment from their betters.

He leaned forward and plucked a ripe strawberry from a fruit bowl, swallowed it and licked red juice from two fingers.

Anne looked away, unable to see strawberries without the image of John Gilbert teasing her filling her mind.

"Good evening, my dear Anne. Although I had planned that we would celebrate this evening with friends, I have decided that it's more important that you and I become intimates again."

He looked at her closely and passed a tongue over his lips. "I hope that you are recovered enough from your cruel captivity to manage a pretty blush at the altar." He smiled at her without rising as courtesy required for a lady of her rank. A woman who'd ridden about the countryside with a rogue and in a man's breeches deserved no gallantry, and would get none from him.

She seemed not to notice what he did, but sat pale faced under the candlelight, toying with her soupspoon. Edward noted that the shamefully low-cut blue gown he'd supplied to her had darkened the emerald of her eyes to the color of cold northern seas.

He signaled for the steward to fill her glass, then raised his own to her. "Long life, my love, and an heir within the year." His eyes glittered over the rim of his wineglass. "And if the spawn have royal blood, so much the better. I am not a man who cares what seed bears my name, so long as that seed is equal to mine." He waited, but she did not pick up her glass.

She laughed instead. "And what if that seed belongs to John Gilbert, a better man than you or the king . . . in all ways."

With a piercing look and a jerk of his head, he dismissed the serving men, and they were alone at the huge table. He gripped the banquet table with his slender white fingers until the knuckles turned red, his eyes wildly searching the middle distance for some new advantage and ultimately settling into a glare, with his thin mouth stretched in an animal grimace, teeth bared.

Anne watched him parade his barbarity, and knew that he

calculatedly used it to smother her feminine will and the love he could scarcely imagine. With startlingly clear insight, she realized that Edward was a man who found that cruelty added to his enjoyment of any game.

"So, my lady, you threw away your chastity on a common dog of a thief." His hands twisted one of his new, imported silver forks until she thought surely it would bend or break.

She watched the fixed smile that froze her blood, watched him toss the fork aside to slide his fingers incessantly up and down the stem of his wineglass. Perhaps he was not as calm or as sure as he would have her believe. He needed her compliance, or his scheme to trade her for Virginia tobacco land could not possibly work, and in giving or withholding her consent, she had some small power, but for only these hours before her wedding. After, as his wife, she would legally belong to him, body and fortune and for life.

"Edward," she said, her voice low so that he bent unwillingly forward to hear it, "I will do in all things as you command."

He laughed and flicked the lace at his wrists. "For love of *me,* my dear?" he asked. "I do remember that I was beloved once."

"And you betrayed my love and my father's friendship," she said.

He tilted his head slightly, his smile aggrieved but even then a sham. "You were ever too harsh in your judgement of me."

She ignored the remark, determined to direct the conversation in the way it must go. "Edward, I here take me an oath to do your bidding with His Majesty, and with great good grace so that he will never know how I loathe his touch. And then, when you have what you want, I do swear to faithfully bear your children. You will no doubt bother me little after that, preferring other pleasures."

She picked up her glass, lifted it to him and drank, replacing it on the white linen with a steady hand. She was icily calm, the new, bloodless Anne Gascoigne, a woman without true emotion and whom she was not certain she would ever really admire.

Edward studied her, then brought his elegant hands together in slow applause. "Ah, I do understand now, my dear Anne, why other men could find you so intoxicating. The role of sacrifice played by a woman is, after all, endlessly fascinating, although like modesty, quite out of date." He shook his head doubtfully. "But I fear that there is more to this sudden womanly resignation than first appears. Pray, tell me that I am wrong, and you give over your self for love of me at last."

Anne sat straighter in her chair. "I am trading you my life for John Gilbert's. Let him live and live whole, and you will have all that you dreamed of, I promise you."

"I will have it in any event."

"Do not underestimate me, my lord. I am not the simple-hearted girl I once was. I do know that the king loves women and is spoiled with the privileges of royalty, but he is not completely unprincipled. I have but to tell him my story, hesitant and weeping. Pillow talk is a sharp weapon in a shrewd woman's hands." She'd heard the Countess Castlemaine say that, and if anyone knew, Castlemaine did.

Waverby stirred uneasily. "The king will believe *me*."

"Maybe, although the king has been led by his cock before, my lord, as you do know well, and depend on for satisfying your scheme." She smiled, equaling him in calculation. "Indeed, why risk all for the dubious pleasure of killing a highwayman? You can see one hang any day on Tyburn Hill."

"Not this particular knave, who did leave me naked in St. James Park, to the laughter of the court and the London rabble. He will pay twice over for that, nay, three times." He drank deeply again before he could continue. "Do you think me such a fool that I would loose him so that he could steal you back from me, eh? I have not forgotten that stealing is his business, and that he is renowned for it."

"Then transport him to the colonies, never to return."

Waverby sneered. "Such tender concern for the rogue does your ladyship little credit." He emptied his glass and refilled it, splashing wine upon the table linen.

A servant entered and whispered in Lord Waverby's ear.

"Yes," Edward said with a laugh, "by all means, let him present himself for my lady's amusement."

A moment later, the door swung open and Philibert Wyndham strode stiffly into the room. Edward was nearly his height seated, and looked quite entertained by his squat visitor.

Philibert glanced at Anne, color flushing his face, but to his credit, he did not attempt to hide his uneasiness from her.

Lord Waverby opened his purse and extracted coins, which he stacked before him. "My Lady Anne, this is the fine young man who helped me to rescue you. You owe to him your safe return to my loving arms. Perhaps you would like to thank him in your own way."

Anne's voice was soft and without rancor, for she pitied the doctor's son. He had allowed fear and envy to rule his conscience, and he would never in this life be easy with it. "I'm sure that any words of mine could never fully convey my feelings for his deed."

Philibert's face was stony as he accepted the gold guineas, and, without another word or a courteous bow, left the room.

"You temporarily have me at a disadvantage, Anne," Edward said, his voice lazy, almost purring and catlike. "God's truth, but I cannot understand your effect upon men. That youth was made momentarily wealthy, and yet he looked as if he were sentenced to the Spanish galleys. If you so touch a man's goodness, then you may have even more worth to me than I supposed." He laughed, merrily for Waverby. "I shall make you deal with all my niggling creditors."

Anne's voice rose steadily. "If I have such worth, then accept my trade. John's life for mine." She slipped her Italian steel from under her bodice and held the point against her own left breast where he could see it, gazing deep into Edward's eyes.

"This is no time to jest, Anne," he said, but there was loathing in his eyes, and the dawning knowledge that she had bested him again, at least temporarily.

She said nothing, just held her gaze steady to his face.

"Give the knife to me," he said.

She didn't move.

He shrugged, pretending to be bested. "All? You say that you will do all I ever ask and with great good grace."

She nodded without lowering the knife.

"Then John Gilbert will have his life, 'pon my word of honor."

She lowered the steel, and then with a swift and impulsive movement stuck it, quivering, into the table. "Your pardon, my Lord of Waverby," she said, her chin high and proud, "but I will need better proof."

The fist holding the glass tightened until she thought that the fragile stem surely must crack. Then the hand relaxed, and he said, "You will have proof before this night is over."

"When I have confirmation of his freedom, then you will have the king where you want him, for I do now know how to rouse and hold a man's passion, and what once I did so very willingly for love of John Gilbert, presently I will do to save him. I would be whore for Beelzebub himself to give John life, and when I am in your bed, my lord, I will know no difference."

Pushing away the cold soup, she stood and left the table, her back rigid as she ascended the stairs to her room to prepare for her wedding. She did not have to look back to know that Edward's hate-filled eyes followed her until she was out of sight.

Soon, it was late into the evening, and Kate had not reappeared. Other maids, chattering with excitement, helped Anne to don the elaborate white wedding dress of fine satin and Brussels lace, its bodice intricately sewn with hundreds of seed pearls. She dared not ask for Kate, fearing that somehow the girl would be compromised, if she had not already been caught.

Near midnight, Edward came to escort her to a waiting carriage, the same one in which she had first kissed the highwayman and felt his passion rise against her body, the one she had driven through a wild, rainy night to Tower Wharf. The carriage's polished gilt shone in the torchlight from linkboys, and cast a glow on three cloaked figures approaching from the direction of the stables to join them. The man in the middle sagged, his knees almost scraping the cobbled courtyard.

Edward bowed to her. "My dear Anne, here is the proof that I promised, a bit the worse, I fear, for having tried to escape."

But Anne had already recognized that long, dark hair and the sculpted features of John Gilbert, although his mouth was hidden under a tightly wound strip of cloth and pistols were pointed at either side of his head. Her heart thudded frantically as John was half lifted into the carriage.

"Get in, my lady," Edward said, "but I warn you, under the most dire consequences for your highwayman, do not speak to the prisoner." He laughed softly. "I am sure that you will not need speech. Aren't the looks that pass between lovers supposed to be the true language of love?"

For once, Edward Ashley Carter, the Earl of Waverby, spoke the entire truth.

As the carriage lurched along the Strand, John's dark, pain-lashed eyes were frantically saying to Anne that she must survive no matter what she had to do, and hers were saying to him that wherever he was, she was bound to him forever. Throughout his life, whatever he felt, she would be feeling; all that he was thinking would be her only thoughts.

As if in answer to their unspoken prayers, one of the linkboys fell back to the side of the coach and the light from his torch revealed their faces more fully to one another.

Anne's eyes clung to John's, and his never moved from hers. "I love you," her eyes flashed, silently but powerfully, her green gaze misting with emotion. "I will give up nothing that is yours to Edward or to the king," she promised without making a sound. "They may have my body, but I will remain pure inside myself for you. My courage will be ever yours, and my belief that I belong with you will never be taken from me."

John flexed his hands, straining against the shackles, and although the cloth hid his beloved mouth, his eyes tilted in the way they did when he was about to smile or kiss her. Slowly, he closed one eye in a good imitation of his old boldness. He had understood all that she had mutely communicated, and would take the knowledge with him.

"So touching," the earl observed, but Anne did not look at him. At that moment, she could almost feel pity for Edward, because he would ever be deprived of the depth of feeling that made life heaven and hell on earth.

They rattled across old London Bridge and stopped by a Southwark pier. At a hail, a skiff stood out from an East Indiaman moored in the river, its bow to the sea. Lord Waverby handed Anne down the carriage steps, while John was thrown to the pier, where his legs were trussed like a pig's bound for market. Despite Edward's foot on his back, he tried to twist his head toward Anne.

A man stepped from the skiff and saluted Edward. "Your servant, m'lord."

"This is the man, Captain. He's to be delivered to the *Chloe* at Southampton, and thence shipped in irons to Jamaica. You may sell his indenture and keep the gain for yourself, but you are to keep him close watched, for he's a slippery sort."

"Aye, sir, it will be done as ye say," the captain said, and touched his forehead.

Jamaica, Anne thought. At least I will know what part of the world he inhabits. Suddenly, she was ashiver with the memory of an overheard conversation. Indentures were put to work in the sweltering cane fields and seldom lived out a single year. It was a death sentence for an ordinary Englishman, but John Gilbert was no ordinary man. She must bethink that whenever she despaired.

Anne watched numbly as John was tumbled into the bottom of the skiff. He groaned, and she took an involuntary step forward. "Johnny!" His name and Edward's iron hand were on her lips in the same moment.

"Slut! Whore!" Edward hissed into her ear, his voice shaking with fury. "I will not have my bride cry after a common felon on the city dock. Do not trifle with me, my lady."

She was propelled quickly back to the carriage, and when she tried to turn about for one last look at the skiff in the Thames, she was most savagely prevented. Finally, she was alone with her soon-to-be husband in the carriage, the two guards taking their place as footmen outside while the linkboys ran ahead crying for clearance. She leaned back in the dimness, turning her head away from Edward. There would be time to mourn John Gilbert later, a whole lifetime.

"To Ludgate Hill and old St. Paul's," Edward ordered, and the carriage heaved forward and crossed back into the city. "There, my dear bride, I have kept my promise before your eyes. He has his life. Now you will have yours, eh?"

"Yes," she said, quietly, "I will have mine."

He looked at her, perplexed and deeply angry. Whatever he did or said did not seem to violate her. There was some new and astonishing strength about her that was absolutely infuriating—in truth, it would be unsupportable in a man, but in a woman, it drove him unbelievably mad.

He laid a package in her lap. "A wedding gift and token

of my esteem," he said quietly, his eyes glinting, narrow and unsmiling, in the faint light of the jouncing vehicle.

She made no move.

"Open it," he commanded.

She unwrapped the festive red ribbons, and the heavy paper fell open at once on her lap, exposing its bloody content. For the briefest moment, she glanced at it without recognition.

The Earl of Waverby watched her eyes widen with knowledge, and waited for her screams and swoons, but she made no sound or movement.

"I promised only his life," he said petulantly. "I did not promise that he would enjoy it."

As they rode on, her waxen face and rigid body worried him. She couldn't be carried like a board into St. Paul's. Even her uncle would not perform the wedding service unless she responded willingly. Curse it! He had gone too far.

"My dear Lady Anne," he said, and his voice sounded most ingratiating to his own ears, "a swift courier to Southampton can yet hang him if you fail me. Indeed, I will dispatch your Gentleman Johnny at any future time you decline your wifely duty of strict obedience." He shrugged, and his words held a scarcely subdued mirth. "You should thank me for having your self-interest uppermost. At least you know that without his manhood, he will never love another woman."

Chapter Seventeen

A Lady Weds

For an eternity, it seemed, Anne stood before the high altar of St. Paul's, trying to answer her uncle's question. "My child," he said, a pained account of duty spread across his face, "you are required to repeat the words of conjugal submission aloud."

In the silence and flickering darkness of the old church, columns and arches seemed to loom over her malevolently, and the odor of ancient dust and damp stones filled her nostrils, but it was Edward's tightening grip on her arm that reminded her she was there to exchange herself for whatever was left of John Gilbert's body and life, more precious to her than her own.

She would have said anything to keep that bargain, and she did. "I will take to husband, to faithfully obey, Edward Ashley Carter, the Earl of Waverby," she repeated after her uncle, the Bishop of Ely, omitting the words "love" and "honor," since she would not lie before God in his house.

It was her voice but she scarcely recognized it, for it sounded like the voice of a very old woman who had lost everything but her ability to croak a few simple words, barely understood.

Other words were said by Edward and her uncle, but she

was hardly aware of them. What did they matter? At this moment, John was sailing out of the Thames into the Channel, and soon south along the coast toward Southampton, and thence Jamaica.

He was out of her life forever, and she would have to make her own way beside her corrupted husband, nourishing a tiny flame of dear memory, the sweet few days and nights of which she would never again speak, for to speak of them or long for them was the way to early madness.

But she could not govern her memories. She would think of those days with John in the cool innocence of a May morning, or when the sharp odor of fresh butter filled her nostrils, or in the face of a sweet william opening to her in the garden. That way, too, lay a slow descent into madness, but there was no help for it.

Until that release, she must cling to her only reason to live. She wanted to witness Edward receiving his due, and if there was a just God, she would see it. And if there was not a just God, she was determined to judge and punish Edward herself, though it took the rest of her life.

Just the thought of revenge hardened her resolve to live through whatever disgrace was ahead for her this night, and she feared it was beyond anything that she could possibly imagine.

What would she not give for just one hour—less, even, just a few minutes—with John on the greensward in Whittlewood Forest? To see that insolent bow, his plumed hat scraping the ground like the old cavaliers of her father's time, to feel that dark, laughing gaze upon her and wonder what he saw and felt. She stiffened in apprehension; she could not, would not, go on in this way. Swallowed tears collected in her throat, nearly strangling her.

"My children," the bishop spoke loudly, tapping Anne's open prayer book to get her attention, "I would speak now of wedded love, and remind you both that it is the Sabbath and, therefore, not to be violated by lust of any kind. It is also required of good Christians that they do abstain during a woman's periodical and pregnancy, and that no unnatural positions or acts be brought to the marriage bed."

Here he looked severely at Anne. "It is well known that the violent passions of women often lead husbands astray from their Christian duty," he explained.

Anne bowed her head in submission. Her uncle was a fool to think that his standard conjugal sermon would stop a vicious cock such as Edward.

"And my Lord Waverby," her uncle continued sonorously, "you will remember that nothing is more impure than to love a wife like an adulterous woman. Modesty and comeliness within marriage are—"

Anne heard no more of her uncle's admonition against physical pleasure. She didn't have to look at Edward to know that there was contempt on his face.

"Yes, yes, Bishop, get on with it," Edward said.

"It is finished, my lord. You have a wife, but it is a part of my holy office to—"

A commotion in the south entrance ended the bishop's ramblings. A curate raced, black robes flying, toward the pulpit. "The king," he cried, "the king is here."

"Curse him!" Edward said.

The bishop's mouth gaped open. "My lord, you speak treason!"

"Go to hell," Edward said, further speaking blasphemy at the high altar, which left the bishop suddenly and totally inarticulate.

The king approached from the wide center aisle, called Paul's Walk for centuries, with the voluptuous and very pregnant Countess Castlemaine upon his arm, and his "night baggage," as he called his entourage, crowding in behind. Anne curtsied low, but she did not bow her head, watching the king stride toward her.

He was thirty-five and taller than the average man, his youthful good looks now marred by a lengthening nose, which gave him something of a sharp and distrustful look, though he could dispel it with a smile, which he now did.

Barbara Castlemaine was not smiling.

"Our long lost Lady Anne," the king said in his slightly French-accented English, holding out his hand to lift her up.

"Your gracious Majesty has found me at last," she responded, surrendering her hand into his, the disparate pieces of a hope beginning to reassemble in the recesses of her mind.

He seemed delighted with her greeting, only slightly frowning as he shifted his gaze to Edward. "My lord earl, it distresses us that you would not include your king upon this solemn and holy occasion. Were it not for our dear Bishop of Ely, we would have heard of your marriage through the penny broadsheet."

Edward shot a poisonous look at Anne's uncle as he bowed low, his hand over his heart. "Your Majesty does me an honor I had not the courage to request."

King Charles's smile broadened. "Come, my lord, we cannot believe that you lack courage in any part. In truth, we come to charge you to use that courage in our service."

Edward looked confused but bowed again. "Sir, as always, I am yours to command."

"Then we are right gladdened to see you." He clapped Edward on the shoulder and motioned to a courtier, who advanced with a document. "My Lord of Waverby, we do not come empty-handed, but with a nuptial gift meant to reward a faithful subject for service past, present and future." He cleared his throat and glanced at the document. "It pleases us to grant entailed proprietary rights to lands in our Virginia colony to the Lady Anne Gascoigne and her firstborn, et cetera, et cetera"—he glanced up from his reading and smiled slyly at Anne—"such lands, we are told, are situated along the bounteous James River, and our advisors do say they are prime for tobacco growing."

Anne curtsied again, her mind wondering at the king's meaning.

Waverby bowed. At last! The grant! But then the full import of the king's words made its way to his brain. Edward held himself very taut. "Your Majesty jests, surely. A grant in entail means that no part may be sold, and to give it to the Lady Anne outside marriage—" He trembled at the insult, and he felt his mouth wanting to abuse his king, a very dangerous desire indeed.

The king tapped his fingers upon the document, "Our generosity displeases you, then, my lord. Do you question our divine right to grant as we choose?"

Waverby bowed again, not too low, but with no hint of discourtesy. "I do not question you in the smallest detail, Your Majesty. It is just that entail is not much heard of since the old queen's time."

"Then it has been heard again tonight, has it not, my lord, unless we are made to regret it?"

Edward bowed lower this time. "Your Majesty will have no cause to regret such ingenious generosity."

Barbara Castlemaine coughed behind her hand. The king laughed. Edward was forced to smile, although he was beginning to know how thoroughly he was the butt of this jest.

King Charles nodded, his eyes flicking to a beaming Anne and back again to Edward. "Ah, Waverby, we do believe that we will have no cause to regret anything from so loyal a subject." He motioned, and another courtier stepped forward with a dispatch case. "We charge you to carry these coded messages to our brother York on the warship *Royal Charles* off Lowestoft. As you know, he defeated the Hollanders in a great battle just days ago, but he came close to losing his own life. In these letters, among other grave matters, we order his return to the safety of these shores."

"It was God's miracle that the Duke of York escaped without injury," Castlemaine observed in her low and mellow voice. "All in his party were killed by a single shot, and he drenched in their blood. Since he is heir—"

Anne watched the king's mistress curiously. No other person but Barbara Castlemaine would have dared remind the Stuart king that his queen, the tiny Portuguese Infanta, was still barren; or, by implication, that her own children bore the king's features and her own constant hopes for their legitimization or preferment.

The king was impatient. "Yes, yes, my dear countess. But we mustn't keep my Lord Waverby waiting. The sooner away, the sooner back to his bride."

Edward had listened to this exchange without much interest, for he had heard it many times. His mind was now grappling with the king's attempt to delay his wedding night, and looking for a way out. He took the dispatch case from the courtier. "Your Majesty, I will be away at first light."

"Our yacht *The Folly* moored across the river from Whitehall Palace stands ready to take you to a swift ship in the Medway, and thence to the fleet. You will leave immediately to catch the tide. In the time before your return, your bride will hold her land grant"—he handed the heavy vellum, red seal dangling, over into Anne's hands—"and to keep her merry, we will take her to our court and under our royal protection."

The bishop started, then spoke, his voice thin but his duty sure. "Your Majesty, my niece is most welcome to await her husband in my residence."

The king frowned. "No, Ely, we would not think of delaying your departure to the country. The plague grows worse with each day, and you must return to your flock. It is our wish."

The bishop blanched at the royal rebuff, but duty done, foolhardiness was never called for.

Edward squirmed, his hands holding the dispatch case, his mind searching for a way out. He had planned to humble

Anne this night, and in the most delightful ways, and his mind did not want to let go of the image of Anne's impaled shrieking upon his plunging cock. Indeed, his sense of instant and grievous loss was almost stifling even in the cool stone vault of old St. Paul's, and quite dispelled his anguish over the king's land grant. But as his reason ran down every remote recourse, they all amounted to denying the king's will, which was plain treason and meant a swift trip to the Tower and its blood-drenched block.

Edward bowed, this time very low, a hand over his heart. At least he'd been bested by a king, and with a grand fee in the bargain. He grit his teeth silently. Let the king have her vial of sheep's blood. Let His Majesty's cod be frozen by that icy maid, so that he never piss again in this life.

Edward sighed, the heartbroken bridegroom. "Your Majesty will allow me to claim my wedding kiss?"

The king laughed. "We are not monsters, my lord."

As Edward bent to Anne's mouth to claim his right, she could not suppress flashing him a look of triumph. She had not expected one so soon, and that it came at the hands of the king did not lessen her enjoyment of seeing Edward bluffed and bested.

She steadied herself for his kiss, and when it came, it was meant to surprise her. Edward's lips demanded something that she could not give. What? A wife's affection? A maid's fear for a husband going to war? But no appeal from him brought heat to her lips or to her heart. They were forever closed to rapture, for the man who could bring her to it was lost to a woman's love. Her lips did not move or open or pulsate, although Edward's did all those things.

Anne was not even astonished as the kiss went beyond propriety and became a contest, him attacking, her parrying. Some innate feminine wisdom told her that a man like Edward could never really believe himself unwanted.

The king looked on with interest, and finally would have

intervened but for Barbara Castlemaine's staying hand. "Your reputation, sir," she murmured.

Shaken, Edward broke off, and bent to Anne's ear. "You will pay mightily for that, my dear wife," he whispered.

Taking Anne's hand, he gave it to the king. "Your Majesty, I leave my love in your tender care."

Charles II placed Anne's hand on his arm, and without another word, escorted her down the aisle, a bride without a husband, and with the Bishop of Ely hurrying after, clutching his robes.

Edward watched them leave and then bowed to the Countess of Castlemaine. "It seems that we have both been left outside the altar," he said sardonically.

Her steely blue eyes flared, and he wondered if he had aroused her notorious temper, but she smiled coldly. "Best be to your mission, my lord, as I will be to mine." She followed the king, trailing courtiers behind her.

With eyes narrowed, Edward regarded her straight back. The woman was not keen to have a new and younger rival. She might yet come to his aid. Smiling, he left quickly by a side door.

On the ancient south porch, the king bade Anne's uncle farewell. "My lord bishop, we cannot wait to hear about our Lady Anne's adventures in the highwayman's camp."

The bishop grasped his crucifix. "My niece brought honor upon her name, Your Majesty. Her piety protected her person from even that thieving rogue, John Gilbert."

Anne forced a smile. "More like, dear uncle, 'twas the Italian dirk I showed him on more than one occasion."

The king laughed, delighted, and put his arm about Anne's shoulders, and it was on this scene that Barbara Castlemaine exited the cathedral.

Anne saw her and quickly looked up into the king's face adoringly. Anne had promised to give herself to the king, and she would if she must, but if there was the slenderest straw of hope, she would grasp at that, too, and that slender straw could well take the form of the king's chief mistress.

There was only one person in all England who would dare thwart the will of King Charles Stuart, and that person was an angry and aroused Countess of Castlemaine.

The Right Honorable Anne, Countess of Waverby, rode in the huge state carriage opposite the king and his mistress, back to Whitehall. The king looked well pleased and hummed a tuneless song, tapping one red high heel in time to his own music, glancing covertly at Anne while holding Castlemaine's plump hand.

Not daring to make small talk, Anne pretended to doze, clutching her prayer book as if it could ward off the devil. It could, she was certain, but she was less certain that it could ward off the most amorous King of England since the great Harry Tudor.

They arrived in a flurry of mounted guards, and Anne saw *The Folly* standing down the Thames for the Channel. She ran forward a few steps, waved and allowed a tear to slide down her cheek.

The king, who was busy greeting several perfumed and curled spaniels with sugar tidbits, saw the tear and responded somewhat peevishly. "Then, Lady Anne, are we to think that you are reconciled to this marriage from which you formerly ran away?"

Real tears fell from Anne's eyes as she followed the billowing sails of the yacht. It was not for her husband that she wept, but for another, also sailing away from her in another ship.

The Countess Castlemaine stepped forward and put an arm through Anne's. "Sir, is this a time to question the poor girl? She has lost her wedding night to duty, and her father's life to scoundrels within a fortnight. She has been harried by felons and made her way back across this, your realm, with great courage to her uncle's bosom. I bethink me that she is simply exhausted."

Castlemaine smiled her brilliant smile. "Your Majesty, I will take her into my own bed this night, and console her until her apartments are readied."

Anne kept her face a blank, but the respite was far more than she'd hoped. Castlemaine was bent on asserting herself, and in so doing had given Anne a momentary reprieve.

The king looked irritated. "You are ever thoughtful of your sex, Lady Barbara," he snapped. "Oh, have your way, my dear. You always do." Then he brightened. "We will order the Countess of Waverby's apartments readied by to-morrow night."

Castlemaine coughed. "Only you, dear sir, could be so considerate."

"My maid," Anne said, and she had been waiting for such an opportunity. "Your Majesty, I would like to have her with me. Her name is Kate and she is at Waverby House."

"But we have many servants from which to choose."

"You are most generous, Your Majesty, but this is a special maid; she is a Quaker and, therefore, quiet and comforting in these sad hours of my privation."

"A Quaker in the palace?" The king laughed, caught up a squirming puppy, and playfully blew in its ear. "That will confound Protestant and Catholic alike, and oppress our little reputation with the Puritans most heartily." He laughed again, louder.

Anne knew that he had good cause to want to irritate the Puritans, who'd beheaded his father and exiled him, penniless, to the mercy of foreign kings until he was thirty years old.

"By all means, then, have your Quaker maid," the king said, and with one last poignant glance at her, walked away, his dogs, courtiers and guards scrambling after in raucous profusion.

Anne sighed with relief, then felt Barbara Castlemaine's

firm hand on her arm. "Come," she said, and without another word led Anne to her sumptuous apartments, past the nursery being readied for yet another new baby, and into a bedroom, which contained a huge curtained bed only slightly smaller than Dr. Wyndham's barge.

Following Castlemaine's lead, Anne divested herself of her gown, and beautiful though it was, left it on the floor for the servants, wishing it to never remind her of her marriage again.

Rather than spar guardedly—sometimes it took women of the court hours to come to a point—Anne decided to confront the question between them. "My Lady Barbara, although I am aware of the high honor His Majesty bestows upon me, it is not my own wish to be his mistress."

Castlemaine had been toying with a porcelain shepherdess being compromised by a porcelain shepherd, but now looked up sharply, disbelief on her face and in her voice. "I have with mine own eyes seen you cozen the king. Could you have played false? If that is so, you are a fool, and even more to be feared because who can comprehend a fool?"

At that moment, Anne had lost everything and had nothing more to lose by telling the truth, which for the next hour she did, even revealing the vial of sheep's blood. At the end of her long tale, both women were seated cross-legged on the big bed, each with a tumbler of Madeira, facing each other.

"And so you see, my Lady Barbara," Anne concluded, her voice trembling earnestly, "I will keep my bargain for the sake of my highwayman, but I will never be a rival to you. As soon as the king tires of me, I will return to Edward, and hope to spend my last years in the country, waiting for my revenge and the end of my life."

Castlemaine shivered. "Someone strolls upon my grave," she said. " 'Tis a story to raise ghosts or jack-o'-lantern himself." She sat back and eyed Anne skeptically. "You are either a greater actress than Nell Gwyn or this Gentleman Johnny is a most remarkable man to inspire you to such forfeit. Tell me more of him. That devil Waverby should be hung for making such a man a eunuch."

Anne nodded, tears splashing on her folded hands.

"Never mind, I will hear more of your love later," Barbara Castlemaine said. "You are weary now. And I am weary. The babe grows heavy, as boys do." She smiled at the thought of a son and possible heir to the throne of England. "We will sleep, and talk again in the morn."

Anne fell almost immediately asleep. She did not resist Morpheus, because it was in her sleep that she knew she would forever be with John Gilbert, replaying endlessly the scenes of their days and nights together, and of the memory of enclosing him inside her, united through the endless hours. He would be there, waking or dreaming, for all her lifetime, to her everlasting anguish.

Drowsily, Barbara Castlemaine watched her sleeping rival with interest. She did not know how much of Anne's story to believe, but she did believe that Anne did not truly desire the king as she had feared. Of course, the child did not know that a woman could grow to love a man, especially one as solicitous in and out of bed as Charles.

If the Countess of Castlemaine had any hope of becoming the Duchess of Cleveland, as she had so long wanted, then she knew that she would have to act, and to act quickly, or the preferment might go to this beauteous young chit. Especially when the king discovered that she didn't want the title, he would be absolutely wild to give it to her. How dangerous a new mistress to the old one could be!

But what to do about the girl, and how? A hundred years before, a mistress could simply have slipped a little poison into a rival's cup, but these modern times were more diplomatic. Damned complicated, too. Sometimes old ways were best.

Barbara Castlemaine found a comfortable place on her

side, and was nearly asleep when she heard the door to the secret entrance slide open. She kept her eyes almost closed and did not greet the king, curious to see what he would do.

His Majesty did not enter the familiar room, but looked upon the two women in the filtered dawn light, one swollen with his child and ripely enticing for all that; the other still miraculously untouched, if that old fool, Ely, be right, her glorious fire-tinged hair spread upon the white pillow, and beneath the silk coverlet, a hint of the pretty little body that left him always, even now, with an uncomfortably stiff cod.

Charles itched, scratched his aching groin and sighed. "I wonder," he mused to himself, pushing the counterbalance to the secret door, "if the queen might now be awake."

Chapter Eighteen

The King's New Mistress

John Gilbert stepped to the stern rail of the East Indiaman to relieve himself, and carefully aimed his cod with the wind.

He smiled ruefully at the memory of what he'd nearly lost. An emerald ring and the natural reluctance of men to take another's living manhood had saved him at the last hour, although he'd had to bear a beating and howl his head off as a gambit to satisfy Waverby. His lordship, it seemed, had been made right pleased with the cod of a poor plague cadaver. Damn Waverby's evil soul to hell!

"And then what happened when ye held up her carriage?" One of his two guards prompted him to continue his tale.

"Why, I asked the lady most courteously to step down," John answered, mimicking a bow, and allowing the salty sea air to blow the last shadows of illness and humiliation from his soul. He would make friends of these sailors, and hope to profit thereby.

"And then," one sailor asked encouragingly, "what happened?"

"She cried," John said, "like a poor babe, and my heart was deeply moved."

The second sailor laughed as John wiped away an imaginary tear. "But you did not give her back her strongbox with the dowry money in it, did you?"

"Aye, but I did, lad. Well, not all of it. I kept a thousand pounds for my expenses, but left her two thousand for her dowry. Any real man, I told her, would love her for herself and two thousand." John laughed.

"But ye said that she walked willingly across the heath with ye, and kissed ye and more," reminded the first sailor, hungry for more details.

"That she did," John said, smiling. "Kissed me most pleasurably and for quite a long time by the new moon, after which I was certain that her betrothed would not abandon such a heated little minx for being a paltry thousand short of her marriage contract."

The first sailor slapped his leg and roared, "I would have given my mother's good name to see the man's face when she told him he'd been robbed of both money and kisses by Gentleman Johnny Gilbert."

John grinned. "Exactly the same thought occurred to me, lads. So in the dark of that night, I followed the carriage to Chipping Norton, always at a safe distance, mind you, and there the next morn overheard the bridegroom take the two thousand but tell the weeping lass to return to her father for the rest, or the marriage was off."

"The bilge rat!" chorused the two guards.

"Precisely, and a man in need of stern correction, you'll agree. Therefore, good lads, I stopped him in full daylight on the Oxford road and relieved him of the two thousand, lecturing him against the ill use of pretty young women for profit. I also took his horse and left that gentleman afoot without his pants, the longer to contemplate his sins."

John laughed with them, for the memory of humbling the pompous young aristocrat was a pleasant one. "It pains me to think that I'll never know if that worthy had to accept a bride with one thousand pounds that he wouldn't take for two."

His guards bellowed heartily at the thought, which brought the captain up the ladder to the high sterncastle.

"The prisoner has taken the air long enough," he directed. "Take him below and watch him close. He is clever beyond the both of you dolts. Have a care he doesn't laugh the last laugh."

"Aye, Captain, sir!" They scrambled to lay rough hands on John.

With one last look at the Sussex coastline off to leeward, John was shoved down the ladder into the hold, along a narrow passageway, through the crew's quarters to the shackles bolted to the bulkhead of a small storage cabin.

"Captain's got a bug up his arse right enough, John," one guard said, chuckling.

John gave the man a playful wink. "Captains and lords, all the same, do loathe to see the commons at their ease."

The man laughed and turned to repeat John's words to the other guard, exposing a knife he carried, sheathed in the back of his canvas breeches. But the narrow passage was the wrong place for John to attempt an escape. Later, he hoped for a better opportunity, since he had managed to amuse the two sailors with his tales of the highroads, and they were often lax in their guard of him. He prayed they continued so.

Each of them carried pistols, and if they escorted him to the *Chloe,* he might have a last chance to grab a weapon and escape short of the promised voyage to the Jamaica colony. It was the only possible plan, because he had nothing precious left to barter for his life. He had already promised to draw them a map of hidden highwayman treasure, but they were too dull to imagine riches they couldn't touch or see.

He sat down in the small cabin that smelled of past cargos of India tea and hemp and spices, overlain with the dank smell of bilgewater sloshing beneath, and was soon reshackled to the bulkhead. Both guards lounged in the gangway, and he half listened to their lewd retelling of what they

would have done with the bride had she fallen under their
tender mercies.

With an occasional appreciative grunt to keep them talking, John gave himself over to thinking of Anne, not of what
might be happening to her at this moment, which was too
painful, but of what had been between them, dwelling on details of sight and touch and smell that transported him back
to those hours with Anne in Nell's house and on Dr. Wyndham's barge, until he could bear them no longer.

Had he been totally wrong in denying her marriage? He'd
tortured himself through the long days and nights with this
single question. Was it always better to live or die together,
even the slow and horrible death of the hangman, rather than
to die a little each day for a lifetime apart? It was one thing
to be the noble martyr when she was beside him; quite another to bear the pain of such nobility utterly alone.

He had been many things in his life of which he was not
totally proud, but he had never been stupid or without honor.
Yet it was clever John Gilbert who lay in irons, about to be
transported to the deadly cane fields of Jamaica, and ignoble
Waverby who had taken Anne and was even now working
his will—John could imagine it only too well, and he sickened at the envisioning and at his last glimpse of Anne's sor-
rowing, lost face hovering always before his eyes.

Damn it! Who now was the stupid man?

Watching his guards, who were deeply engrossed in an
endless game of dice, he tested the bolts on his shackles. He
had almost immediately discovered that one was loose, and
at every opportunity he had moved it back and forth in the
old sea-weathered wood.

On into the evening, he sat upright with his hands behind
him, working the bolt with sore and bloodied fingers, keeping an eye on his oft-dozing guards.

Sometime in the night, John became aware that the ship
was no longer climbing the troughs of the Atlantic. The mer-

chantman began to ride longer swells and seemed to lose headway, as if entering a harbor.

He worked faster. Perhaps with one heave, he could pull the bolt loose. But if he was wrong and the bolt remained fast to the wood, the noise of the chains would alert the guards and they would replace the ring bolts.

Dimly, he heard the watch calling the time and knew it was near morning. At first light, they would stand into the harbor of Southampton and he would be transferred to the *Chloe*.

Just before dawn, one of the guards woke and left to break his fast. The other continued to doze.

John tested the bolt. It moved, but a determined pull did not rip it from the wood. His spirit plummeted, and he rested his head on his knees, exhausted.

The guard returned with ale and bread and a measure of cold porridge. "Eat hearty, John. Indenture ships be not good feeders for a man of your size. E'en children do starve on the voyage out."

A bell rang faintly, and they heard the call from the crew's quarters. "All hands aloft!"

The two guards jammed their food into their pockets and scrambled to their feet, disappearing down the passageway.

John couldn't believe his good fortune. Quickly, he took the porridge spoon and began digging at the wood around the bolt. How much time would he have? Minutes, maybe a half hour. The pewter spoon bent and the bowl broke off. Calculating the advantage against the time spent, he took the handle and sharpened a point against the iron shackles.

Afterward, the digging went faster, and he hid the mounting pile of wood chips under his upturned porridge bowl.

At last, one bolt fell out, and he frantically began to work on the other one, stopping to resharpen the spoon with every few gouges. Finally, the second bolt pulled out and his hands were free.

Above him, he could hear the sails being hauled in and

the anchor chain making a fierce, screeching clamor as it dropped onto the harbor bottom. Shortly, he heard voices in the passageway; he quickly lay down in front of the bolt holes and pretended to sleep.

"Look at 'im, would ye," one of the sailors said, "asleep like a babe. The man has iron nerves, I tell ye. I'd venture the highroad with such a one to lead me."

Keys clinked together. "Come, John, it be time, and we be right sorry to see ye go."

John didn't move.

"John Gilbert? Wake, man!"

Still, John didn't move, but sensed them shuffling closer, bending under the sloping overhead until both of them leaned curiously over him. Lunging suddenly, John walloped their heads together. With a whoosh of escaped breath, they collapsed in a heap.

"Sorry, good lads, but I have no wish to taste the balmy climes of Jamaica at a time not of my choosing," John said. He unlocked the dangling shackles with their own key, took their pistols and backed down the passageway.

Expecting to be confronted at every turn, John reached the hatch that opened amidships and raised it enough to look out on the deck. The leeward rail was lined with sailors. With more luck than any man had ever had before, he might just be able to sneak over the other side while their backs were to him.

But at that moment, a heavy drum tattoo began, and a mate from the *Chloe* hailed the ship and climbed aboard. The mate and captain held their hats above their heads in salute. "We're come for the prisoner, John Gilbert," said the mate.

"Good morning, Captain," John drawled, exiting the hatch, bowing his most extravagant bow but holding a pistol each on the mate and captain. "I thought I'd save you gentlemen the trouble of an irksome descent into the hold. Now, be so kind as to row me ashore. No, you, too," he said, as the captain moved toward his cabin door. "I'll take you with me to ensure your crew doesn't fire on the gig."

As John was rowed away from the merchantman, he felt better than he had for several days. A new determination filled him: If he had to storm Waverby House or Whitehall itself, he would find Anne and free her. He owed her that, and he could not deny that he had to see her once more, hold her close against his body one last time before he met whatever fate had ordained.

John Gilbert thought to force the sailors from the *Chloe* to swim for it, but several could not swim so he landed all, protesting loudly, on a headland, and rowed himself to the Southampton dock where he found a stable and traded the two pistols for a dray horse that looked to be the great-grandfather of Sir Pegasus.

Anne sat before the small inlaid mahogany supper table laid with silver plates for two, and awaited King Charles. She had hoped that Barbara Castlemaine's jealousy would postpone this night, but it was obviously not to be.

Upholstered chairs lined one wall, and several gilded mirrors hung above, reflecting light from nearby wall sconces. Settees, after the French style, ringed the fireplace, and odds and ends of other pieces of furniture were arranged about the room. When the king had escorted her to the small apartment that afternoon, he had apologized for its disarray and pressed upon her an ardent and long-winded account of his eagerness to find less cluttered quarters in due time.

Anne looked around her now, a faint, ironic smile playing upon her mouth. Perhaps this was a storage apartment, and new royal mistresses passed their trial period here, graduating to sparser and sparser accommodations as they rose in the king's esteem.

She shrugged and rubbed a temple. Her thinking had grown lunatic in a deliberate attempt to avoid the crazed reality she was facing. She had escaped Edward temporarily, but there was no way she could escape the king in his palace of Whitehall, not with guards patrolling the halls and gardens.

"My lady," Kate said, moving silently to her side, "what should I do when the king arrives?"

Anne sighed. "You should do whatever the king asks. That is what your mistress intends."

Kate watched Anne closely. "Then, mistress, what would thee have me do until the king arrives?"

Without looking up from the hands folded in her lap, Anne replied, "You know what I wish," she said, her voice low and intense. "Tell me again how he looked when you last saw him."

"Most handsome, my lady, e'en though he had straw in his long black hair and lay trussed on the stable floor. He looked most tall and vigorous withal."

"And what did he say when you repeated my message?"

"He smiled a most bountiful smile, Lady Anne, and swore that he would send thee a kiss if he but had his hands loose. He said"—Kate blushed—"that a kiss be not a proper kiss unless a man may use his hands."

Fire flashed through Anne's body. Would she always remember with this much clarity her Johnny's kisses at Nell's and on the barge, and his hands on her everywhere? A kind deity would disperse such memories. Perhaps soon she would pray for oblivion, but like St. Augustine praying for abstinence, she would pray for it to come later. "Go on, Kate," she said softly, "leave out nothing, not a word or a look."

"Then he took the emerald ring, my lady, and I hurried away. It was at that time I was caught and whipped for breaking servant's curfew. They never suspected me of more."

"I'm sorry yet again that you had to bear that for my sake."

"It was nothing, Lady Anne. Servants are whipped all the time," Kate said resignedly.

"Never in my service, I swear," Anne said, wondering if she'd be able to honor that vow when Edward returned. He thought to rule everyone through fear.

"Be that all, my lady?" Kate said with a bobbing curtsy.

"Go back to your embroidery. And Kate—"

"Yes, my lady?"

"If I ask about John Gilbert again, do not tell me more, even though I beg."

"But, Lady Anne, that's what thee said not an hour gone."

"I know." Anne nodded, acknowledging the hopelessness of her request.

The *tick-tick*ing of tiny dog toenails on marble signaled the king's approach, and a moment later he burst in. The dogs immediately descended on a settee and began shredding its satin upholstery.

"Down, Fubbs," the king commanded the fattest of the lot, who obeyed only to hurl herself upon another settee, rolling over and presenting a very round, nippled stomach for the royal tickle. The king obliged and bent to kiss his favorite's muzzle. "If your deportment improves so that the Lady Anne is impressed with you, we will give you a sweetmeat." But he handed it over indulgently, without waiting for the change in behavior.

Anne had risen and curtsied to the floor at the king's entrance, and watched the scene with interest. Why, he adores his little dogs more than any mistress, she thought, and although she couldn't love this king, she could no longer quite hate him, either.

"My dear Anne," he greeted her, slipping a rope of translucent pearls around her neck, his hands lingering about her bare shoulders.

She curtsied again, escaping his fingers. "Let us sup and talk, Your Majesty. I would tell you everything of my adventures. I think you will be right well amused."

"By all means," the king said, "and spare us no paltry detail." Smiling, he helped Anne to her seat, and then took the chair opposite, motioning for Kate to serve them.

Anne couldn't tell him everything, but she did tell him the stories that he could repeat to the court, such as her confession that she participated, however unwillingly, in highway robbery. He liked his women somewhat notorious. Had he not, he would have sent Barbara Castlemaine packing after the shameful affair with Jacob the rope dancer, whose gymnastics had aroused her sensual curiosity.

Especially, the king loved the story of Anne's escape from the highwayman in groom's clothes, extracting every particular and exclaiming that she could very well play a breeches role at the Theater Royal, for not only had he allowed women to play women's roles on the stage, but even men's roles. "Tell us again, dear countess," the king said, laughing mightily, "how you played the beldam restored by the elixir. We would write a verse of it."

She repeated the story, adding additional detail as she could make it up. "More wine, Your Majesty?" she asked.

He nodded and removed his doublet. "Damned hot in these inner apartments," he muttered.

"Perhaps a stroll in the river air?" she said hopefully.

He frowned and sulked. "We do not wish a stroll." He pulled at the ribbons on his shirt, his eyes lustful upon her. "Help your mistress," he said to Kate, who, wide-eyed, was watching her king disrobe.

Anne stood. "Excuse me, Your Majesty."

The king grabbed her hand and kissed it hotly. "Do not keep your king and master waiting without for long," he said, his breath coming in short, hot puffs.

She curtsied low and walked into the adjoining bedroom.

"Is there nothing thee can do, my lady?" Kate said, a little breathless.

"Nothing, good Kate. Help me with these hooks."

Anne kept her mind a blank as she undressed, until she

stood in gauzy smallclothes. Although she had been unsuccessful in forgetting John, and knew that she always would be, still she hoped that this night with the king and the ones to follow would eventually be an empty space in her memory. In that way, she would keep her mind, if not her body, pure for her highwayman.

An impatient knock came at the bedroom door.

Anne climbed into the bed that Kate had prepared. "Close the bed curtains and leave me," she said.

Kate was crying.

"Stop that! I do not cry, and you are not to cry for me. If I should start, there would be nothing to stop me flooding all this world."

"Yes, my lady." Kate wiped her eyes and nose on her sleeve and withdrew through another entrance.

A moment later, the door to the bedroom opened. "My sweetheart, we are here at last."

"Your Majesty," Anne said, the words muffled against the back of her hand.

The king threw open the bed hangings, and Fubbs jumped past him and into the bed, snuggling against a pillow.

Anne stared at her king. He was naked, his thin legs and knobby knees giving him the appearance of an unformed lad. But that was all that was unformed, for his cod stood out like a royal guardsman's parade pike. The stories that he was well suited for lovemaking were apparently truer than most such stories.

The king crawled toward her and lay over her breast, breathing heavily. "My dear countess, we will be most lenient of your maidenhead, for are we not known throughout our land as the gentle King of Hearts?"

He kissed her moistly, sucking her lips, and his hand fumbled at her breast.

Anne stopped breathing and quivered, wanting to run but

not daring to. The moment had finally come, and she wasn't as ready as she had thought herself to be.

"But you must remove these smallclothes," the king ordered fretfully.

"Of course, Your Majesty." Taking a deep breath and mastering her trembling hands, she undid the red ribbon at her shoulder, but no sooner had she done so than the little dog roused herself, pounced on the ribbon and began a tug-of-war.

"Fubbs!" the king roared. "Unruly jade!" He picked up the dog, scrambled across the bed on his knees and padded to the bedroom door, opening it.

Barbara Castlemaine stood on the other side in a deep curtsy. She wore a white maternity apron, and there was a smile behind her heavy-lidded, sensual eyes. "Good evening, Your Majesty. I trust you are well amused."

The king covered his surprise but not his anger. "We would know what marks this behavior, Countess Castlemaine."

"Your Majesty mistakes me," she said, smiling, her knowing eyes swiftly taking in Anne, sitting upright in the rumpled bed, the coverlet pulled tight across her bosom. "Although jealousy be but love raised to the extreme, I come not for love of you, though I carry its true proof before me"—she caressed her swollen abdomen in a kind of tender self-mockery—"but to deliver this message just come by swift courier from the fleet."

"Yes, yes," the king said impatiently.

"*The Folly* has been engaged in a terrible battle by a superior force of Hollanders, Your Majesty, and sunk. Only one man escaped to tell the tale."

"Waverby?" the king asked, casting a sharp glance behind him at Anne, who was now sitting at the edge of the bed, her eyes on them, unbelieving.

"No, Your Majesty. The Earl of Waverby was reported

killed by cannon shot, and his body went down amongst the ship's wreckage."

Silently, Anne collapsed, the light snatched from her eyes. She slipped into a swirling black whirlpool, hitting the floor in a swoon.

"Curse it, Babs!" said the King, disappointment tugging heavily at his shoulders.

"Alas," Babs murmured, gently taking the king's head upon her own welcoming bosom, "my poor Charlie."

Chapter Nineteen

Castlemaine Weaves a Plot

Anne sat up straighter, pounding the mattress for the second time, and for the same reason. God's bowels! Would she never stop dreaming of the pool in Whittlewood Forest and John Gilbert holding her against his long, brown, naked body? It was a body—she quivered suddenly—of which a certain important part no longer existed in this world, a part that she knew she would always remember as she had first seen it, noble and upright.

"So for sweet pity's sake, let be!" The sound of her own heartbroken voice assailed Anne's ears.

"My lady," Kate said, replacing the plaster on Anne's forehead. "Thine uncle, the bishop, awaits in the anteroom. He has come to offer thee prayerful comfort."

Anne frowned. Her uncle? Why was he here? Then the memory of Barbara Castlemaine's announcement returned with renewed force. Anne, the new Countess of Waverby, was a widow.

Without a second thought, Anne murmured a short prayer for the repose of Edward's soul, although she suspected that his soul would require her earnest and lifelong prayers if she could, in Christian charity, manage such, and she wasn't at all sure she could.

She tried to feel some sorrow at his death, for the sake of the girlish love she had once borne him, but she could not. He had taken her father's life and John's manhood, destroying the two men she loved most in this world. Surely Edward's crimes were the most despicable on earth, and fit him to occupy the lowest level of hell's inferno for all the ages.

"Will thee see thy uncle now, Lady Anne?" Kate urged.

"I will see him, Kate," Anne said, her head suddenly hammering. She touched the plaster and frowned. "Tell me again, how did I come by this?"

"Thee hit thy head in a swoon," Kate explained, her poor, pitted face full of worry. "Stay quiet, my lady. There is a knot the size of a hen's egg." The maid moved to open the door and announced the bishop.

Anne's uncle bustled in, wearing his ecclesiastical robes and every symbol of office. He sat in a chair beside her bed, taking her hand. "My dear child, how you must have suffered. I do blame myself—" He began a confession, but he could not quite bring himself to the finish of it.

"Edward is dead," she said in a flat, toneless voice, withdrawing her hand from his.

"Dreadful business," her uncle responded, shaking his head solemnly. "I will pray for him."

"And for yourself, Uncle."

He twitched. "You are overwrought, Niece"—he pointed to her head—"perhaps befuddled from your injury."

"Nay, Uncle, you bear a responsibility beyond anything you'll ever know." Her fingers trembled upon the coverlet.

The bishop bowed his head and clasped his hands. "Anne, I am a man of the cloth, not a man of the sword. Waverby threatened my person most viciously."

"And promised you rewards, as well, if I remember my late husband aright. He offered both the cudgel and the sugar teat, when he spotted a need he could use for his own ends. He employed my love for John Gilbert so."

The Bishop of Ely's head remained bowed, his lips moving silently.

He prayed for a long time while she watched, her heart strongly moved. Wretched and a coward though he was, he was the last of her family, and he had come to her in her need.

"Amen," he said.

"Amen," she repeated.

"Her ladyship, the Countess of Castlemaine," Kate announced at the bedroom door.

Anne sat up straighter still, holding her throbbing head.

The bishop stood respectfully.

"My dear Lady Anne," Castlemaine said, bustling to the bedside. "You are obviously unwell. I do think that we must call a physician. A possible broken head is naught to trifle with, brain fever even less so."

Anne didn't know how, but she believed that the countess was trying to help her, that Barbara did or said nothing that did not have a double meaning. Like many wantons, she was drawn to the true heart of another woman, as long as that heart's rescue agreed with her own interest.

"Your ladyship is graciously thoughtful," Anne said. "I do most sorely need the services of my own personal physician, one Josiah Wyndham, residing on a barge near the London bridge."

"Then you shall have his attendance this day. His Majesty will allow me to send the guard. The king is most concerned for your welfare," Barbara said, a smile dancing in her eyes. "It did take me near all night to console him for your sake, and, of course, for the loss of his friend, your late and much lamented husband, the earl."

Deigning to notice Anne's uncle for the first time, she nodded. "My lord bishop. I do so look forward to your funeral sermon for poor Waverby."

Anne's uncle coughed. "If the king grant me leave to re-

main with my bereaved niece, I will, of course, officiate—
but, er, I haven't considered a topic for my sermon."

Castlemaine's eyebrows raised slowly. "Have you not,
my lord bishop? The Old Testament scripture regarding
King David's sending of Bathsheba's husband to war because David lusted for her is a caution for all the ages, even
this one, don't you think?" With a smile at the bishop's appalled face, she swept from the room, surprisingly agile for
one huge with the king's bastard.

John Gilbert rode through the dusty day and misty night,
pushing away hunger and exhaustion, a picture of Anne before him in every cloud. He took the lesser-traveled roads
northeast to London, skirting towns and hamlets, and several
times eluded sheriff's patrols, since he had neither rapier nor
pistols with which to defend himself. Twice he exchanged
his horse for one grazing in a field, the cottagers gaining a
better plow horse with each trade.

It was early morn again when he reached London Bridge
and made his way to seek out Dr. Wyndham's barge for news
of Anne.

John hailed the barge, and the doctor opened the cabin
door, his gaze unbelieving. "Come inside quickly, man. Your
likeness is still posted throughout the city." John thanked the
horse and slapped its flanks, watching it trot off down a
Thames side street, sure to have a new home by nightfall.

The doctor insisted John sit, and poured him a great
tankard of wine. "Is there aught I can do?" he asked. "Do
you need treatment?" he added, making a vague motion toward John's privates.

"How did you know?" John asked.

"Waverby spread the word. He needed to redeem himself
with the commons. They laughed as his carriage passed in
the streets after you left him naked as a newborn in St. James
Park."

Before John could tell him the truth, the doctor was

hailed from the riverside. Motioning John to stay out of sight, Dr. Wyndham answered the hail from the barge window. "I am Dr. Wyndham of the Royal College of Physicians. Who is in want of my skills?"

John heard the answer. "The Countess of Castlemaine does command your presence at the palace to treat the Countess of Waverby, who is sore taken. You are to come at once by water to Whitehall, and we are to escort you."

While the doctor answered the palace guard, John was on his feet, rummaging in the chest he knew contained the doctor's robes. He donned one that had all the signs of the zodiac embroidered on it, and grabbed what must have been Philibert's wig and put it on.

The doctor, seeing him, shook his head so vigorously that his own towering periwig tipped to one side. "You cannot go to the palace, John Gilbert, unless you do want your head to go the way of your . . . well, you take my meaning."

"Only too well, dear doctor, but I have no choice in the matter. If Anne is there and taken ill, then my fate is to be with her."

The doctor sighed a much bigger sigh than his small frame seemed capable of producing. "It was an ill day when a doctor of my standing became a pawn of aristocracy and rogues. . . ." he rumbled in his low voice. "But I would not go back and change a whit e'en if I could."

John lay a friendly hand upon his shoulder, stooping a little to reach it, and later helped the doctor into the riverboat and under the royal canopy. And thus on silk cushions they were rowed, the oars slapping the water in rhythm with John's pounding heart, toward the Westminster water steps and thence to the Horse Guards parade ground and beyond the walls of Whitehall Palace.

An hour later, Barbara Castlemaine hurried to the private quarters of the palace guards across the promenade. The captain was waiting for her. He bowed low. "My lady, follow me, if it please you."

She handed him a purse rattling with guineas, some of her winnings from several long nights of cards, at which she never lost if her fellow players wanted to retain her favor and therefore access to the king's majesty. "Reward your men for their swift journey and for their future silence," she said, knowing that precious few coins would ever see the inside of their pockets.

The captain opened a door, bowing her in, and she dismissed him.

A very short man with a tall periwig sat upon a stool. When he spied her, he grabbed his medical case and stood quickly, scarcely taller for the standing.

"Dr. Wyndham, Josiah Wyndham?" she asked.

"I have the honor, your ladyship, to be that physician you sent for, member of the Royal Society and graduate of the University of Padua"—he eyed her condition—"specializing in painless and swift childbirth."

She smiled. "Then you must be prized by women above all your profession. Alas, I am not your patient, at least not yet. I called you here to care for the Countess of Waverby."

"My lady is ill. . . ."

"Yes. She swooned at news of her bridegroom's death, and you will find upon examination that she has a broken head, and must retire to the country air at once for fear of the brain fever and even of her life." Castlemaine held out a small purse of guineas to assist the diagnosis.

The doctor looked at it and shook his head. "Lady Anne is my friend, and I take not a farthing for her care"—he smiled slyly—"though I would not want such unprofessional conduct to become common knowledge."

Castlemaine eyed him skeptically. Nobility was usually not so reliable as gold. Still, nobility had its uses. She shrugged. "As you will, Doctor, but I think me that you are doubly rare in your occupation."

Outside the guard room there was a commotion in the hall. The door burst open and John Gilbert was shoved inside, doctor's robe half off his broad shoulders, his wig gone.

"I ordered only one physician. Who is this?" she asked the captain.

"He tried to run for the palace, your ladyship."

"This man is my assistant, Countess," Wyndham rumbled in a commanding voice for so small a man.

"Leave us," the countess commanded the guards.

"But . . ." the captain began.

"Leave us," the countess repeated in a tone that was not used to being disobeyed.

As the door closed behind the captain, Barbara Castlemaine faced John. He swept her a generous bow, considering that he had no plumed hat to doff and the tatters of his breeches dangled below his robe even to the stone floor. "My lady Castlemaine," he said.

"Sir, your visage and manner are like no physician or apothecary that I have ever seen."

John smiled. "I am very recently come to this work."

Dr. Wyndham cleared his throat as if to speak, but she waved him away.

"Your face is known to me. Where have we met?"

"We have not, my lady, or I would never have forgotten."

"You have a pretty tongue and way, but I do not believe you."

"It is known that you cannot be made the fool, my lady. I am John Gilbert, and I beg you to allow me one word with Anne. I will be ever in your debt."

"Before this day ends, you will owe me still more, if we are both under the influence of our lucky stars," she said, circling him. She liked what she saw. "So this is the famous Gentleman Johnny, whose cock *was* as long as his sword." She sighed, facing him, her interested fingers tracing the line of muscle on his exposed shoulder. "Waverby deserved his death for unmanning such a one as you."

John could scarcely believe his hearing. Waverby dead? And what of the king? Had he concluded the bargain made with Waverby?

The countess went on in a musing voice. "Waverby—the jealous wretch—met his own doom at sea after he gelded you and gave his bride to the king, although without that chastity the king valued. I had the story entire from Anne, though she was near hysterical in the telling of it."

John lurched past Castlemaine toward the door. "Take me to her. If the king has—"

Castlemaine raised her hand. "Stay, highwayman. I'll hear no word against my Charlie. Foul Waverby, to his good, did save her from far worse than the king's attentions by his timely death." She wondered at the castrated man's obvious relief. What could it matter? "Remember, the guard is outside the door, and if you wish to see your Anne again, you'll hold your ardor for her sake." She watched him cannily. "For a man with no jewel for the ladies, you are as bold as any of your sex."

John smiled again. "I am not castrated."

Josiah Wyndham started, but Castlemaine motioned him back down on his stool. She frowned. "You lie. Waverby was not a man to make mistakes."

"But he *was* a man to send other men to do his dirty deeds."

"I do not believe you. Waverby did present Anne with your severed cod."

At that, a look of anguish suffused John's face. If Waverby were not already dead, he would need killing for that awful cruelty.

Then John bowed to her ladyship, a cool smile on his lips. "I humbly beg your pardon, my lady, but I cannot bear it that a beautiful woman of your vast reputation should doubt my manhood. How do we resolve this?"

Still frowning, she placed her hand on his crotch and left it there. She did not remove it for some time, and he half enjoyed the play of changing emotions upon her face, nor was he surprised when he stiffened. How better to prove himself to this particular countess?

After a sufficient examination, he politely stepped back and bowed. "My lady, I don't know what you plan for me, but I must tell Anne that I am whole. It is barbarous to allow her to think otherwise."

"It may be barbarous, but I think me that it is a tool"— she smiled, suggesting a deliberate use of the term—"to save your life."

Castlemaine began to pace, resting her hands upon her belly as pregnant women in near full term do. "Sir Highwayman, for now I think it will be shock enough for her to see you here. And we must use that shock, if you are game to challenge a Stuart king for her."

Dr. Wyndham bowed to the bishop sitting with his prayer book by a window, parted the bed curtains and looked inside. Anne was pale, her lips blue tinged, and her hand lay listless upon the coverlet.

"My lady," he said softly, "it's Josiah Wyndham come to tend you."

"Good doctor," she said, "I have much need of your miracle salve this day." She smiled slightly, inching her hand across toward the sound of his voice. He took it, and she opened her eyes, comforted by the familiar small, round face under the towering wig. She blinked hard against the bright sunlight that streamed through the windows.

"Do you see two of me, my lady?" he asked.

"No, but I have a fearsome headache."

He checked her eyes, his surprisingly gentle fingers examining her head. He smiled. "It is better than I hoped."

Slowly, her eyes adjusted to the light. "Who is that behind you, Doctor?"

"My assistant, Lady Anne."

She tensed. "Philibert," she whispered.

"No," he said, the doctor's usually loud voice a low rumble. "He confessed his perfidy, and I sent him away. He is no longer my son."

"Oh, Josiah," Anne said, distressed, "he is not to blame for his actions."

"Your ladyship, a man is always responsible for his own disgrace."

"I'm most truly sorry for this further injury I've brought upon you," Anne whispered, distraught at this news. "I have much to regret of my life, and I would rather have done with it than . . . oh, Doctor, help me if you can! If I cannot have my Johnny, then give me that final potion that brings eternal sleep."

The bishop leaped to his feet. "I will not countenance such talk! Niece, there is nothing in your life so bitter"—he indicated the palace with his free hand—"that you should think of such a sinful thing and court hell."

Anne sighed. "Uncle, you speak as a man would speak of comfort and protection. Women want more. Do not censure us for our need of joy over treasure, or our despair at joy's irretrievable loss."

There was a rustle from the foot of the bed, and she strained to see the assistant who remained beyond the curtains. "Why will your man not show his face?" There was more than curiosity in her voice.

Before the doctor could answer, John Gilbert stepped into the window light, the streaming sun highlighting the dark and light planes of his bronzed face, a face that was filled with uncommon pleasure. "You'll forgive me, Anne, but I did not want to risk a meeting until the doctor had pronounced you past danger."

She did not hear what he said; she heard only his voice, the voice that she had thought never to hear again. "Johnny! But you are on the sea even now. How came you here?" She fought the tangled coverlet to reach him, but he came to her first, and sitting upon the bed, took her completely within his arms, his face buried in her soft hair.

The bishop slammed his prayer book shut. "Listen, my man, you cannot do this, not here at Whitehall, with the king's—"

"I am not yet the king's mistress," Anne replied to her uncle, but she was looking deep into John's eyes so that he could see her truth. Then neither Anne nor John paid the bishop the slightest further attention, and Dr. Wyndham's black scowl stopped any more complaints from the clergyman.

"This is some fantastic fancy," Anne said, moving her hands about John's face, determined to know if he was a dream and she was once more deceived as she was each night.

"Here is my proof," he said, and kissed her, with such longing that the doctor turned away and even the bishop looked momentarily melancholy.

Anne pulled back from John's embrace so that she could look into his face and be sure of his answer. "You are in pain, John?"

He shook his head. "I was, but no longer," he said, and held her tighter and closer. He knew she spoke of his mutilation, but he had promised Castlemaine that he would not tell Anne he was a whole man until they left the palace—if they ever left the palace. And he was not certain at this moment that he could follow Castlemaine's plan to deceive the king into thinking Anne might die unless removed to the country at once. Unless a highwayman received a royal pardon, there was no future for him or the woman he loved. But the risk was great. Had he suffered all to end on Tyburn, after all? He had been willing to die to see her, but now having seen her, he wanted to live.

Anne heard the yapping first, but she had hardly time to gather herself for the onslaught when the chamber door

opened and the *tick-tick*ing of toenails gave way to a perfumed fur ball flinging itself on her bed, as the king's favorite spaniel nestled against her with a doggy sigh.

John stood and steeled himself for the meeting that could
end with his neck in a noose.

"Fubbs! Naughty Fubbs!" The king stood tall and vastly
elegant in the doorway, a sugar treat dangling from his fingers.

The fat little spaniel did not move but whined for the
treat, and obediently the king crossed to the bed and gave it,
allowing the dog to lick his sticky fingers clean.

"We thought to find you desolate for company, dear
lady," the king said fretfully. "And yet we find you surrounded and from your high color, much entertained. Who
are these people?"

The doctor bowed. "Josiah Wyndham, physician, Your
Majesty, with a specialty in the care of wounds of the
skull"—for a moment the doctor looked flustered, but then
he brightened—"and small dogs, particularly as to nourish-
ment for a long life."

"Ah," the king said, "then both your patients are in one
bed." He pointed to John. "And this man here?"

Anne spoke, picking up her forgotten plaster and placing
it upon her forehead. "The doctor's assistant, sir."

John stepped audaciously forward. "That is true, my
king, but it is not my primary occupation."

The king eyed him inquisitively. "We would know what
that might be."

"I am, until lately, John Gilbert, chief thief upon Your
Majesty's highroads, and under your royal sentence of
death."

The king grabbed up Fubbs and stepped back, almost
ramming the Bishop of Ely. "Guards!" he called.

The bishop stammered. "Your Ma-majesty, you must believe me when I say that I knew nothing of this man's true
identity. I came only to succor my—"

His explanation was interrupted by the arrival of two guards with pikes at the ready.

"Arrest that man," the king said, pointing to John.

Anne cried out, and in her descent from bed, she almost ripped her nightdress from her breasts. She placed herself in front of John, her arms outspread. Confused, the guards shifted their pikes toward Anne.

Ignoring them, she cried, "Your Majesty, I beg you for his life, as you have any regard for me."

Startled, the guards recovered and shifted their pike points back to John, whose large frame was an easy target behind her slight body. "Your orders, Majesty?" one guard inquired.

The king stared at John and Anne, and barely hung on to the wriggling Fubbs.

John picked Anne up firmly and put her back upon the bed. "Allow me, please, Anne, for once, my sweet, to speak for myself." Then he fell on one knee before the king.

It was on this scene that the Countess of Castlemaine arrived with a voluptuous young girl, her bosom spilling over her bodice onto the Spanish guitar she was holding.

"Shall I play now?" the girl asked.

"A little later, perhaps," the Countess said, her glance taking in the high drama.

The king eyed Castlemaine with cynical but obvious relief. "We see your hand in this, Babs. No one can produce a farce to equal yours. But you go too far. This man says that he is the highwayman Gentleman Johnny Gilbert, who has harried my subjects for years, and who comes now to assassinate me."

John stared fearlessly at his monarch and spread his arms wide, exposing his breast to sword or bullet. "Never would I harm your person, sire, but I have on occasion harried your subjects. Yet neither have I stolen from the royal couriers, nor from an army paymaster. Nor have I assaulted plain citizens, butchers or farmers on their way to market. I have taken only that which my victims had in excess."

The king had listened with undisguised interest, but suddenly turned angry. "That is not true, highwayman. You have stolen the affections of that which we have only one—the Lady Anne."

Heedless of John's warning, Anne advanced and fell heavily to her knees beside John, pale and shaking. "Then, gracious Majesty, punish me with him. Allow me to share his fate on the gibbet. If I cannot live with him, then I would die with him."

The king drew back in horror. "You would have your dead body hang in chains on Bagshot Heath, the crows picking at your flesh until your bones fell to earth." He buried his face in Fubbs's curly coat.

"Your Majesty is most picturesque," Castlemaine said, clearing her throat. "May I have a private word?"

"Watch the fellow," the king ordered his guards. "Nay, watch all of them."

Castlemaine placed her arm on the king's and guided him to the window that looked upon a narrow courtyard, dislodging the bishop with one look, then whispering in her sovereign's ear long and intently.

"This is no fancy of yours?" the king finally asked aloud.

"Indeed not, Your Majesty. My late Lord of Waverby did show the grisly object to the Lady Anne before their wedding. She recounted the story in every detail."

The king looked sickened. "Waverby's humor did ever cut too deep for our taste."

"How true in this case, Your Majesty," Castlemaine said wryly. "If you will allow me—for I do know how compassionate your mercy can be—the man, John Gilbert, has suffered beyond most men already."

"But the Lady Anne?" the king asked, obviously unwilling to let her go. "I would have no unwilling virgin, Babs, but I cannot believe that there is such."

Castlemaine smiled in agreement. "My lady," she said to Anne, "is it still your wish to remain chaste the rest of your life-long?"

Anne scrambled to her feet with eagerness and yet cautious of her words to make them truthful. "Yes. That was my vow when I fled from Lord Waverby, and I renew it, especially now that there"—she halted herself from almost saying too much and insulting the king—"especially now," she finished lamely.

John's dark eyes glinted, and he avoided Castlemaine's amused gaze. Standing, he moved to Anne's side and placed his arm about her shoulder.

The king stared at them both, and then for a long time at Anne, the hurt of unfamiliar loss marking his face. And thus, in a very theatrical tone, for he was ever a theater-loving monarch, he quoted a couplet of his own devising, which Andrew Marvell, the poet, had praised extravagantly, " 'Oh, then, 'tis oh, then, that I think there's no hell like loving, like loving too well.' "

Anne curtsied, unwilling after all that had gone before to believe that this long nightmare might be coming to an end. "Your most gracious Majesty," she whispered, and kissed his hand. He allowed it, but with petulance.

The king bent his head and nuzzled Fubbs, perhaps the only female that sensed his need for affection that demanded no return, and the little spaniel licked his cheek. "You have injured us, my Lady Anne," the king said sorrowfully. "It is a hard thing to know in one to whom we have given so much of our favor."

Castlemaine signaled the guitarist to play, and the girl began singing softly in a low but clear vibrato. As she strummed a Spanish dance, her breasts jiggled an accompaniment to the music.

"Charming tune," the king said, his eye drawn to the singer. He continued to stare.

"Your Majesty," Castlemaine whispered, "these young people await your royal wish."

With a sigh, he nodded to John, his voice still peevish. "Oh, very well. You have our pardon, as long as you do not thieve upon our highroads again."

John bowed. "And for my men, if they wish to follow me in renouncing villainy."

The king, close to losing patience, snapped, "And your men!"

Castlemaine summoned a secretary from the anteroom, who soon produced a document of royal pardon, which the king signed without taking his eyes from the guitarist.

John bowed gratefully, accepting the parchment. "Your Majesty, many thefts of which I was innocent were laid to me, and will be again, but I do promise you that for the sake of my Lady Anne's neck, I will lead an exemplary life from this moment forward."

The king nodded, but his eyes strayed again to Anne. "And you would share his life, such as it is in his, er, state of health?"

Anne nodded determinedly. "My renewed vow of chastity says that I do not need what he does not have, Your Majesty."

John dropped his head in seeming humility, his shoulders shaking obviously with pent-up emotion.

The king was moved. "Then we will order a coach made ready to take you on your journey. You will be safe from highwaymen"—he glanced archly at John—"when you are under the royal arms."

"We thank Your Majesty," John said, "but the royal arms would be a magnet for every thief upon Oxford Road."

The king shrugged. "As you will. We cannot hinder ourselves from wishing you both very well." But he was already turning away. "What is her name, Babs?" the king asked Castlemaine, watching the singer during a particularly vigorous, bouncy chorus.

"Mary Green of the Duke's theater, and she is eager to play your favorite tunes in your private closet, to your complete content."

Once the guards, the king and the singer were gone, Anne pressed her thanks upon the Countess Castlemaine.

"Do not thank me," Castlemaine said, and on her face was a mixture of love and pain. "The king adores a woman with intelligence and the courage to challenge him. This Mary's head is as empty as her bosom is full, and therefore she will be soon dismissed. You would have been a more formidable adversary, Lady Anne, especially since you do not desire him or his preferment. There is no spur to the male heart like rejection." She smiled slyly. "Now, all of you, quit the palace quickly while the king is besotted with—the music."

Chapter Twenty

She'll Go to Hell!

"Mistress, please take me with thee," Kate begged, tears welling in her eyes.

"I would never leave you, dear Kate."

"Nor I," John said, smiling down at the plain young Quaker girl. He bent and kissed her cheek, while she blushed furiously.

Anne had not loosed John's arm and seemed determined not to, as if he might fly away if she did not hold him to the floor next to her. It was not a clinging that he wanted her to stop anytime soon.

The bishop confronted Anne, ignoring John. "I cannot believe that a Gascoigne would court such a misadventure," he said sternly, his hands clasped before him prayerfully, holding his cross high as if to ward off evil. "Return with me to Ely at once, and after your mourning, a suitable marriage can be arranged, with the king's gracious permission, of course. It will be a simple matter, when sufficient time has passed, to convince His Majesty that a young flibbergib came to her senses."

Anne tightened her grip on John's arm, obviously in no agreement with her uncle's thoughtful offer.

"Come, Niece, you must know that I could never bless a

union with such a man," he added with an uneasy glance at John. "Marriage is for procreation, and if there is no chance of that, then there is no basis for marriage."

John studied the bishop, a half-smile lurking about his mouth. "And what about romantic love, Reverend?"

The bishop huffed. "A spurious passion, one for triflers and the foolishly wanton. True marriage is the union of two families, and I doubt not that you have Anne's land grant well in mind."

"I renounce her property," John said, his face darkening despite his determination to indulge this man in his calling, and because he was Anne's family.

Anne looked at her uncle, her eyes steady. "Do you think me such a poor, sheepish creature that I do not truly know the character of the man who holds my heart?" Before her uncle could speak again, she rushed on. "I hate lying even for convenience, Uncle, so I will not." Her fingers tightened on her highwayman's sleeve. "John and I are married already, by all the words the church uses to unite a man and woman. I do love and honor him above all men, and I will faithfully cleave to him and to no other throughout my life."

She watched her uncle's mouth gape open, and she knew that her next words would not make him feel better. "It was truly bigamy that I committed before your altar with Edward, Lord Waverby, because I had already given my heart and soul and body to John Gilbert."

"Niece, fear for your immortal soul in hell for those words!"

She drew herself to full height, which was almost the equal of her uncle's. "Better hell later than hell on earth!" Then her tone softened. "I do ask for your blessing, Uncle, as you are my beloved father's brother."

He almost strangled on the word. "Blessing! You ask me to bless a wanton travesty, and that I cannot do."

"Then you have *my* blessing, Uncle, and my leave to go."

"I beg you to think carefully, Niece," he intoned in a penetrating voice he usually used at the high pulpit. "You will change your mind in years to come, and women do not have a second chance if they lose their reputation."

Anne looked up at John, smiling. "I already have my second chance, Uncle, and I do not mean to lose it, not even for my soul's sake. I could not love God if he allowed me these sweet feelings only to condemn them."

John swept her into his arms, nearly crushing her, and she covered his face with her kisses. "Sweetest Anne," John murmured against her cheek, and then he held her at arm's length, because he felt his cod rising beneath his doctor's gown. There was no way he could hold her close and control that which had no wish to be controlled.

Anne could not take her hands from him, needing to feel his muscled arms, throbbing with the life that was in him. "My love," she said, her voice breaking and her green eyes swimming with the joyous, loving tears that she had withheld from Waverby and the king, tears that John began to kiss away.

The Bishop of Ely left without another word. No clergyman could save a soul that did so obviously wish to wallow in abominable sin.

Dr. Wyndham cleared his throat when the kissing seemed unlikely to stop, as John, his eyes beseeching, seemed to beg him to intervene. "I think 'twould be a good thing to follow my Lady Castlemaine's suggestion and be quit of the palace as soon as ever we can. Stuart kings have been known to be changeable."

Dressing hastily with the help of Kate, who also found more suitable attire for John in a chest, Anne was about to leave the apartment when she remembered the pearl necklace. She placed it carefully on her pillow, where the king and the buxom guitarist would surely find it that evening.

John picked it up. "Well matched," he said, holding the pearls to the light. "Lustrous, and worth a hundred pounds at

Cutpurse Mary's shop in the Fleet Street. The baggage would love to fence this piece."

Anne took the pearl strand from him and put it firmly back onto the pillow. "I would take nothing away, but a gown to cover my nakedness."

John smiled. "Old habits die hard, my sweet Anne."

"But die they must, John," she said firmly.

He smiled. This was a new Anne, more sure of herself; perhaps a woman needed to be if she thought a man less than a man. He smiled again. "Anne, you must help me adjust to this new way of thinking," he said, looking boyishly wicked.

For answer, she kissed him lightly on the lips. He suspected that he would get an uncommon amount of her help in the future.

Guards waited in the hall, and the four were quickly escorted across the parade ground and out of Whitehall Palace. A short sedan chair ride and they were at a Bankside inn, where John had stabled Sir Pegasus many days before.

The horse nickered and danced in the stall, eager for exercise. Anne threw her arms about his neck as far as she could reach and kissed his muzzle.

"We can't ride three together all the way to Whittlewood," John said, retrieving a brace of pistols from a saddlebag and thrusting them into his breeches. "I'll see if the landlord has a young cob to sell for Kate." With a shrug, he began to twist his father's ring from his finger to pay, but Anne stayed his hand and removed Edward's wedding ring, forgotten in the drama of the past twenty-four hours. He smiled into her eyes and was rewarded with a doting flash of green through a glint of auburn-tinged lashes, caught perfectly by an unshuttered lantern's light.

"I guess this is fare-you-well, Wyndham," John said to the doctor. "We owe you much more than we can ever repay." He held out his hand to the little doctor for a shake, an act that had been made popular by old Cromwell's idea that all Puritans were equal before God, and now becoming a symbol of equality among men.

"I take your hand, John Gilbert, and gladly," Dr. Wyndham said, "but not in farewell. If you have need of my skill, I have need of such true friends. Besides, my lady will need my salve for her head, although the fresh country air will work its own miracle."

"Then come with us, and welcome," John said heartily, noticing Anne's delight. "There may be broken heads aplenty before we have done."

"Agreed!" The doctor pumped John's hand. "I'll share your fate, and the beauteous young Kate may share my horse to your highwayman's lair."

Kate reddened and glanced at Anne, who smilingly gave her permission.

"But your barge, Doctor," Anne said.

"I'll send a message by yon groomsman to Philibert at his lodgings in Cheapside. It is all the patrimony he will get from a brokenhearted father."

A bell rang in the clear morning air.

Josiah Wyndham lifted his head. "Strange. I thought the king had banned the funeral bells tolling for plague victims."

John nodded grimly. "Those aren't plague bells. It's the bell of St. Sepulchre ringing for the condemned on their way from Newgate Prison to Tyburn. It rang thus for me once not so long ago."

Anne clasped his hand, shivering. "Let us find another way to Oxford Road, John."

"'Tis the shortest way to the west, Anne, and we must take it if we are to reach Whittlewood Forest in two days hence. I have too long neglected my men, and am uneasy in my mind."

Mounted at last, and with saddlebags of provender—wine, bread and cheese—they made their way to High Holborn and thence by St. Giles's to Oxford Road. The stench and dust were nigh unbearable as the sun climbed higher.

Plague or no plague, the way was jammed with men, women, children, beggars, jugglers, pickpockets and apprentice boys laden with wares, going to the fair that surrounded the place of execution. Printers were hawking the confession and last testament of Jack Clinch, the highwayman.

"Broadsheet, sir?" a man asked, pulling on John's breeches. "Jack Clinch does name a hundred men he made cuckolds."

John looked down from his horse on the man's face. "Then, good printer, Jack did cheat you of at least one hundred more names."

They came up a gentle rise, and Anne saw the famed triple-armed tree of Tyburn, dangling corpses. Below one hanged man, who occasionally gave a spasmodic kick, two men pulled hard on his legs.

Anne cried out in horror. "John, what are they doing to that poor wretch?"

"A kindness," John said grimly. "He'll die faster with their added weight."

Incongruously, a trained she-bear in a woman's gown danced nearby to sprightly lute music, and Anne turned her face away. "Is there no other way for felons to die, John?"

He kept his dark eyes on the scene. "Probably not," he said. "Until common men live with dignity, they will not be allowed to die with any."

To amend the hopelessness from his tone, he kissed the top of her head, but he watched until he could see the corpses no more. Tomorrow up to twenty-four men would take their place, and the next day another twenty-four. Since the theft of property worth the sum of five pounds was a capital crime in Charles Stuart's England, Tyburn had an endless supply of men and ofttimes women, even children.

Hanging or worse had been his own ultimate fate for the seven years that he'd been on the road, and Anne had saved him by her love. He owed her his life twice over, and though the old John Gilbert would have laughed at the sentiment, he intended to make her proud that she loved him.

His promise to the king had been no idle token to gain a pardon. And yet he was equally sure that it was not in his stars to abide in Whittlewood Forest. Every robbery on Oxford Road would be laid to him, and sooner or later, he would be forced by a constable to defend himself.

Beyond Tyburn, the crowds thinned until at last the horses were making good progress, and great Oxford Road west lay before them.

Anne sat as straight as she could, her leg wrapped about the saddle's pommel. She wanted to lean her aching head against his chest as she had done on the night ride from Burwell Hall almost a month now past. She dared not, because she feared that his frightful wound could not possibly be well healed, although he was far too courageous to show pain before her.

She shifted to a softer perch. There were things that she needed to say to John, delicate things, and she wanted to say them now at the beginning of their new life together, so that they would not gain further strength until they became impossible to discuss. She glanced behind and saw the doctor and Kate in an animated conversation. Steeling herself, she determined to speak of what they both must have uppermost in their minds. "John?"

"Yes," he said, bending close to plant the word in her ear.

She shivered a bit from the heat of his breath. "I don't want you to misunderstand what words I am about to speak." She looked back and up into his face, and somehow she could tell that he knew the subject of her discourse already.

"My sweet, I will try to listen with the understanding the subject requires," he said, his visage serious.

John knew what was coming, and he thought for a moment to forestall her words with the truth. Although Castlemaine had sworn both he and the doctor to silence, there was no longer a need for it. Until now, there had been no adequate opportunity to discuss what the king had called his "health." A man just didn't announce before his lady love and a room full of other witnesses that his cod was intact and, indeed, full of life whenever he looked upon her. It was a matter that needed privacy between a man and woman. He would pick the time and the place, and as soon as possible, but not on the road, where she might swoon or become hysterical.

He smiled to himself. Anyway, if all truth be told, he had been curious what Anne would say when inevitably she broached the subject. It was an opportunity that few men in the world were given: to discover what a clever, beautiful and passionate woman really thought of that most intimate and obvious of male appendages.

Anne cleared her throat repeatedly, though it was a hot, moist day with a storm on the way, one of the many that had bedeviled England this plague summer. "I am not entirely" —she coughed again—"John, you are certain that you will not misunderstand?"

"Most certain," he said, and nuzzled the nape of her neck. "Pray, continue, my sweet."

"You must pay me close attention so as not to mistake my meaning," she said, sounding in tone a bit like his theology professor at Oxford.

"Go on, Anne, before you forget what you must say."

"I would never forget," she said, half understanding that he was teasing, and a bit discomfited by it. This was no matter for laughing, but for serious discourse.

"Then straight out with the words," he said, his baritone voice attempting sternness.

She drew back her shoulders, and her tongue engaged the words again, only none of them, once spoken, sounded as high-minded and reassuring as she had intended. "In a way, I'm not sad about your—" She stopped, searching for the right word.

"My, er, health," he prompted.

"Yes. But, oh, John, I simply mean that you will know forever that I love you for the excellent man you are and not—not for any reasons of lust or animal pleasure, not that such pleasure as I remember, indeed, will always remember, to be . . ." She stopped, although she was not certain that she should finish.

John was silent, waiting for her to continue a rather enjoyably pretty speech. But she fell silent, and after a furlong or so, his arms tightened about her. "Well said, sweet Anne. I am indeed a lucky man in spite of, well, my condition. Shall we call it that for delicacy's sake?"

"If you wish it." She sighed. "John?"

"Yes, my angel."

"I am worried in my mind that in some way, breaking my vow of chastity might have aroused the fates—that I am even more responsible for what has happened to your . . . to you than I imagined."

Since he was holding her close, she could feel his body shaking with emotion, and in respect for his feelings, she did not turn about.

Indeed, she was finding it increasingly difficult to remember that his lack of a male part should make maintaining her return to chastity perfectly simple. The body that had aroused her before aroused her still.

"John?"

"Yes, my love?"

"You remember when we were at Nell's . . ."

"I do have some memory of it."

Was he teasing her? Could he not be serious about such a serious subject? "We were before the fire and you were feeding me strawberries."

"They were red ripe and plump," he said, and smacked his lips, as if he were deliberately missing the point.

"John!"

"Yes, my sweeting?"

"God's bowels! I am not talking of strawberries, but of

words you said about . . . about more to lovemaking than . . . than just the male . . . well, than the lower parts." She was out of breath from pushing out such difficult words, and her stomach ached.

"Ah, I do remember something of the kind, dear Anne."

She was becoming more exasperated from trying to suppress her exasperation. "Well, then, tell me what you did mean."

"Let me think," he said, beginning to regret the teasing, which had probably gone too far.

"You have forgotten?

"Nay, but it is something that needs a quiet time, not jouncing along Oxford Road with dust in our faces."

"You will tell me when we are alone," she said hopefully.

He leaned forward and put his tongue in her ear, slowly moving along its tender circles until he nipped her lobe. "I will show you, dearest."

She shivered but not with cold, since her woman's part sent heat into all her limbs. Oh, God, would she be strong enough to bear John's affliction, since it was now her own?

His arms and strongly muscled frame were as yet most distractingly hard. She had heard that men castrated by war or to become eunuchs in some infidel seraglio became soft and fat. She drew in breath sharply at the thought. Oh, and his smooth baritone voice would no doubt become like the *castrati* of Italy—vaguely soprano. She closed her eyes. God's bowels! She would never in this life make a stupid vow of chastity, or any other!

The four travelers stopped beyond Bagshot Hill and its gruesome line of gibbets meant as a warning for highwaymen, and shared a quick slice of bread and cheese and a quaff of watered wine.

It was there, from behind a small copse of woods, that a man dressed as a gentleman appeared on horseback, pistols drawn. "Have a care, all of you," he shouted, approaching.

"Keep her calm," John told Wyndham when Kate mewled

in fear. "Let me speak to him, Anne. The man is not to be trusted."

John dismounted, held the head of Sir Peg, and waited until the highwayman was a few feet away. "Tom Barrow, isn't it?"

The man laughed. "Sink me if it isn't Gentleman Johnny Gilbert. I met you once, riding with Black Ben."

"State your business with me, Tom," John said, interrupting a reminiscence he would just as soon Anne didn't hear.

"Well, dog will eat dog, eh, Johnny? I could lift your valuables, or you could join me." Tom Barrow surveyed the group. "I heard you had style, John, but a doxy, a doctor by his carrying chest, and a maid-of-all-work is fashion enough for a traveling duke. What say you to a partnership?"

John bowed. "I'm deeply complimented, Tom, but I carry a royal pardon, and have solemnly promised the Lady Anne here to be quit of the road."

Tom Barrow sat his horse, pistols leveled at John's breast, digesting this information. He bowed his head to Anne. "My lady, I beg your forgiveness. I should have recognized your quality."

"You should have," Anne said haughtily. "With such poor judgement you'll have no success from your profession."

The man's eyes narrowed. "You are not afraid of me?"

She shrugged. "Why should I be, highwayman? I have faced marriage to a man I hate, the plague, the king's wrath and the gibbet, all within a fortnight." She omitted castration, since she did not want to shame John before his colleague.

Tom Barrow thrust his pistols into his belt. "Then I have no hope of frightening such as you," he said, laughing, mightily amused.

His horse reared at the unaccustomed sound of mirth, but he shortened rein and brought the beast under control. "John, I think now that the *three* of us could take every coach on Oxford Road."

John nodded, glancing a warning back at Anne. "You may be right, Tom. 'Tis a shame, but I have sworn an oath, and this lady is dogged about oaths."

"Under what petticoat tyranny we men must live," Tom Barrow mused.

"How true," John agreed, though he felt Anne's pointed slipper jab his back.

Tom lifted his hat. "I leave you then, John Gilbert, in full possession of all your goods, to war with cupid's demands. I think you do have the harder profession." And smiling, he rode past.

John shouted after him. "Any news of my men, Tom?"

Tom half twisted in the saddle. "Black Ben rules your roost now, John."

"What petticoat tyranny?" Anne asked, as John swung into the saddle behind her.

He stopped her pouting mouth with a kiss, and she seemed content with that answer.

John gathered the reins into his hands. "Doctor, we must make haste. We will water and feed the beasts at an inn that I know, but I would ride on to Whittlewood Forest this night."

They set off at a brisk pace. "Your poor head, Anne. Can you bear this?" John asked.

"This and more," she said.

He kissed the nape of her neck. "I do think Tom Barrow was right. You would have made the best highwayman of us all."

They reached Whittlewood Forest well after first light the next morning. At the first guard post high in a tree, John's halloo was unreturned. And at the second tree. And the third.

At the place where they turned into the stream bed, John shifted Anne up behind him and told Dr. Wyndham to do the same with Kate. "We know not what we face, Anne," he said. "For once follow orders, and hold tight to me."

She had no trouble doing so.

They reached the bramble copse, and John dismounted, finding the black iron ring and sliding open the entrance to the cave dug through the hill. The lanterns were not lit, and once the door closed behind them, they were in inky darkness.

John remounted. "Stay close, Wyndham."

"Kate, do not be frightened," Anne said. "Nor you, good doctor."

Wyndham's deep voice rumbled behind her, in what she was sure he thought was a whisper. "As you do know so well, my lady, I have had my adventures along the river, but this surpasses all, for now I have the agreeable company of a delightful young maid."

Anne heard Kate's giggle. So the sober Quaker girl might find those love feelings that she had so longed to know. For all Anne's apprehension about what lay on the other end of the tunnel, she was happy for Kate.

They rode first into half-lit shadows, where John checked the prime on his pistols, then into full sunlight.

Anne squinted her eyes to make out the smithy, the pretty bowling green and dairy barn, and at the far end of the open common, the small, thatched cottage where she had determinedly fended off first Black Ben and then, unfortunately, John Gilbert. In a way, she had been looking forward to seeing it all again, as if she were coming home. Since her leavetaking, most of her memories of the outlaw village had turned to fond ones.

Silently, they rode to the smithy and dismounted.

"Where is your village, John Gilbert?" Dr. Wyndham asked.

John surveyed the burnt-out cottages and barns, where random wisps of smoke still rose from their embers. "Ashes, all ashes. This is the work of that mongrel Black Ben."

Anne looked about silently, for she would not for the world allow John to see her disquiet. "Beth and Joseph?" She said the names softly.

"If he has harmed them or others of my band, I will cut out his unnatural heart!"

"What must we do, John?" Anne asked.

"First, we will break fast with the last of our victuals," he said, "over here under this tree. Thus fortified, we will set to work and see what we can salvage from the ruins."

John apportioned the food. "This is a sorry homecoming, Anne."

She lifted his hand and held it to her cheek, slowly shaking her head. "Perhaps Whittlewood is not meant to be our home," she said. "Remember, John, as Edward's widow I do own Virginia land."

"Never could I live there at your suffrage, Anne."

Before she could ask why, though she knew his answer, Josiah started to his feet beside her.

"Who comes there?" Dr. Wyndham asked, staring at the woods.

It was at this moment that a ragged crew of five left the line of trees and walked down the green hill toward them, Joseph and Beth in the lead.

Chapter Twenty-one

She Would if She Could

A thick silence descended on the clearing as Joseph and Beth ran before three men toward Anne and John, a silence that was broken by Joseph's rasping cry: "Johnny, we thought ye dead for sure!"

John slapped the blacksmith on one huge shoulder. "I thought myself dead more than once, Joseph, but the Lady Anne here can charm the angels out of heaven or deceive wily Satan himself."

Joseph stared at Anne and slowly smiled. "I never thought to see ye again in this world, but I'm happy to be mistook."

"I'm happy, too, good Joseph," Anne said, her delighted expression agreeing with her words.

"Joseph," John interrupted eagerly, his arm now around the blacksmith's shoulder, "I return with the king's pardon for all my men and women, too, who do agree to forsake the road. Will you follow me?"

Joseph gawked at John, as did the others. "Do ye speak true, Johnny?" Joseph asked wonderingly.

John removed the parchment from his doublet and showed them the royal seal of red wax and the king's signature.

One of Joseph's companions stepped forward. "We did not wish to ride with Black Ben, Johnny, but if we ride not at all, how will we earn our bread?"

John folded the parchment and replaced it carefully. "We will decide that in council."

"What council?" Joseph asked. "The men be gone."

"Not for long, if I know Ben," John answered grimly. He uncorked the last ale jug, and it made a quick round.

"My lady," Beth said, sinking to a low curtsy in front of Anne, "every night I prayed ye'd be safe."

Anne raised the milkmaid, embracing her plump shoulders. "It is Anne now, Beth, just plain Anne. And this is Kate." She took Kate's arm and tugged the shy young Quaker woman forward from Dr. Wyndham's side, including her in the embrace. "We are all equals in John Gilbert's band."

Anne hadn't known that she would say such words until she did, but when she heard them issue from her mouth, she knew that she had been thinking such words for some time, and that they sounded right to her ears. Here were no servants to fulfill her every whim, no fine French and Spanish wines, no courtiers who spoke for hours with endless wit about nothing at all, no viols playing Lully overtures in shining marble rooms. Here hardship stretched as far as she could imagine, and yet here she was loved and needed. Here she had friends. Here was her true happiness. She smiled quizzically up at John. "I have a vote now, don't I?"

"Aye," John said, the pride in his eyes shining down on her, "but I do expect to regret it."

They looked at each other and held the look, and it was clear to Joseph that this Anne was not the same person as the arrogant Lady Anne Gascoigne, who had so neatly escaped them on Oxford Road, nor was John Gilbert the same man who had followed her, although outwardly he seemed so. Joseph would have given a month's plunder to hear what had happened between the two.

John hastily introduced Dr. Wyndham, whose black carrying chest proclaimed his profession, then questioned the blacksmith. "What happened here, Joseph?"

"Black Ben happened, as ye can well imagine, John. He persuaded some of the lads that ye'd gone off with yon minx—your pardon, Anne—then he got most of them to sign his articles, not without threats, mind ye, and thence he took them out on the road. We five escaped into the woods, and watched him torch the village in a rage because ye had escaped him." Joseph pointed to the woods. "We have a shelter and a cellar full of supplies, powder and shot"—he grinned—"e'en the last cool crock of the good, sweet butter your lady didst churn while here."

Anne smiled through her fatigue. " 'Twould pain me to think one mouthful had been lost."

Dr. Wyndham stepped forward and examined the arm of one of the men. "Lad, that sword slash wants stitching to heal aright. Kate, you look a sturdy lass who does not swoon easily. Will you assist me?"

Kate looked at Anne.

Anne nodded. "If you wish it, Kate. You are free to do as you please. Indeed, we must all turn a hand as we can."

John was already striding away toward the ruined smithy, and he and the men spent the rest of the day unearthing the cache of arms buried underground beneath the ash, while Beth showed Anne the camp in the woods.

Shyly, Beth motioned to the lean-to propped between two large tree trunks. "Ye'll want another place for—" She stopped, embarrassed.

"Yes, John Gilbert and I will want to be together." Anne knew this was true, although she didn't know what form this togetherness would take. She had half decided that it might be better for them if they continued as dear friends, close yet apart in all but normal speech. The thought of lying near John Gilbert's body each night, unable to feel aught but the cruelest of constrained passion—well, she could simply not bear the thought, especially if she had to feel infernally guilty about it forever. Although he had hinted on Oxford Road at other delightful ways to make love . . . she shook her head to lose the curious thoughts that crowded in, for to allow them might do greater harm, if he meant them as a kindness.

Beth stared at her. "What be wrong, my lady"—she corrected herself with difficulty—"I mean, Anne?"

"Nothing, good Beth," Anne said, noticeably sagging, "I'm—"

"Exhausted is what ye be, my poor dear, and hurt, too, if that black bruise there on thy head be any sign," Beth said, and began to gather fern fronds and leaves into a nest that she tucked between two bushes, and then over all stretched a blanket and afterward suspended a large piece of green linen from a nearby clothes chest to make a closed tent. "Now," she said, taking Anne's elbow and guiding her firmly to the makeshift bed, "ye rest snug here. And for a woman's privy necessaries, my Joseph dug a trench past yon copse," she announced, pointing down the hill.

Anne heard a particular pride in Beth's voice. "You and Joseph?" she asked. Was all the world sick with love?

"Yes," Beth answered, this time not bowing her head modestly. "He is a strong man, and kind for all his strength."

But Anne was asleep before Beth could say more, and the onetime milkmaid turned back to the rabbit-and-leek stew she stirred in the kettle hung over the fire.

Sometime later, Anne interrupted sleep long enough for Beth to spoon some hot broth into her, and later still, she sleepily watched John and the others hunch around the fire, their loud voices arguing about something called an article, but Anne couldn't understand the argument, and soon slept again, deeply and, for once, dreamlessly.

She awoke with a start, more a reaction to the absolute stillness about her than to the occasional crack of a banked fire log spitting sparks. Rising on one elbow, she surveyed the small campsite, bathed in full moonlight, noting the sleeping forms, and guessing, in a rather distressed way, that one was John. Although he must have been wondering, as she had, what kind of closeness theirs would be, he had chosen to avoid rather than confront the question this night.

Anne felt especially troubled by this evasion. It was time to face his condition, no matter how painful to both of them. She could see all this plainly. Why couldn't he be interested in details?

Anne stood and swiped angrily at her wrinkled gown. God's fish! It had been she who had boldly broached the subject on the road from London; hence it was now John's turn, most definitely, to make all clear. She wondered which sleeping form was his; she certainly couldn't shake them all. If she awakened the wrong man, what explanation could she offer? Every possible reason was embarrassing, and probably not to be believed.

Undecided but wanting to do something, she stood outside her small tent, smoothing the tangles of her curls, longing to wash the dust of hard travel from her hair and body.

Joseph and Beth propelled her to action.

From the lean-to across the tiny clearing, the unmistakable sounds of vigorous mating assailed Anne's ears, and she found herself, moments later, with her feet upon the path to the stream pool. The moon made it an easy walk through the dense undergrowth; her endless dreaming of the place added a certain caution. Could she face the memory of such exquisite dream-passion when there was no possibility that it would ever come true?

Yes, it was time, she told herself, to set aside girlish fancies of what she would do in the pool if she could, to face life's hard reality, and, thus hardened, to help John face it, as well. He seemed, well, not to have grasped the full implications of his condition, although, she admitted reluctantly, it might just be his stubborn male desire not to discuss unpleasant things with a woman who was eager to explore them thoroughly.

Anne reached the huge rock jutting into the stream where she and Beth and the other maids had cleaned the milk churns and buckets, and where she had met John in countless images of lovemaking. Below her, the cool water was just as she had remembered it through so many dreaming nights.

Moonlight glinted off the ripples, lighting the gentle downstream flow. And from faint crystals half buried in the smooth stones that lined the streambed, moonbeams sent pink sparks at sharp angles into the night. Over all, the earthy musk-green scent of close-growing trees and water lilies and bracken pervaded the air.

She scrambled out onto the rock and stripped off her gown and smallclothes, hanging them on a tree branch.

Then, slowly, she slid up to her waist in the water. A little gasp escaped her when the cool stream enveloped her warmer body, its gentle current tugging at her buttocks, but almost at once she was thoroughly used to its cool, clean smell.

In the gentle night breeze, the o'er-arching trees met to rub their branches together, their leaves whispering secrets in the night. She stood for some time, her arms floating out at her sides, her fingers splayed upon the surface, water weaving through them, replaying all those loving scenes at Nell's that had finally revealed her true feelings for John Gilbert to her.

But she conjured those scenes far too well, and ultimately she shrank from any further remembering. It was just too painful, and she must be practical. What was not to be must not ever be thought of, especially in such tantalizing particulars.

She ducked her head under the water, scrubbing briskly at her scalp, as if to harshly knuckle away any thought of what had been and might still be if not for Edward's perfidy.

Flinging the curly mane up, she squeezed excess moisture from it between her hands, then tossed it behind her shoulders. Water drenched her eyelids, droplets hung from her lashes and she rubbed them to clear her vision.

John Gilbert stood on the bank—no, actually his feet were already gliding into the water—and he was naked.

"Johnny," she cried, or thought she cried, and her throaty voice caught on his name, although she was pleased that he had joined her dream. So pleased, in truth, that she called him again. Why shouldn't she? This *was* a dream. In reality, they were both back at the campsite, sound asleep, because there before her, John Gilbert was a whole man; in fact, he was whole enough for two men.

Could she be feverish or mad? No, of course not. She had seen him naked before at Nell's and on the doctor's barge, thus this was a mere memory projected into her sleep. A woman could not encounter John Gilbert's privy parts without afterward remembering them in detail quite well indeed. Even ill unto death near London Bridge, John Gilbert had been magnificent and somewhat mysterious, as men are without their clothes.

She smiled and closed her eyes, giving herself over more completely to her sleep fantasy, knowing that all too soon she would awaken to a more bitter reality.

Later, she promised she would absolutely not chastise herself for this dream. It was perfectly understandable that in this harmless way, her sleeping body reached out for what her real body would never know again. It might even be a heavenly compensation to help her face the future with a man who would year by year become less and less a man and more a—she shuddered at the despised and pitied name that she banned from her lips—eunuch.

"Thank you, God, for this one last dream, then, but I pray you, send me no more," she murmured, hearing John move through the water toward her; in fact, she could feel the push of water against her legs. Truly, this was the most authentic of all her night visions of him. Eyes wide now, she determined that she would make this one last as long as she could. She took two steps toward him.

John wrenched his gaze from the quivering orbs of her rose-tipped ivory breasts and the ripples lapping at the full curve of her hips and the tantalizing dark triangle just beginning below her gently swelling stomach, and waited for her cry of happiness. None came, though he could see she stared straight upon his stiffened cod, no mistake. Instead, her lips held a trembling smile, and her arms were opened to him.

The foxy chit! She had guessed all along, and all that earnest talk by Oxford Road on their trip from London had been a great jape. He had fallen for it like some young bumpkin. The jest was truly on him.

He threw back his head and roared a rogue's laugh, the hearty sound bouncing from bank to bank and then back to her ears again.

Anne's eyes opened wider. "You've never laughed in my dreams before."

Her eyes were glazed and her face held a strange out-of-this-world look, and thus John knew that he'd made a mistake.

Her hand reached out and touched his arm. Then she grasped it and pinched hard.

"Sink me, Anne," he yelled, flinching away, "but you have fingers strong enough for a witch's imp."

"You," she said, her voice quavering. "You!" she said again, and it was an unspeakable accusation.

Regret twisted his heart because her surprise at his lack of a "condition" was obvious. He had perhaps misjudged her; at the least, he owed her an explanation. "Anne, you must try to understand why I did not tell you. There's been no time—"

"Time!" she shrieked, her damp hair flying about her shoulders, her eyes two eddies of green wrath. "There's been

time to make a fool of me, to laugh at my most earnest re-
flections. Oh, how you must have reveled—"

"Never!" he said. "Listen to me." He laid both hands
firmly upon her arms, but she wrenched away like some
slippery eel and flailed through the water toward the bank.

John caught her as she reached the shore in the only way
he could: by grabbing her ankles and pulling her halfway
back into the water. He was having great difficulty keeping
his grasp on her; in her fury, she coiled and twisted like a
fish on a hook.

He crawled onto the bank, and because she was clawing
at him, he had to crawl over her to protect himself from her
punishing hands and feet.

"Stop it, Anne. You must listen to me," he panted in her
ear, and finally, she lay subdued, her face a thundercloud of
wrath under his. But just in case she planned a further attack,
he held both of her wrists in his one hand, and with his other,
he accommodatingly broke off a fern frond, which she was
furiously trying to blow away from her mouth.

"Thank you," she said, though the words held no gratitude.

"One would think," he replied, his heated lips close to
hers and his naked body pressed against the full, fragrant
length of her, "that you actually meant those saintly words
you spoke on Oxford Road about loving the excellent man I
was and not needing me for any reasons of animal lust or
pleasure."

"I did mean them," she said, pushing the words between
clenched teeth, her proud head thrown back, her chin thrust
high as best she could manage.

He kissed her then, a long and lingering kiss that left her
aquiver. Indignant, she tried to bite him, and he nipped her
lower lip in reprisal. "Admit it, minx," he said, "you only
wanted to mean them."

She pressed her lips together, her irate eyes, caught by a
moonbeam, flashing up at him. "I might have known that a

coarse jester like you could not possibly understand the tender feelings of a—um, a—" She sputtered to a stop.

"Martyr," he finished for her, then began kissing her again, and this time her lips seemed warmer and just a bit less rigid to him. Yes, decidedly less rigid. "I will not apologize for standing before you more a man than you thought," he said, lifting his head at last to look full in her face, and trying to keep his tone serious, although he was full aware of the ludicrous nature of having to defend the presence of his cod to a lady whom he wanted very much to bed again, and unless he was sorely mistaken, wanted him as much. "I am sorry that you are disappointed, my dear Anne," he said, feigning sadness.

She shook her head, totally nettled. "Of course I'm not disappointed! How can you say that? I suffered mightily when I thought—" Remembering the extent of her suffering, her face softened, and she began to feel quite a bit silly. "Loose my hands now," she said softly.

He did so, and on his knees beside her, he lifted her completely out of the water and pulled her gently up the bank where he'd left his clothes. He spread his shirt on the tender young ferns and sat her upon it. She shivered slightly, although the night air was full of warm zephyrs. Shyly, she closed her legs and crossed her arms about her exposed breasts.

"How?" she asked, and the trembling word held all her wondering.

"Your emerald ring for a bribe, my sweet Anne, and the cod of a poor dead wretch for proof."

She shuddered. "Edward was so sure."

John nodded grimly. "It never occurred to his late lordship, Anne, that commoners and servants would dare thwart his will."

Forgetting her nakedness, she caught his hand up in both her own. "In truth, John, how could you possibly think that I would be disappointed that you escaped such a horrible indignity? It's just that I had—well, I had made up my mind to be brave, and now I have to get used to—"

"More?" He grinned at her, and the white of his teeth was contrasted against his bronzed skin most agreeably. "I will see that you do not get too used to it, Anne."

Anne watched him, her face accepting but not yet quite forgiving. She dropped his hand. The knave deserved a dose of his own medicine. "In time," she said, shifting her arms to cover more of herself. "In a few months, perhaps mere weeks, possibly, I think that I could forgive your deception."

But she could not continue the pretense, because she was becoming more and more painfully aware that they were both as naked as babes. Clothes provided a barricade between woman and man, and without those defenses she could not hide her body's yearnings from him. Two spots of red flamed in her cheeks, a white heat racing through her blood. She watched fascinated as his restless fingers danced upon his knees where he knelt, and his hungry eyes swept her up and down and side to side.

Through the treetops she saw the moon and stars glittering high against the dome of the night sky. If she did not touch him, or he her, she felt that the world would turn empty and cold, to stay that way evermore. But how to give in after his deception without it seeming to be in utter capitulation?

Anne smiled slightly with what she hoped was just the right amount of encouragement. "Do you remember on the barge after your illness?"

He didn't nod or shake his head, but continued to watch her. One hand did snake out, and his finger began to trace the inner line of her arm. It didn't seem deliberate, just a thoughtless gesture, but he didn't stop.

"I told you," she continued softly, without shifting her arm, "that I had decided to forswear my station in life as I had my oath of chastity."

"I remember," he said, "and I thought that I had nothing

to offer you but a felon's death." His lazy finger made the figure eight at the hollow point where her shoulder met her neck.

She thought she ought to tell him to stop, but he aroused the most amazing sensations with just the tip of one finger. Perhaps she shouldn't be too hard on him after what he'd almost been through, even though he had played the most appalling trick on her, one that no true gentleman would. . . .

John's one finger became his entire hand, and he slid it around, under her damp hair to the nape of her neck. Although he applied no pressure to pull her face to his, she felt as if he could at any moment, and tipped slightly toward him to thwart the move.

"You must know what you're doing," she said, and although she had meant for her voice to be sharp, it was not. Rather, it sounded languid and distant, especially when he cupped her breast with his other hand.

The hand on her breast didn't move in any lascivious way; it seemed a harmless, even friendly gesture. One finger played with her nipple, until he lowered his mouth to kiss it. She shuddered violently.

"Are you cold?" he asked, and gently lay back with her upon his shirt, and took her against his body, which was not cold.

Anne could feel his breath coming in great whooshes. Or was it hers? "I have never been warmer," she admitted, her voice faraway and strange to her own ears.

They lay there, silent, trembling against each other, until with a groan John rose, and hung suspended on his hands over her. "Is there aught more that I can do for your comfort, my lady? If there is, you must ask politely."

She stared at him, no longer trusting her voice. Nothing she meant to say seemed to come out the right way, and all the time there was a burning, radiating fire below her belly that made talking at all seem lunatic. Was she moving back into her dream, helpless to stop it now or to want to? She lifted her body to him.

He kissed her softly but insistently and she longed for more, but a lady could not ask. Could she? God's bowels, but his face was handsome in the moonlight.

"Are you glad," he asked, "or are you sorry that I am whole?" He shifted his body closer still to hers, although she would have thought it impossible.

"Glad, my Johnny," she said, half mocking him with words he might have said himself, "although mightily inconvenienced at times." She heard him chuckle softly, and felt disinclined to argue further. "Perhaps it will not take weeks to forgive you, after all," she said, her arms creeping up his hard muscled back.

"How long, then?" he asked, pinning her closer to him, his mouth finding the most tender parts of her, and she didn't care that she heard the bedeviling in his voice.

"As long as it will take to truly know that I am loved."

"Do you not know it now, sweetest Anne?"

Her mouth stopped his rush of words as she pressed herself against his lips, felt the hardness of his ripe manhood against her stomach, felt the wild racing of her blood and promptly forgot the question.

John Gilbert was burning as he felt her pink-and-white body join with his. He touched her, kissed her everywhere at once, although he could scarcely bear the distance between them that permitted such activities.

As her moans increased, he sucked at the air for fear he could not get enough. Blood pounded through him, and its pulsing seemed to match hers. His fingers dug into the flesh of her hips, and she lifted to him. Fleetingly, he thought that she was delightfully helpful for a highborn lady, and then was lost in her for good and all.

For long moments, Anne arched against John on the riverbank as they dwelled in one another, suspended under the moon. John thrust into the empty secret part of her, his cod swelling and filling her completely, deeply. Her fingers dug into his back, and her voice called out his name, begging him not to stop, never to stop.

What she had once girlishly feared as a conquering invasion was actually something quite wonderfully different. In a searing, sweet instant, she gave the precious gift of all herself to him that would now go to no other man, whether she married John Gilbert or not. She was filled and complete again, with more sense of belonging than she'd ever known, as his scalding torrent of love poured into her.

A cry of ecstasy hung for a long moment above the moon-silvered pond. Anne cried out, or John cried out; perhaps the cry came from both of them together. A time passed while they clutched each other as though newly born twins fearful of separation.

"Does it still hurt you, sweetest angel?" John asked, his voice catching on each word.

Anne breathed deeply, relaxing a little as her breath returned, although not enough to release her hold on his cod. "It was a most wondrous hurt, John, a right warming sensation."

He pushed an auburn curl from over one of her lovely eyes. "A sensation that you would care to repeat?"

"Oh, yes, Johnny," she said, her face luminous with reflected moonlight. "Haven't I always said it? You are a most excellent man."

"Then I take it," he teased, "that you still have no regret forswearing your oath of chastity."

"It seems a miserly treasure now, and almost forgotten to memory," she said, her fingers roaming upon his face and twining through his dark hair, so that he began to stiffen again inside her. "But think you not that I have given up chastity forever, darling Johnny."

"A woman is either chaste or not. To be both seems impossible e'en for such a determined woman as you," he said, amused by the wonder of her, drinking in her face, cradled below him in the crook of his arm.

"In truth, not impossible," she said, and her lustful green gaze did seem to devour his form. " 'Take me to you, imprison me, for I—' "

John took up the next line from John Donne's sonnet: " 'Except you enthrall me, never shall be free—' "

" 'Nor ever chaste," she whispered, "except you ravish me.' "

And so to content her, he ravished her again, but this time slowly, letting her lead the way, allowing her to guide his hands and cod where she wanted them. And where she wanted them made him smile.

The moon was very low, and in the east the first hint of morning sunlight shone on the treetops before John and Anne could bring themselves to think about returning to the campsite. For hours they had lain, talking and swearing their love with their eyes, lips and hands, without any weariness; he declaring that there was never a woman so fair or fearless, and she that never was a man so handsome or gallant.

And as women often do, when the moment came to end a night of love, she clung to him, while tears of joy spilled from her eyes.

He began to kiss them away, to reassure her. "Nothing has ended, sweet Anne. Everything has started." He cleared his throat. "If you are serious about giving up your title to become plain Mistress Gilbert, then I will marry you. . . . For your promise of obedience."

"Won't you ever be serious?" she asked, smiling happily.

"I have not heard your answer, minx. Whisper it in my ear."

He bent close to her mouth. "Yes, oh, yes, and soon," he heard.

And for both of them, their lust began once again to rise.

It might have taken hours longer to return to the clearing had not pistol shots rung through the clear morning air.

"Dress yourself," he ordered, and began to hastily don his clothes and sword. Her gown in place, he handed her his pistol. "Stay here and wait until I come back for you."

But when he started for the campsite, she was close behind him, pistol cocked. He knew it was useless to try to stop her.

Chapter Twenty-two

A Fight for Love and Life

Without hesitation, John stepped from the shelter of the thick woods into the clearing. Running to keep up with his long strides, Anne was not two steps behind him, her pistol at the ready. From all the signs of disarray, Black Ben had overwhelmed Joseph and the others in a dawn raid.

John and Anne left the woods unseen. Everyone was watching Black Ben fumble greedily through the contents of Josiah Wyndham's case, and the doctor was saying, "—And a graduate of the University of Padua, with a specialty in the secret and sacred alchemical arts of the transmutation of base metals into gold."

Anne couldn't help smiling at the familiar bravado, but Black Ben was not entertained. He waved a long dirk in the doctor's face. "Ye canting rogue," he sneered. "Can ye cut a purse, steal a portmanteau, slit a throat? Those are the arts I prize."

The doctor drew himself to his full height. "Then I have naught to interest you. I do not take without return, for that would be pure villainy. If I cannot cure, I leave behind confidence, an art sadly lacking in most common men."

Kate struggled against the arms that held her pinned. "Thee must know, Friend Ben, that thee addresses the most

famous physician, Josiah Wyndham, late of London, called
to Whitehall Palace by the king himself."

A smile played upon Ben's wickedly scarred face. "A
Quaker doxy, as I live. If ye talked such a one to your bed,
Doctor, ye may have special powers as ye say." He flicked
the dirk close to Wyndham's nose before the doctor could
deny the slur on Kate's honor.

Ben slowly and deliberately stuck the tip of the knife into
one of the doctor's nostrils. "If ye and the lass would live,
surgeon, and join this rogue's company, we would test thy
skill here and now. I will cut off thy nose, and for sport
watch ye sew it on again. 'Twould be better than a cockfight.
What say, lads?"

Ben whirled to face the semicircle of men, and spied
John Gilbert and Anne advancing from the woods.

"Loose the doctor without harm, Ben," John said, in a
voice deepened with command, not interrupting his stride.

"Ye be giving no more orders here, Gentleman Johnny,"
Ben said, his face a blotched mix of triumph and rage. "Take
him, lads, and bring his wanton to me, for she be wanting
another straddle, from the looks of 'er!"

"Have a care, John!" yelled Joseph, being held down on
the ground by three men sitting atop him.

John faced some of his own former band now under
Ben's command, his sword point dancing, and they were obviously reluctant to advance on him further.

"Good day to you, young Francis," John called, "and you,
Alexander and Dick. Is this the way you greet a sworn
brother of the society, and your elected leader? I thought I
taught you better manners." He smiled at them, and hesitat-
ing but an instant, they smiled back in right good humor.

Francis spoke, a bit shamefaced. "Ben said ye wouldn't
be back, Johnny; he said ye'd lost thy nerve over yon woman."

John shrugged, a friendly smile upon his face. "As you
see with your own eyes, lads, I am back. If Ben is wrong
about my return, mayhap he's wrong about my nerve."

Anne was happy to hear a slight murmur of thoughtful agreement from John's old band, who seemed to hold themselves somewhat aloof from Black Ben's men.

Ben drew a pistol and pointed it at John. "I'll kill yon bleating cock—the devil take me if I don't!"

Swiftly, Anne stepped from behind John and pointed her pistol at Black Ben.

"Nay, Anne," John said without taking his gaze from Ben. "Stay out of this."

"If you die, Johnny," Anne said calmly, sighting down the barrel, "I'll send Black Ben to hell and save the hangman a pleasure."

"Mark ye, lads," Ben roared, his head bobbing exultantly, "how John Gilbert be ruled by this doxy, and unfit to command brave men of the road."

John laughed, rather too raucously, Anne thought. "Ben, you were ever mistaking the ladies. Any good man can command men, but no man alive can command e'en one good woman unless she wishes it." John flashed a grin and a wink at his men. "But we know how to help her to wish it, don't we, lads?"

"Do you, indeed?" Anne said, not too quietly from the side of her mouth.

"I'll have to show you later, when I'm not quite so occupied," John replied, his rapier in constant, dancing motion.

The men facing them laughed and nodded at the banter, and their hands were relaxed upon their weapons.

With a bellow, Ben stuck his pistol in his belt and bolted to within a few steps of John, there drawing his sword. A few of his own men moved up behind him in support. Ben eyed John's old band, his face seething with black rage. "Ye be but a gutless crew, the lot a ye; I'll have ye up on articles as soon as I've carved my name on the arse of this bastard son of a nobleman's poxy milkmaid."

Although the warming sun was rapidly burning off the early morning forest haze, John felt icy cold when he heard the detested word "bastard." He held himself rigid for a moment, while some of Ben's band edged along behind him. Mentally, he shook himself to be rid of all anger; he'd have to use all his wits if he would rid the road of Black Ben, and somewhat more importantly, if he would save his and Anne's lives. Since Anne had said yes to marrying him last night by the moonlit pool, living had suddenly taken on a far greater significance for him.

John watched every expression on the evil highwayman's face. "Black Ben, I deny your right to lead my men." John's clipped voice rose again in command. "You did use lies and promises of gold to entice them to sign with you, and under Article VII, I have the prerogative to challenge your election."

Black Ben roared, his tongue stumbling over the word. "What's this prerogative?"

Under the weight of a man sitting on his chest, Joseph the blacksmith managed to gasp, "In truth, John Gilbert has the right of duel. When a patrico be unmade *in absentia,* he may challenge the new man to a fight and choose the weapons."

"Shut his month," Ben raged. "He be no London lawyer."

Young Francis stepped forward now, his hand on his sword hilt. "I can read, lads," he announced to all the assembled men, "and that be what the article rightly says."

One of Ben's own men, emboldened, added, "It could bring shame on all the fraternity if ye fight him not, Ben."

Ben's face was swollen and red when he pulled the pistol from his belt, and shot his own man where the man stood, although from the sound of his outraged screams, not fatally. Two friends dragged him to one side, and Dr. Wyndham and Kate went to his aid.

John smiled, his eyes and voice cool. He knew how the highwayman used bursts of violence to intimidate. "Ben, you seem not to remember a great many articles of the brotherhood you claim to lead. There's likewise one about punishment coming from the will of the majority."

Again, there was a general approving murmur from the crowd, and although obviously wary, some of the men turned stern faces to Black Ben.

Anne had kept her pistol on Ben, but now she was quivering with both fear and pride. Ben was a mad brute, killing and maiming from pure bloodlust, but he was cunning, too. He must know that her brave John was maneuvering him into a position where he should fight or lose stature with his men. Strange. It seemed that no one set more store by their law than these outlaws, who themselves broke royal decree every day.

Ben swaggered a few steps along the line of men, ignoring the pitiful cries of the man he'd just shot. "Ye'd have me fight this dainty Gentleman Johnny, then, lads, fight this feeble bird in a tart's cage." He circled yet again, his back to John.

Without warning, Ben whirled, his sword clearing his baldric, and lunged at John. But John had expected a trick and sidestepped, shoving Anne into friendly hands in the same movement. "Hold her, Beth!"

John leaped lightly across the fire pit, gaining the seconds he needed to strip his shirt and wrap it quickly about his sword arm to shield the flesh. A man could fight with a wound anywhere but on his sword arm.

Anne struggled briefly against Beth's hold on her.

"Stop, Anne," Beth said. "Do ye not see that sometimes we must let our men fight alone?"

"Nay," Anne said, panting, "I do *not* see. I do not want to see."

A huge lump formed in her throat, past which she could scarcely swallow or breathe. Ben was huge in weight, many stone heavier than John, although John had about the same height and reach. But Ben had another advantage. He carried a heavier saber, while John favored the lighter, faster French rapier.

"Lay on!" The clearing rang with the vigorous male cry as Ben and John crossed swords.

At first John seemed to be losing. He parried, over and over, backing away from the bigger man's overwhelming two-handed slash and thrust. It was several minutes before Anne realized that John was fighting with his wits as well as his good right arm.

"Stand and fight, Johnny, if ye be a man," Ben puffed, windy as a big man who loved his ale and pipe too much. "Ye run about like a little minx with a tattle to tell."

Some of Ben's men cheered at this taunt, but John didn't change his strategy, smiling and retreating, motioning insolently for Ben to catch him if he could.

Infuriated, Ben lunged repeatedly, slipping once on the blood of the man he'd shot. He hit the ground hard and lay sprawled on his back, the breath temporarily knocked out of him.

John did not move in for the kill. Instead, he grabbed Anne and twirled her into a dance step, and then back to Beth, where he soundly kissed them both. It was just the kind of bravado that had made his men love him.

"Are you lunatic, Johnny?" Anne asked, much to the delight of all who heard, except Ben, who was finally lumbering to his feet, nearly blind with frustration and sweat.

He swiped at his eyes with his sleeve. "Stand still, you playacting dog," he bellowed, charging.

John bowed slightly, gesturing elegantly like a gentleman actor in the King's Company, and jumped away, circling ceaselessly just out of reach of Ben's bulk. John couldn't allow the big man to corner him, because speed was a swordsman's greatest weapon. For precious minutes, he parried and danced just beyond his enemy's slashing saber.

"Huzzah, Johnny! Huzzah!" The cheer roared in John's ears each time steel rang against steel. At least he was winning back the loyalty of his own men.

But Ben's men rallied to their leader. "Make him eat dirt, Ben!" yelled a lieutenant. "Show him the better man!"

John laughed, taunting Ben from atop a rock outcropping. "He's a man of breeches only, lads. E'en the devil himself can't correct a life of defect and fault at this late hour."

But Ben, though he was gasping as if his lungs could not get enough air, wasn't finished. Stooping, he grabbed up a handful of dried and crumbled leaves from the forest floor, tossing the whole in John's face with a mock of his own. "I'll straddle thy wench yet this day, Johnny! Think on that!"

Blinded by dirt and leaves, John heard Anne's warning shout an instant before he felt the white-hot, sharp bite of Ben's blade in the flesh at his side, and the jarring impact of metal bouncing off his ribs.

Devil take it! John blinked furiously, swallowing a cry of pain, and cleared his vision just in time to parry a blow aimed for his gut. It seemed Ben planned a slow death for John Gilbert.

He clutched his side, trying to close the wound with his fingers. If he slowed or if he lost too much blood, Ben would win the day. There were too many ways for Ben to prevail.

Determined to end it while he yet had strength, John whirled and caught Ben a glancing blow upon the shoulder of his sword arm. Ben twisted to the right, but John reversed and came up on his left side, thrust, felt the flesh of Ben's breast open, then pushed his blade through that huge body as hard as he could. Ben grunted inches from John's face, and he tasted Ben's sour spittle upon his lips.

For a moment, the forest stayed its ceaseless movement. Branches did not wave in the breeze, birds did not fly, no men or women in the clearing shifted in their tracks.

Black Ben stood straight, very still, his eyes terribly alert, his body leaning forward as John pulled out the rapier, almost as if he desired it to remain to fill the small, round, bloody hole its removal revealed.

A thin trickle of red edged from between his lips as he

stood there, sneering at John. "Bastard, you'll never keep her. Waverby lives and works for the Hollanders. . . ." he whispered, and then fell, dying on his way to the ground.

For a moment, John was as dazed as the men in the clearing, hope draining away faster than the blood from his wound.

Anne, fearing the calm would not last, cried out, "Huzzah!" and at once several of John's old band took it up. Even Joseph was on his feet, shouting, his guards having left him to examine the body of their slain leader, and pull it out of the way under a tree. But not all joined the cheer, and Anne feared that John and his loyal men would be badly outnumbered if Ben's band decided to fight.

"Beth," Anne said, "where is the arms chest?"

Beth pointed to an open coffer not twenty feet away under the big lean-to.

Anne raced for it. "Follow me, Beth," she called, but didn't wait to see if Beth followed.

Anne knew that she would have at best a minute, not enough time to load the pistols. She snatched up a sword. She heard the faithful Beth behind. "Good Beth, arm yourself and Joseph. John will need all of us."

Anne ran headlong into the menacing circle that Ben's men were forming around John. She did not think, but brandished her sword, remembering the heft of it and the stance John had taught her, all the while smiling at him helplessly. Somebody shouted her name, but she could not tell who. Then the warm green smell of Whittlewood Forest in her nostrils connected her to John again, and she heard and saw no other.

John groaned, holding his wound. "For God's sweet pity, Anne! Won't you stay out of this?"

She placed her back against his. "Censure me later, my best beloved. Do not let them think we disagree." She waved her sword at the sullen men whose mouths were now agape with surprise.

John smiled, his teeth held tight. "Would I think of dis-
agreeing with you?"

"You might," she said, shifting slowly about as he moved
cautiously to face Ben's crew. "You might imagine that I can
only sigh and lament, love and preen. Is that what you
think?"

"Only in my most demented fancy, my lady," he said.

"Well, I am no such woman!"

His bloody hand left his wounded side and reached for
her hand, and she took it. "No, you are no such woman, nor
is such a woman what I wa-nt." The word broke apart and
she heard it, but she also heard the sadness in what followed.
"In truth, Anne, though all be for nothing, did I ever have a
second choice?"

"No," she whispered, love warming her voice again. "Nor
did I, but what do you mean all for nothing?"

Young Francis, Alexander, Dick and some of the old band
stepped into the circle. "We be with ye, Johnny. If thy fine
lady will fight with ye, then we can do no less. Right, lads?"

Armed, Joseph and Beth marched into the center of the
small group. And Josiah Wyndham, holding Kate, stepped
courageously into the closing circle, without a weapon.

A quick count and Anne realized that they were still outnumbered two to one.

John faced Ben's chief lieutenant. "I have no quarrel with
you, Izaak. Tell me, why should we fight and kill each
other?"

"For the treasure," the man growled. "Ben said ye had
buried enough gold bars and jewels for to suit the king's
whores."

John shook his head. "Ben lied out of pure meanness or
madness, God rest his rotten soul."

Izaak didn't have the look of belief on his face.

John boldly took a step nearer the man, keeping Anne behind him. "Answer me, Izaak. How much treasure do you
and your men have buried?"

"None, as ye well know," Izaak sneered in a good imitation of his dead leader, glancing about to see where his support lay.

"Well then, sink me, Izaak, if I understand how you think me wealthy. The road is a rich enough place, but expenses are high and pleasures come dear. Between the innkeepers and the lasses and the bribes, what highwayman has more than a guinea at a time in his breeches?"

Some of Ben's men nodded in agreement, some even smiled, and John shifted his arguments to them. "We're all beggared, lads, long before we swing on Tyburn. That is why I am quitting the road."

Izaak frowned, reclaiming his right to speak for Ben's men. "It be true, then, Johnny? Ye have a royal pardon?"

"Aye, Izaak, I do, for me and any man who docs wish to follow me to a more righteous life."

"Breaking my back on some cottager's farm for three pounds annum."

"Aye, or breaking your neck on the last long step at Tyburn. 'Tis a man's choice." John lifted his voice so that all could hear. "Either way, lads, what good do we gain fighting each other at this place? I welcome any man who joins me, and I leave Oxford Road to any who don't. You know me well, and you know me as no mean trickster. What could be a fairer offer, I ask you?"

From their faces, it was clear to Anne that John's bold arguments appealed to the majority of Ben's old band. Alive, Ben would have fought to the last man's blood, but Izaak seemed to have been made of sounder mind or weaker stomach. A score of Ben's men stepped away with Izaak from John's small group. They stood at a distance, whispering together earnestly.

Anne was determined not to give way to her fears for John. "Your wound," she said, modulating the tremor in her voice.

He stared down at it. "The bleeding is almost stopped."

"Do you want some ale?"

"I shall drink later, and well, when the good doctor sews me up."

She was quivering inside, and she despised the weakness that made her want to fall down in a heap of tears now, or worse, to run away and hide. Facing death was not so difficult, she'd learned well of late. But afterward was hell. It must be the incredible and sentimental realization of how close she had come to losing everything so recently gained: love, pleasure and the desire for a long life with one man. Would it have been better never to know such feelings?

Ben's men were edging toward them again. Anne raised her sword point, scorning her moment of cowardice and indecision.

"What say you, Izaak?" John asked, seemingly at ease, but Anne could sense his terrible vigilance.

"John Gilbert, ye affirm that we have all brotherhood rights to contributions on Oxford Road?"

"I do, and heartily."

Izaak nodded. "Powder and shot, too," he said.

"Take half our supply, and welcome," John answered.

Izaak smiled, and tossed his head at his men, several of whom began to pick up more than half the supplies. "We thank ye, Johnny. Now, we'll just take the doxies and be on our way right peaceable."

John smiled easily, but there was steel in his voice. "The ladies stay unless they vote to join you."

"They have no say in this," Izaak said, and his manner was menacing. This was the first challenge to his authority.

"Our articles say they have a vote. Even Ben knew that," John replied, his soft tone deceiving no one, least of all Izaak.

"I vote to stay by John Gilbert," Anne said hastily.

"I vote to stay," Beth said, and an openly shocked Kate managed the words firmly, as well.

Izaak watched the women with resentful eyes, and Anne

thought for a very long moment, watching his hand creep toward his pistol, that he would defy John, but the highwayman suddenly stumped off out of the clearing. "There be doxies aplenty, boys," Izaak roared with forced heartiness. "It's bad luck to e'er take them on the road." Ben's men trailed behind him, Ben's body and the man he shot forgotten under a tree.

"Now to that wound," Dr. Wyndham announced to John. "You'll not be able to travel for several days, mayhap a week."

"I cannot wait so long," John answered, and there was no arguing with his tone.

Though Anne looked at him in puzzlement, this was no place to dissent.

After the time of deadly uncertainty in the forest clearing, the afternoon and evening hours were almost worse for Anne. By the time the doctor had cauterized, stitched and bandaged the wound, John was thankfully very drunk. They carried him to the tented sleeping place and laid him beside the man Ben had shot. Anne watched for signs of fever through the hours while John slept soundly, and while Ben was buried with words said by Joseph that were more suitable than the evil highwayman deserved.

After dark, Anne sponged the still-sleeping John's face once again, kissed his lips and then joined the others around the fire for a quick meal.

Later, John woke and saw the man Ben had shot, lying beside him, eyes open and staring at him. John's side was throbbing, so that he dared not move too quickly. "What is your name, man?" he asked, slowing inching up on one elbow.

"Mathew, sir, and I had no love for that dog, Black Ben, and I long to leave the road."

"Then stay with us, Mathew, and take up the king's pardon."

The man spoke eagerly. "Gladly, Gentleman Johnny, if yon men of yours be giving me a place."

"I will speak for you." He slowly extended his hand to shake and seal the bargain. "Now you can help me. Ben said Lord Waverby survives and spies for the Hollanders against his own king and country."

"Aye. They were a pair, old Ben and his lordship. Ben said that Waverby didn't die on *The Folly* but be captured by none other than Admiral de Ruyter himself, and gone over to the Dutch."

"Why would he risk exile or a traitor's death?"

"There's much I be not knowing but what I heard when Ben and Izaak thought me sleeping. The Hollanders be giving Lord Waverby a ship and slave trading rights in Guinea for spying on the court. The king will think him a great hero for escaping the Hollanders, and no one will know he plays a double game. Waverby promised Ben a free hand and protection in the county for a thousand a year, since ye were meant to dance at the end of a rope once you took ship to Jamaica."

John smiled without mirth. "We'll see, Mathew, who is the better dancer."

With a great effort, John pulled himself to his feet and walked out slowly. Joseph, coming from the necessary house, handed him a slender packet. "I took this from Ben afore he be buried, Johnny, and ye know I do not have my letters." John nodded his thanks as Joseph joined the others but stayed just beyond the firelight to listen.

"Where be we going now?" Joseph asked one and all, his worry obvious. "Johnny is right that we'll be blamed for half that Izaak's men do, or more like twice their felonies. Even with the king's pardon, we'll swing in short time. The Sheriff of Oxfordshire is not a friend without our guineas in his pocket."

Dr. Wyndham sat close by Kate. "Too bad we are at war with the Hollanders, or we could settle there."

"And I hate the Frenchies and their ways," young Francis said.

"Quakers can be put to death in France and Spain," Kate said quietly.

"Not in the colonies," Anne said.

"Aye," Kate said sadly, "in Boston colony they have hanged."

"But surely not in the Virginia colony," Anne said hopefully, watching the sparks from the fire rise and disappear into the black night above her.

Kate looked at her. "I don't know about Virginia."

"Tell us, Anne," said Beth.

"It is a wondrous place; the king himself did tell me," Anne said. "I have a royal grant of land in Virginia. We'd be safe, all of us, and we could build a new life."

Joseph pounded one huge fist into the other. "I want no new country or new life," he said, looking at Beth, who nodded agreement. "This be my home. Here in Whittlewood Forest, I be staying to rebuild all that Ben destroyed."

"I am most sorry, Anne," the doctor replied, putting his arm around Kate, "but I am a man of science. There are medical advancements coming to this land, wonderful and astonishing, and I would be a part of them. I could not be who I am in a wilderness," he added, dropping his voice to a rumbling whisper, "or find a market for my miracle salve amongst the savages."

A little breeze rose from the center of Whittlewood and cooled them as Anne looked about, resigned. She had never seen faces more determined than the ones before her, shining in the firelight as if in a rare and lovely new dream of the future. "It was but an idle thought," she said.

She had not been aware that John had come from the lean-to and stood listening to her. When she did see him, something in his face caused her heart to beat a sudden alarm in her breast. Still, she spoke cheerfully, as if words alone could erase doubt. "John, shall we tell them our plans?"

For answer, he turned on his heel and disappeared silently into the dark woods.

Chapter Twenty-three

We Love but Cannot Dream

Anne knew where John had gone, and followed the path to the stream pond, lit by the same bright moon that had shone on their love the night before.

She came upon him as she had hoped, sitting in the fern bower, the fronds still crushed and wilted from their feverish bodies. Was it just a few hours ago that they had lain together as if they would never again lie apart, and now in some way she could not divine they were separated?

Although John did not turn or greet her in any way, she saw beneath the dark locks that lay about his shoulders a tensing of the muscles on his bronzed back, bare except for the white undershift bandage wrapped across his ribs, a dark red spot centered on his side.

She sat down very close to him but without touching. "Johnny, tell me what have I done to anger you so?" she asked, half not wanting to know the answer, and half a bit wrathful that she had need to ask.

He studied his hands flat on his knees, glancing at some papers spread upon the ground in the bracken, and when he spoke his voice was a stranger's voice. "I love you, Anne, but we cannot wed."

"Why?" she asked, and attempted to postpone with amusing argument what he might answer. "You may not make the best of husbands, but you would suit me quite well."

"Waverby lives."

She was smiling, but it faded at his words. "What jape is this, Johnny? Edward went down with his ship. The king himself acknowledged me a widow."

John nodded, a terrible concentration in his voice. "The king was wrong."

Anne didn't want to hear him, and so she didn't. "I know aught but that I love you." When a look of utter despair crossed his face, Anne rushed on. "In truth, I do not come to you with the large portion that my father settled on Edward. It seems that English widows do not fare well by the law. My uncle, the bishop, explained to me while I lay hurt abed in the palace. I may have my pin money from the marriage settlement and the right to hearth and food with Edward's family, but all of my father's estate goes to them, and all of Edward's property outside London, as well. I could go to the Court of Chancery and claim Waverby House in London, but his younger brother would sue and it could take years and a fortune to the lawyers." She shuddered involuntarily at the thought. "The Virginia land is all that I have in this world in my own name, but it is yours, too, if you will but reach out and take it, John."

She took his hand, and his fingers immediately twined through hers as before. But when he looked at her, he stared as though she were a child to be placated with fatherly reason.

"Anne," he said, and his voice caressed her name as if he'd never truly spoken it before, "it's not your widow's dowry that would stop me. You must listen e'en though you don't want to hear. Waverby is alive! You are no widow."

Anne gasped. "I don't believe. . . ."

"Hush, sweeting, and listen close. Ben taunted me with the news before he died, and his wounded man, Mathew, and letters on Ben's body both confirm its truth. Waverby was captured and turned traitor. He works for the Hollander Admiral de Ruyter, and he will make his way back to the court to spy for them. The foxy Dutch bought his continuing loyalty with a ship and a piece of the Guinea slave trade to repair his fortunes."

Anne shivered. "I didn't think it possible to loathe him more, but . . ."

"Anne, the king will demand your return to court when Waverby appears."

"But you could show the king Black Ben's letters."

"Waverby could easily claim them forgeries, and the word of a lord is greater than that of a highwayman, even one so reformed as I." His mouth widened in a smile that was more a grimace. "I must think me well what is to be done." He stared out far across the stream sparkling in the sunlight.

"Then all the more reason that we depart for the Virginia lands."

"There is no place on this earth that we could escape Waverby's hatred. He would come for us, for he will never allow me to best him, and he will never allow your happiness." His voice grew bitter. "So I must do for the traitorous rogue. And bastard that I am, nameless and landless, I will kill him, or die in the trying. . . . For my honor."

She clung to his hand, her heart almost breaking, for the passion that had flowed between them so ceaselessly just hours earlier seemed to have disappeared as though it had never existed, burned away in the heat of his purpose. "Johnny, it is you who do not hear me on this. Edward matters not. Your birth matters not. Your honor matters not." She had gone too far and immediately knew it, and made haste to speak again.

Anger shook him, but he put a finger to her lips, barely touching them. "But your safety matters very much to me, and I have sworn an oath to protect you with my life."

"I asked no such oath from you."

"I gave it to your father that first night at the inn. My oath did not die with him. It will only die with me."

Anne had no argument remaining, and she refused to be shut out. "What are your plans?"

He picked up two letters, the wax seals broken, seals that Anne saw were imprinted with Edward's signet ring. "Ben was instructed to go to Burwell Hall and deliver this to Waverby's majordomo." John's voice was flat when he began, but as he spoke the words, his tone lifted and the words had more meaning. "The majordomo's letter instructs him to proceed with five of Waverby's men to Southampton and take ship for the port of Le Havre at the mouth of the Seine River. Waverby will be in the harbor on a Dutch gallot named the *Ere,* pretending to be a captive. I will get aboard and . . ."

Anne gasped at the thought of John fighting against many. It was a desperate dead man's plan. "Take me with you."

"It is far too dangerous for you. I would not ask my men to follow me when there is no benefit to them." His jaw tightened. "This is my fight."

"After last night, I thought we were together in all things." She fought the angry tears that threatened to engulf her words, the tears that would seem to beg, but beg she would never do.

He frowned in concentration. "Don't you see, Anne? Our happiness is not possible with Waverby in the world."

Her words emerged softly, but her eyes narrowed. "I am trying to understand, John. If you die, you have destroyed my world in order to make me safe in it. Is that your argument?"

He did not answer, but his shoulders sagged perceptibly.

Hope fueled by desperation grabbed her. "Take me with you. You have seen me stand my ground with Black Ben. I will not leave your side."

"It is a lunatic idea! The answer is no."

Fury at his obstinacy and at the bleak picture he drew of their future overwhelmed her at last, and she lashed out at him. "What is all this fine talk about each man and woman having a vote, and yet, like Black Ben, you presume to speak for everyone without any consultation? If dishonoring your oath to your company is your craven wish, John Gilbert, then it is best I discover it now before I commit my affections further!" Even to her ears, the words were ridiculous; she was far beyond feeling mere affection for him.

He shifted a bit to face her more squarely, and she could see that it pained him much to move. "You twist my words like a devious woman," he said, scowling.

Her heart moved her to compassion for his wound, but her head was still wrathful at the wound he meant to inflict on her, indeed, on both of them. "In truth, sir, I only point out your man's falsity, as any logical woman could."

John drew a long breath, so deep into his lungs that he felt his wound issue a sharp reminder to breathe easier, which Anne's presence was going to make increasingly difficult. The moon seemed to pour its beams down on her hair and turn it to curls of dancing flame, but nothing to match the hot fire that shone on her proud face. Desire fanned through him as if borne on a sea gale, and his gaze was riveted on the pounding pulse in her flawless throat. He longed to touch it with his mouth, feel it moving against his lips, as he had so many times the night before, but he could not. Anne Gascoigne was not yet his, but a living man's wife.

Despite her obvious anger at him, she was remembering last night, too; he knew it as he knew what he must do. Although it might be difficult for both of them—and at the moment, he was finding it the most bitter thing he'd ever done—in time it would prove best. Although he was not so old-fashioned that he believed women had no voice in their own affairs, as a man he was her leader, as he was the leader of his band of men, and it was up to him to show this woman good lordship. It was a powerful argument, one he had heard debated at Oxford many times, and he had it on the tip of his tongue, but in response to the defiant expression on Anne's face, he decided it best not to speak it.

Anne watched him, her eyes missing nothing, and for a moment she feared that her body, heating at the touch of his hand despite her anger and distress, would betray her. She was afraid that she would slide into his arms, yielding every principle she knew to be true, just for the sake of his tender kiss.

But ultimately, John's stubbornness proved too infuriating. It seemed to yield to no words of hers. Well, he hadn't heard all of them yet.

"Very well, John," she said, arranging her very rumpled gown primly about her ankles. "You take my chastity, then refuse to save my honor"—she was pleased to see him glower at that—"so you leave me no choice but to save it myself. I will confront Edward alone with my dagger at Whitehall, if I die in the attempt."

A look of extreme pain that did not come from the injury in his side crossed his face. "Black Ben could not make me eat dirt, but you can." His voice was broken and harsh. "You present me with naught but bitter solutions, Anne."

"Bitter?" she challenged, an anger forged from hurt filled to overflowing. "Last night you swore to marry me and love me forever." She made her voice contemptuous. "Or was that just the cock lusting to plow the maiden?"

He struggled to his feet, his face turning ashen with the effort. "As you wish, it was lust and nothing more."

Here was proof of a perfidy beyond belief, and the sound of those words threatened to destroy her. But when she looked into his dark, haunted eyes, she saw an entirely different proof. "I don't believe you, John Gilbert."

"Believe what you must, as you always do, Anne, but I will never have it said that I was beholden to a woman's weapon!"

She stood and faced him, resolution stiffening her back.

"Would you deny me revenge from a false lord who toyed with my affections, sold them to the king, killed my father, a . . . a man who tried to unman you?"

"A woman's revenge is different," he said, his voice indicating that these words ended the matter.

But she would not let it end. "Howsome different, John Gilbert? Different because you say so. Different because your false pride does make it so."

"Enough!" He grabbed her by her upper arms, his fingers sinking into the firm flesh that he remembered only too well, but he shook her nonetheless. As much as it pained his wounded side, he shook her in his rage to make her understand, to make her stop her confusing disputations, to keep her safe. A man could not always explain the right of a thing, but he always *knew* the right. He had already grieved her enough by taking her chastity, making her unfit for a suitable marriage. He would not take more by allowing her to risk her life for his sake. That was, indeed, the noble choice. Couldn't she see that? "Leave be, Anne. I will go after Waverby alone, and that's an end on it."

She struggled against his hold, but then stood still and faced his hard gaze with one of her own, and the only argument she thought might reach through his pride to reason. "Is this your democracy for which I glorified you?" she questioned him. "There is a vote when you think it will go your way, but when you doubt—"

He loosed her arms, but his imprint was so strong that it was as if he held her still. The words that followed were almost without feeling. "I will call for a vote," he said, and scooping up the letters, started slowly back down the path to the clearing, holding his side.

She did not follow him immediately. She had won the last argument, but she felt empty of all victory.

When she returned to the clearing, after thoughtful prayer and no clear answer that she was wrong, Anne found John standing by the fire. A dozen faces were turned up to him as he spoke. "I am taking ship to France to find and bring back the traitor Lord Waverby for the king's justice. . . . Or kill him, if I must, or be killed in the trying." He handed the two letters to Beth, who haltingly read them aloud. "I say this is my fight and none of yours, so I release you from your brotherhood vows to me."

Anne sat down quietly between Beth and Kate and listened to John practice the arts of persuasion. Even wounded and in some obvious pain, he was their leader without question, and it would be difficult for them to go against him.

Finally, unable to be silent longer, she stood, her eyes shining in the firelight. "I will go." The words were calmly spoken but echoed throughout the little clearing.

Slowly, one by one, Joseph first, they rose. "Your fight is our fight," Joseph said, and each followed, saying the same words, even Francis, Alexander and Dick, who'd been lured away by Ben's promises. Although the doctor swallowed hard before he spoke, his vote was never in doubt. In the morn all would leave for Southampton and thence to the coast of France.

Anne left the fire and walked swiftly to the small lean-to and lay down on the bracken-and-leaf pallet, her back to the entrance. Minutes later, she heard John crawl inside.

"Anne," he whispered.

Because she was a woman and they had quarreled, she thought not to answer as a torment to him, but it was against her nature to stay silent long. "Try to understand, John. Those who love you want to share your danger. Only a craven kind of love would not."

His hand reached for hers, and her heart warmed to his touch. "You swear you will follow my orders in all things?" he questioned, and there was a lift to his voice that said he already doubted her eager agreement.

Once more the distance between them, the barrier of his pride and her determination, dissolved in the intense memory of the moon-swollen pool of mere hours before. Anne felt life rush through her once more. Why was love ever doubtful? Silent tears of relief coursed down her cheeks and dropped one by one onto the matted floor of Whittlewood Forest, mixing with the rich leaf mold and loam.

John bent slightly and stopped one tear with a kiss, and she lay through the night, nestled carefully on his arm, waking frequently to ensure that his wound had not fevered, and that it was, indeed, John Gilbert beside her, and not a lovely dream.

John made one more effort to dissuade his band from the danger he was sure they'd face, but when each swore again to follow him, he thanked them with good grace.

After Dr. Wyndham changed John's dressing and pronounced that his wound showed no sign of putrification, hasty preparations followed and they departed midmorning, leaving Mathew provisions until he could fish and hunt. Anne, Beth and Kate wore boots, breeches and swords under their traveling cloaks, hair covered in long red woolen caps, their gowns and shifts tied in a carrying bundle, although Kate worried that her disguise might be against scripture. Still, she couldn't remember either chapter or verse, so she reluctantly donned the attire, Anne and Beth helping with the unfamiliar buckles and ties.

Sultry summer downpours made the roads south a slog of mud, tiring the horses, most already carrying two riders, and requiring frequent stops and nights at wayside inns. After three days, the six men and three women were still two days from Southampton harbor.

"My lady?" Dr. Wyndham inquired one morning as they left the Berkshire hills and headed toward Winchester on the last leg to Southampton. He and Kate reined alongside Anne and John up on Sir Pegasus, Anne riding, as always, in front of John, one leg hooked over the pommel. The good doctor sat his own horse well though the stirrups were drawn up high to accommodate his short legs. "I would have a word for your ear, Anne. Begging your pardon, John."

John nodded.

"You have all my attention," Anne replied, twisting carefully so as not to hurt John's wound, which, though healing well and bandaged tightly, was still painful.

"With your permission, Kate and I would like to marry before we take ship in Southampton. If aught befalls us in France, then we would die as man and wife." He thoroughly studied his hands on the reins. "I have been long a widower, not for want of the desire to marry, but for lack of a proper woman." He paused, but Anne said nothing, and so he continued. "There's some as might think that I am too old for Kate, but I am scarcely in my forties, and, I wager, more able to husband than hotheads half my age."

Anne smiled, and encouraged, he went on in his deep, rumbling voice.

"As for our difference in religion, Kate has a gentle faith, and I have an almost total lack of dogma, so that we would seem to suit in that regard."

"I am genuinely delighted," Anne said, and from the corner of her eye saw Kate's face lit with the possibility of the love for which she had so longed on that first day they'd met back in Waverby House.

"This is wonderful news," Anne said to her, "but you do not need my permission. Kate, you are no longer my servant."

Kate stretched her hand to Josiah and he took it. "But I would feel the better for thy blessing, Friend Anne," she said.

"Then you have it, and with all my heart."

"And mine," John said, wondering what he could read if he could see Anne's face.

Kate smiled and tightened her hold on Josiah Wyndham. "He is a wondrous clever man, and generous of spirit," she said. "He has given me a miracle salve for my complexion."

Kate turned a radiant face to Anne, and it did seem to Anne as if Kate's skin showed much less the scars and pits of smallpox than it had. "Love, dear Kate, works true marvels beyond any concoction of Josiah's."

Josiah grinned. "If that be true, then I will add it to my formula."

They rode alongside, silent for a while, until Kate spoke. "Friend Anne, Friend John, it is none of my place to say it, but it pains me to see thee both in such despair. Mayhap Josiah can prescribe an elixir?"

Before the doctor could recount the magical properties of his elixirs, John smiled at the earnest Quaker girl. "Good Kate, not even Josiah Wyndham has physician's skill enough to take a Dutch ship in a French harbor with his bare hands, for that is near to what we must do if we cannot lure Waverby to land."

When Kate and the doctor dropped back, Anne rode on in the same silence that enveloped John.

Despite her troubled thoughts, the morn was glorious. Being so close to John, feeling his arms around her, seeing his strong brown hands on the reins, aroused all that made despair difficult. It seemed to Anne that when she closed her eyes, she could see the pool in Whittlewood Forest. She could hear the gently flowing stream lap against the big rock, and she knew that the sun beating down on her now beat upon that stream, and that sometimes in the night years hence another soft breeze would blow over the memory of parched and hungry bodies that had lain together on its bank.

Anne wrested her mind from such thoughts and did try to feel true joy at Josiah and Kate's happiness. But the look of bliss on their faces seemed to loose a mighty flood of jealous regret and mock her heart's best intent.

That night, John came to her in their room in the inn. She was brushing her hair, happy to have it free of the stocking cap. "We have been asked to stand as witness to a wedding."

She sighed. "Of course. Josiah and Kate have my best wishes."

A moment passed. "I speak of Joseph and Beth, too."

Anne was little surprised, but she laughed bitterly. "Marriage, it seems, is all the fashion in John Gilbert's band."

"To those who are free to think on it," John replied in a clipped voice, having no doubt of her meaning. Then impulsively, he placed his hands on her shoulders as she sat before the cloudy mirror. He took her brush and began to stroke her hair, lifting it to watch the candlelight dance upon it. "Pique ill becomes you, sweet Anne."

The sharp words were out of her mouth before she thought enough on them. "Really, sir? Oh, I think pique becomes me right excellent well, so that I plan to wear it often." She saw how ugly these words were in her reflection, and would have recalled them in another moment.

"Sink me!" John said, dropping the brush and stalking from the room, his face dark with anger, a bit of doggerel leaping to mind: *If of herself she will not love,/Nothing can make her; The devil take her!* But he did not allow the words to become speech. They were, after all, unfair to Anne, who loved very well, but this admission only increased his helpless fury at the woman.

She passed him on the stairs, her head high. How dare he flaunt multiple marriages in her face and expect her to be sweet-natured about it? Were men insane to think that once an argument was settled to their satisfaction, it no longer mattered to a woman? She urged her mouth into a genuine smile when she saw her friends Kate and Beth once more wearing their simple gray stuff dresses, gathered below with a Puritan divine. Later, she found a lone place and cried out her anguish.

That night, John and Anne lay in their gallery room, together yet apart. "Are you sleeping?" he whispered, and she did not answer lest she begin to sob and rob him of sleep.

John lay awake for some hours, aching to comfort Anne, but having no healing words. Damn Waverby!

Two days later, tired and travel worn, at last the band reached Southampton and sat momentarily atop a small hill, looking down into the busy harbor, swooping gulls screaming overhead.

"There is much to be done," John said, "and a ship for France to be found as soon as possible. We cannot afford to deplete our guineas by idling in port."

"Then, sir," Anne said, primly, "we women will find a clean family inn not so much given to ale and roistering."

With only a grumble or two at that, John, Francis, Alexander and Dick took the horses to sell at the local horse fair, except Sir Pegasus, who was boarded at the inn. Taking the horse sale money, they bought supplies and extra pistols, and arranged for passage to Harfleur, a small, ancient port near Le Havre, on the fast brig *Merry Chance*.

A week later on a mid-July day, Anne braced her feet on the deck of the ship as it stood out to sea, bearing under shortened sail toward the harbor mouth. Clinging to the railing, her hair all of a tangle about her head, she watched England slowly slip astern and knew that she might never see it again. They passed the headland, and her spirits were strangely lifted as the bow raised in salute to the Atlantic before they tacked about to head for France.

She knew there was little chance that she would live to spend her life with John Gilbert or, indeed, that their lives would be long ones. This mad adventure to find Edward might end the love and laughter, even the sharp words and squabbles that were almost as dear, but something drove her to risk what John risked. Old Shakespeare had said it well: The miserable have no other medicine but hope.

She watched sailors run up the port rigging as the *Merry Chance* piled on more sail, and the long ocean rollers began breaking over the bow. She breathed deep of the salty sea air and felt very much alive. Around her were good companions, and before her an adventure unknown to any woman, even Lady Castlemaine, who had experienced most of the world's adventures. And by God's bowels, Anne Gascoigne would make the most of it, whatever befell.

The captain, a heavy, much-weathered man, appeared at her side, pulling on his forelock. "If ye will follow me, lady, I'll show ye to my cabin, so that ye may retire in some comfort during our crossing."

Surprised, Anne hesitated. "I thought we would have but a place in the cargo hold."

The captain grinned. "That be true for most, my lady, but not for such a one as ye, for your quality shows. Ye may have my cabin, and welcome."

"I thank you, captain, but I would not dream of being so burdensome to you."

"Nothing of the kind. The gentleman"—he pointed to John, standing amidships—"paid right well for it."

"Then you must tell the *gentleman* that I refuse to be separated from the rest of the company."

The captain was obviously not happy at losing the extra passage money. "Ye will not like it, the hold. It be full of rats, and there be only one chamber pot for privy convenience. Think again on it, my lady. The Channel can be right choppy. Think on it."

That was exactly what Anne was trying to keep herself from thinking.

She glanced at John and saw that he was looking at her, and she thought she detected a slight smile on his lips, although it could have been a dancing reflection of the light on the water.

Anne drew herself as erect as the pitching deck would allow. "Nay, Captain, I do not need to think further on't. I'm sure that the short journey in the hold with the others of my company will be a thrilling and instructive affair."

"So, Lady Anne," John said for her ears, as she passed

him, "we will see how you practice democracy with one chamber pot."

Anne's words to the captain and their haughty surety came back to haunt her during the next days and nights.

Early on the second daybreak, Anne stood at the railing of the sterncastle, trying to cleanse her lungs in the pure sea air. The dark hold had become impossibly noxious, and she spent as little time there as possible. The wind was thundering in the canvas sails above her head when suddenly poor Beth rushed past her and retched over the stern rail.

Finally, Beth wiped her mouth on her apron. "Oh," she croaked, her entire body quivering from the effort, "I am sure to lose my babe."

"Nothing of the sort," Anne said consolingly. "Go now and rest. Later, Josiah will attend you, and I'll try to make some broth to renew your strength."

Beth made a face at the thought of food, but smiled weakly and retreated to the cargo hatch, climbing down the ladder into the hold.

She was scarcely out of sight when Anne, unable to contain herself longer, bent over the rail and repeated Beth's performance.

Chapter Twenty-four

My Lady Pirate

Anne walked away from the dock with John and the others, trying to regain her land legs and control her wretched stomach, where the stale ship's biscuit and watered ale with which she'd broken her fast swirled relentlessly. "Why Harfleur, John?" Anne questioned to cover her discomfort. God's bowels! She must hide what she suspected from John Gilbert.

"Best we not draw Waverby's attention to an English ship sailing into Le Harve," he said, smiling because she looked adorable in tight breeches, weaving down the road like a drunken sailor.

With the help of a passing hay wain and Anne's French, which had been her second language in Charles's court, they made their way to Le Harve's waterfront by nightfall. They broke into groups of two and three as they walked in the faint lamplight of the docks, pretending to be drunken townsmen and their whores. They found the *Ere* berthed apart from other ships at the end of the harbor, bow to the sea.

John pulled Anne back into the deep shadows, and the others disappeared against a warehouse. He saw one lookout forward on the galiot, no one up its single mast and no other movement on deck. "Count the oars, Anne," John whispered.

"I make it eight," she answered, the words trembling with her excitement.

"That makes sixteen oarsmen, so they'll have a crew of maybe twenty-five to defend her, counting officers. . . . And Waverby."

Joseph and Dr. Wyndham had sidled up and joined their bulk to John and Anne's shadow. "We're but six men against so many," Joseph said with none of his usual heartiness.

"You forget the women, good Joseph," Anne chided him, only half in jest.

"Nay, lady, I do not forget. I yield to no man in my admiration for ye and for Beth, although I think me it be unlikely that Quaker Kate be making much of a fight of it. If willing be all, I'd take ye all three, but we need strong sword arms with that number of men against us."

"Fighting is against my wife's religion," Wyndham said in Kate's defense, and Anne liked him the more for it.

At that moment, three men wearing the red cockade of the port gendarmerie rounded the corner and stopped under a lamp scant yards away, one lighting a long clay pipe, another carrying a flintlock on his shoulder. John put his arm about Anne's shoulders, pulling her to his chest, and she inhaled the familiar scent of him, now mixed with the freshening night breeze off the Atlantic Ocean.

On board the *Ere,* softly at first and then louder, they heard voices singing a song that they all knew: *"Oh, the roast beef of olde England, the roast beef of olde England, oh!"* But instead of the roistering tavern song John had known since a youth at Oxford, it sounded more like a hopeless dirge to his ears.

"Anglais," said one gendarme, jerking a thumb toward the galiot.

"Les chiens," another said, and they laughed, and moved back down the wharf.

Anne was stiff with rage. "*Dogs?* They dare . . ."

"We'll see who the dogs are," John said against her ear, feeling an identical rage.

"How do Englishmen come to be on that ship?" Anne whispered.

"Mayhap captured during the battle of Lowestoft in June and now chained in the galley of Waverby's ship," John replied, his teeth clenched around the words. "There is truly nothing that man will not do for gold."

Anne shivered even with the warmth of John's body close to her, conjuring Edward's face, the face that stood between her and a life with John, at its most evil.

Joseph grabbed John's arm. "Look, Johnny lad, there's a small boat putting out from the ship."

Anne stared hard. A lantern swung from a pole in the stern shone on a white face she knew well. "Edward," she murmured, shivering again in spite of the warm night, and felt John tighten his arm about her in reassurance.

"Don't worry, sweeting," he said, his voice made sure for her. "I had thought to lure Waverby off the ship, but if we can release good English seamen, we have a better chance than ever I hoped."

Anne's fast-beating heart was not calmed.

The dinghy pulled up to the dock, and Waverby was first to step out. He and an officer stopped in the lamplight to look back at the *Ere*. "Captain, I expect my men and a ship any day, and then you can sail for the Guinea coast. If you make it a fast journey, I will reward you and your men with an extra share."

"My lord," the captain replied in English with a thick Hollander accent, "my men are paid vell enough. Another share vill make them bad sailors. . . . But me a better captain."

Waverby smiled, a triumphant smile that never failed to chill Anne in her bones. "Captain, though we are from different countries, often at war, I think me that we may be brothers."

The Captain bowed. "As you say, my lord. I see now why you named your ship the *Ere*."

"Do you, Captain? Damn me, but I think your Hollander word for 'honor' is most fitting for our plans."

Both men walked off laughing, and as soon as they were out of sight, the remaining two sailors in the dinghy tied it to a ring bolt by the dock where other boats rode high, climbed ashore and fast disappeared into the nearest alehouse.

John held Anne, who was shivering, though the July night was warm. "You can stay safe ashore, and I will send for you if all goes well," he said.

"I go if you go," she answered, squaring her shoulders, using what she was certain was the last drop of her bravado, but she wanted to use it. A man like Edward must be sent to the devil for the sake of all.

"As you will, Anne," John said, and knew that he admired her as he had admired few men. He stepped into the faint lamplight and motioned everyone to him. "We've been called land pirates; now we'll be pirates in truth, eh?" he said, flashing confidence he was far from feeling. "We've taken many a carriage on Oxford Road. Howsome is this different? And yon ship has no wheels!" They all laughed. "Quiet, lads. We'll take one of the boats tied to the wharf and row to the *Ere* without a light. If they hail us, I will answer. Anne, Beth and Kate, once aboard, you open the hatch, go below and free the prisoners, no matter what is happening on deck. Can you do this?"

"Aye, sir," Anne said, and pulled her forelock as she'd seen the sailors on the *Merry Chance* do in answer to their captain.

John handed Anne one of the primed and charged pistols. "If there's a guard, try not to shoot him and rouse the town, but if he needs killing . . ."

Anne nodded her understanding, now too tense to speak, her hand aching under the unaccustomed weight of the pistol. She had only the briefest moment to wonder how a lady of the queen's bedchamber had come to piracy, dressed in breeches and armed with pistol and sword. Even Castlemaine would not dare so much.

John issued orders as they raced forward to the small boats tied at the dock. "Joseph, you silence the lookout, then keep guard on deck against Waverby's return. Dick . . . Francis . . : Alexander . . . Doctor . . . forward with me to the crew's quarters. Quickly now, into the far dinghy. Waverby may be back at any time."

They rowed across the narrow strip of water to the *Ere*'s anchorage, the oars scraping the oarlocks. "Ahoy, the *Ere*!"

The return hail came in the Hollanders' tongue.

Anne was astonished when John answered in Waverby's exactly pitched drawl. "Captain, instruct your men to answer a noble earl properly. Damn me, but I'll have him flogged."

"I would have liked to see you on the stage," she whispered, turning up her face admiringly.

"You just did," he said, kissing her rather dirty cheek, then checking his pistol's priming. "Doctor, as last man up, push the dinghy off so Waverby won't know he has unexpected guests."

John was first up the ladder, Joseph behind. As the lookout raised his head from the water butt, Joseph grabbed him in his massive arms, squeezing him insensible and dropping him like a puppet to the deck.

Silently, John helped Anne over the rail, pointing to the galiot's hatch, which was partially ajar, and motioning to Francis, Dick and Alexander, he went forward, wondering how many crew remained aboard and how sober they were.

Anne helped Beth and Kate to the deck, giving Kate a hard shake to bring her out of her wide-eyed terror. She dared not think what her own face revealed, but prayed her nerve didn't fail her. She could not bear it if she showed cowardice in front of John Gilbert. It was one thing to be defiant as she had been when first in the highwayman's hidden village; quite another now that she had more, much more to lose, indeed, the love of that same highwayman and mayhap his babe growing in her belly. She wondered as she crept to the hatch leading below, her heart pounding in her ears, if she had only a small amount of courage and that already used. She would soon know as few women were given to know.

Quietly, they opened the hatch fully and Anne stepped upon the ladder, motioning Beth to follow and Kate to stay on guard. In a narrow space, she wanted sturdy Beth at her back, who was now drawing her sword like a proper pirate, and looked to well remember her lessons upon the Whittlewood green.

The guard was sleeping heavily on his arms, his pistol beside him, a pot of ale and a lantern with a guttering candle before him. Anne crept down the stair, stopping as one creaked under her foot. She waited, not breathing for a moment, then moved down again as an Englishman dozing on the first oar raised his head. She put a finger to her lips for silence, but she needn't have. The sailor was speechless at sight of Anne with her pistol thrust ahead of her.

With Beth following, Anne poked the barrel in the guard's neck. He woke with a sleepy start, speaking in the Hollanders' language, but she held steady on him the weapon, which spoke in a language of its own and was well understood by the look on his face.

She reached for the keys hanging on his belt, and he knocked the pistol from her hand, uttering some Hollander oath. Then he knocked her to the floor as she clawed for the pistol, which had skittered along the deck to come up against the bulkhead.

"Beth," Anne yelled, as the Hollander pointed his own pistol at her, although she had scarce breath enough.

But Beth was already leaping from the ladder onto the

guard's back, and as he whirled to dislodge her, Anne kicked out, her heavy boot heels connecting painfully with his ankles. Beth and the guard went down in a heap, he losing his grip on his weapon, as Anne's hand closed firmly around her own pistol.

She tossed the keys under the first rower's bench, and they quickly passed from shackle to shackle. The sailor who'd first seen her saluted. "I be Robert Howe, and nevermore thinking women unlucky aboard ship, as God be my witness. Bless 'e, lady, whoe'er ye be."

Keeping an eye on the Hollander lying on the deck, she smiled, regaining her breath. "I am a countrywoman who does not like to see good English sailors in chains, especially to a rogue like Waverby."

"He be the worst kind of traitor, lady. . . . For money," Robert said, tying and gagging the guard, who ceased his struggles after Anne applied a pistol butt hard to his head. "Be ye two ladies our rescue party entire?" he asked, shaking his head in wonder at her.

Anne thrust her pistol into his hand. "Go at once to the crew's quarters and help John Gilbert."

"Gentleman Johnny, the highwayman?" Robert asked, his mouth now farther agape.

"He is your true rescuer. We plan to take Lord Waverby to England and the king's justice. Are you with us?"

All the sailors raised their arms to cheer, but Anne shushed them. "Silence, lads, until we take the ship," she said, thinking she sounded a right pretty pirate authority.

A guard was posted on the Hollander, and one by one they crept up the ladder to the deck, two rescued sailors now armed with pistols.

Kate looked relieved when Anne emerged on deck. "Friend Anne," she said, "there be fighting where John Gilbert and my Josiah went."

Without a thought, Anne raced forward, her sword raised, as John backed out of the forecastle, with his men coming soon after. The clang of sword on sword followed them as the *Ere*'s Dutch crew tumbled on deck, seven men squinting in the light of the lantern hung on the mast.

"I'm at your back, Johnny," Anne yelled, her tangled auburn curls cascading about her shoulders, having lost her stocking cap struggling with the guard below. She was nearly breathless with an exhilaration she'd never before experienced, one that made her tremble inside and yet steadied her hand. She had spent her years learning courtly manners and womanly ways, fine embroidery and household duties, which at this moment were quite useless. John Gilbert had given her the only lessons that mattered.

Dr. Wyndham came up out of the crew's quarters, nursing a swollen eye, and stopped near the hatch to the galley, shielding Kate with his body. "Kate, I must help in some way."

"Ye be a doctor of medicine and unarmed, Josiah!"

"Nay, I have a cure that's never failed me." He pulled a crockery jar of his miracle salve from his kit and tossed the contents at the deck under the Hollanders' feet.

Anne parried an awkward saber thrust, as her barefoot opponent slipped on the salve. John jabbed the man in his sword arm, disabling him. "You're a born pirate, sweeting," he said, claiming her mouth in a kiss heated by battle and too much separation. Then they both turned as one and saluted the doctor with their swords, while Kate looked very proud and the doctor no less so.

English sailors, armed with clubs and bare hands, swarmed the Hollanders, the two English pistols holding a distinct advantage over Dutch cutlasses.

"Shackle them to the oars below and keep them quiet," John commanded, his arm tightening around Anne. "Quickly now, all of you find a hiding place before Waverby returns."

The faint quarter moon was low in the sky when John heard oars splashing, the bump of a small boat alongside and the sound of Waverby's voice, low and angry. "I'll have their hides, Captain, if our oarsmen returned to the ship without us. Otherwise, they can stay in a foreign port and rot!"

"My lord, I vill have another hide if the watch sleeps!"

John knelt behind the water butt, Anne behind him, both of them armed with pistols looted from the captain's cabin. He saw the shadows of his men and the English sailors not guarding the Hollanders below, some aft and some forward.

First Waverby and then the captain came over the rail, dropped to the deck and looked about them. Anne was filled with loathing as she watched Waverby, his eyes suspicious, slowly draw his blade. "Captain, something is amiss."

John stepped from behind the butt into the light of the masthead lantern, pistol in hand, Anne following, her own pistol pointed with both hands at Waverby. John bowed slightly. "For once, my Lord Waverby, you are in the right of it. You and the good captain are our prisoners. Drop your weapons!"

The captain complied immediately.

For several heartbeats, Anne waited, watching Waverby casting about in his mind for an escape, all of his thoughts parading across his once handsome face, now beginning to be stamped with the wickedness in his soul. A strong odor of sandalwood reached her nostrils, and his languid voice followed. "Ah, the eunuch still lives." He frowned at Anne. "Have you no kiss of welcome for me, my Lady of Waverby?"

"No, nor ever shall," she said, her voice overfull of emotion at the sight of the tall, slender figure who was her husband, and then softly added with some delight, "John Gilbert is no eunuch, my lord, as I can swear with certain knowledge."

Edward stepped forward, idly weaving his sword in tight circles, as if testing its metal. His eyes flicked to John and then to Anne, and a look of vicious ill, so totally aligned with evil, crossed his cold face, so that Anne felt as if a powerful hand squeezed her heart.

"When last we met, my love, you were in the king's tender care, and your highwayman on his way to a yardarm. What a tale you must have to tell. But have a care, my lady countess: Adultery is still a burning offense for a woman in England." He smiled, not seeming the least concerned. "But I am a generous man and will forgive even cuckoldry if you return to my side and my bed. All you need do is *turn your pistol on that rogue,* if you don't wish to put yourself outside the law with him."

Edward looked very pleased with his argument. As practiced as he was at hiding any small emotion he might feel, he could not hide self-congratulation, since it was his right to best the rabble.

"The king has granted his royal pardon to John Gilbert," Anne said softly, savoring the words as she said them.

"I see. So this is not a merry welcome for a returning husband. You are more clever than I thought, Anne. But a noble peer of England does not surrender so easily, and never to a rogue and the king's mistress." His voice had a strange assurance, as if he could not accept that anyone could defy him or interfere with his plans.

Slowly, emerging from their shadowy hiding places, John's band and all the English sailors rose, the sailors muttering their triumph. "Let me slit 'is traitor's throat," said one. There was a cheer that would have chilled a man who grasped his situation.

The Hollander captain stepped away from Waverby.

John shook his head. "Nay, lads, his throat belongs to the king."

"But you belong to me," Waverby said through clenched lips, "as does that whore by your side. Both of you will hang for piracy from the Deptford docks. Think you the king will hear aught against me . . . on the word of a landless rogue bastard?"

The Hollander captain put his hand out to John. "I vill tell the king his earl is traitor who decoded English dispatches for Admiral de Ruyter. . . . All for my parole."

Waverby whirled on him and ran him through, neatly between the eyes, loosing a thin stream of blood, which arched over the deck. "By Christ's wounds!" Edward said petulantly, wiping down his sword with his sandalwood-scented handkerchief, "you have cost me a good trading captain for my ship."

John lurched forward, drawing his sword.

Anne cried a warning. "Johnny, he is master of the sword."

"Stay safe, Anne," John ordered.

Waverby's sword taunted John, turning in little circles, daring him to come within reach.

John danced away, o'erleaping the captain's body. "Is this an example of your aristocrat's honor, my lord?"

Waverby's sword sliced the air with a whooshing sound. "Bastards cannot call up the rules of gentlemen, so expect no mercy."

John sidestepped a thrust. "Then if you call yourself noble, I am honored to call myself bastard, my lord." And so he was for the first time. Born without distinction, he would so live, or die if need be, that distinction would cling to his name, as it would never in this world or the next cling to Waverby for all his pure ancestry.

As his lordship advanced in the *en garde* position, John sidestepped swiftly because he knew that Waverby's longer arms gave him more extension. John would not fight Waverby's fight of fancy fencing school parries, but fight a good English street brawl, using his sword as a shield, twisting away, again and again, then coming up on Waverby's other side.

John could see Waverby was frustrated and angry as he turned to meet him, and when his gaze dropped to John's feet, John knew what was coming. He leaped into the air as

Waverby lunged, and his slicing sword passed harmlessly beneath John's feet.

Waverby was off balance as John's feet landed lightly on the deck, his sword passing through the shoulder of Waverby's sword arm. The sword fell, stripped from him as if by a just God, and his arm hung useless by his side, his elegant cloth of silver doublet slowly staining red.

A wild huzzah rang from the deck as Anne ran to John. He kept his sword at Waverby's throat, as she blazed her defiance at the man who had sold her love for self-gain. "Take him below, lads," she said, triumph filling her voice, "and chain him to an oar as he chained you. Doctor, see you to his wound, if it please you."

As he was being led away, Waverby stopped and stared at Anne. "He used a commoner's tricks on me. I am not beaten."

Anne threw back her head and placed both hands on her hips. "Then, my lord, you would do well to study his method, since it seems the better of the two in my eyes."

A pistol nudged Waverby, and he was forced to the galley hatch below. "You're mine, damn you, Anne," he said, looking back at her as he disappeared down the ladder, and she shuddered at the surety in those words.

John took Anne's hand and they climbed to the forecastle. He leaned over the railing, looking down amidships. "Lads," John called, gathering all together before him. "We will take this ship to England and present her to the king, along with his lordship's neck. Are you with me?"

"Huzzah! Huzzah! Huzzah!" The men who had hats waved them in the air.

John addressed them again. "Since the captain is dead, we need a navigator."

Robert Howe stepped forward. "I was third mate of His Majesty's warship *Royal Charles,* sir, and can plot a true course."

"Then plot a course, Captain Howe, and take us up the Channel to the Thames. Let's put on all sail for England!"

Three sailors leaped to the ratlines and up the mast to the sails furled on the spars. Others began to haul in the anchor. All were singing, "Oh, the roast beef of olde England, the roast beef of olde England, oh!" and it sounded to John's ears like an anthem of endless joy.

And for Anne's ears alone, he whispered, "Let's hope His Majesty is in a mood to listen to a pirate lady and her highwayman."

"He will," she said, pulling herself to him. "He must." But she was not certain she believed her own words.

Anne had been unable to break her morning fast, despite gaining her sea legs more quickly while crossing the Channel in the *Ere*. She drooped briefly against the smooth railing, feeling it surge rather too strongly against her stomach. She straightened, swallowed hard and stared at the horizon until the churning sensation passed.

There was no longer any way to deny to herself that she was breeding, for Beth provided an uncomfortable mirror image that was impossible to disown.

She gripped the rail, trying not to see the choppy Channel waters around her. She would not tell John. Oh, no! For the man who so hated bastardy, the knowledge that he had sired one himself would be too much to bear. It might also make him too cautious with her, and she was determined to be part of whatever happened next.

Anne closed her eyes against the sharp sting of salt spray, which had nigh ruined her complexion except for applications of the doctor's last jar of miracle salve, though he assured her that he would make more as soon as they reached land and he could collect the early morning dew from under a country oak.

"Sail, ho!" sang out the masthead lookout.

"Where away?" the newly minted captain boomed.

"To larboard!" came the response from overhead.

The captain trained his glass on a distant sail, and without warning, Anne heard John's familiar footsteps as he hastily mounted to the high poop deck. She composed herself, hoping she showed no signs of the green sickness.

"Can you make it out, Captain Howe?" John asked.

"Not at this distance, except she be a large galleon—maybe two gun decks, and that be at least thirty cannons. A Hollander, by the look of her broad beam."

"Fly their flag," John ordered.

"Aye, that might stop 'em, but maybe not. They'll be like fighting cocks since they lost at Lowestoft, especially if they be catching the scent of English blood close by." The captain shrugged and shouted down to the deck, "Break out the Hollander colors."

Anne felt the warmth of John's body as he moved closer to her, and she took heart, especially after his fingers gently settled on the exposed flesh above her cloak, their touch telling her not to worry.

"We're the faster ship, Captain," John argued, "and my men will fight well if need be. And Anne here is worth any man in a fight."

The captain nodded. "We be faster, John Gilbert, if we have the wind behind us, but they can pile on more canvas, and at thy peril forget it—they be a man-o'-war and we be unarmed. This be their game."

The captain put the glass hard to his eye once more and swept the horizon. "Heavy weather be making up in the sou'west." But his glass moved back to rest on the Hollander ship. "Hurry," the captain said, and raised his voice above the rapidly freshening wind. "Best get the women below, for these Channel blows can be bad 'uns."

John climbed down the larboard ladder to the main deck, and held his arms aloft to assist Anne. She climbed down into his arms. They might be captured and Edward released. They might both die this day or be separated. She would not go to her maker without feeling Johnny's hands on her one more time.

"Anne." He breathed her name, and the warmth of it enveloped her ear, and though a strong breeze was sweeping the deck, she heard him clearly.

He stepped closer, and she felt again the imprint of his body, made leaner by weeks of worry and travail that she had brought upon him. "I will not let Waverby take you," he told her fiercely.

"Together, Johnny . . . always."

"Always," he repeated, his voice breaking. Anne looked up and saw his distress framed against the day and a sky that seemed to have a cold whiteness about it, and the morning sun appeared huge and red over his shoulder. She had not seen such a morn before.

A sailor rushed toward them. "Cap'n wants 'e, sir."

John released her, and with an outer show of calm she was far from feeling, Anne made for the captain's cabin. When she looked back, John was climbing to the forecastle deck, and she wondered if she would ever see him again in this world.

For a moment, watching him, she was terrified at how easy it would be to tell him all, to give name to the tiny heart that now beat below her own, but she could not bring herself to burden him further.

John felt cold in his loose shirt as he mounted the ladder. And for the first time in his life, he knew helplessness. If he had been on land with Sir Peg under him, he could have led Anne and the others to safety, Hollanders or no.

On the upper deck, the captain handed John his glass. "Take a look."

John raised the brass telescope to his eye and squinted.

"See," Robert Howe said, "they be gaining fast. They'll board by noon."

John could see the full sails of the big ship, make out tiny figures scurrying on its deck, and on the main mast flew the

Hollander flag. He handed the glass back to the captain. "My men will be ready," he said grimly.

"There be another way if ye have the stomach for it," Howe said. The wind blew stronger, dark clouds massing overhead.

John jammed his hands in his breeches. "Can we make for the nearest land, then?"

"Nay, they'd have us boarded and under tow before we could raise safe harbor."

"Then what?" John yelled above the wind, which was blowing harder with each minute.

The captain jabbed his finger to the southeast. "It be a bad Channel storm making up, or I be a landlubber. We could run for the storm, John Gilbert."

"And the Hollanders wouldn't follow," John said, thinking out loud.

"We be sure to drown, every man, Jack, and woman, too."

"But it's a chance," John said.

Robert Howe shrugged. "Only if there be one of the old religion's saints aboard, or we have the devil's own luck."

Chapter Twenty-five

The King's Justice

Anne hung on the edge of the captain's berth in the *Ere,* its swaying lanterns throwing a wildly dancing yellow light over Beth and Kate, both pale and seasick. As the galiot began to plunge into the heaving Channel seas, the two women clung to the small table bolted to the deck. Joseph had wanted to tie them to it to spare them broken bones, but they'd refused. Better a bone broken than to drown like a rat, they'd told him.

Kate's eyes were closed, her lips moving, and Anne knew that she was praying. Even Beth was staring at the planking over her head, as if she could see directly through it to God and his angels. Praying seemed to be all that women could do, while the men were all topside, fighting to keep the ship afloat.

Well, it was not all that Anne Gascoigne could do. If she were to die, she would die facing death. She would die next to John Gilbert. *Together.*

Ignoring the pleas of her friends, Anne climbed to the deck, using all her strength to push the cabin door open. A sheet of rain beat about her shoulders, stinging her face. Somehow she struggled onto the deck, and kneeling, wrested the door back into place.

It was all but impossible to see, but she could dimly make out the captain and another English sailor on the forward deck, both lashed to the wheel, straining to keep the galiot's bow into the wind. For an instant, she heard the frantic calls of the men shackled below, but they were drowned in the sound of splintering wood as the dinghy broke from its moorings and swept past her, over the side.

She tried to make for the quarter deck, where John might be, but fell and skittered back along the deck to the galley hatch like a leaf in an autumn breeze. Her hands were raw and bleeding now.

John was nowhere in sight. She'd been a fool to think that she could help; she couldn't do much of anything but hang on to a hatch cover in the towering seas, each wave threatening to swamp them. The ship's bell was tolling madly, as if all the plague bells in London rang at once, and this time, she knew, remembering the poet Donne's promise, the bell tolled for her. She would die alone in front of all eternity.

"JOHN!" She screamed his name over and over, but each time it was whipped away in the wind that picked up her wet hair and flogged her face. The wind mocked her, wailing his name through the rigging, and she cursed the wind, but the storm swallowed even her curses.

Then suddenly, he was there, water streaming from his face, and in his strong arms she felt herself being lifted and half carried to the mast, and he was tying a thick rope around them, and hitching the rope's ends to the mast.

For hours they stood as the wind howled and drove the ship at a furious speed before it, first east, then west, tearing every shred of furled canvas from the spars, unraveling rigging lines as big as a man's forearm as if they were a child's kite string.

At first they tried to talk, but it was impossible and the rain beat upon them so fiercely that they could not raise their faces to each other and talk with their eyes.

Finally, they sank to the deck in each other's arms, her

face shielded against his broad chest, and there they talked with their clinging hands. And his said, *Forgive me for bringing you to this*; and hers said, *I'm content to die with you.*

Once, when the ship heeled dangerously and the wild gray Channel seas broke over the scuppers, she clutched him with all her strength, thinking that if they went down, she would never lose her grip while she had life. Terrified, her head fell back, and he wiped the hair from her face and laughed, his teeth shining white even in the stormy darkness. At that moment, she loved him as much as woman had ever loved man.

At times during that day, it seemed to Anne that the galiot must founder in the whirling, thrashing seas or break apart as the winds drove the ship first west, then east. The mast creaked incessantly and straining pine-pitched seams sprang leaks, but by some divine destiny or Friend Kate's prayers, the storm at last blew itself out, and they were still afloat and yet alive with the chalk cliffs of Dover in sight, and the Dutch warship nowhere on the horizon.

After the storm passed, from every hatch and cabin battered English sailors and John's band crawled to the deck. Relieved, Anne waved to Beth and Kate, who emerged from the cabin on wobbly legs, supporting each another. The doctor, his wig wet but towering over him, staggered from the galley.

Kate led prayers for the sailor swept from a yardarm during the first minutes of the storm, but no one had to remind the survivors to thank God for the miracle of surviving.

Anne and John knelt side by side on the deck washed clean and white as if scrubbed by a giant hand. Above them the sky was a cloudless blue, the sun warm on their backs, and the tamed sea rolled gently beneath them. Both prayed silently what was in their hearts.

Joseph found some ship's biscuit, and their instant appetite was like a celebration of life.

They all gave a hand to helping jury-rig a sail, the women donating shifts from their kits, carried all the way from Whittlewood Forest, which the English sailors made into a curious sail that had them all in a merry humor as they sent it flying.

The *Ere* sailed north in the Dover Strait, and by morning had rounded Margate and moved with the incoming tide up the Thames, a Hollander ship with a petticoat sail, flying English colors.

Looking aloft, John smiled and pulled Anne close as if he'd never let her go again. "I think me word goes well before us that a strange sight approaches London."

"We must get these proofs to the king," Anne said. John sat across from her on the deck of the captain's cabin, searching through Edward's chest, which had produced some interesting papers.

"We can scarcely storm Whitehall," John said, a mischievous quirk to his lips, "though damn me, but I think you well might." He bent forward and claimed her lips, his hands circling her waist, and liked the feel of it without the undershift that now flew from the mainmast.

Anne looked up with a curious smile. "What weekday is it, John?"

He thought for a moment. "Friday, since we did sail from Southampton on last Lord's Day. Why, sweeting?"

Anne smiled. "We *can* storm Whitehall, John."

"You are especially dear when you are plotting," he said, one side of his mouth curving up in that way that made her feel weak in her nether parts, which she would never reveal in this world.

"Today is Friday, and after the midday meal, His Majesty touches for the king's evil and all skin diseases as is his divine authority."

"So I can gain entrance to the palace," John said, understanding completely.

"No, *we* can gain entrance," she said, her tone brooking no argument. He leaned to her and kissed her rather thoroughly, she thought, and she touched with her hands where no lady would.

The captain knocked as the sound of the anchor chain rattled past them. "We're docking at Deptford, and I be seeing the captain of the port's gig approaching."

John reached for his sword, but Anne laid her hand on his sword arm. "Allow the Countess of Waverby to greet the port captain."

Quickly arranging her hair and smoothing the green velvet gown with gold lace she'd carried in her kit from Whittlewood, she followed John on deck just as the port official's gig came alongside, full of armed men. In two minutes they were up the ladder and on deck with pistols drawn.

Anne did not allow him to speak. "My thanks to you, sir, for this greeting."

The port captain, resplendent in black velvet and gold braid, recognizing quality, bowed. "Lady . . ."

"Anne, Countess of Waverby, lady of the queen's bedchamber," she said in her most imperious tone, "and near captive of the Hollanders, but for these brave English sailors."

"I am all amaze, my lady," the port captain said, his eyebrows reaching almost to his wig, "but . . ."

Anne stamped her foot as a lady used to her own way would do, and as she had done in other days. "I have important papers for His Majesty and require transport immediately to Whitehall for all my crew."

The port captain hesitated.

"At once, sir, or the king will hear of your discourtesy and replace you before the sun sets." She dared not look at John, lest she see the glint of laughter in his eye.

The man bowed much lower than before. "As you wish, my lady." He motioned to a lieutenant. "A barge for her ladyship's party."

"I thank you for your assistance, sir. We also have Dutch prisoners, which we would give into your hands for safe-keeping. Bring them up," she said to John, who pulled a forelock, dipping his head to hide a grin almost out of his control.

An hour later, they were rowing down the glassy smooth Thames, between the tides, toward Whitehall's water stairs, with Lord Waverby bound and gagged in the bottom. His clothes were torn and dirty, his gaze like a sharp weapon as he looked from John to Anne and back again. John gripped his pistol, for he knew that if the king did not receive them or believe Waverby's treachery, then Tyburn's triple tree would be his fate and Anne's, and he would not allow her to suffer.

"The touching will be well along when we get there," Anne said. "Row faster, lads!"

"Aye, lady," the recent captain of the *Ere* said, and set a faster pace.

When they reached Whitehall, John ordered the English sailors to keep Waverby at their center, with a knife pricking his back so that he could not be recognized by the courtiers strolling along the garden river walks. Except for Dr. Wyndham, who had met the king and gained the confidence of the king's mistress, Lady Castlemaine, all the Whittlewood band stayed with the barge for their own safety, with strict orders to leave the city if John did not return by evening.

John, Anne, Josiah and the sailors surrounding Waverby made their way to the Banqueting Hall near Whitehall, and joined the line of scrofula sufferers waiting for the king's touch, which was known from ancient times to heal even the worst afflicted.

Charles II was seated on a dais at the far end of the towering, many-windowed hall that most frequently hosted feasts for Garter knights, broken sunlight streaming in through the tracery of thick glass panes, two assistants in surplices attending, one wearing a bishop's miter.

"Johnny," Anne whispered, her eyes wide, "'tis my uncle, and Edward did always have him under his sway."

A man at the head of the line went forward, knelt and the king touched him on his neck, then hung a gold medallion on an azure ribbon around his neck. The divines murmured prayers. Courtiers applauded politely.

The English sailors crowded forward to see the king, and at that moment, with a strangled cry, Edward, Lord Waverby, sprang forward, raced across the hall and threw himself at the king's feet.

Guards rushed toward the king, pikes at the ready.

"Hold!" Charles commanded, starting from his seat, looking as if he'd seen a ghost. "Loose him!"

Guards removed Waverby's gag, and he spoke quickly as they removed the bindings on his wrists. "Your Majesty, arrest those traitors!"

The king looked to where Edward's head had indicated, and saw John and Anne, standing at the head of their band of sailors with Dr. Wyndham. Several courtiers drew their weapons and advanced on them. The king held up one hand. "Hold, we say." And he motioned John and Anne to come forward, where they knelt, bowing their heads.

"We are most glad in our heart to see that you live, my Lord of Waverby, but we would know what means this intrusion upon our royal duty."

Waverby was shaking with rage. "I was kidnapped by this rogue John Gilbert, Your Majesty as . . . as I was escaping from the Hollanders. And I accuse my wife, the Countess of Waverby, of joining him in piracy. Hang them!"

The king frowned, his face darkened. He motioned to a servant with a bowl of scented water, and when it was extended, swirled his fingers in it. "Dismiss the penitents for this day, my lord," he said to the Bishop of Ely.

"Anne . . ." her uncle said, taking a step toward her.

"My lord bishop!" the king repeated, and there was no

mistaking a tone that demanded immediate compliance, and sent Anne's uncle, skirts lifted, scurrying across the room.

"What means this, my lady?" the king asked Anne, a certain eagerness in his voice, which was not yet intrigued, but ready to be. "We expect to be entertained by your answer. We have never met a lady pirate."

John rose and gave Anne his hand. As she also rose, she prayed for the right words.

Waverby took a half-step forward. "Do not listen to her lies, Your Majesty. She hates me and will say what she will to save that rogue John Gilbert."

"He speaks truth for once, Your Majesty," Anne said. "I would give my life for John Gilbert, but I do not have to lie. Edward is the traitor, gone over to the Hollanders."

Waverby started to speak, but the king silenced him with a look.

John reached inside his doublet and brought forward several sheets of paper with hanging seals. "Here are the trading warrants Admiral de Ruyter gave him for decoding English dispatches after his capture, and his promise to spy within your court." While the king examined the papers, John reached again into his doublet and drew out a small book. "Here, Your Majesty, is the Dutch naval code he planned to use to communicate with de Ruyter, for as long as he sent information, he would be allowed to profit from the Guinea slave trade. The Lady Anne and I and these good English sailors"—he pointed to the men at the back of the hall—"took the ship from him and brought it home to Your Majesty."

The king looked most favorably on Anne, who was prettily flushed and even more prettily in some disarray, despite efforts at her toilet. "You are bold beyond most of your sex, my lady. Babs could not best your tale, and will surely make a court play of your adventure." He leafed through the code book and slowly raised his eyes to Waverby, his good humor instantly gone. "My lord, this is damning evidence."

"Evidence against *them,* Your Majesty," Edward said in his practiced languid voice, well in control of himself and showing all confidence. "They are forgeries, of course."

Anne turned to the English sailors still at the back of the hall. "What say you, lads? Is my Lord of Waverby a traitor?"

"Aye!" shouted the sailors, every one, the recent captain of the *Ere* detaching from the group and coming forward. "Your Majesty," he said, his voice wavering, attempting an awkward bow, "Robert Howe, late third mate of the *Royal Charles.* " 'Is lordship here be chaining us to galley oars in the ship the Hollanders be giving him, and we be Your Majesty's loyal seamen taken at the battle of Lowestoft."

"Your Majesty," Waverby said, his voice a little shrill, "you cannot believe this rabble against one who has served you well."

"We believe our own eyes," Charles said, waving the documents in his hand. "Guards, take my Lord of Waverby to the Tower to await our royal will."

"Your Majesty! I am a peer of your realm. Show mercy."

"And so I shall, my lord. Though your title and lands are forfeit to the Crown, you will not die under the ax, but a sharp French sword." The king turned his face away, regret vying with revulsion.

As Edward, Lord Waverby, was marched at pike point out of the chamber, he looked back, helpless now, at Anne and John, hatred strangling him like the rope he had wished for them.

The king's head was bowed, until the English sailors crowded toward the dais.

"Hats off to good King Charlie! Huzzah! Huzzah! Huzzah!" they chorused, and threw their hats into the air, making the king merry again.

"Now," said the monarch, "we would know the whole tale, from the first."

And taking turns, Anne, John, Josiah and Robert Howe told their story, and when they came to the part about hear-

ing captive English sailors singing of home, the sailors
began singing and Charles joined them right heartily, the
song boisterous as it should be, echoing about the Banqueting Hall: *"Oh, the roast beef of olde England, the roast beef
of olde England, oh!"*

When the whole tale was told, Charles II stood and all in
the chamber bowed. He stepped down and confronted John.

"Your Majesty," John said, wondering what to expect.

"How may we reward you, John Gilbert?"

"Your Majesty, my father, the Duke of Lakeland, left
Burwell Hall to me, but it ended in Lord Waverby's hands."

The king looked thoughtful. "You and the Lady Anne and
these our good sailors have served me well. We are inclined
to generosity, and would give the Lady Anne an honored
place in our court, and return her dower lands with all rights
and rents."

Anne smiled, seeing a somewhat wistful look on the
king's face. "Your Majesty, I am grateful for your kindness
and the honor you do me, but it is still our wish to marry—
in spite of . . . er, impediments."

John nodded. "When her ladyship is free, Your Majesty,
it is also my heart's wish."

"Ah. Well, then, kneel, John Gilbert. 'Tis fitting this marriage be between equals." The king withdrew his short ceremonial sword as John knelt, nearly overcome by many
emotions he had no time to sort through and mayhap never
would.

John felt the light tap on first one and then the other
shoulder. "Rise, Sir John Gilbert, Baronet, Lord of Burwell
Hall and all lands pertaining thereto."

They did not remain in London for the execution of Edward,
Lord Waverby, nor bear witness to it, though they heard
from a broadside cryer as they rode from London onto Oxford Road that the earl had been carried in a faint to the
block.

The king rewarded his loyal sailors with a gold guinea each, and Robert Howe with command of the *Ere,* renamed the *Lady Anne,* to the delight of its namesake.

After a hard ride, the Whittlewood Forest band reached Burwell Hall three days later. John and Anne rode up the long avenue to their perfect jewel of a manor house, with its stone tracery windows and red chimneys, through the arch into the forecourt, he with his arms about her, she leaning back in the saddle against him, as she hoped she would ever ride.

"Welcome to Burwell Hall, my lady."

"Thank you, Sir John," Anne replied, and she felt the delight that tightened his arms about her.

They were married the next day at the waning of July in the small stone church in the deer park, a tame doe looking curiously in an open window as the vicar presided in sonorous tones.

Anne listened to the official words of the ritual of holy matrimony once again, and received again the ring that read "You and No Other" only this time she was not desperately and coldly alone, as she had been when standing on the hard stones of London's old St. Paul's, next to Edward. This time, a tiny life existed, a living spark of her love for John and his for her.

"Johnny," she whispered as they walked back down the aisle, "I am with child."

John did not miss a step, although the soft words were like a hammer blow to his heart. It was all he could do not to disgrace them both with a leap and a whoop that would put to shame any savage in Anne's New World lands.

"Well," Anne said, half twisting toward him, a frown worrying the soft flesh between her great green eyes, "aren't you at least surprised?"

"No more nor less than any man who becomes husband and father in one day."

She dug her elbow through his fine new doublet and into his ribs.

He satisfied her womanly chagrin with an exaggerated flinch, but smiled and nodded to his people from Whittlewood Forest—Joseph and Beth, Josiah and Kate, young Francis, Alexander and Dick—and the cottagers waiting at the church door to escort them to their wedding feast. "Remember your reputation, my lady."

"Hang my reputation!"

He rubbed his throat ruefully. "We'll have no more talk of hanging, if it please you, my sweet, but we will observe public decorum. The name of Gilbert will mean something in the shire one day soon."

Anne groaned. "*You* talk of decorum! Whatever happened to my bold highwayman?"

His hand slid up the back of her bodice, hot as a branding iron, while he showed an innocent face to the crowd. "Be assured, wife, your Gentleman Johnny will come out and most confidently—tonight and tomorrow night, and—"

"Despite the vicar forbidding lust in marriage?"

"Nay, because of it," he said, and they were both laughing as they were swamped with congratulations and hearty kisses from cottagers who had come to honor their new master and mistress, some of them remembering John as a lad. In the great hall on a long trestle, a wedding feast was laid of fresh sturgeon in dill sauce, a jugged hare, a bowl of radishes, hot caraway-flavored jumbals with butter and honey, and a Banbury wedding cake with a rich currant filling, accompanied by many toasts in wine and ale to the bride and groom, which they endured with good grace until, with the usual ribald jests, they were put into their wedding bed.

Josiah finally pushed everyone out and then, somewhat the worse for wine, stuck his head betwixt the bed curtains. "Do not worry, dear friends," he said in his rumbling whisper, "if you get with child, I will swear to the king that it was my miracle salve." His wig, never fully recovered from the Channel storm, tipped to one side, pulling his head with it. "If it can make old young again and pox scars disappear, a new cod would not be so impossible. I think me that my cure will make me famous."

John and Anne laughed, Anne near to choking. "Josiah, the king is oft foolish, but no fool."

Josiah's head bobbed. "Right you are, my lady, but the king is a man. Half the great physicians of London do treat cods to make them grow longer or stronger, and the other half do treat the ladies to enlarge their bosoms or make them fertile. Those who *want* to believe will believe. Who can say, my lady, that faith does not work miracles, as the divines do so often tell us?" The doctor grinned and backed away, closing the door behind him. The sound of great laughter following him down to the hall, where all were warmed by it.

Chapter Twenty-six

The Milkmaid Returns

Anne quietly opened the bed curtains on the four-poster to the chill morning air. Somewhere between the linsey-woolsey sheets, a pair of white gloves, given to her by Beth to symbolize the bride's purity, lay discarded and near forgotten.

She sat on the great bed, cross-legged and naked, looking down at John as he slept in the master's chamber at Burwell Hall. The rogue was smiling.

"Will it be this way forever?" she asked softly of herself or of love. It was a fate-tempting question, but one a woman asks in the first hours of her marriage, for this was the rest of her life sleeping next to her.

John opened one pretending eye. "Forever is a long time," he said, and the smile was still upon his lips. "At least until you grow too old and rheumy to . . . let me see, one leg was over here, wasn't it, and the other was there?" His eyes sparkled, and he put his hands behind his head as he had done in Nell Gwyn's room, his dark eyes tempting her. Daring her to make love to him.

She watched with delight and with pride, unable to keep her hands from his hard, sculpted body. He was the handsomest, most glorious man she had ever known. She pitied those English brides who did not bed a passionate man with a light heart—young women, some little more than girls just reaching their monthly, who were driven shy or frightened to marriage with old men they scarcely knew. Why did families continue, in these enlightened times, to think that titles and property made loving marriages?

Anne entangled her fingers in the tightly curled dark hair on John's chest. "I was just thinking how wonderful you are, husband," she said, the new word rolling sweetly from her tongue.

"Perfectly acceptable behavior in a wife of John Gilbert," he said, sitting up, pretending laziness. He pulled her astraddle his lap, facing him, her extended nipples touching his chest, and she gave a little groan of satisfaction and anticipation as she once had back in Nell's room. "What am I to think of a bride," he said, kissing the hollow of her neck, "with so little maidenly reserve?"

"You are to count yourself a lucky man," Anne said, feigning her courtly hauteur.

"Am I?" he teased. "You take a free knight of the road and make of him a country gentleman bound to the land, and call him lucky. Only Lady Anne Gilbert, mistress of Burwell Hall, would think so."

"But the story is told by all in this land that you gave up the highways for love of a lady pirate."

He sighed. "'Tis true. I must find my excitement elsewhere now, must I not, but where?" He pretended to search the room.

She slid closer yet to him, and her sense of joy was like a thirst unquenched. She lifted her head to present her entire throat for his kisses, and then she reached for his mouth, which opened to her, and the parry and thrust of their love assault began again. All too soon, his tongue moved her to impale herself upon his upright hard cod, certainly in no need of Josiah's miracle salve now. His hands were hard on her buttocks, pulling her toward him until not even a light summer breeze could pass between them. As he filled her, completing her, and they rocked together, the bed curtains danced about them like mad things.

Plea . . . ease, John," she begged him, longing for heated desire to sluice down her in molten waves.

Groaning, he lapped at her breasts as they brushed back and forth past his lips, until they came again to hard points. Soon his slightest movement set her to quivering at her core, and that turned his cod to all sensation.

John could hold himself back no longer, and he poured all his love and manly strength into this woman, the most beautiful in the world. His wife. Carrying his babe. In many ways, she was the most exasperating woman he had ever known, and yet with her and only with her, had he found heart's peace for the first time in his life. He couldn't explain it. Perhaps, like heaven and hell, it was unexplainable.

Finally exhausted, they lay close together for half the morn and only rose when the duties of the Lord and Lady of Burwell Hall could no longer be ignored.

When they entered the hall, John and Anne faced the customary wedding-morn jests, he with great good humor and pride and she with appearance of modesty she no longer truly felt in any great measure. They spent the day riding their fields and greeting all their cottagers, who were relieved to hear that their high rents would be reduced, and each expressed happiness that the Lord of Waverby was no more, his head, as was reported, already rotting on a pike over London Bridge.

By noon that day, John had sent a fast rider to fetch Sir Pegasus from Southampton while Joseph and Beth gathered all the goods needed to live and prosper in the hidden village they meant to rebuild in Whittlewood Forest. Anne could not dissuade them as they loaded powder, lead for shot, nails, axes, kettles, a plow, salt for preserving venison, apple tree seedlings—all necessary items to start their new life in the burnt-out encampment.

"We be fixing your cottage, John," Joseph said, giving John a hearty clap on the shoulder, "and ye and your lady be ever welcome."

John smiled, shaking his hand. "We will come soon. And often."

Joseph unwound the reins from the cart. "Josiah, ye and Kate be welcome to join with us, as well."

"Nay, Joseph. I thank you, but Kate and I are for London. If the plague be still with us, then good Londoners have need of a graduate of the University—"

"—of Padua!" they all shouted in unison.

Joseph and Kate drove away in their cart with the merry sound of laughter following after them.

When a hard winter passed into early spring 1666, a babe was born to Sir John and Lady Anne of Burwell Hall, and barely had the birthing chair been removed than the warming scent of a late March morning called Anne, and she struggled to see out the bedroom window. "Help us to sit up, Johnny," she said.

He shook his head. "The babe is but hours old. Josiah said that you should be flat abed at least a fortnight. He came all this way to help you."

She made a rude noise. "Josiah is a doctor and knows nothing of birthing. He admits it is midwives' work."

"Beth did well, and I'm happy she was with you, but—"

"She has brought calves into this world, and counts babies easier," Anne informed him. "And Beth says I should move about or risk the milk fever."

"On all fours?" he teased.

With an exasperated sniff, Anne struggled again against the confining coverlet. John surrendered his objections and gently lifted her and the baby, crooked in her arm, suckling at her breast, and sat with them against the massive pillows, facing the window.

"There, Johnny, now I can see it," she said, and her pale

face was alight with joy. "Our fields are beginning to green, and what is that a-building in yon pasture?"

"It's a surprise for you, sweeting," John said, laughing. She could feel him move his arm behind her shoulder, and the hard muscle reassured her that he could do anything that took strength and will.

"When can I see it?"

"Sooner than you should, I fear, for I will not be able to keep you abed."

A cloud seemed to cross her face, and John, who could read her moods, held his wife and babe tighter. "Don't let Waverby haunt you, Anne."

She relaxed against him. "Soon, I pray, he will be gone e'en from my night frights."

John opened the babe's swaddling clothes and again marveled at the most perfect tiny girl, all pink and cream, with a mass of curly red-tinged hair, and under those tight-closed eyelids, he expected the sea green eyes of her mother.

"I have named her," he said.

Anne's face grew paler yet. "But that is bad luck before the first natal day. Babes do die of anything."

John shook his head. "Not Anne junior. She will live long and exhaust us."

"But I thought to name her Prudence, for my mother, as custom decrees."

John laughed heartily. "That is a name no daughter of yours could ever grow into."

She laughed with him, and together they set up quite a racket, waking the babe, who demanded more refreshment in an even louder voice.

On an early morn scant days later, as an April dawn warmed the land, Anne made her way into the pasture to find that John had built for her a perfect little dairy barn with cows, milkmaids, churns and all she'd need to make her own sweet butter. She tucked up her gown into her bodice and set to work at the churn, with bright eyes and a smile for the maids who watched their mistress with disbelief. When she started back to the manor, she carried before her a cloth-covered pottery crock of the sweetest butter she had ever tasted. One day soon, her Burwell butter would be famous in the shire, perhaps in all of England.

John walked through the pasture toward Anne, not wanting her long from his sight. He was carrying their daughter, the babe never far from his arms since her natal day, feeling the pulse of her tiny life and its promise that his blood and Anne's would reach into eternity.

He had never been so happy as at this moment, not at his first lying with Anne, not at their marriage. Nothing had equaled being with Anne every day, looking upon her whenever he wished, touching her hair as he passed her by, catching the message of her eyes meant for him alone. A life of such moments would be enough for John Gilbert, he thought, as he felt the rich earth of Burwell Hall give way beneath his feet.

He called Anne's name as she walked from the dairy, and she heard him, lifting her face, warm and rosy from the churning. He hurried to her and bent to kiss the butter from her willing lips. "Better far than the sweetest oatcake," he said, enclosing her, babe, crock and all in his tight embrace.

Their laughter reached the house and Dr. Wyndham's ears. "Ah," he murmured, "my friends have discovered all they have to love, or I'm not a graduate of the University of . . ." He left the rest unsaid, and went out, smiling, into the sun-warmed morn to greet them.

Read on for an excerpt from

Lady Katherne's Wild Ride

by Jeane Westin,
coming from Signet Eclipse in
August 2006.

When Lady Katherne's uncle, her
guardian, Sir William, tries to seduce her,
she knocks him over the head and takes
to the open road with her trustworthy
servant, Martha. But with the authorities
after them for attempted murder, they may
never make it to London, where Charles II
rules during the bawdy period now
known as the Restoration. . . .

"If ye be the devil," said a shaky voice, "I have me fowling piece to hand."

Katherne smiled reassurance at Martha. "No devil knocks, good Thomas, but an old friend who more than once gave you cider from the first pressing."

The door opened, and a wrinkled man with thin white hair and a sunken, toothless mouth lisped, "My lady, I would know the woman from sweet memory of the child. It be ye for certain, or be I dreaming." He bowed her in.

"No dream, Thomas, and this is Martha, my . . . friend."

"She be welcome, too, my lady," he said.

"We be hungry," Martha announced, sniffing the air.

A fire burned in the fireplace and a bubbling pot hung on the hook, filling the cottage with the smell of rabbit stew and wild onion, strongly reminding Katherne that she'd had nothing to eat for all the day.

Thomas bowed them to backless stools around a plank table. A bed and thick mattress sack and chest were the only other furnishings in the single room. He got out two wooden bowls and ladled them full, then reached to the dried thyme hanging from his ceiling and added a pinch. Thick slices of dark bread and a tankard of strong ale finished the meal.

Katherne saw a hundred questions in his eyes, but he squatted on his haunches before her and asked nothing until they had finished the first bowl and started on the second.

"What troubles have ye, my lady? I would give ye a place to rest and hide for yer sake and for love of the old master, your father, God rest his soul. I cannot take ye to the manor, for I be forbidden that house by Sir William on pain of death."

"Why, good Thomas?"

"The new master does not abide questions, but cottagers be shot at who wander close."

Katherne stood. "We must be gone from this place, Thomas. I can only tell you that I did no wrong but was sorely wronged against, as much as any woman can be. Now we must away quickly this night before the sheriff comes this way. I have no wish to put you at risk for your head."

"The sheriff's men were here at an early hour, Mistress Kit. I opened the gate and they be searching the manor grounds, trampling Sir Robert's knot garden with much merriment." He took an old apple sack and began to fill it with fruit and the remaining bread. "This be all I have, but ye be welcomed to it." He reached atop his mantel and brought down a small stoppered vial of green glass. "This be an herbal for those bruises, my lady."

Katherne felt tears starting their slide down her cheeks. "Remember, you have not seen us, Thomas."

He opened the door and she threw her arms around him, placing a kiss on his weathered cheek as she had from a small child, though she was now a full head taller than he. "I won't forget your kindness."

"Wait," he said, quickly going back into the cottage and opening a chest at the foot of his bed. "This be my wife's, God rest her soul," he said, holding out a yellowed cloth day cap. That lace cap ye wear will not pass for a servant's."

He called one last time as they walked beyond the gate. "God bless ye, my lady, and take ye in His care. There be gypsies about, and worse—strolling players."

She was too choked with gratitude to say or do more in fear of breaking her heart, and so without a backward look, Katherne and Martha started south following the road in the half-moon's light. She had not been this near to her home, Rosevere, for many years, but she could not bring herself to stand and study its long shadows. There was too much pain behind its ancient battlements. Memories of the day news had come that both her older brothers had died at the battle of Worcester, their bodies thrown into a common grave, and horror upon horror, the word that her father had been given up to Cromwell and hanged. Finally came the day she had lost even her home, when Sir William's allegiance to

Cromwell had earned him Rosevere and Katherne's wardship and dowry.

They walked on quietly for hours in the pale moonlight and enough sparkling stars to light a thousand candelabra; drenched by a sudden shower; meeting no one except for a straying cow, which Martha knelt and milked, drinking from the teat.

When Katherne was offered a teat, she laughed softly. "We are running for our very lives, but you find food everywhere."

Martha wiped her mouth on the back of her sleeve. "We be doing for ourselves and best be eating when we can. That be part of this freedom from masters, Mistress Kit, as ye be now called by me."

Katherne smiled. "I was so named by my brothers, being not so tall in those days. Come, we must travel more miles before daybreak if we would keep from the sheriff's men."

They walked on, Martha's sturdy legs never seeming to tire, although Katherne's slippers were now past repairing, the dainty soles flopping with every step, her feet bruised and beginning to bleed.

"We must get ye new shoes," Martha announced, "or I be riding you on my back before we get to Chelmesford."

Katherne sat down by the side of the road and looked at the hopeless ruin of satin slippers. "I will be no burden to you, but will go in my bare feet, if I must," she announced, "or crawl on all fours like a babe."

Martha put her hands on her ample hips, incredulous. "When hens make holy water!" But there was a new admiration in her voice.

Kit laughed, and Martha joined in until Kit shushed her, and they walked on, Kit without shoes, near-dancing over the pebbles and hard ruts that tortured her narrow tender-skinned feet. They passed some sorry cottages with sagging thatch and tossed some of their precious bread to quiet a dog tied to one.

"Wait here," Martha said, turning back toward the cottages after going a few paces beyond.

"No. We stay together," Kit said to Martha's back disappearing behind one of the cots. Against the shed used for a closet of ease in the back—the odor proclaimed it—hung several fishing poles.

"I hoped so," Martha whispered, picking up a pole.

"We cannot stop to fish," Kit said with exasperation.

Martha stifled amusement, although her ample bosom shook with it. "I be angling for something better, although a nice tender sturgeon would not go amiss," and she crept toward the cottage before Kit could say more.

They advanced toward an open window, its shutters ajar, stepping carefully around the barnyard clutter of abandoned tools and some nesting boxes empty of ducks since the spring. The only noise she heard was the swoop and rustle of bats in the thatch overhead. Martha looked inside, then stuck the pole and hook in, and with great care inched her catch out the window and into Kit's hands.

A monstrous loud snore that seemed to rattle on forever shattered the night's peace and caused Kit to stifle a hapless laugh.

After waiting quietly for some time, Martha then stuck the pole in again and slowly drew out a second item, a worn leathern shoe to match the first. Kit could hear the uninterrupted snores from inside, but afraid to breathe herself, stayed Martha's hand when she raised the pole to fish again.

"Sausages!" Martha mouthed.

Kit shook her head and drew a gold guinea from her handkercher, leaving it on the window's sill in extravagant payment. The cottager would surely think the fairies had come in the night. She guided the unwilling Martha, still mourning sausages, toward the privy house, replacing the fishing pole.

Back on the road a light showing in a cot sent them scrambling some distance to a log where Kit could put on her new shoes, much too large for her. They were hard pressed against her sore feet.

"Here," said Martha, reaching into her basket, "take these thick wool hosen. Those silk ones be for fine ladies and their dancing slippers, not for the likes of us."

"Thank you, Martha," Kit said, realizing that she had learned much from a kitchen maid, a woman she had never thought to converse with at any length. "Where did you learn to—"

"Be an angler? From my brother Jacob, who was a right good thief until they caught and branded him on his thumb and forehead, then transported him to the Jamaica plantations. That be when my indenture was sold to Sir William," she said, and walked on, carrying what Kit thought must be a sad story of a starving family forced to sell their daughter's youth to service.

"Sorry about the sausages," Kit said quietly to her back, vowing never again to tease Martha about her appetite, since the only hunger she had ever known had been nothing to compare.

Before first light, they began looking for a barn or shed to hide in, and found an abandoned cottage, its thatch having collapsed onto its dirt floor, leaving a skeleton of rafters exposed to the sky. A hollowed-out log trough outside the byre at the back of the cot was filled with fresh rainwater. They drank their fill, then washed their hot feet to cool them. Kit bent over the clear water and saw a face she hardly recognized as her own: dirty, bruised, with yellow hair escaped from her cap to swirl wildly about her face.

She found the herbal balm Thomas had given her and spread it on her face and feet. She must heal before they appeared in a town, or the constable would mark her as a vagrant or thief, both of which she realized she now was or soon would be.

They ate the last of the bread and each an apple. Kit spread her torn and dirty cloak upon the hard-packed ground where once a family had lived and worked their small holding. She wondered what had happened to them. So many had been carried off by plague or driven off by lords enclosing land for sheep runs. But exhaustion soon conquered curiosity, and she lay down next to Martha to sleep under the ridge pole, where enough thatch still clung to give them shade.

The sun was high overhead when she opened her eyes, her back stiff from the hard ground, no softer on this second day than on the first. She tried to sleep again, but her mind went racing down the road ahead of her. What would happen to her if she escaped the perils of travel and finally came to London town? There were only two ways for an unwed woman to make her way in that world: as servant or as prostitute. Perhaps, with her gold pieces, it might be possible to set up a dame's school, though she would have to be careful not to attract the attention of parish constables or curious competitors. She took a long, trembling breath and let it go slowly. This solution gave her little sense that she would be her own master.

She stood up and stretched her aching muscles, walking out to the ancient wooden trough. The sun sparkled upon the clear rainwater, and she felt a great desire to bathe her bruised and violated body . . . to wash away the last memory of William's perfidy, the man-scent of him she had carried in her nostrils these many hours.

Overwhelmed by the need to be clean and fully rid of him, she stripped off her bodice, gown and shift, stepping into the water warmed by the sun, slowly sinking into its shallow depths with a groan of pleasure though the wood scraped her skin. She wished for some good lye soap but settled for scrubbing herself and her hair between her hands until it was as clean as it could be. It was the first time in her life that she had bathed without a bathing gown, and she thought never to wear one again.

Raised on her elbow, Martha called softly from the cottage floor, "Ye will catch yer death, Mistress Kit. It be only July and not a bathing month."

"Then I will die with a clean skin if not a conscience," Kit said, laughing, and dipped her head into the water, coming up with her dripping hair blinding her. Tossing it back, she opened her eyes and turned toward Martha, then immediately covered her breasts with both hands, swallowing a scream.

Martha was not alone at the cot door. A tall man, wearing a fancy French rapier in a gold-embossed baldric, held a cocked pistol to her head. His eyes were in shadow, but Kit saw smile creases in both cheeks and an arrogant tilt to his mouth as he bowed slightly in her direction.

"I would agree, mistress, that skin such as yours should never be unclean. As for your conscience, I would beg you to never allow it to hinder pleasure . . . as you find it."

The bastard mocked her!

Although he did not move the pistol from Martha's temple, the ruffian bowed again, and she saw corded muscle ripple along his neck to disappear inside his open shirt. Kit gathered herself to leap. She had not come so far to lose all now.

"Do not think it, mistress," he said, aiming the pistol at her head, "since you cannot outrun my powder and ball."

Still, she could not see his face in the shadow formed by his wide-brimmed hat. What she did see were two long, well-muscled legs covered in fine silk hosen the color of bluebells and knee-high black Spanish boots turned down. Some dandy out for a lark? Perhaps she could cozen him. . . .

"You must come up and out of the trough," he said in a tone of voice that did not seem easily fooled. "It does not suit you, though I must admit to never seeing a finer young filly."

She spat the words, "Sir, I have need of my clothes."

"So you do," he said, walking Martha to them with a sidestep as deft as any French dancing master.

Kit didn't move to come out of the water. Whoever he was, a sheriff's man or no, she would not stand naked as a babe before him, though she was shivering now. "Sir, allow me to cover myself," she said, trying to keep a note of pleading from her voice, which she now knew inflamed men.

He prodded Martha, who was staring wide-eyed and openmouthed into his face. "Help your mistress to maintain her . . . modesty."

Stung by the laughter beneath his words, Kit flung a challenge. "A gentleman would turn his back."

He laughed openly as she struggled to exit the horse trough, her hands slipping on the wet wood. "Nay, mistress, you cannot think me so slow-witted, nor could I turn my back on such exquisite loveliness," he said in a musical baritone that made a confection of every word.

With Martha shielding her, Kit left the trough quickly and dressed faster still, watching him as the pistol never wavered. She had barely returned the old cap to her head when he walked forward and studied her for a very long minute in which she found herself holding her breath. Before she could chastise his impudence, he introduced himself.

"Jeremy Hughes, Jemmy to those fortunate ladies who love me, a peddler of poetry, of words to charm, to persuade or to command." He bowed again even more gracefully and continued, his voice stroking the words, while Kit tried not to stare at the wide, full mouth saying them. "I am, sweet lady, a strolling player to neither of Their Majesties as yet, but that is their loss and soon to be remedied," he added, crowning his pretty speech with another bow, sweeping his fashionable wide-brimmed black hat, adorned with red ostrich feathers, before her to the ground. "And dam'me, Lady Katherne Lindsay, if I would give up that lovely neck of yours to the sheriff's hangman for the ten guineas on offer . . . though I think me I can bargain for more."